PRAISE

Everything We Keep

A Top Amazon Bestseller of 2016 and *Wall Street Journal* Bestseller

Liz & Lisa Best Book of the Month Selection

POPSUGAR and *Redbook* Fall Must-Read Selection

"This fantastic debut is glowing with adrenaline-inducing suspense and unexpected twists. Don't make other plans when you open *Everything We Keep*; you will devour it in one sitting."

—*Redbook* magazine

"Aimee's electrifying journey to piece together the puzzle of mystery surrounding her fiancé's disappearance is a heart-pounding reading experience every hopeless romantic and shock-loving fiction-lover should treat themselves to."

—POPSUGAR

"You'll need an ample supply of tissues and emotional strength for this one . . . From Northern California author Kerry Lonsdale comes a heart-wrenching story about fate sweeping away life in an instant."

—*Sunset* magazine

"Gushing with adrenaline-inducing plot, this is the phenomenally written debut every fall reader will be swooning over."

—*Coastal Living*

"A beautifully crafted novel about unconditional love, heartbreak, and letting go, *Everything We Keep* captures readers with its one-of-a-kind, suspenseful plot. Depicting grief and loss, but also healing and hope in their rawest forms, this novel will capture hearts and minds, keeping readers up all night, desperate to learn the truth."

—*RT Book Reviews*

"A perfect page-turner for summer."
　　—Catherine McKenzie, bestselling author of *Hidden* and *Fractured*

"Heartfelt and suspenseful, *Everything We Keep* beautifully navigates the deep waters of grief, and one woman's search to reconcile a past she can't release, and a future she wants to embrace. Lonsdale's writing is crisp and effortless and utterly irresistible—and her expertly layered exploration of the journey from loss to renewal is sure to make this a book club must-read. *Everything We Keep* drew me in from the first page and held me fast all the way to its deeply satisfying ending."

—Erika Marks, author of *The Last Treasure*

"In *Everything We Keep*, Kerry Lonsdale brilliantly explores the grief of loss, if we can really let go of our great loves, and if some secrets are better left buried. With a good dose of drama, a heart-wrenching love story, and the suspense of unanswered questions, Lonsdale's layered and engrossing debut is a captivating read."

—Karma Brown, bestselling author of *Come Away with Me*

"A stunning debut with a memorable twist, *Everything We Keep* effortlessly layers family secrets into a suspenseful story of grief, love, and art. This is a gem of a book."

—Barbara Claypole White, bestselling author of *The Perfect Son*

"*Everything We Keep* takes your breath from the very first line and keeps it through a heart-reeling number of twists and turns. Well-plotted, with wonderful writing and pacing, on the surface it appears to be a story of love and loss, but just as you begin to think you've worked it out, you're blindsided and realize you haven't. It will keep you reading and guessing, and trust me, you still won't have it figured out. Not until the very end."

—Barbara Taylor Sissel, author of *Crooked Little Lies* and *Faultlines*

"Wow—it's been a long time since I ignored all of my responsibilities and read a book straight through, but it couldn't be helped with *Everything We Keep*. I was intrigued from the start . . . So many questions, and Lonsdale answers them in the most intriguing and captivating way possible."

—Camille Di Maio, author of *The Memory of Us*

All the Breaking Waves

AN AMAZON BEST BOOK OF THE MONTH: LITERATURE & FICTION CATEGORY

LIZ & LISA BEST BOOK OF THE MONTH SELECTION

"Blending elements of magic and mystery, *All the Breaking Waves* is a compelling portrayal of one mother's journey as she grapples with her small daughter's horrific visions that force her to confront a haunting secret from her past. Examining issues of love, loss, and the often-fragile ground of relationships and forgiveness, this tenderly told story will have you turning the pages long past midnight."

—Barbara Taylor Sissel, author of *Faultlines*

"With a touch of the paranormal, *All the Breaking Waves* is an emotional story about lost love, family secrets, and finding beauty in things people fear . . . or simply discard. A perfect book club pick!"

—Barbara Claypole White, bestselling author of *Echoes of Family*

"A masterful tale of magic realism and family saga. With its heartfelt characters, relationships generational and maternal, and a long-ago romance, we are drawn into Molly's world. While her intuitive gifts may be ethereal, her fears and hopes for her daughter and personal desires are extraordinarily relatable. Woven with a thread of pure magic, Lonsdale crafts an intriguing story of love, mystery, and family loyalty that will captivate and entertain readers."

—Laura Spinella, bestselling author of *Ghost Gifts*

EVERYTHING WE LEFT BEHIND

ALSO BY KERRY LONSDALE

Everything We Keep

All the Breaking Waves

EVERYTHING WE LEFT BEHIND

KERRY LONSDALE

LAKE UNION
PUBLISHING

Published by Lake Union Publishing, Seattle

www.apub.com

Amazon, the Amazon logo, and Lake Union Publishing are trademarks of Amazon.com, Inc., or its affiliates.

ISBN-13: 9781477823972
ISBN-10: 1477823972

Cover design by Damonza

Printed in the United States of America

For my parents, for keeping the faith

PROLOGUE
JAMES

Six Months Ago
December 18
Puerto Escondido, Mexico

He dreamed about her again. Blue eyes so bright and hot they branded his soul. Waves of brunette curls stroked his chest as she moved over him, kissing his heated skin. They'd be married in two months. He couldn't wait to wake up with her each morning and love her as his wife, exactly how she was loving him now.

There was something important he had to tell her. Something urgent he had to do. Whatever it was remained elusive on the foggy edges of his mind. He narrowed his focus, homing in on the thought until he could . . .

Protect her.

He had to protect his fiancée. His brother would hurt her again.

He saw his brother, the conviction in his expression. It bordered on insanity. They were on a boat. He had a gun and was making threats. His brother pointed the gun at him, so he dove into the water. The ocean was wild, dragging him under. He felt himself sinking. Bullets sprayed the surface and shot past his head and torso, narrowly missing their mark.

He swam hard and fast, his lungs burning. He had to protect her.

Large, powerful waves tossed him against rocky cliffs. Searing pain tore at his face and limbs. The ocean wanted him, but his will to protect the love of his life was stronger. He had to get to her. The current sucked him below the surface. He floated, drifted. Back and forth, up and down. Then darkness came.

"*¡Papá! ¡Papá!*" a small voice squealed.

His eyes shot open. A small child jumped over him, messing the sheets. He looked at the boy. Giggling, the child leaped around the bed.

"*¡Despiertate, papá! Tengo hambre.*"

The child spoke Spanish. He racked his brain, delving back to his college Spanish courses. The kid was hungry, and he'd called him "Dad."

Where the hell was he?

He shot upright and backpedaled, slamming against the headboard. He was in a bedroom surrounded by framed pictures. He saw himself in many of the photos but had no memory of them being taken. To his right, windows overlooked a balcony and the ocean beyond. *What the fuck?*

He felt the blood leave his face. His body broke out in a cold sweat. The child jumped closer, spinning full circles when he launched in the air. "*¡Quiero el desayuno! ¡Quiero el desayuno!*" the boy chanted.

"Stop jumping," he croaked, holding up his hands to ward off the boy getting too close. He was disoriented. Fingers of panic slithered around his throat. "Stop it!" he yelled.

The child froze. Wide-eyed, he stared at him for two heartbeats. Then he flew off the bed and out of the room.

He squeezed his eyes shut and counted to ten. Everything would return to normal when he opened his eyes. He was stressed—work, the wedding, dealing with his brothers. That had to be the reason. This was only a dream.

He opened his eyes. Nothing had changed. Labored breaths blasted from his lungs. This wasn't a dream. It was a nightmare, and he was living it.

On the bedside table he spied a mobile phone. He picked it up and launched the screen. His heart stumbled as he read the date. It was supposed to be May. How the hell could it be December . . . six and a half years after his wedding date?

He heard a noise at the door and jerked his head. An older boy stood in the doorway, his espresso face pasty. *"¿Papá?"*

He sat up straighter. "Who are you? Where am I? What is this place?"

His questions seemed to frighten the boy, but he didn't leave the room. Instead, he dragged a chair to the closet. He climbed atop and retrieved a metal box from the upper shelf. The older boy brought the box to him and punched a four-digit code on the keypad. The box's latch popped open. The boy lifted the lid, then slowly backed from the room, tears streaming down his face.

Inside the metal box were legal documents—passports, birth certificates, a marriage license, along with a death certificate for a Raquel Celina Dominguez. Thumb drives and several data-storage discs were tucked at the bottom, along with an engagement ring. He knew this ring. She wore this ring. He held it to the light, staring, uncomprehending. Why wasn't she wearing his ring?

He returned the ring to the metal box, and an envelope caught his attention. It was addressed to him. James. He ripped the envelope open and extracted a letter.

I write this on borrowed time. I fear the day's coming I'll remember who I was and

3

forget who I am. My name is Jaime Carlos Dominguez.

I was once known as James Charles Donato. If I'm reading this note without any recollection of writing it, know one thing: I AM YOU.

CHAPTER 1

JAMES

Present Day
June 21
San Jose, California

Dying is a whole lot easier than coming back to life. The amount of paperwork required to reinstate his identity is enough to suck the life back out of him.

Maybe he should have stayed dead. Because there sure as hell isn't anything worthwhile left for him here.

The thought skips through James's mind like a grounder across a baseball field, slamming hard into the outfield wall. It leaves a dull ache in his temple and a hollowness in his chest.

He stares at the San Jose skyline outside the window of his brother Thomas's office at Donato Enterprises. Glass buildings reflect the setting sun in radiant displays of gold and orange. Six and a half years lost, and there isn't a damn thing he can do, medically speaking, to recapture that time.

But he remembers the day he left Aimee as though it were yesterday.

He paces in front of the window, plagued by the conversation they had the night before he left. "I'll be away for less than a week, barely enough time for you to miss me." He then kissed her and made love with her. His fingers had caressed the moonlight in her hair as he reassured her their future would be the one they wanted, with him free of his obligation to Donato Enterprises. He wanted to pursue art. His mouth had traced the supple lines of her thighs, the curve of her calves, as he promised to care for her for the rest of his life.

But he failed to keep that promise. He failed her.

So much time has been lost. So much of his life lost. His home. His art. His identity.

The love of his life.

Aimee.

Her name whispers through him.

Does she know he's back in the States? Does she know *he* is back, her James?

She hasn't seen him since she found him in Mexico more than five years ago. She'd discovered he was still alive, not dead like his brother Thomas had everyone believing. The jackass even organized James's funeral and bought a headstone at the family plot.

For his protection, Thomas has told him, else Phil would have tried to kill him again in order to save his own ass.

Thomas took advantage of his amnesia, which, in James's case, had been a total whiteout of his autobiographical information. His brother went so far as to create a new identity for him, a new life.

Jaime Carlos Dominguez. Artist. Widower. Father.

He doesn't have any memories of Aimee's trip to Mexico. He doesn't have any memories of falling in love with his physical therapist, Raquel; marrying her; adopting her son, Julian; fathering their son, Marcus; and her death from birthing Marcus. He doesn't have any memories of

6

anything Thomas told him about what he, as Carlos, did in Mexico. He can hardly recall *how* he ended up in Mexico.

He doesn't remember anything about the hours leading up to his wandering into Playa Zicatela, bloodied, dazed, and confused, with no idea who he was or where he was from.

What he does have, though, is more than six years of Carlos's journals, all tidily filed on a thumb drive. Daily entries that stopped two days before James surfaced.

The damn man kept a diary.

James makes an odd noise in the back of his throat. It's ironic. Anytime he curses Carlos, he's only cussing at himself. But thinking of himself as separate from Carlos has made it easier to accept the loss of time.

There is much about the man Carlos was that James doesn't understand. The one thing he can relate to, though, is Carlos's paranoia of losing his identity. For when James surfaced from the fugue state to magazine and newspaper stacks, framed picture mosaics crowding the walls, and a lockbox bursting with the details of the man's short life, Carlos was lost to this world forever.

James thinks of the items in that lockbox. Photos, birth and death certificates. Aimee's engagement ring.

His blunt fingers rub the edges of the diamond solitaire ring tucked deep in his trouser pocket. The thin gabardine wool dress pants scratch thighs long used to board shorts. And the ring is a solid, cold reminder that for the rest of his life he'll pay for his mistakes with more than the physical scars marring his thirty-six-year-old body. The angry ridge from right temple to jawbone, the not-set-just-right nose bridge, the slash of rigid tissue across his hipbone—a bullet trail, he surmises. Those scars he can handle. What he can't get past, what he has yet to come to grips with, is that he'll never share his life with Aimee because he fucked up.

James thinks of his sons waiting in the conference room. Eleven-year-old Julian hates him. He's convinced James doesn't want to be their father, that he'll ship them off to Hawaii to live with their aunt, Raquel's half sister Natalya Hayes. Six-year-old Marcus has been wary of him since that first day when his dad started speaking English. James is not the same *papá* as before.

God knows how he'll manage getting his sons settled in a new home, let alone a new-for-them country, and trusting him as their father, all the while trying to start a new life together.

A life Aimee will not be a part of.

James breathes through the ache deep inside his chest.

"She won't see you."

He fists the engagement ring and slowly turns from the window to glare at his brother. Thomas sits behind his desk, erratically bouncing a Montblanc pen against the glass surface. James's ears flex, capturing the noise. The sound grates. He tightens his grip and the diamond bites into his palm. The desire to punch Thomas, feel the sickening crunch of cartilage vibrate up his arm—that feeling consumes him. Almost.

Get a grip, James.

Thomas meets his glare, a brow arched as though challenging James to object.

"How would you know?" James asks, turning back to the window. "You haven't seen her in five years."

The tapping stops. "I haven't spoken with her."

Last December, when James bombarded Thomas with questions about Aimee, he couldn't answer them. Aimee had filed, and the court had awarded, a temporary restraining order against his brother upon her return to the States. She didn't want anything to do with Thomas or the Donato family, so other than a few e-mail exchanges after the order expired, Thomas has left her alone.

James doesn't blame Aimee. If he wasn't so reliant on Thomas's help to get reestablished, he'd write his brother off, too. He'd even contemplated suing Thomas for violating his human rights. But his own shame, as well as his respect for his mother, had stopped him. Claire Donato's three sons has already done enough to screw up the family. Besides, James deserves what happened to him. It is because of his own mistakes that he ended up where he did, abandoned and practically forgotten.

"I have seen Aimee," Thomas murmurs.

James flips the ring onto his pinkie. He leans his forearm against the window, taps the glass with a finger, and wonders if Thomas is right. Would Aimee want to see him?

Chair wheels roll across tightly woven carpet, and the distinct rustle of rich, tailored fabric disturbs the air. Thomas comes to stand beside him at the window.

"Los Gatos is a small town. I walk past her café almost every day. Hard not to see her or Ian. Or their daughter."

James leans his forehead against the bent arm supporting his weight.

"She had to move on," Thomas says. "Kid. Husband. She loves Ian. She's happy."

James knows this, has known since the day he tried calling her last December only to reach a disconnected number. He'd never been so scared in his life.

He reached Thomas, though. His brother had answered on the first ring. Then he was there in Mexico, twenty-four hours later, and told him everything.

Thomas claps James's shoulder. "Don't fuck up her marriage."

"Like you fucked up my life?"

Thomas flinches. "I told you, I tried to fix it. You, when you were Carlos, wanted nothing to do with me." He angles his face toward the evening traffic below. Hands in pockets, he fidgets with the pen. "I couldn't force you to leave Mexico no matter how hard I tried to convince you."

The sun disappears below the horizon, and the sky darkens. Their reflections against the glass grow more distinct with each passing moment. James notices for the first time in their lives he is larger than

Thomas. He also looks much younger than the two years separating him from his older brother.

That was what surprised James the most when he first saw his own reflection last December: how much he'd aged. The surfer-length hair and scarred skin on his face had been a shock. Six and a half years had deepened the creases around his eyes and mouth, tightened the skin around his ribs as though it had baked frequently under the Mexican sun. But Carlos kept his body in top form. Between running and mountain biking, he maintained an active, outdoor lifestyle.

Thomas hasn't fared so well. He wears his stress in the dull-gray hair cropped close to his head, blanched skin deficient of vitamin D, and a leaner frame James surmises survives on caffeine, cigars, and a liquid diet. The wet bar in Thomas's office is well stocked, and the burned, musty smell of cigars is unavoidable when Thomas stands near him. The sharp smoke scent in Thomas's suit hits the olfactory, almost making James's eyes water.

Hard to believe Thomas will be forty in less than two years. He looks years older.

"I don't plan to see Aimee," James says on a resigned sigh. Not yet, anyway. He isn't sure he can handle seeing her, knowing she's no longer his.

He moves away from the window and stops at Thomas's desk. A large envelope rests on top, addressed to him. "Is this it?"

"Yes, it came in this morning."

James opens the envelope, flips through the items. Deed and keys to his parents' house. His mother moved out several years ago to an upscale retirement community after his father's passing. Now the house is his, a place to raise the boys. He intends to sell it as soon as possible.

He scans the rest of the paperwork. A list of bank- and investment-account numbers, school registration forms for the boys. Car keys. A new life.

If only it were that simple.

James thinks of his sons. Thanks to him, everything familiar about their lives is gone: their home, their school, and their friends. They've lost their mother and, more recently, the father they knew. And according to Julian, James is a poor excuse for a replacement.

"As of this week, I've sold off your remaining interest in Donato Enterprises. Mom and Dad's place is yours to do with as you want," Thomas explains. "Everything you shipped from Mexico is there. I kept your canvases boxed."

James pulls out a document. Thomas joins him at the desk and taps the form with his pen. "The boys are enrolled at Saint Andrew's." The private academy down the road from where he and Thomas grew up. The same school they attended.

"They have an excellent English-as-a-second-language program."

"They speak fluent English. Apparently I made sure of that," James scoffs.

He stuffs the paperwork back in the envelope and slaps it against his thigh. He wants to leave. He's tired and hungry, and knows the boys are, too. They came straight here after their flight from Mexico landed. "Anything you need from me?"

Thomas shakes his head.

"We're done, then. I'll call if I need something. Otherwise, don't expect to hear from me." *Ever,* James would like to say. But it seems almost every life play he runs downfield to catch, Thomas is there to intercept the ball. *Pass interference,* he wants to cry. He just needs Thomas to leave him the hell alone.

James turns to leave.

"Phil's prison term ends next Tuesday," Thomas remarks when James reaches for the door. "He's out. A free man." He extends his arms, palms out.

"You're just telling me now?" James stares pointedly at his brother. He thought Phil had another few months to serve. His eyes narrow. "How long have you known?"

Thomas takes an interest in the pen he holds.

"Damn you." He's known about it long enough for James to move anywhere that isn't here. Thomas has been determined to set right everything he can about James's life, which includes getting him moved back to Los Gatos.

"I already told you Fernando Ruiz, the Hidalgo cartel leader, has been captured, tried, and convicted. I doubt Phil has any further association with the Hidalgo cartel. Still"—Thomas taps the pen against his thumb knuckle—"keep your eyes open. We have nothing but my gut telling me he tried to kill you and I have no idea what he'll do when he gets out. He still doesn't know you're alive."

James fist-bumps the door. "Jesus, Thomas, really? You were supposed to tell him." James thought he would have time to visit Phil *before* he got out of prison. "Do you really think he'll come after me again? What's the point? Everything's resolved. The Feds got their man and you got Phil in prison."

"Phil will seek you out if you have something that implicates him in your attempted murder."

"We don't know if he, or anyone, for that matter, tried to kill me," James points out. "I can't remember a goddamn thing."

"Nothing at all?"

"No."

Thomas swears under his breath. "You'd tell me if you remembered something, right? Make sure you get in touch with me the second you do."

James gives him a clipped nod. It might be important to Thomas, but to James, what happened, happened. He messed up, chasing after Phil without any sort of plan. He'd been furious Phil assaulted Aimee, disgusted Thomas showed no interest in stopping Phil's laundering, and he was angry at how Phil planned to ruin the family. In the end, James failed everyone, especially Aimee.

He yanks open the door, a solid mahogany slab.

"James."

He angles his head toward Thomas but doesn't look at him.

"It's good to have you home."

James walks out of the office and quietly shuts the door behind him. He glances across the lobby, relieved to see his sons are still in the conference room. Boys Carlos didn't trust James to raise.

CHAPTER 2

CARLOS

Five and a Half Years Ago
December 1
Puerto Escondido, Mexico

He lurked outside Casa del sol's beach bar, that guy who came with Aimee. Ian, that was his name. Camera slung over his shoulder, he looked at me every so often. Why was he still here? He should have left with her.

Imelda Rodriguez, the hotel's owner and the woman who posed as my sister, told me Aimee had flown home the day before, a few hours after I'd dropped her off at the hotel. The only reason I knew that was because I'd come by the hotel again this afternoon to deliver Imelda a clear message: Stay away from me and my sons. She was not my sister or their aunt. I didn't want her in our lives. She'd schemed, she'd manipulated, she'd lied. All so she wouldn't lose her hotel, of which she was behind on payments. Thomas Donato had paid her to keep up the fabricated life he created for me.

I still didn't know why he felt the need to involve Imelda. And at the moment I didn't give a flying crap about him. Sitting at the bar, I tossed back a shot of Patrón and swiped my mouth with the back of my hand.

Two days before, Imelda had confessed I was not Jaime Carlos Dominguez. My name was James Charles Donato and I'd been living in a dissociative fugue state for nineteen months and counting. Anytime, any day, anywhere, I could snap out of it. Boom! I'd be James again. The real me. When that happened, I'd lose every memory I'd had since that day I woke in the hospital to the whir of machines, tubes snaking from my arms, and the gagging stench of dried blood, antiseptic, and my own unwashed body. I didn't have any idea who I was or where I was from. I didn't have a single memory in my head but for that first one. That of a doctor looming over me and asking for my name.

When I would emerge from the fugue, I'd forget how much I had loved my deceased wife, Raquel, and my sons. I wouldn't remember Julian's hug when he learned I'd adopted him as my son, or recall the first time Marcus squeezed my finger and gave me a toothless smile.

I would forget who I was now. Jaime Carlos Dominguez.

For nineteen months I hadn't been living a lie. I'd *been* a lie. A man with a false identity and no past.

As for my future, it seemed I might not have one. My brain would flip the switch from Carlos to James, and the man I was today would disappear tomorrow. And when I did, my sons would have a father who didn't know them and might not want them.

¡Dios! What will happen to my sons?

I slammed back a few more shots and swallowed the tequila's burn. I swore I intended to go home after seeing Imelda, but hell. I needed a drink, or two. I emptied another shot glass. Make that five.

The tequila knotted in my esophagus. I hissed through my teeth, pounding my sternum with a fist, then coughed.

I glanced at my watch. Good, I had some time to hang around before returning home. Natalya, my deceased wife's half sister, was watching the boys. As a representative for her father's business, Hayes Boards, she was in town for Puerto Escondido's annual *torneo de surf.* She planned to leave this morning but given the nuclear bomb that went off this past weekend, she'd stay another week. I needed to deal with the fallout without worrying about who was caring for Julian and Marcus.

I needed another drink.

Pouring more shots, I emptied them in quick succession—one, two, three—striking the glass on the counter after each round. After downing my ninth shot, I stared at my reflection in the mirror behind the bar. Bloodshot eyes embedded in a face with three days' growth on my jaw stared back at me. The mirror tilted.

"Whoa," said the guy on the stool beside me. He pushed me back in my seat.

"Lo siento." I leaned on my elbows and lowered my head into my hands.

"No worries, dude." He clapped my sweat-drenched back. Sun-bleached hair fell over his brows. He tossed it back with the flip of his head and grinned.

"You're done here, Carlos. I'm cutting you off, friend," Pedro the bartender told me in Spanish. He swiped my glass off the bar and underhanded it into the sink, where it clattered against the other dirty glasses.

I snagged the bottle of Patrón, the finger of liquor left inside sloshing around, and stumbled off my stool. Pedro yelled at me as I left. I waved a hand behind my head. "Put it on my tab."

I took a long step off the bar's deck and dropped into the sand. The early evening sun scorched my face, temporarily blinding me. Squinting against the glare, I trudged across the sand, and sought refuge under the shade of a lone palm. It offered no reprieve from the dry heat.

Neither did the tequila, I thought, wiping the sweat off my forehead. I was still the guy with the fake name and doomed future. And I didn't have an ounce of control over it.

Leaning back against the palm trunk, I gazed at the sun taking a dunk into the ocean's horizon. Bile thickened in my throat, and my stomach gurgled in that unsettled I-have-to-vomit sort of way. I rubbed the front of my shirt and eyed the trash can nearby. A camera clicked.

I scowled at the photographer.

Ian lowered his camera, letting it hang from the strap over his shoulder. He used his hand as a visor, shading his face. "The lighting's phenomenal. It was a good shot."

I flipped him off.

He held up his hands, palms out. "Hey, I should have asked."

"Forget about it." I probably would. One day. I offered the near-empty bottle. "Drink?"

He grabbed the bottle's neck, wiped the lip with his shirt, and drank. His lips spread thin over his teeth as the liquor's sourness made its way to his stomach. He returned the bottle, now empty.

"Why are you still here?"

He clipped a cap on the lens. "Imelda's looking up some information for me."

I overhanded the Patrón into the nearest trash can and missed. It dropped into the sand. *Shit.* "I wouldn't trust anything she tells you."

"My situation is unrelated to yours."

"You mean she hasn't been paid to lie to you?" I pushed away from the tree and the horizon tilted.

"Steady, man." Ian snagged my arm. He scooped up the Patrón and waved the bottle at me. "Did you drink the entire thing?" he asked, tossing it into the trash. It crashed onto a pile of empty Corona bottles left over from the *torneo*.

I shook my head. *No, thank God.* I was drunk, not comatose. The bottle had been less than half-full when Pedro started pouring me shots. Speaking of shots . . .

"I need another one." I stumbled away from the tree.

Ian folded his arms. "You're just like him, you know."

"Of course I look like James." *You idiot.*

He nodded his head in the direction of Casa del sol's lobby. "I was talking about your brother Thomas."

The asshole who choreographed my mess of a life. Definitely not the person I wanted to see. I couldn't be responsible for what I'd do to him if I did. He'd find out firsthand what it was like to recover from reconstructive facial surgery and pulled shoulder ligaments.

That had been my second memory. Opening my eyes to a woman sitting beside my bed. She'd worn a white blouse and gray skirt, her shapely legs crossed and leaning to the side. Breathtakingly beautiful, that was my first thought of her. Like an exotic model from an upscale clothing catalog. Or the ones airbrushed to perfection on the glossy pages of a magazine, like the one she flipped through. I lifted my head to see what she was reading and groaned at the laser-sharp pain that exploded in my shoulder.

Her head snapped up. She tossed aside the magazine and leaned over me. Her hand found mine, soft and cool to the touch, and when she smiled, her cocoa eyes sheened. "Don't move; you need to rest," she said in a soothing voice. "Your nose and cheekbones had to be reset. The less you move, the less pain you'll feel." Her fingers fluttered over my face, drawing my attention to the bandages wrapped around my head.

She nodded toward my right shoulder. "You dislocated it." She explained that the swelling had finally diminished enough for Dr. Mendez to pop the joint back into place. I had to keep it immobile, then I'd need therapy.

My gaze skimmed her face, the sharp angles of her cheekbones and straight line of her nose, hinting of European descent. I frowned. How could I know that when I didn't even know who she was, let alone my own name?

"Who are you?" I whispered through chafed lips.

"Imelda." She smoothed her palms over the front panel of her skirt. "Imelda Rodriguez. I'm your sister, and I'm going to take care of you, Carlos. *Sí?*"

"*Sí.*"

I had a sister.

I didn't know why it was important. It was more like a feeling I had. This woman would watch over me while I healed. For the moment, I felt safe.

As I eyed Ian a few paces away, an uneasy feeling rippled through me, adding to the queasiness brought on by downing too much liquor in the span of twenty minutes. I wondered if I was any safer today than I had been before I entered my fugue state.

Pedro left his post at the bar and went around the back, probably for a smoke. He'd never know I'd slipped back into the bar for one more shot. "I'm getting a drink. Want one?"

Ian shook his head and shoved his hands into the pockets of his cargo shorts. "Drinking yourselves to oblivion won't solve your problems."

I snorted in disgust.

"Yeah, your bro's fairly wasted, too. He's been a permanent fixture in the lobby bar since he arrived two days ago."

"I don't give a fuck. As for my problems, those shots have done a phenomenal job making me forget them." I started to walk away.

"May I give you a word of advice?"

The warm sand under my feet and the alcohol I'd consumed were turning my body to liquid. I swayed as I stared at him. He didn't say anything, just tilted his head and lifted both brows, waiting. I sighed, circling my hand. *Come on, man, spit it out.* I needed to move on.

"Talk to him," Ian advised.

"For real?" I scoffed, and started to turn away again.

"Then go beat the crap out of him. Trust me, you'll both feel better."

"I don't want to see him," I said around a thick tongue. Maybe I shouldn't have another drink. I didn't need Imelda to cart my ass home.

"Suit yourself." Ian made the briefest eye contact before touching his brow and giving me a two-fingered salute in the direction he started walking. He was probably going to go pack for his flight back to the States. Back to Aimee.

"You love her," I said when he reached the bottom steps where the hotel's patio kissed the sandy beach.

He swung around and leveled his gaze with mine. "Yes, I do. Very much."

"Treat her well. Apparently, I didn't do such a great job."

He gave me a brief nod and jogged up the steps, taking them two at a time.

My phone buzzed. A text message from Natalya.

Will you be home for dinner?

I wiped the sweat from my eyes and texted back.

No. Not tonight.

I didn't want to show up drunk. Not before the boys went to sleep. They didn't need to see how messed up their father was. But Natalya . . .

Wait up for me.
Please.

She pinged back within seconds.

I will. Be careful.

I worried her. She told me as much when I laid out my tragic story like a freshly caught fish split open, skinned, and deboned. I felt like that fish out of water. Flapping around and gasping. Floundering as I tried to make sense of it all. The lies, the deceit. The abandonment. My family had left me here, like a discarded flip-flop lost in the sand. Natalya had stared at me, her eyes the size of the full moon outside my bedroom door, her jaw unhinged. Then she cried and tried to comfort me. I didn't want her sympathy, and I especially didn't want her pity. I punched the wall instead and went for a run. I ran hard, and fast, and for miles. Because if I stayed with her she'd see me cry, too.

Slipping the phone back into my pocket, I looked at the ocean and debated where to go next. Beside me was the beach bar. Behind me was the hotel. Ian had disappeared into the lobby and Thomas was somewhere inside. Most likely the lobby bar. *You're just like him.* Ian's words returned like waves that kept on coming. Forget the tequila. I needed to paint.

I flipped through my prefugue paintings, the ones Thomas had shipped here under the guise they were mine. I studied them as though seeing them for the first time. These were his. I mean, mine.

James's.

Whatever.

I snapped through the canvases, leaning one after the other against my shins. Paintings of landscapes I could only assume I'd once seen. A forest of oaks in the evening light. A meadow at sunset. An ocean cast in the hues of slate and stone. Where were these places? What meaning had they held for him?

Not him. Me, I corrected. What meaning had they held for *me*?

Nothing. Abso-fucking-lutely nothing.

I slammed the paintings back against the wall and shoved open the window. The evening breeze, heavy with salt from the ocean and smoke from the grills parked on the sidewalks below, exploded into the room. I sucked in the pungent air and a palette knife of pain sliced through my skull as though my brain were a glob of acrylic paint. I pressed the heel of my hand against my forehead. Tomorrow's hangover would be nasty.

In the far corner of my private studio, paintings of Aimee's likeness mocked me. I'd been painting her for over a year, the woman I reached for in my dreams. Her image morphed painting after painting until it had become almost an exact replica of the woman I'd found crying outside my studio.

That had been the ultimate mind-screw, seeing her sitting there; to touch the woman who left me baffled on the nights she came to me. Always the same dream—always my reaching for her, kissing her soft lips until she faded away, leaving my arms empty and soul wanting. Longing for something. Or, had that been that other part of me, the James me that longed for her?

Those dreams stirred a mixture of baser emotions. Joy, sadness, anger, and fear. All but the fear dissipated when I jolted awake, gasping for breath. Fear clung to me long after I woke in a sweat, damp sheets tangled around my calves. Some nights it took hours to fall back to sleep. Other nights I remained awake until the first light of dawn. I'd lace up my running shoes and hit the pavement to burn off that fear.

But it never completely went away. Now I knew. In all honesty, I'd been afraid since the day I woke in the hospital. I thought the memory loss triggered that fear, when perhaps it had been something else warning me that everything Imelda and the doctors had told me about my past had been manufactured. Some buried part of me understood it was all a lie. *I* was a lie.

I scrubbed my face with both hands, hating that nightmare. I hated that image of Aimee luring me toward her. She represented everything

I couldn't remember and everything I would lose. Damn her. Damn her to hell.

I roared, grabbing one of the older versions of her image, and slammed it against the table. The wood frame splintered. I smacked the canvas again. Again, and again, and again. God, I hated her. I hated that I dreamed about her. I hated that she came looking for me. She ruined my life. *No!* I slammed the canvas against the tabletop. Imelda ruined my life. Thomas screwed me over. They screwed up my sons' chances of having a normal life.

Sweat broke out across my body and veins popped up on my arms as I did what I could to annihilate the painting. The wood frame fell apart and the canvas shredded. I lunged for another canvas.

"James!"

I whirled, teeth bared. Thomas stood in the doorway, suit pants wrinkled and white dress shirt unbuttoned at the neck, sleeves rolled up his forearms and jacket slung over his shoulder. His hair was uncombed and brown eyes wild. We had the same color eyes.

I sneered at him. He clutched the door frame, his chest heaving as though he'd been running. How long had he been there? How many times had he called my name?

No, he didn't call *my* name. I wasn't James.

"Don't, James. Don't destroy your paintings."

"That's not my name," I spat. "I'm not *him*." I didn't want to be him. *I am* me. My body, my life.

"Fine. Carlos. I don't care what name you go by. You're still my brother."

I jabbed a finger at him and ate the distance between us. "You're no brother of mine." I punched him in the jaw. His head snapped. He staggered back a few steps. White-hot pain radiated from my knuckles to my shoulder, rattling my arm. *That hurt.* I shook my hand.

Thomas gripped the door frame to right his balance. He pressed fingers to his chin, worked his jaw. "Damn. Guess I deserved that."

He deserved much more where that came from. I wanted to hit him again, beat him until *his* nose shattered and cheekbone cracked. He needed to leave. He needed to leave *now*. I pointed at him. "Get out." I had two sons to worry about. If I came home drunk, bruised, and bloodied, Natalya would be fuming and Julian would ask questions. He was almost six, and he was smart. He'd know his dad got into a fight and he'd want to know why.

¡Mierda! How do I tell them about me?

I don't. Not yet. They're too young to understand. I could barely wrap my own damaged mind around it.

Flexing my fingers, I gave Thomas my back. I picked up the damaged canvas from the floor. It had split down the middle, right through the beautiful eyes that had bewitched me for months. I tossed the ruined painting on the table, wondering if Aimee would visit me again in my dreams now that I knew who she was. Would that other part of me still try to communicate while I slept? Because that was what I believed James was doing. There was something he wanted me to know.

Thomas came into the room, edging the table. He stopped on the opposite side. "We need to talk."

"No, we don't. Imelda and Aimee have told me enough."

"They've only told you what they know."

Which was more than I cared to understand. The more I knew about James, the greater the chance I'd snap out of the fugue.

"I don't want to hear anything more, especially from you."

"I don't care what you want," Thomas snapped.

"Obviously. That's why I'm here," I scoffed, pushing off the table and extending my arms to encompass the room, the town. Oaxaca. This whole fucking country.

"God dammit." Thomas pounded the table. "Would you just listen? *Please.* Hear me out."

"Why now? Why not nineteen months ago when I was flat on my back in a hospital bed? Why not when my face was swollen and shoulder busted and I was going out-of-my-mind crazy wondering who the hell I was?" My mind flashed back to the hospital, to a man standing outside my door. Aviator glasses, expensive suit, and face etched in grief. Anger sparked, flaring hot like a struck match. "You were there, in the hospital."

Thomas shifted. His mouth parted briefly then flattened. He nodded.

"You gave Imelda the envelope with all my documents."

"Yes."

"You didn't say a damn thing to me and you paid her to lie!" I grabbed the jar of paint on the side of the table, the Caribbean-blue color I'd worked hard to customize so that it matched the eyes of the woman in my dreams. Aimee's eyes. I lugged the jar across the room. Thomas's brows shot up into his hairline. He ducked. The jar shattered against the wall behind him. Paint oozed like a Jackson Pollack painting, down the wall, puddling on the floor.

Thomas lunged out of the way. Paint stained the back of his shirt, dotted his hair. Blue polka dots like the cartoon animals in one of Julian's children's books. His shirt was ruined.

I shoved my fingers through my hair. "Go. Just go away."

Thomas hesitated; then he pulled out a card from his breast pocket and left it on the table. "I kept you hidden to keep you safe. Phil tried to kill you."

"The same guy who attacked Aimee? Where's he now?"

"In prison."

"Then I don't need to worry about him."

"There's more—" He stopped when I held up my hand. He scratched the side of his nose. "Suit yourself. Call me when you're ready to talk. But for now, I'm thinking it's probably best you remain in Puerto Escondido."

"I never intended to leave."

Thomas shot me a look before walking to the doorway. He picked his suit jacket up from the floor where he'd dropped it after I punched him. He folded the garment over his arm. "Promise me you'll call if you change your mind."

"About talking or leaving Puerto Escondido?"

"Both." He gave me a sad smile. "Take care of yourself and . . . watch your back." With that, he left the room.

CHAPTER 3

JAMES

Present Day
June 21
San Jose, California

"*Papá* will be angry."

"Who cares? He's always angry. He's also not our real *papá*."

Julian reprimands Marcus for what James thinks is the millionth time. Marcus, or Marc, as he's come to call him, must be sick of his brother's attitude. James sure is.

From the conference-room entrance, he watches Julian launch a spitball at the window. He's been busy while James was with Thomas. Spitballs dot the glass like falling snow. Julian shreds a napkin, wads the paper in his mouth, and blows through the plastic straw they found for their sodas in the lunchroom. The gooey wad splatters against the window and sticks.

Enough.

"Julian," James snaps with authority, a tone he adopted too quickly after first "meeting" the boys last December.

Julian jolts. He tosses the straw under the conference table.

James narrows his eyes on the wadded masterpiece. What a mess.

Most of the office staff has gone home. He left the boys alone in the conference room with chip bags and sodas from the lunchroom vending machines. Probably not the brightest idea he's had, but his lack of good ones has been on a downward slide since before he left the States years ago.

He glances down at where Marc sits. Doritos fragments litter the floor around his chair like speckled paint on a drop cloth. "Let's clean up. Time to go."

Julian chuffs—a short, sharp exhale that fluffs his bangs. "Go where?"

"Home."

"We sold our home."

"Don't start, Julian," James warns. "Now, clean up."

Julian groans and picks up the straw. He launches it into the trash.

"Nice aim," James compliments. The kid's a natural athlete. He's seen him dribble a soccer ball in the sand with his friends and shoot consecutive three-pointers on their driveway back in Puerto Escondido.

Julian slides James a look and pulls his backpack over his shoulder. He rises from his chair and starts walking to the door.

"Forgetting something?"

Julian's shoulders slump and he turns around, dragging his feet. James gestures at the window.

"Fine. Whatever." Julian drops the backpack into the chair he vacated.

"You too, Marc." He points to the floor.

Marc looks at the floor. His mouth forms a small circle, surprised at the mess. He slides off the seat and picks up the pieces, popping a couple into his mouth.

"Don't eat them."

His son looks up at him. A chip hangs from his lower lip. He wipes it off. "*Lo siento, Pa—*. I mean, sorry."

James drags a hand down his face. He kneels beside Marc. "No, it's my fault. I didn't mean to snap. Here, let me help." He cups his palms and motions for Marc to give him the chip fragments. "People have walked all over this carpet. What if they'd stepped in dog doo-doo?"

Marc scrunches his face. "Doo-doo?" He giggles at the funny word, then cocks his head. "What's doo-doo?"

"Dog shi—" James catches himself with the shake of his head. "Um . . . *caca*?"

Marc's mouth stretches wide over his teeth.

"Gross, huh?"

Marc nods vigorously and wipes his tongue on the back of his hand. James laughs. "I think you'll be fine."

He tosses broken chips into the trash, then picks up the colored pencils scattered across the table. Marc's open notepad catches his attention. The sketch of a wolf head is rudimentary, but well beyond the talent of an average six-year-old.

"You did this?" James points at the sketch.

Marc drags the pad toward him and flips the cover closed, sliding it into the open mouth of his backpack.

"It's very good." James gives him the pencil case. Marc averts his gaze as though embarrassed by the compliment. He adds the pencil case to his backpack and zips the pack closed.

James sighs, wondering how he'll ever get through to the kid. Aside from the lack of memory, he's still the same guy. He's still their dad. Someday, hopefully, Marc will see that. Julian, too.

James joins Julian at the window. He plucks a few spitballs. Their hands brush.

Julian shifts away. "I've got it."

"Fine," James replies in the same short tone. Six months living under the same roof together in Puerto Escondido and they were starting to sound alike. Maybe they always did. He lets Julian finish the rest.

His son dumps the soggy wads into the trash, brushing his hands together, then wipes them dry on the back of his jeans. Snatching up his backpack, he leaves the conference room. Marc walks in a wide circle around James and jogs after his brother.

James blows out a breath and grabs Marc's pack, tossing it over his shoulder. One fun-filled day of parenthood in the States down. A gazillion more to go.

⁓

James stands with the boys in the empty hallway of his childhood home. Aside from a few pieces of furniture—his mother's Henredon & Schoener couch in the living room and the antique Italian walnut table in the dining room—the house is empty.

Julian drops his backpack on the floor and kicks it against the wall. "This sucks. Where are we supposed to sleep?"

Good question. Hopefully there are beds.

It's past ten. Too late to find a hotel in an area that typically has a 100 percent occupancy rate during the workweek. He leads his sons through the house, tossing the pizza box with their leftover dinner on the kitchen countertop.

Marc sniffs the air and scrunches his face. "It stinks in here."

Yeah, it does. James noticed the stale, sour "old house" smell he once associated with his dying father as soon as they opened the front door. He also smelled a subtle, powdery aroma as though his mother's perfume had gone bad. It reminded him too much of growing up here and why he spent so much time at Aimee's house.

"The house has been closed up for a long time. It'll go away when we open the windows," he tells his son.

Marc wanders over to the great room's French doors and presses his nose and hands to the glass. He peers into the darkness of the backyard. "Where's the beach?"

"There isn't one." Julian flops onto a leather couch. That piece is too new to have belonged to his mother. Thomas must have brought it over from the Donatos' warehouse. Hopefully he had beds delivered, too.

"There is a beach." James cuts Julian a look and joins Marc at the door. "But it's twenty minutes from here. Back there is a forest. I'll show you in the morning. We can walk the trail. We might see a bobcat if we're lucky."

Marc's fingers curl against the glass. He gnaws his lower lip. James takes it as a sign of interest.

"So, where *do* we sleep? The floor?" Julian slips on his Beats and cranks up the music on his iPhone.

James sighs. God, he hopes they don't have to sleep on the floor. Thomas said he stocked the house with the basics. Towels, dishware, milk, a few dry goods. He hopes he remembered sheets and pillows. And beer.

His mouth salivates. He could really use a cold, dark brew after today. They've been awake for almost twenty-four hours. The boys caught a few hours of sleep during their layover in Mexico City, but James had been afraid if he closed his eyes, the boys wouldn't be there when he woke. So, he stayed awake.

Selling their home and his gallery in Puerto Escondido had been an easy decision for him. He would have returned to California sooner if it hadn't been for his sons. They didn't want to leave. After he first told them, he only mentioned their "grand adventure" every so often, giving them a chance to get used to the idea. He also had them finish the school year. Better to wait for summer when they had time to get used to their new surroundings. Besides, he had to wait on the boys' visas and his own identification paperwork.

Soon, Julian and Marcus took to the idea of a big move, until the FOR SALE sign was posted in their front yard. That was when the idea became reality and James became the instant family "bad guy."

33

And he's tired of being assigned that role. All he wants is to get settled and get on with his life. Kids adjust. Eventually they'll get used to the move, and to him. He hopes.

Marc yawns. James gives his shirtsleeve a gentle tug. "Come on, kiddo. Let's find a bed for you."

They find queen-size beds made up with sheets, blankets, and pillows in James's and Thomas's old rooms. Marc whines. He doesn't want to sleep alone. After a bit of prodding from James, Julian reluctantly offers to share a bed with his little brother.

James retrieves the luggage from the car his eco-conscious brother bought him—a freaking Prius—and leads the boys down the hallway. "Which room?" He points to his old door, then Thomas's.

"This one." Julian walks into the room on their left. James's old room. He's surprised how good that makes him feel, and he doesn't breathe a word about that to Julian. The kid will just change his mind.

James shows them the bathroom, then waits nearby as they ready for bed. Once they're under the covers, James leans over as if to kiss Marc's head. Marc's fingers squeeze the sheet he's pulled to his chin. James hesitates, hovering over his son. All of Julian's talk about James not being their "real dad" has left Marc confused and withdrawn where James is concerned. The kid was more affectionate with his teachers and the neighbor's dog. At least he hugged them. James can't remember the last time someone has hugged him, let alone touched him, other than resting a hand on his shoulder, or poking an arm to get his attention.

James straightens and does his usual hair ruffling. Anything more than that and he chances Marc's receding further than he already has.

Marc smiles and shimmies deeper under the covers. The air is cooler here compared to Puerto Escondido's dry, salty nights.

Julian is sprawled on top of the covers on the other side of the bed, sporting a ratty T-shirt and gym shorts that reach his knees, still plugged into his music. James points to his own ears and motions for Julian to put away the headphones. "Sleep. Now."

Julian exhales, cheeks puffing like a fish. Rolling to his side, he slips off the Beats and tosses them, along with his phone, onto the side table. He keeps his back to James, and within seconds, his breathing evens. He's already fallen asleep.

"Good night," James murmurs from the doorway. He flicks off the light and closes the door, leaving it cracked to allow in a ribbon of light from the bathroom down the hall.

A whispered "Good night" reaches him as he turns away. James stills, blinking away the burn. As Marc's words sink in, James sends up a silent prayer.

He gives the door frame a couple of knocks and returns to the kitchen. When he puts the pizza in the fridge, he finds a six-pack of Newcastle on the top shelf. *Thank God.* Popping the top, he breathes in the ale's roasted-nut aroma. Muscles bunched from traveling unwind. He tosses back half the beer before leaning against the countertop. He crosses his arms, letting the bottle dangle from his fingers, and inhales, long and deep. His eyes drift close.

He is finally home, but not really home.

This isn't his home.

But he didn't belong in Mexico either, so he left that life behind. Not just because California is familiar, but because Carlos had every-thing James wanted before the accident—an art gallery to display his work, a classroom to teach others, and a studio ideally situated to take advantage of a full day's natural light. Then there was Carlos's artwork, paintings well beyond James's expertise.

As ashamed as he is to admit it, James is jealous of the man he was in Mexico.

He pushes away from the counter and stretches his arms overhead. His back pops and cramped legs ache. Feeling restless, he glances out the windows and considers going for a midnight run. He'd do it if he felt comfortable leaving the boys alone. They're still too young, and it's their first night in a foreign country and a strange house. A house that had been home to Phil during the months leading up to his arrest.

Beyond the glass, he stares into the dark woods of oak and pine, which looks peaceful during the summer months. A place of rebirth and renewal. But in the winter, it's dark and sinister, with branches bare and bent like bones.

Skeletal like Phil's frame.

Six days until he's released. Six days to figure out how to avoid him, along with the rest of his family. Would Phil come here since it's the last place he lived?

His gaze jumps to the dead bolt on the back doors. Swearing under his breath, he e-mails himself a reminder.

CHANGE THE LOCKS.

He slips his phone into his back pocket and looks around the room. Pent-up energy channels from jittery fingers to cramping calves. Maybe his old treadmill is in the garage.

James makes his way there, flicks the light switch. LEDs flood the four-car garage and his chest rises sharply. He knew his belongings were there, what he had before and what he shipped from Mexico. But knowing and seeing are two different things.

The bulk of his items take up the expanse of two car spaces, cardboard boxes stacked like fat square pillars. They hold everything he wanted to keep from a life in Mexico he wished had never happened, and a life before that he never intended to leave. Basking in the LED glow, his two lives converge atop the smooth concrete.

He moves into the garage, drawn by the thick black Sharpie lettering on a stack of boxes. ART SUPPLIES. He slowly sweeps his hand along the words, recognizing Aimee's handwriting. When did she pack his stuff? Before or after she found him? He can't imagine how difficult the months after Thomas announced his death had been for her. The need to hold her from just thinking about it nearly stops his heart.

The words blur and for the second time that night, James's eyes dampen. Knowing Aimee, she would have packed his supplies neatly and orderly, even with the knowledge he would never use them again.

And he most likely won't. The hunger inside him—that drive to create, to share his interpretation of the world—is gone.

So is Aimee.

He punches the box and returns inside.

CHAPTER 4

CARLOS

Five and a Half Years Ago
December 8
Puerto Escondido, Mexico

It was dark when I stumbled up my driveway. Fourth night this week I'd spent with Patrón, liquid gold and the only remedy that got me through the lonely evening hours. After mucking through another day teaching art classes, organizing the gallery's next season of showings, and finalizing contracts on several commissioned works, I left my car at work and landed on a stool at La cantina de perrito, a bar down the street from my gallery. Natalya wouldn't be happy. The boys had been asking why I hadn't been around much.

Because your dad's a ticking time bomb, that's why.

Glancing up at the second floor, their bedroom windows black squares against the house's white stucco paint, I craved a sense of normalcy. To go back to the way things were before Aimee had shown up.

Face angled toward their windows, I stepped backward and stumbled over a planter edge. My shoulder slammed hard into the adobe wall lining my property. Pain spiraled like fireworks across my deltoid, waking up the old injury. I hissed and punched the bricks. *"¡Mierda!"*

I needed to get myself together. *¡El pronto!* If not for me, then for Julian and Marcus. I sucked the torn skin on my knuckles and shook my hand, trying to lessen the pain.

Thomas had left for California six days ago. Imelda texted me when he checked out of the hotel. True to his word, which said nothing of his character, Thomas didn't contact me again. Imelda had tried to reach me daily. I sent her calls directly to voice mail where the number in the red notification circle on my phone app had crept up all week.

I fumbled with the lock. The front door flew open. Natalya stood there, hands on hips, scowling. She wore a fitted white tank and a tie-dyed skirt that dusted the floor. Damn, it was colorful, just like her long copper hair. Bright and lustrous with multiple shades. I blinked hard, trying to focus, and stumbled through the door. She caught me before I face-planted. My chin dipped to her sunscreen-slathered shoulder. Coconut and salt. She'd been at the beach with the boys. Heck, she practically lived on the beach, even after years spent competitive surfing. She'd been a rock star on the board, just like her father, world-class surfer Gale Hayes.

Natalya stumbled under my weight. "You smell like a dirty bar mat."

I straightened, focusing on her head to keep the room from spinning, and gently tugged a few strands of her hair. "So pretty," I murmured about the colors. She was fair to her sister Raquel's dark. They shared a father, but both had taken after their mothers.

Natalya nudged my hand away. "You're drunk. Again."

"Yep." I lowered my hand and swallowed, my throat drier than the hillside behind the neighborhood. "Need water."

She followed me into the kitchen and rummaged through the cabinets. I filled a glass from the fridge water dispenser. She popped the cap on a bottle of aspirin she found next to the boys' vitamins and dropped two tablets in my palm. "This is becoming routine."

I smirked at her, popped the pills, and drank the water.

She watched me drink, her gaze zigzagging from the glass to my face and then to my hand. She sucked in a breath. "Carlos." She took the glass from me, setting it aside on the counter and cradling my hand. She brushed a thumb gently over the torn flesh. "What did you do?"

I pulled my hand from her grasp. "I had a run-in with a wall." Tonight was another low for me. I'd been punching things all week. My bedroom wall when I first told Natalya about what I'd learned from Imelda, then Thomas earlier this week, and now the bricks outside. It was time for me to dry out and do . . .

My thought tapered off. *Do what?*

What in God's name could I do to make my situation better? How could I ensure my sons were taken care of should I happen to one day wake up as James?

Natalya sighed and I raised my head as though looking to her for an answer. Realization dawned like the eastern sun, bright and luminous. Maybe she was the answer.

She curved an arm around my back. "Come on, let's get you upstairs."

She stayed with me while I washed up and brushed my teeth. Then she went to crack open the slider to the balcony and closed the screen, giving me a moment of privacy while I shucked my clothes and pulled on boxers and a shirt.

I flopped onto the bed, arms spread wide. My head spun in the opposite direction of the ceiling fan overhead. I groaned and closed my eyes, listening to Natalya move around the bed. The jangle of the sterling-silver bracelets she always wore. The steady patter of her bare feet walking on hardwood. The wisp of cotton sheets as she yanked them out from underneath me. Grunting, I lifted my hips for her. She stood near the end of the bed. I grinned and waggled my brows. She flopped her arms, giving me a disgusted look, and the similarity in that one gesture hit me in the chest, almost killing my buzz.

"You look like her." Her expression turned sad, and I wanted to take back the words as soon as they left my mouth. Damn alcohol. Liquor loosened my tongue.

"I'm not her."

No. You aren't.

Natalya pulled the sheet up, letting it float over me. She sat on the edge of the bed. "Do you always see her when you look at me?" she asked, her face searching mine.

Did I see my deceased wife when I rested my hand in the small of Natalya's back? Did I see her when I longed to kiss Natalya? Even though I hadn't yet tried, Natalya saw the desire to do so in the way we both knew I looked at her.

I missed Raquel, and always would. She was the mother of my sons. But it wasn't Raquel I saw when Natalya came to visit.

"I see you."

Her shoulders lowered and I reached for her hand. Our fingers twined and a terrible thought spilled into my head, oozing outward like watered-down oil paint until it covered me completely, making me desperate for an answer. "Was it real? Raquel and I?"

Has anything about my life here been real?

Natalya studied our joined hands. She flipped mine over and traced the lines in my palm. The pressure of her finger tickled. "Nat," I pleaded, my heart racing faster. I squeezed her fingers. Had Thomas bribed Raquel, too?

"I think what Raquel felt for you was very real." She folded my hand in both of hers. "I'd never seen her as happy as she was with you. She gave you both of her sons."

Air rushed from my lungs. "Good." I settled back on the pillow. "That's good."

She pressed my hand against my chest. "Get some rest, Carlos," she said, rising to her feet. "I leave in the morning and the boys need you."

"They need you, too." I lifted my arm toward her. "So do I."

"They have me." She opened her mouth, briefly hesitated with a short intake of breath, and said, "So do you. I like you, Carlos, very much."

I shook my head. "That's not what I meant."

She blinked and averted her face, cheeks tinged with embarrassment.

"I like you, too. But listen." I tunneled both hands into my hair.

Natalya sat back on the bed. "What is it?"

Eyes darting toward the hallway in the direction of Marcus's and Julian's rooms, my chest tightened. I'd told Aimee she'd never have her James back. It had already been almost two years, and I was convinced I'd be this way permanently. I'd always be Carlos. But it was nine days ago when the full impact of my condition had barely carved its hole in my chest. I understood now there were no guarantees. I could remain as Carlos for the rest of my days or wake up as James tomorrow. It all depended when my mind was ready to deal with the trauma that had triggered my condition.

"When I stop being me, you're all they'll have."

"That's not going to happen," Natalya said.

"But it can. It's a real possibility that it will. I don't trust anyone in the Donato family, so how can I trust the man I should be? I don't know what I was like. I could be just like Thomas, or that other brother he told me about—Phil. The one who'd sexually assaulted Aimee. I don't want someone like that anywhere near my kids, let alone raising them."

"How can you talk like that? You and James are the same person. Same body, same heart."

"But not the same mind."

"You have the same soul." She rested a hand over my heart and I clamped it to my chest with my own. "I can't believe James would do

43

anything to hurt them. You'll love them as James just as much as you love them as you."

"I wish I had your faith."

She splayed her fingers on my chest. "Maybe you will someday. Until then, how can I help? What can I do to put your mind at ease?"

"I want you to adopt my sons."

She jerked back. "What?"

"You heard me."

She stared hard at me. I stared back. "You're serious."

"Very. I want you to raise them should something happen to me."

"Nothing's going to happen to you. You're drunk. You don't know what you're asking."

"Yes, I'm drunk, and yes, I know exactly what I'm asking. You're their aunt. Julian is more related to you than to me, and Marcus adores you. It makes perfect sense."

"It makes absolutely no sense," she objected. "I live in Hawaii. You expect me to take your sons away from you, the only father they've known, when you're still alive?"

"But I won't be *me*." I gripped her hand. "I won't know who they are, and there's a very good chance I couldn't care less about them, not to mention the danger they might be exposed to if James takes them back to the States. I'd rather have them living with you in Hawaii than in California with the Donato family."

Natalya slid her hand from mine and stood. "I leave early in the morning. Can I think about this?"

I groaned, frustrated. Then I nodded. "Take your time. We'll talk in a couple weeks." She'd be back for the holidays.

She leaned over me, her face less than a foot from mine. She cupped my cheek. "You should think about this, too. You may feel differently tomorrow."

I doubted I would.

She kissed my forehead and I clasped the back of her neck, urging her lips to linger longer on my skin. She lifted her head a few inches and caressed my cheek with her thumb. "Take care of your boys, Carlos. And take care of yourself."

"That hasn't been an easy task lately."

"I know. But try. I'll be in my room downstairs if you need me, otherwise I'll see you in the morning." She moved to the door, her bare feet a whisper across the floor. "Good night," she said.

"Good night, Nat."

CHAPTER 5

JAMES

Present Day
June 22
Los Gatos, California

James should have known returning to his childhood home would reward him with a restless night. He floats in and out of sleep. The cold, deathly quiet interior of a house that's too large for the three of them keeps him awake. So does his overactive mind.

He tosses in the bed, the sheets tangling around his legs. He worries about his sons adjusting to their new country. He's concerned they'll never see him as the father they once had. He's paranoid he'll hear Phil walking down the hallway. And the person he wants to talk to the most, the one he used to talk to every day, is the one person he can't call.

James groans, rolling to his feet. He pads barefoot through the house, triple-checking the locks, then flips the thermostat switch. The fan rumbles to life. Vents creak, stirring the air, erasing the oppressive stillness in the house. Maybe the white noise will help him rest. Remarkably, he misses the ocean outside his bedroom windows.

He misses Aimee.

A memory moves gracefully through his mind the way Aimee did while in his arms as they danced. And suddenly, she's back there, in his arms, as he spins them around the crowded floor at Nick and Kristen's wedding. Her smile is dazzling and meant just for him. "I love you," she tells him.

He leans in to kiss her and the clock in the dining room chimes off the hour. James tenses, then sighs, a frustrated sound of longing. He punches the wall. Not hard enough to do any damage, but with enough strength to bring on the sharp sting of reminder that he is alone in this new life. He doesn't have anyone he can rely upon, or lean on, not in the way it had been with Aimee for most of his life.

God, I miss her.

He rubs his sternum with the base of his palm to relieve the ache and returns to the guest bedroom where he's been sleeping, or trying to sleep. He powers on his laptop and launches the browser. He should go to LoopNet and search for commercial properties. But what's the point? He has no desire to paint, and without painting, he doesn't have any art to show and sell, which means he must find a job. His interest in Donato Enterprises that Thomas sold on his behalf is enough for them to live off for now, but the money won't last forever.

James brings up the career-search website Ladders and stares at the home page. He graduated from Stanford with a double major in finance and art history, and because of his father's expectations of him in the family's import-and-export business, he completed Stanford's Spanish-language program. Thanks to his experience at Donato, he's more than qualified to apply for upper managerial positions. He can also return to school and get credentialed to teach high school or college-level art courses.

Both ideas sound utterly unappealing.

James opens a new browser window and finds himself staring at the satellite view of Los Gatos. He has two sons to support, needs to find a job, wants a new house, and definitely needs to exchange his car. He really should get back into painting. But he doesn't have any motivation to do anything other than look at the house he once owned with Aimee. This isn't the first time he's checked out the house, a three-bedroom, two-bath bungalow in the heart of downtown. He doubts it'll be the last.

He zooms into the photo until the roofline fills his screen. He doesn't recognize the car in the driveway. The sycamores in the backyard are overgrown and the grass left to brown. His index finger erratically taps the edge of the laptop. He doesn't like how the yard has deteriorated and he wonders if the same has happened inside their house.

He and Aimee were supposed to raise their children in that house. They had grand plans to expand—add on a second story and push out the back. And they were supposed to fall more deeply in love as they grew old there together. Instead, she married another man and now has a daughter.

What did she name her little girl?

He swears at himself and slams shut the laptop.

Thank God she doesn't live there anymore. He's not sure how he'd react with her there with another man. But damn, he feels like a stalker every time he Googles her, or the house. Or her café. He can't help it. The same craving that drove him to paint now drives him to learn everything he can about Aimee.

He doesn't deserve her and deep down he knows he must stop obsessing over her, but he can't help that either. He wants her back, *needs* her back, as much as his body needs air to breathe.

⤳

After an early-morning walk with the boys through the reserve behind the house, James finds himself on the sidewalk outside Aimee's Café. He didn't intend to stop here, but the nearest parking spot was three doors down and the boys are hungry. Starving, rather, as Marc pointed out during their excursion. It's well past breakfast time.

A sign squeaks overhead and James looks up. He recognizes the logo instantly. A coffee mug under a tornado-swirl of steam. He'd scribbled the logo, a crude drawing nowhere near what he could have designed. he had wanted to spark Aimee's interest to open a restaurant like he planned to open an art gallery. They'd both been working for their parents at the time. He never intended for her to use that rough sketch, but it touches him profoundly. It's as though she wove pieces of him into her dream.

Dressed in a wrinkled DC Comics *Suicide Squad* shirt, chino shorts, and Adidas slides, Julian cups a hand alongside his face and peers through the glass. "This looks good. Let's eat here," he says in Spanish, blatant defiance to James's request they speak English. School starts in two months, so they'd better get used to speaking the language regularly.

"No," James snaps. It's late morning and he's starving, too. But under no circumstance will he set foot inside the café.

Julian scowls and clamps his ever-present headphones over his ears.

"I'm hungry," Marc whines in heavily accented English.

"Me too, bud." James reaches for Marc's hand and almost stumbles in amazement when his son's smaller hand clutches his.

"I can't see the menu from here." Julian slips inside the café.

"Julian!"

Marc tugs his hand free and follows his brother.

James swears, glancing down the street toward the diner where he planned to take the boys. *Now what?* Does he wait here on the sidewalk like an idiot and hope the kids come back out when they realize he didn't follow? Or does he suck it up and go inside?

Through the glass he sees Julian placing an order.

"Shit." He sucks it up.

James yanks open the door. The bells overhead swing in a wide arc, hitting the wood-framed glass. Heads turn in his direction, exactly the attention he doesn't want. He gives the diners a clipped nod and freezes. A montage of photographs, stencils, and paintings cover the far walls. His paintings.

She kept them, after all these years. He stares at them until his eyes dry out—scenes of rustic barns in the foothills and meadows covered with morning dew overlooking the ocean, forests with sunlight breaking through a canopy of trees or moonlight reflecting off the waterfalls of Yosemite. He pushes a long, steady stream of air through his lips and his hand slides into his front pocket, fisting the ever-present engagement ring like a lifeline.

"James?"

The tendons around his ears tighten at the sound of his name. He slowly turns around and faces a woman with a distended belly. She gazes up at him as though he returned from the dead, and in a twisted sort of way, he has. Her lips part on a gasp at the same time she falls back a step, eyes growing large. He'd recognize those cornflower blues anywhere.

"Kristen," he rasps. She looks the same, yet different. Seven years has matured and enhanced his best friend's beautiful wife.

"It's you. It's really you." She launches herself into his chest and folds him in her arms, holding him as tightly as her pregnant stomach allows.

It's the first hug he's received in longer than he cares to remember. James's face tightens as he fights a sudden well of emotion, and ends up holding himself back. He doesn't return the hug, but awkwardly pats Kristen between the shoulder blades.

She leans back to look up at him. "Nick told me you were coming home and I didn't believe it. Then I could hardly wait until you got here. And now you're here." Tears spill over her cheeks. A silly grin stretches her lips wide; then she excitedly jumps up and down. "Oh my God, you're here!" she squeals.

James cringes. His gaze jumps to the swinging door that leads to the kitchen, then to the hallway in back before returning to Kristen.

She's still jumping and squealing. A smile fights its way onto James's face. No, Kristen hasn't changed much at all, except for her stomach. He stares stupidly at her belly. "You're pregnant."

She snorts. "Again. I know."

Nick visited him once in Puerto Escondido. When he couldn't reach Aimee, James had called Thomas. Nick's number was the third one he dialed. He had to hear from Nick that everything Thomas told him was the truth. Unlike the lies Thomas had been telling him for years, the one he'd hoped was a lie, that he'd been abandoned in Mexico, was the absolute, horrifying truth. Nick confirmed this with one sobering statement. "Yes, it's true, all of it."

Within a few days, Nick was with him in Mexico, filling him in on the six and a half years missing from his life. James learned about Aimee, how she never gave up on him, eventually finding him, only to let him go so he could live his life as Carlos. Nick then sat him down, because he'd been pacing the length of his living room like a crazed man confined in a prison cell, and gave him the cold, hard facts about Aimee. She's in love with another man. She's married and has a daughter. Of all the news he heard, that was the most heartbreaking. It nearly destroyed him.

James had thrown his glass of scotch against the wall, where it shattered into slivered fragments, just like his heart.

Now, Nick's own wife is pregnant with their third child.

Kristen rubs a circle around her stomach. She grimaces. "Four more months to go."

"You look good," he tells her honestly.

"So do you," she says, her exuberance from a moment ago gone. "It's good to see you. I never thought—"

Pots bang in the kitchen. Voices reach them, drawing his attention. His heartbeat accelerates. "Is she . . . ?" He looks anxiously at Kristen. "Is she here?"

Kristen shakes her head. "She didn't come in this morning."

He makes a noise in the back of his throat. She's not here, which is for the best. When he does finally see her, he doesn't want an audience.

James feels a tug on his shirt hem. He looks down at Marc. "May I have a doughnut, please?"

"We're not eating here, Marc."

"Anything else for you, sir?" the cashier calls over to James. His older son, standing at the head of the ORDER line, tosses James a challenging look.

"Julian," James barks. So much for not eating here. He glares back at his son.

"What? I'm hungry." Julian holds out his hands, silently asking what's the big deal. His expression morphs into feigned innocence as he walks past him and Kristen. Kristen's brows reach her ponytailed hairline as they both watch Julian meander his way through the maze of disordered tables. He flops into an empty chair.

Kristen smirks. "I see I'm not the only one who has my hands full."

James grunts, but the corner of his mouth tugs upward at their shared connection. Parenting.

"Why don't you join us? We just sat down." She points out a table near Julian where a toddler in a high chair exuberantly eats her oatmeal. Another girl with jelly-tinged lips stands in her chair humming.

"Sit down, Nicole," Kristen orders.

The girl sinks onto her chair.

"I'm so happy this one is a boy." She pats her stomach.

"Boys aren't much easier," James admits, thinking of the circles Julian and Marc run around him.

Kristen sighs. "Just different, I guess, right?" She tilts her head toward the counter. "Go order and come eat with us."

Marc scans the dining area. James nudges him in Julian's direction. "Sit with your brother. I'll get your doughnut."

At the counter, James scans the menu and orders a coffee and omelet. Trish, according to the chalkboard-style name tag, repeats back his order. Anger crawls up his throat as Trish rattles off the items. "That'll be ninety-five fifty," she concludes.

Julian had ordered enough for all three of them, for breakfast, lunch, and dinner. James yanks the wallet from his back pocket and shoves the chip card into the slot. *Pick your battles, man. Pick your battles.*

"Outside of the omelet, doughnut, and pancakes, pack the rest to go."

"Sure thing, sir." Trish smiles and hands him the receipt.

James doesn't bother calling the boys over to Kristen's table when he sits down. Let them eat alone. They could use this brief respite after the past couple of days.

Kristen passes her older daughter a napkin. "Say hello to Mr. Donato, Nicole. He's Daddy's friend."

"Hey-whoa." Mouth full of food, Nicole waves jelly-stained hands.

James returns a wave to the little girl who's a mirror image of the mother he's known since their youth. After a round of introductions where he learns Nick's youngest daughter is named Chloe, and a brief conversation about their kids, their ages, and favorite activities, Trish brings their drinks. Regular coffee for James and two giant mugs of hot chocolate under a mountain-size glob of whipped cream for the boys. She also sets down a large Mexican coffee and espresso shot on Julian's paper place mat.

"You've got to be kidding me," James grumbles.

Kristen leans over, shaking with silent laughter.

He looks at her. "I didn't ask for this," he admits without considering the deeper meaning of his words.

Kristen rests her chin in her hand. "I know you didn't. But sometimes, the best gifts in life are those we didn't know we needed."

James glances over at his sons. Both have whipped-cream mustaches. A quick chuckle vibrates his chest and he feels a slight lift in spirit.

"So, what *are* your plans?" Kristen asks, pulling his attention back to their table.

He drinks from his mug. "My plans?"

"You know, what you're doing for work, schooling for the kids, where you're living." She circles her hand, inviting him to share.

"You want my life story."

"I do, but the moment we're done with breakfast, I'm calling Nadia. She's in SoCal this week on business, but she'll want to know everything."

Nadia, the glue that binds the Aimee-Nadia-Kristen trio. James watches the steam rise from his mug as he considers Kristen's questions. "Do you plan to call Aimee, too?"

She is quiet for a beat. "I'm not sure. She's having a difficult time, James. She loves Ian and they're very happy together. But knowing you're *you* now, it's brought the past back." She crumples Nicole's dirty napkin and studies the wadded paper as though it holds all the answers. "You'll both have to figure out how to move forward in your own separate ways."

Soon, breakfast arrives, and after he finishes eating, they make plans to meet again. Kristen invites them to barbecue and swim at their house that weekend. On the way home, James drives around town. He shows the boys the school they'll attend and points out a local skate park crowded with kids Julian's age. His son sits up straighter to get a better look out the passenger-side window and James makes a mental note to purchase a skateboard. Julian surfs so he might like boarding.

It's past noon by the time they get home. Scents of toast and bacon assault their senses as James shuts the front door. The boys raise their noses and sniff. Julian scrunches his face at the hard-boiled-egg-and-vinegar odor.

James and Julian look at each other for a heart-pounding few seconds. Someone is here.

James sets the bag of take-out food on the floor. "Stay here," he orders the boys and cautiously moves through the house. Sweat dampens his armpits. Has Phil been released? He swore Thomas said six more days. Five now, since that was yesterday. He clenches his hands. Damn, he wishes he had a baseball bat. Or a gun. The scar on his hip throbs.

He rounds the corner where the hallway opens up into the kitchen and comes to a dead stop. He blinks as his mind attempts to process the sight before him. Standing at the marble-topped center island slicing hard-boiled eggs is his mother, Claire.

"What are you doing here?" He should be overcome with joy at seeing her for the first time in years. Any good son would be. But he wasn't a good son, and Claire had never been the kindest of mothers.

He really needs to change the locks to be certain other family members don't show up unannounced.

Claire sets aside the knife and gives James a critical look. He didn't shave this morning and his shirt is untucked and unpressed. He doesn't have to ask whether he passes inspection. Her pinched face is all the answer he needs. She taps her chin, a silent message that he should have cleaned up before he left the house.

He's thirty-six years old, for crying out loud. He won't be made to feel guilty about how he looks. He's already swimming in a cesspool of guilt as it is.

"What's all this?" He lifts a palm at the food.

"I've made lunch," she says, neatly brushing crumbs from her hands. "Welcome home, James."

He hears the boys come into the kitchen behind him. Marc squeals. Julian gawks before the first smile since they landed in California appears on his face. His expression goes full wattage. "Señora Carla, what're you doing here?"

CHAPTER 6

CARLOS

Five Years Ago
June 17
Puerto Escondido, Mexico

Marcus upended a bucket over his head. He squealed, kicking his chubby legs as sand spilled over his naked body, sticking to patches of sunscreen-soaked skin. I added another tower to the castle that I was building and Marcus was determined to destroy it. He waved his arms, knocking over another wall.

"Marcus." I grabbed him by the armpits and planted his bare ass farther from our sand masterpiece. I passed over his bucket and shovel. "Here, knock over your own castle." He grinned and stuffed a fistful of sand in his mouth. "Don't eat it." I grabbed his wrist and swiped my fingers across his tongue.

Marcus started to chew and I heard the crunch of coarse granules. His face scrunched up like a wad of paper and his brown eyes widened as he looked up at me in confusion.

"See what happens when you eat sand?"

He blew raspberries. Saliva-drenched sand drooled from the corners of his mouth.

I chuckled, turning back to the sand castle, determined to fix the wall Marcus just blasted. Near the entrance to our backyard, Julian passed a *fútbol* to his two friends, Antonio and Hector. He narrowly missed our new neighbor lounging under the umbrella she'd painstakingly erected in the sand about a half hour earlier. I finished the wall, added one more tower, then went searching for my phone in our pile of towels. Natalya wanted a picture of Marcus's latest sand castle.

I watched Julian steal the ball from Hector. He kicked it, a beautiful pass that soared over Antonio's head, landing smack-dab in the middle of our neighbor's sun umbrella. The umbrella toppled over, burying its owner underneath. She shrieked.

"Santa mierda," Antonio swore.

Pale legs shot out from under the toppled umbrella, kicking like eggbeaters. "Help!"

Julian's jaw unhinged.

I grabbed Marcus. "Help her out," I yelled to Julian.

"Oh, right," he said, shaking off his surprise. He followed my lead speaking English. Judging by the screeches emanating from underneath the umbrella, our neighbor was American.

I deposited Marcus in the sand with a stern warning that his butt better not move.

"Get it off, get it off me!" Legs kicked maniacally. A hand shot out.

I pointed at Hector and Antonio. "Grab the post." I moved behind the woman and gripped the top of the umbrella. "Now lift." I closed the canopy as we did so, making sure the aluminum spokes didn't snag in her hair or clothing. We side-shuffled and dropped the damaged umbrella in the sand.

Our neighbor lay sprawled in a beach chair that teetered on its side. The feet had sunk into the sand. She removed the wide-brimmed hat smashed low on her head and pushed back damp silver hair plastered over her eyes and forehead. Breathing heavily, face flushed, she pointed a bony finger with a sharp maroon-tinted nail at Julian. "You . . . ," she started, leaning forward. Her chair wobbled and both hands flew out to grip the arms.

Julian shifted back and forth on the balls of his feet. He ran a hand over his sweat-drenched, sandy head, shifted some more, and again ran his hand through his hair. The thick, short mass stuck straight up. *"Lo siento, señora."* His gaze jumped to me before casting to his feet. "I'm sorry," he repeated in English.

"And well you should be." She pushed from her chair and stood over him. "I was going to holler 'fantastic kick,' but you need work on your aim."

"Sí, señora. I mean, yes, lady." Julian swiped his hand across his chest, leaving a trail of sand. He brushed it off, scratching his skin.

I grabbed his wrist and gave him a stern look to stop fidgeting.

Our neighbor smoothed her paisley-printed tunic. Colors swirled across the sheer material. Gold sequins edged the sleeves and dress hem, sparkling in the sunlight. "I seem to be short an umbrella," she said, glancing over her shoulder at the mangled shade structure. She squinted at the sun. It blazed down on us, the air dry and stifling today. Sweat dripped down my chest and back. Perspiration glistened along our neighbor's hairline. Julian and his friends continued to shift, the sand burning the soles of their feet.

"Well, then." Our neighbor brushed her palms together, wiping off sand. "I guess I better head inside before I burn."

"We'll buy you another umbrella," I offered, my eyes narrowing on Julian. He'd be spending the next few Saturday mornings assisting my gallery receptionist, Pia. Floors needed to be swept and displays dusted.

Julian mumbled another apology.

Our neighbor's mouth knitted. "That won't be necessary. But, perhaps"—she looked over the sandy crew, tapping her chin—"your son and his friends will help me carry my chair and bag inside."

I wholeheartedly agreed. It was the least they could do. "Boys?" I prompted when no one moved.

"I have lemonade and I picked up some . . . what do you call them?" She snapped her fingers. "*¿Bizcochitos, sí?* I think that's what the cookies are called. You're welcome to some."

"*Sí, señora,*" the boys chimed in unison. They gathered her belongings—chair, bag, and towel—and ran into her yard.

I scooped up Marcus, who had just rubbed sand in his hair. "I'm Carlos, by the way. Your neighbor." I tilted my head in the direction of my house and extended my hand in greeting. She didn't take it because she didn't see it. She stared fixedly at Marcus. Her eyes sheened. I wondered if she had grandchildren; then I realized the sun blazed behind me. I shifted to the side so that neither of us looked directly into it.

She blinked a few times, briefly shifting her gaze toward me before landing on Marcus again. "I'm Cl—" She cleared her throat. "I'm Carla. Is this your son?"

"*Sí.* This is Marcus." I juggled him under my arm, and he giggled. "*¡Mas! ¡Mas!*" He clapped, begging me to bounce him again.

Carla clasped her fingers, holding her joined hands at her chest. "How old is he?"

"Almost seventeen months." I glanced at Marcus, who waved at Carla with both hands. "I think he likes you."

The corner of her mouth lifted slightly. "I like him, too."

Marcus squirmed in my arms. "*Por, papá!*"

A breathy laugh broadened Carla's smile. "*Papá.*" She watched Marcus squirm in my arms. Her eyes welled further and she looked down at the sand. "Ah, I better go." She wiped her hands against her hips. "Your son and his friends are waiting for their treats."

"It was nice meeting you." I offered my hand again. This time she took it.

"You, too, Carlos." She said. She sounded lonely.

"Señora Carla," I called when she reached the gate to her yard. "Join us for dinner tomorrow night? It's taco night. I barbecue lingcod."

Her fingers fluttered to her tunic's neckline. "I—I have plans to eat out."

"Should they change, just come on over. Six o'clock."

She lifted her hand in a half wave and proceeded into her yard.

"Come on, Marcus. Let's get you cleaned up."

∽

Five Years Ago
June 18

The sun hovered low on the horizon, kicking up a dry breeze. It offered little relief as Julian and I passed the *fútbol* in the backyard. With each return kick, Julian inched closer to the barbecue.

"Watch out. It's hot." I kicked the ball to the far side of the yard, away from the grill. It rolled to a stop by the gated entrance to the beach. I went to check on the grill.

Julian dribbled the ball to the center of the yard, cranked back his foot, and kicked, connecting hard with the leather. The ball soared into the air, over the adobe divide, and into Señora Carla's yard. Julian groaned dramatically.

I waved a grill brush in the air. "Go get it before Señora Carla returns," I said, assuming she went out to dinner as planned.

Julian darted through the wrought iron gate and ran to the neighbor's. I scraped clean the grate and closed the lid so the grill could warm a bit more. "Ready for tacos, little man?" I asked Marcus. He pushed a toy truck across the grass.

"*¡Un taco!*"

"Say, 'I want a taco.'"

"Taco!" he repeated, grinning.

"Close enough." I smiled back.

Julian returned, ball tucked under his arm. He held open the gate for Carla. "The lady was sitting in her yard all by herself." He blurted the words and slammed the gate. Carla jolted. She shot him a look and Julian grinned. "I told her she could eat with us." He dropped the ball to the ground and juggled it across the yard, where he left it in the dirt.

Carla remained at the gate, even reached for it before her hand fluttered up and smoothed her hair. She'd clipped the slate tail at her nape, an elegant accent to her white-linen trousers and pale-pink blouse. She looked uncomfortable and ready to leave. She reopened the gate.

I set the grill brush aside and strode quickly across the yard. "You'll stay for dinner?"

"I had plans to go out, but they . . ." She kept her gaze focused somewhere on my chest. Her fingers flexed around the wrought iron.

"They what?" I searched her face for why she seemed indecisive about joining us.

Her expression briefly darkened, turned sorrowful. Then she schooled her features and lifted her chin. Her eyes didn't meet mine. "They fell through." She offered a small smile.

"Then stay," I insisted. "We have more than enough fish." I gently closed the gate when it occurred to me her reluctance might not have anything to do with her embarrassment over her plans falling through, or that we were strangers. "You aren't allergic?"

"To fish? No. I love fish." She wrung her hands.

"Then you'll love our fish tacos. They're *el mundo famoso*." I led her across the yard and pulled out a chair at the patio table. "Drink?"

"*Sí.*" She sat down.

I grinned, studying her. "I bet you don't drink tequila." I tapped my nose and pointed at her. "Gin."

She inhaled, the gasp just audible enough.

I clapped my hands. "Gin it is. One gin and tonic coming up." I waved a finger, retreating toward the house. "Lime?" I called out from the kitchen slider.

"Sounds lovely."

"Julian, come get the chips and salsa."

After I mixed her drink and grabbed a beer for myself, Carla watched the boys while I grilled the fish. "What brings you to Puerto Escondido?"

She circled the plastic stirrer inside her glass. "It's a place I've never been."

"Have you been to a lot of places?" Julian popped a salsa-loaded chip in his mouth. He crunched loudly.

Carla frowned. "Yes, many."

"Do you travel a lot?" Julian asked with his mouth full of chip.

Her eyes narrowed and I caught Julian's attention, motioning at my mouth. Julian swallowed loudly. "Do you travel a lot?" he repeated.

Carla set down her glass. Condensation glistened on the base. "I used to."

"Really? Where have you been?"

I tested the fish's readiness, curious myself.

"All sorts of places." She dreamily sighed. "Italy, France, England. I've also been to Hong Kong, Tokyo, Saint Petersburg."

"Where's that?"

"Russia."

Julian whistled.

"Business or pleasure?" I removed the fish from the grill.

"Mostly business. But this trip . . ." Carla removed the stir stick. She squeezed the lime in her glass. "This trip is for me. I'm here for the summer."

"Hmm." My mouth turned down as I considered what she said. Typically, a steady stream of foreigners rented the house next door throughout the summer months. Surfers, vacationers, college graduates traveling Central and South America before returning home to start their careers. At least once a week I lodged a noise complaint. The excessive partying kept my sons awake. I doubted we'd have that problem with Carla.

I set the fish platter on the table between the tortillas and cabbage. Carla moved her glass out of the way and her wedding band reflected the waning sunlight. "Will your husband be joining us?"

Carla flinched. She gave me a blank look. I pointed with the tongs at her wedding band.

"Oh." She splayed her fingers and stared at the ring. "I always forget it's there. No, no, he won't be coming. He passed away several years ago. I've worn it for decades. It doesn't make sense to remove it just because he died." She tucked her hand in her lap. "I don't have any interest in meeting anyone else."

"You never know," Julian said, fixing himself a taco. "You're old, but you can't be that old."

"Julian." I firmly set down the tongs.

He jutted a shoulder. "She's still pretty."

"Julian," I harshly whispered.

Carla's cheeks took on a rouge hue. She shifted uncomfortably in the chair.

"He's six and a half," I told Carla as though his age was an excuse. I handed her a plate and glared in warning at my son. "Please apologize."

"Sorry," Julian muttered. He flopped into a chair and stuffed a chip in his mouth.

Marcus toddled over, catching Carla's attention. "Your son is beautiful. I see you in him," she said.

I glanced down at Marcus. He had my brown hair and eyes. But his cheekbones and skin tone favored his mother.

My breath tripped up my throat, the tightness fainter now than in the past when I thought of Raquel. She'd been gone for nearly a year and a half.

Marcus raised both arms, trucks in his hands. I lifted him into his high chair. "How about you, Señora Carla? Any children?"

Her eyes remained fixed on Marcus. Her expression turned sorrowful. "I had three sons. Once."

༄

Late that night, I stared at the framed photo of Raquel and me, the one I kept on the bureau in my room. Our foreheads and noses pressed together, we shared a laugh. About what, I didn't remember, but Raquel's dry wit often left me lurched over, stomach cramped and eyes watering. Laughter dissipated the shadows that lurked in the recesses of my mind, even if only for a short time.

We'd just been married on the patio of Casa del sol overlooking the wild, chaotic surf of Playa Zicatela. Our love had been like that. Swift and dynamic. I often wondered if I would have fallen so deeply and quickly had I not been terrified and broken. But I had loved her from the moment she walked over to where I waited in the physical therapy office. She pushed her hair behind an ear, where I caught a glimpse of the unadorned divot in her lobe, and extended a hand in greeting as she introduced herself. For me, that first touch peeled off the outer layer of anxiety that had kept my heart racing since the moment I woke up in the hospital a month before. A rush of air left me, and I recognized the inklings of hope. I would be all right.

Within moments, she coaxed me out of my sullenness and the chair with a determination I initially envied and rapidly adopted. If I couldn't fix my brain, then I needed to focus everything I had within me to repair my body.

My wounds were mostly superficial. Facial bones knitting, lacerations healing to pinkish scars, and soon my shoulder would improve. Judging by the condition of my body, Raquel remarked on that first day, I'd been athletic my entire life. Doing what, I had no clue, but within four months I was running 10Ks. I'd been training for a marathon when Aimee showed up and knocked my world on its ass. On race day, a week after she'd left, I nursed a hangover and wallowed in self-deprecating grief, rising from bed hours after the starting-line gun fired.

I smoothed a thumb across the glass, tracing the line of Raquel's loosely coiled updo sprinkled with baby's breath. Golden-brown tresses and honey eyes, she'd never looked more stunning. Dressed in white silk, the waistline loose over our child growing inside her, she radiated happiness. I'd been drawn to that joy. Raquel had been a bright light, the beacon in my dark world.

I missed my late wife, more so tonight than in past months. But I always longed for her whenever I tucked in the boys. Some nights I saw her there, seated on the edge of the bed, her long, graceful fingers tracing the lines of Julian's face as she sang a lullaby. Tonight, the illusion seemed real enough that I swore I heard her voice. How often I'd wished Marcus had the chance to hear her say "I love you."

She'd died on his birthing bed, of an aneurysm, while I watched as my newborn son, freshly cleaned and swaddled, wailed in my arms. We both cried.

I returned the photo to its spot on the bureau and thought of Carla. Her despair over losing her loved ones—how, I did not yet know—had been palpable. It got to me.

The air inside my room had become hot and stifling. I flipped on the ceiling fan, snatched my phone from the bedside table, and slid open the door to the deck off my room. Boards groaned as I strode across the rough wood. Leaning against the rail, I swiped aside a notification from Imelda—Please come see me after you close Monday—and called Natalya.

"Hey, you," she murmured. The dusty softness of her tone washed over me, easing the emptiness. Her voice did that to me, calmed and soothed.

"Did I wake you?"

"That's okay." She yawned. "I fell asleep on the couch." Fabric rustled, a lock clicked, and a door slid open. Wood creaked and she sighed. I pictured her easing into a patio chair, gazing at the same ocean before me, thousands of miles away.

I parked my elbows on the railing. "Long day?" It was midnight here, making it seven o'clock in Hawaii.

She hummed an acknowledgment. "I went paddleboarding with Katy and her students," she said of her friend. Katy ran a surf-and-paddleboard summer camp in Hanalei. "We fought the wind the entire time. The sunset was unbelievable, though. It looked like an orange-cream Popsicle melting into the water."

The corner of my mouth lifted. "Now I'm craving ice cream."

She laughed softly. "Me, too. What flavor?"

"Chocolate chip."

She groaned. "That's so boring."

"What do you suggest, then?"

"Poi."

"Poi?"

She hummed again.

"As in the taro root?"

"Yes." She laughed.

I made a face. "Sounds disgusting."

"It's to die for. You'll have to try it."

I made a noise of objection. *When?* I thought. You couldn't get poi ice cream here and I wouldn't travel. For the past six months, I'd refused to leave the state.

Under the moonlight, the tide lapped the shore like a dog's tongue in a water bowl. Lazy and rhythmic.

"I didn't mean to imply—"

"Nat, don't." I pinched the bridge of my nose. "Don't apologize." She hated reminding me about my condition. For a few moments, neither of us spoke. We listened to the rhythm of our breaths and I longed to have her here.

She sighed. "Since you didn't call to chat about ice cream, what *do* you want to talk about?"

I had so much to say to her, and something bigger to ask, but the words dissolved in my mouth the way water does on hot pavement. "Nothing in particular," I said. "I just wanted to hear your voice."

A throaty laugh reached my ear. "I sound like a frog."

"I should let you go. What time's your flight?"

"Too early." She groaned. "And I have meetings in LA all afternoon. See you in a few days?"

"Yes. We're looking forward to it." Because the way I saw it, Natalya was the only way I could keep my promise to Raquel, the one I'd made when I kissed her lifeless body for the last time.

I'll keep them safe.

♋

Five Years Ago
June 22

I found Imelda exactly where I expected at two forty-five in the afternoon: working on her laptop at La palma. Casa del sol's open-air restaurant had the best view in the entire hotel. The Pacific Ocean stretched far to the horizon, and the breeze coming off the water, fanned by the surrounding palms, was always welcome. On days like today, where the air smelled of wood smoke and the heat could singe eyebrows, my shirt was often drenched by noon. The loose sky-blue, button-down linen I'd changed into only an hour ago already had a sweat spot where my back had been pushed against the leather car seat.

Imelda ate lunch at La palma every day. At the same time and at the same table. She'd linger over her meal for hours, meeting with staff and updating spreadsheets. I trusted Imelda as much as I trusted Thomas, which pretty much amounted to zilch. *Nada.* But there was one thing I could rely upon, and that was her schedule. If anything, Imelda was consistent.

I veered around tables until I stood opposite her, my back to the ocean. She typed rapidly on the laptop, a Bluetooth in her ear, her brows pinched. She wore a white silk blouse and one of those super-straight, fitted skirts in gray. Basically the same type of outfit she wore every day, including that day in the hospital she introduced herself as my sister.

God dammit.

Just like that, I was angry with her all over again.

From behind the polarized lenses of my Maui Jims, I silently counted to ten, watching a surfer disappear into the hollow of a tube, then rapped my knuckles on the table to get Imelda's attention. Time to get this over with.

She looked up with surprised impatience. Then her eyes peeled wide. "Carlos. What are you doing here?" She stood, snatching a ballpoint from the table. She held the ends of the pen between her fingertips and thumb, rolling it back and forth, and smiled.

"You called me. What's so important that you can't tell me over the phone?"

"*Sí, sí,* of course." She gestured at the chair beside me. "Please sit."

I made a show of looking at my watch, then sat down, knees spread, back pressed into the chair, and elbows parked on the chair arms. My leg bounced.

Imelda returned to her seat. She clicked the ballpoint. "How are the boys?"

My eyes narrowed on that pen. She'd had one like it, annoyingly clicking away, while she confessed that she wasn't my sister and told me I wasn't Carlos. Between her sobbing and the compulsive clicking, it had taken an excruciatingly long time to get the entire story from her. Either it seemed that way or time slowed, I couldn't recall. That whole week was a blur.

Looking back, I think I always suspected she'd been hiding something from me. Those infrequent dreams of Aimee and my obsession to paint her face. That alone should have been motivation enough to realize something wasn't right. I could blame my reasons for not asking questions on any number of things—recovering from my injuries, falling for Raquel, caring for my sons, everyday life. But those were only excuses. When it came down to it, I had been afraid. Which only made me more disgusted with myself.

I smoothed a hand down the back of my damp head. "The boys are fine. They're at the Silvas' house."

Imelda spun the pen like an airplane propeller. Her mouth parted. She wanted to ask more questions about them but a waiter approached. He presented the menu.

I held up a hand.

"Are you sure? Diego's lemon sole seviche is light and delicious. Perfect for this god awfully hot day." She fanned her neck with a file folder.

I shook my head. "I have to leave in twenty. Nat's flight lands in an hour." Imelda dismissed the waiter and I gave her a bemused look. "Why *do* you work out here?"

She shrugged. "Habit. How's Natalya?"

"Good." She was flying here on business but planned to stay several weeks, which was typical during the summer months. She spent her vacation time with us.

Imelda sighed, knowing she wouldn't get any further details from me.

The waiter returned with a cappuccino she'd ordered before I arrived. He set the cup and saucer beside her laptop, bowed slightly, and left. Imelda ripped open a raw sugar packet and stirred until the crystals dissolved. She lifted the cup, blew across the surface, and sipped, testing the temperature.

I jiggled my knee and tapped the chair arm.

"Thomas signed over the deed."

I stilled. "When?"

She took another sip and set down the cup. "Last winter. The hotel is doing better than it was two years ago." As part of her deal with Thomas to portray my sister while I physically recovered, and to waylay any interests I might have had to learn who I really was, Thomas loaned her money, but on the condition his name be added to the deed.

She got to keep her hotel and I got a glorified babysitter.

"Is he still sending you checks?" Thomas had also compensated her.

"Not since December. I stopped cashing them over a year ago."

"Why did he keep sending them?"

She sipped her cappuccino. "Guilt would be my guess. He hates himself for what he did to you."

I wouldn't know. I hadn't spoken with him since he left Puerto Escondido last December.

"He's under investigation for faking your death. I guess your friend Aimee mentioned something about your being alive when she filed a restraining order against him."

"He told you this?"

She returned the cup to its saucer and picked up the pen. "*Sí*. We still talk."

"After everything he's done?" I bit out the words. She clicked the ballpoint and I swore. "He's keeping tabs on me."

"He cares about you, Carlos."

"I don't give a shit about him. He can rot in prison for all I care." Good riddance.

"He won't go to jail for faking your death. There's no law in your country—"

"My country?"

"I didn't mean . . ." She cleared her throat. "You're right. I apologize. The United States. Apparently designing a fictitious death isn't illegal, and that's what Thomas did. Your funeral and burial were for show. The authorities are looking into the consequences of your death. They want to know if Thomas gained financially."

I pinched off the sweat from the bridge of my nose and pushed the Maui Jims back into place. "The Donatos are wealthy. I'm sure he has."

"Quite the opposite. Donato Enterprises hasn't fared well since Phil's arrest. Your portfolio is still intact. Thomas has it all in a trust and has been managing it. He never collected insurance upon your death."

"How kind of him."

Imelda lifted her eyes toward the ceiling with an air of big-sister impatience. "Your investments, your accounts, everything. It's all there when you want it."

Which I didn't. She clicked the pen. I wanted to snatch it from her hand and fling it over the balcony. "Thanks, but no thanks. When you get word of Thomas's arrest, feel free to text the good news." I pushed up from the chair, wood legs scraping on the tile floor.

"Sit down, Carlos." There was the big-sister tone. I bristled, stopping midrise. She pointed her pen at my chair. "*Por favor.* This affects you. Hate me and Thomas all you want, but believe it or not, we both care about you. And I love your sons."

I eased back into the chair, my head cocked as a chill swept over me. "What does this have to do with them?"

Imelda looked left, then right. She set down the pen and leaned forward. "The authorities are asking Thomas questions about your death. I'm concerned they might come looking for you to verify everything Thomas has told them. You and I are the only ones here"—she gave the tabletop two distinct taps—"who know about you. Thomas gave me your identification papers. I have no idea where or how he got them. They can be legitimate, for all I know, but if they're not . . ."

I didn't breathe. Couldn't breathe. My back slammed into the chair. "I can be imprisoned or deported." Because I might be here illegally. Fake ID and no visa.

"No one can find out I helped you. I'll lose my hotel. And you, Carlos," she said, panicked, "you could lose Julian."

CHAPTER 7

JAMES

Present Day
June 22
Los Gatos, California

"You're Señora Carla?"

"Well . . . yes," she says as though this revelation shouldn't be a surprise to him.

James swears. He can't believe it. Claire vacationed in Puerto Escondido every summer and Christmas holiday for the past five years. She'd become close enough to Carlos and his sons that she was practically family. She hadn't once told them she *was* family.

James clamps his hands behind his neck and glances wildly around the kitchen. When would the lying and deceit end?

Marc shoves past him and hugs Claire around her waist. He presses the side of his face against her belly. Claire gasps; then the biggest smile James recalls seeing on her appears. She rests her hands on Marc's back, holding him against her.

"You love him." The words sound like an accusation. A pulling sensation ripples through him. He jerks his gaze away, envious of the affection his mother doles out for his son. *Her grandson.*

James shoves down the sour knot in his throat. As much as he wants to keep the truth from Julian and Marcus, he'll eventually have to tell them who Señora Carla really is. How will this news affect his sons on top of the other changes?

They won't trust anyone, he thinks somberly. Imelda wasn't their aunt. Carla wasn't a random neighbor. And Carlos wasn't their father's true identity. The only genuine person in this mix is their aunt, Natalya Hayes. Thank God they at least have her.

Claire folds her legs until she's eye level with Marc. She clasps his shoulders. James sharply inhales through his teeth. *Will she tell him? She better not breathe a word.*

He's outraged. These are his kids. There's no way he'll let his family screw with their heads. Between the death of their mother, and their father forgetting everything about them up until six months ago, they've dealt with more heartache and upheaval than any children should be expected to handle.

"I've missed you," Claire tells Marc, and James relaxes slightly, even if only momentarily. She rains kisses on Marc's forehead. "I have something for you. Julian, too." She smiles at his older son.

Julian has managed to maneuver around James to hug Claire. Then his sons wait, anticipation making them fidget, as Claire dips her hand into a reusable shopping bag. She presents Marc with a watercolor paint set.

James almost falls back a step. A paint set, from the woman who made him return the very first set he'd received. It'd been a birthday gift from Aimee. She made it very clear during his adolescence that he needed to remain focused on studies and sports, not frivolous hobbies.

A memory lurches across the field of his mind. His thirteen-year-old self, sweaty T-shirt plastered to his chest, grass-stained football pants hugging his hips, scuffed helmet dangling from his fingertips, arriving at his bedroom after football practice to find Claire riffling through his drawers.

He had stopped in the doorway, heart pounding in his rib cage. "What're you doing?"

"Miranda found paint on your shirt." Claire slammed a bureau drawer, moved on to the next one.

The housekeeper. She must have seen the shirt in the laundry. Oil pigment stained, so he made sure that when he painted at the Tierneys', he only wore ratty shirts—ones his mother wouldn't miss should he have to throw them away.

Her hand disappeared into another drawer, pushing aside sock balls. One dropped to the floor. She wouldn't find any more stained clothes, or paintbrushes, or pigment tubes, if that's what she was looking for. He'd become quite the expert at keeping his frequent visits to the Tierneys' a secret. His reason for spending so much time there was twofold. He really liked Aimee. She was cool and fun to hang out with. But he really loved to paint, and Mr. and Mrs. Tierney had given him a space in their home so he could do so. They even replenished his art supplies.

Why couldn't his parents do the same? Why couldn't his mother encourage him to pursue his passion like the Tierneys? His skill had flourished through their support.

Claire paused and leveled her gaze at him. "Are you painting?"

Why did she despise that he was?

He forced down that thick feeling in his throat and looked her in the eye. "No." He'd also become skilled at lying.

"Then explain the paint on the shirt Miranda found."

"It happened at school during a class project." He wanted to retract the words as soon as they left his mouth. Like a fumbled handoff, he'd dropped the ball. He wore a uniform to school. "Sister Katherine gave us permission to take off our shirts if we had on an undershirt," he embellished. "She didn't have enough smocks for the whole class."

She closed the drawer and approached him, unintentionally kicking aside the sock ball with the pointed toe of her designer heel. She cupped his dirt-crusted cheek. Her gaze pinged from his stringy hair to his chapped lips and back up to his eyes. Her lips parted on a resigned sigh.

"James, the shirt Miranda showed me is old and stretched out. Don't wear clothes like that to school. You have a drawerful of clean, white undershirts." Her nostrils flared slightly. "Go shower." She patted his cheek and left.

James looked at his grass-stained, sweat-drenched socks, wishing she had as much interest in his art as she did in his attire and hygiene. At least the Tierneys framed his artwork. The most recent one he painted of a quarterback in the throwing stance right before the ball is released made him think he was better at wielding a paintbrush than passing a football.

∽

James watches his son inspect the paint set. Marc doesn't have any idea how monumental a gift this is.

"You'll want this, too." Claire shows him a pad of watercolor paper.

Marc makes grabby hands and takes the paper. *"Gracias, Señora Carla."*

"You're an excellent artist, just like your father."

"What the—" James bites off the curse. He should be enjoying this moment with Marc. He should be happy Marc has an activity to keep him occupied as they get settled. Instead, anger and envy wrap their viselike grips around his chest.

He hates feeling this way. He's read Carlos's journals. He knows why his mother despised his painting.

It still hurts, though.

Claire ventures a glance up at James, but her eyes slide away when she registers his dark mood.

"This is for you, Julian." Her generally steady voice wavers. She gives him a soccer ball.

"Cool." He tucks the ball under his bent arm. His other soccer ball is packed up in a box somewhere in the garage.

"This, too." Claire reaches inside the bag. "It's a football."

Julian snorts. "That's not a *fútbol*."

"An American football," she clarifies with a quick smile. "Your father used to play. He once had a good passing arm. You'll have to ask him to show you."

Julian shrugs one shoulder. "Sure. Whatever."

"Julian, go kick the ball around with your brother out back."

"Why?" he asks, startled. "I haven't seen Señora Carla in almost a year."

"She and I need to talk."

"I want to talk with her."

"Julian," he snaps, loud and sharp. The name bounces around the kitchen.

Julian pales. He looks from his father to Claire and back again. He swallows, and James knows he senses something is off. How does his dad know this woman if he can't remember her? He shuffles his feet and angrily slams the soccer ball into the floor. He catches it after one bounce and tucks it against his waist. "Come on, Marc, let's get out of here." He clamps a hand around Marc's nape and pushes his brother out of the kitchen.

When the French door to the backyard slams loudly, James swings around to glare at his mother. Claire twists her lips. She picks up the knife and slices into the egg sandwiches. "You would have sent me away had I told you the truth," she explains about her time in Puerto Escondido. "I wanted . . ." The knife stills, hovering above the next sandwich.

James tightly folds his arms over his chest. "Do tell, Mother." He sneers, any patience for his family long depleted. "What did you want?"

She raises her chin. "I wanted to meet my grandchildren."

A troubling thought moves through him like a cold front. Gooseflesh bubbles the skin on his arms. *Did she know from the outset Thomas faked his death?*

"I know what you're thinking," Claire says, aligning sandwich halves on plates. "Thomas didn't tell me about you or why he kept you hidden until after Aimee found you. He also told me what Phil did to Aimee, and that he thinks he tried to kill you in Mexico." She pauses, wiping a mayonnaise drip from a plate edge with her fingertip. "Needless to say, your brothers and I aren't on the best of terms."

I had three sons. Once.

Carlos documented many conversations with Señora Carla. James remembers reading that one small confession. Carla's loneliness had appealed to Carlos's own desolation. He yearned for genuine companionship but had a difficult time trusting. He and Carla developed a sort of kinship. An openness evolved between them that wouldn't have occurred had he known he was her son.

Claire wipes down the countertop and rinses the knife, sliding the blade back into its slot in the knife rack. She motions toward the sandwiches. Four of them. "I made lunch."

A peace offering, James surmises. "Don't expect to pick things up where you left them off. I'm not the man you knew in Mexico."

Claire blinks hard. Her fingers flutter to the top button of her blouse.

"You're also not the woman my sons believe you to be." His voice is a whisper of warning.

Their gazes fuse across the marble kitchen island. After a moment, his mother's determined expression slides away, crestfallen. Her chin dips in a slight nod. She empties the shopping bag, gummy bears for Marc and Oreos for Julian. Their favorites.

She nudges a flat rectangular box tied in a red ribbon toward James; then she collects her keys and purse. James watches her leave.

She stops at the kitchen doorway. "Welcome home, James." She doesn't wait for his reply, and a moment later he hears the front door click shut.

He stares at the box in front of him. His mother never gave *just because* gifts. Outside of birthdays and holidays, she never gifted him anything. Curiosity piqued, he unravels the ribbon. He hates how his heart races with anticipation and he despises he feels like his sons did a short time ago. Elated.

He lifts the lid and takes in the set of Filbert brushes, their feathered pig-hair bristles ideal for blending oils and acrylics. A fist-size lump clogs his throat. His mother bought him art supplies, after all these years.

Well, Mom. It's a little late. He has no desire to paint again.

He tosses the box back onto the countertop and the fourth sandwich into the trash. The rest he wraps for later since he's still full from breakfast. The boys probably are, too.

Later, he and his sons spend the afternoon unpacking and organizing their rooms. They shipped only clothes, toys, important documents, and a few mementos, like photos of their mother. Aside from a couple of small boxes of books and files, James leaves his own belongings untouched. His taste in clothing is different from what it had been as Carlos, and he can't stomach seeing the custom suits and shirts Aimee elected to box rather than donate. Those clothes from his time *before*.

He now sees his life divided into three periods. The time before the fugue and the time after. The third period, the *in-between*, will always be shrouded in mystery, like the moment before dawn when the world isn't dark or light, just a hazy gray. He'll only know what Carlos elected to write about in the journals. And reading about it is entirely different from experiencing it.

His gaze darts over the remaining cardboard boxes in the garage. The rest are his. He'll start his *after* period from scratch and go shopping tomorrow.

The locksmith and alarm company arrive after three. While bolts are changed and the alarm system inspected and switched to a new service, Marc paints at the kitchen table. Hoping to appease Julian, James sets up his Xbox. His son declines his challenge to a game and promptly launches into a single-man game of Halo.

Julian hasn't mentioned Señora Carla, and while that worries James, he's thankful Julian doesn't want to talk about her. At least not yet. He isn't ready to talk about his mother either. Underneath the surface, he's still seething over how she deceived them for five years. But more so, he fears the truth will crush his sons, Julian especially. He was fatherless the first four years of his life, and the father who adopted him doesn't remember why he took him in. He knows only what Carlos wrote. James needs to handle this situation like a fish caught with bare hands, else he'll slip away.

They eat breakfast leftovers for dinner, and after the boys are in bed, James paces the hallways, desperate for a late-night run. He needs to buy a treadmill.

He needs to get out.

He grabs a beer from the fridge, pops the cap, and debates calling Nick to join him, as he continues to wander through the house, restless. It's late, already past ten thirty, and a work night, reminding James about his other dilemma. He must get serious about finding a job, he thinks, pacing by the front window and catching a glimpse of the night outside.

He stops, beer poised against his mouth. His phone vibrates in his back pocket, but he ignores it. It's been sounding off all day, and the last person he wants to speak with after the unexpected visit from his mother, is Thomas. The guy won't let him alone. Besides, his full attention is focused on the SUV parked in front of his house, headlights on, motor running. He hears the engine through the open window.

Movement inside the vehicle sets his heart into supersonic speed, a fist hammering into his sternum. The gesture is so familiar, it's startling. Electricity dances across his skin, and air surges from his lungs, carrying one word: *Aimee.*

CHAPTER 8

CARLOS

Five Years Ago
June 22
Puerto Escondido, Mexico

My heart slammed in my chest the way it had the day my wife died, when the nurse had placed Marcus in my arms and Raquel had put her trust in me. My past was as much an unknown to her as it was to me, yet we'd fallen in love and married. She'd given me her son Julian.

And now I could lose him.

I gunned the open-top Jeep on the Costera, shifting to a higher gear. The wind dried the sweat in my hair but offered no escape from the heat, let alone Imelda's concerns about my documentation. And those concerns were valid. Though I hadn't had issues, I did wonder about the cards in my wallet. Alarms didn't sound and the authorities hadn't come running when I married Raquel, adopted Julian, and paid my taxes. That didn't mean my paperwork hadn't been forged. It only meant I hadn't done anything to show up as a blip on someone's radar screen.

I could carry on with my modus operandi: maintain the gallery, socialize with the neighbors, and actively contribute to the community.

But that didn't resolve the big *what if* about Julian, especially since the state of my mind was already questionable. Was Julian legally my son?

Red flags would fly high if I started asking questions. I could find my ass hauled to the nearest prison or drop-kicked over the border. There was one person who had the answers, and it enraged me that I'd have to seek his help. It also scared the hell out of me.

I grasped the gear stick and downshifted, swerving right toward the airport. My conversation with Imelda had lasted a lot longer than the twenty minutes I had to spare. Natalya's flight had landed forty minutes ago, and that impatient streak that ran through her veins probably had her in a cab on the way to my house. I'd texted her while leaving Casa del sol, asking that she wait. She'd already left a voice message wondering where I was.

I snatched the phone from the center console, and her most recent message flashed.

Turn around. Got a cab.

I swore, tossing the phone on the passenger seat. I'd just passed her. Couldn't she have waited five more minutes?

There were times during her visits we felt like a married couple. Our schedules slid into place as we navigated around each other throughout the day. We shared meals and chores while juggling the kids' activities and bickering about each other's annoying habits. She picked at her teeth with her fingernail and I used the coffee mugs to clean my brushes. I also saved too much crap, stuff she considered trash, like old newspapers and magazines. I looked forward to her visits, loved having her here, and missed her when she was gone. She made me feel like me, whatever that was supposed to feel like. And I hated that I wanted more from her. She wouldn't move to Puerto Escondido and I'd turned down her invitation to relocate to Hawaii where she'd help raise Julian and Marcus. I haven't driven farther than the state line since December. Fear of travel is a bitch.

But despite the distance, what we did have in common kept us together.

Natalya had been in the delivery room with me when Raquel flatlined. It had happened so fast. Her blood pressure dropped like an airplane shot out of the sky; then chaos broke loose as we watched what should have been one of the happiest days in our lives career in a downward spiral. The next thing I knew, the doctor was offering condolences for my loss in the same tone he'd tell patients to stay off their bandaged feet and rest. He grasped my shoulder, nodded once, then left the room. The nurse adjusted my arms around Marcus, and when she was sure I wouldn't drop him, she mumbled a halfhearted congratulations and followed it with an apology, her eyes darting away. My gaze met Natalya's over the jet-black hair of my newborn son. Her expression mirrored my stunned disbelief.

Natalya had come for Marcus's birth and planned to stay a couple of weeks to help with Julian as we adjusted to life with a newborn. Instead, she stayed two months as we adjusted to life without Raquel. We didn't have experience handling an infant and we blundered our way through feeding schedules and diaper changes, exhausted and grief stricken. Her fierce loyalty kept her home with us and her compassion ensured Julian and I kept an open dialogue about his mother. How did you tell a five-year-old his mother was never coming home? There was no easy way.

But Natalya's compassionate nature brought her to me the night before she returned home. The boys had long gone to sleep and she had said good night, going to her room. I took a shower, alone with my thoughts, wondering how the hell I was going to single-handedly raise two boys when I had my own head full of problems. I twisted the handle and the water dropped a few dozen degrees when the glass door opened with a gust of cold air. My skin beaded and I pulled in a sharp breath at the feel of her hands on my hips. I turned, the water pelting the back of my head and shoulders.

"What are you—?" The question lodged in my throat. Water drops camouflaged her tears but not the redness and swelling around her eyes. She'd been crying.

For two months Natalya put our needs before her own. She held my young family together and kept us moving forward as we worked through our grief, rarely showing that she was hurting as much as we were. She stared up at me with glassy eyes and damp lips, exposed in more ways than a lack of clothes, and I realized for the past eight weeks, no one had held her.

I grazed my fingers into her hair and squeezed. Her lips parted on a gasp. She hadn't come to me for reassurance or comfort. This was a moment for raw emotion, where the need to take transcended the desire to give.

My mouth landed hard on hers. The taste of her anguish was as palpable as the ache to feel alive. In a flurry of limbs and hands and mouths, Natalya's body melded solidly against mine. I groaned, shocked at the possessive sound deep in my throat, and gripped her thighs, lifting her. Her arms and legs coiled around me and I turned, pressing her back to the cold tiles. I slid into her and our eyes locked. Something unspoken passed between us, connecting us in the way that shared loss does. But it wasn't my deceased wife I saw in the lines of her face or arch of her brow. It wasn't her I thought of as I started to move. It was all Natalya.

An undeniable emotion surged in me. Holding her close, I slammed into her. We jerked against each other, hard and rough, until our minds and hearts were stripped as bare as our bodies. I eased her down and we leaned into each other. She cried on my shoulder, shaking in my arms, and I kissed her damp hair, the dip in her temple, the curve of her ear. She trailed kisses across my collarbone and down to my rapidly beating heart. Then she left me, cold and naked and bewildered.

Natalya flew home the next morning. Neither of us had the courage to mention the previous night, and she barely made eye contact with me when she kissed Julian and Marcus good-bye. But at the airport, after I retrieved her luggage from the back of the Jeep, after she briefly hugged me and kissed the side of my neck, I grasped her wrist when she started to walk away. I didn't want her to go. But those weren't the words that fell from my mouth. She could be pregnant. We hadn't used protection.

A sad smile touched her lips, and she gave her head a slow shake. "I'll text when I land."

She returned to Puerto Escondido several months later and we eased into a comfortable rhythm as though we'd been lifelong friends. After that, she visited several times a year, and we talked on the phone a couple of times a week. We texted almost daily. But I wondered if she ever thought of those moments in the shower when she looked at me. Did she see me or her deceased sister's husband? Because I sure as hell hadn't forgotten those fiery minutes, the way her body fit to mine and the throaty gasps she made as I rocked inside her. My name on her lips when she came. The memory sent my pulse thrumming. I should have felt guilty about having sex with my sister-in-law only a couple of months after my wife's death. But I didn't. I had to move on, keep pushing forward into the future. What I did feel guilty about was that I couldn't stop thinking about Natalya in that way. I'd been lusting after her like a horny teenager.

I downshifted to first, pulling to the side of the road, letting a cab pass by on its way to the airport. Then I swerved around and headed home.

∽੭

Natalya had showered and left for a meeting before I arrived home with Julian and Marcus. We'd finished dinner and Marcus had already been put to bed by the time Natalya wrapped up her meeting. I was picking up after the boys, making my end-of-the-day rounds through the house, when the front door opened.

"Tía Natalya!"

"Julian, I'm so happy to see you." Natalya sank to her knees. Julian ran into her arms.

Over their heads, I watched the taxi back out of the driveway. A discarded shoe about the size of my palm lay on the porch. Juggling kids' books, a wooden train, and a lonely flip-flop, I picked up the shoe and turned to Natalya.

"I want to show you a new trick I learned." Julian took off to the kitchen. I heard the slider open and slam shut.

Natalya rose to her toes and kissed my cheek. "Hi."

I smiled. "Hi back."

Copper strands fanned across her face, tangling around her neck. A few caught on her lip. I brushed them aside, knocking her chin with the shoe.

"Ow."

I chuckled, apologetic. "That was a rookie move."

She blushed and glanced behind her. The taxi had left. My neighbors Raymond and Valencia Navarro were out for their evening walk. They waved and I waved back, then shut the door.

Julian barreled up the hallway, dribbling a *fútbol*. "Watch this, Tía Nat." He toed the ball into the air and juggled it with his knees. Natalya counted to sixteen before the ball bounced off the edge of Julian's thigh and nearly collided with a table lamp.

"Whoops." Julian chased after the ball.

Natalya clapped. "That's impressive."

I dumped my armload into the laundry basket of items to go upstairs.

"Your moves are looking great, kid." I prodded him from the room. "But the ball belongs—"

"Outside. Yeah, yeah, I know."

Natalya and I followed Julian outside, where we passed the ball, comparing kicking accuracy and blocking skills. Julian pointed out mine were the worst between us, but I wasn't entirely focused on the ball. My mind was on my conversation with Imelda and how that played into Julian's future.

"Dude." My son gawked at me when he caught me staring at him. I'd missed the ball again.

Natalya looked at me curiously and I shook my head. "My bad." I jogged after the ball and drop-kicked it to her. With the coordination of a professional athlete, she stopped the ball with the ball of her foot and passed to Julian. My son rattled off stats for the Albrijes de Oaxaca, a Mexican *fútbol* team, as we continued passing the ball. Eventually Natalya yawned loudly. She covered her mouth with the back of her hand. Julian followed suit. He rubbed his eyes with his fists.

"Let's go, future pro fútboller, off to bed." I picked up the ball and tossed it onto a patio chair.

Julian hugged his aunt good night. Natalya dropped a kiss on his head. *"Buenas noches."*

I helped Julian with his nightly ritual of picking up his room and brushing his teeth; then I read a quick story. He fell asleep before I reached the last page. Setting the book aside, I kissed him good night and ruffled his hair, letting my fingers linger. He'd lost much in his short life. Abandoned by his birth father and the death of his mother. Then there was me.

I rubbed the dark walnut strands, the hair coarse from salt and the summer sun. There were three scenarios about Julian, two with Marcus that concerned me. The authorities could remove Julian from my care, assuming the adoption wasn't legal. I could abandon them. It could be tomorrow or years from now, but one day I'd wake up without any memories of them. What if I didn't want kids? Would I walk away from them? I had to consider that possibility. What would happen to Julian and Marcus if I returned to California?

Then there was the final scenario, the one I'd been trying to come to terms with since last December. I wasn't sure I wanted James to have custody.

Julian's hair slipped through my fingers and I wondered when the same would happen to my memories of him.

∽

I found Natalya in Marcus's room. She stood over his crib. "I can't believe how much he's grown," she whispered when I came to stand beside her. "He's beautiful."

Marcus stirred. He grunted, lifting his rear into the air, the sheet sliding off him. He smacked his lips and Natalya smiled. She pulled the sheet up to his shoulders and lightly patted his back. "I've missed him."

And I missed her. I wanted to tell her that she was beautiful, too. The startling color of her green eyes, even here in the dim glow of the hallway light that spilled into Marcus's room, always caught me off guard the first time I'd see her after months apart. But the thing about Natalya that touched me in places I never had the opportunity to experience with her sister was the way she cared for my sons. She loved them as though they were her own. It always surprised me she'd never married and had children of her own. She would be an incredible mother.

"Do you want a beer?"

She hummed her acknowledgment.

We went downstairs. She slipped out the kitchen slider and I retrieved the brews from the fridge, popping the lids. She was gazing at the stars when I joined her. "The moon's bright tonight." It cast her face in blue light.

I passed her a bottle. "Thanks." She cheered and took a long drink, then sighed.

Cicadas sang their evening song and palms swayed in the breeze coming off the water, enough to chill what the day had melted away.

I caught the delicate scent of soap in the salt-heavy air. Natalya had showered while I put Julian to bed and she'd changed into a dress that looked more like a large T-shirt. The bottom barely skimmed the top of her thighs. She crossed those amazing legs at the ankle and leaned against a support post for the wood balcony above us.

I looked away and took a huge gulp of beer. "Tell me about your meeting."

"It went well. Dinner was phenomenal. We ate at the new seafood place on Avenida Benito Juarez."

"Luna's?"

She nodded. "I had mahimahi tacos. Mari's agreed to do three exclusive designs for us. We're meeting up in a few days to go over some concepts."

"Is Gale on board yet?"

Natalya laughed lightly at my pun, shaking her head. She could have been laughing about her father, perhaps both. "Not entirely and he's not going to like Mari's counteroffer."

Hayes Boards, a premier surfboard manufacturer founded by her father, Gale Hayes, and based in Hawaii, was known for its proprietary finishes and cutting-edge designs. Their stock boards lacked any unique artwork. Too masculine and generic in color, in Natalya's opinion. The number of young girls taking to surfing had skyrocketed in the last decade and she was determined to expand Hayes Boards's target audience by introducing a line of custom boards with designs that appealed to that generation. Natalya found that opportunity in Mari Vasquez, world-renowned surfboard painter. As artists, Mari and I ran in the same circles and I introduced her to Natalya last November during the *torneo*.

She took a lingering sip. "Dad agreed to commission Mari for three designs." She held up the same number of fingers. "We'll digitally print the designs on a fiberglass wrap and apply them on a limited number of long boards and see how they sell."

I pressed my back against the opposite pillar and faced her. The temperature was dropping and I finally felt comfortable in the linen shirt I'd worn all day. My jeans were another matter and I itched to pull on shorts. "What's Mari asking for?"

"Her name on the board, which I expected and don't have a problem with. Dad, on the other hand, will see it as a sellout. The boards should speak for themselves, not the designs on them or the professional surfers riding them. That's why we don't have our own pro team where many of our competitors do."

"Gale shouldn't have a problem with Mari's autograph when the boards sell faster than you can manufacture them."

She flashed a smile, her teeth bright against her face. "That's when he'll pop a vein. She doesn't do a flat up-front fee. She wants royalty payments."

I brought the beer to my lips and laughed, the sound vibrating in the bottle. "Gale's going to pop more than a vein." I cheered the bottle at her and drank.

She grimaced. "What about you?" She tapped her forehead. "Something's on your mind."

I crossed my arms. "What makes you say that?"

She finished her beer. "You weren't with us when we passed the ball around earlier. You were distracted. Care to share?"

I wasn't sure yet. I was still working it out.

"I'm fine." I held out my hand, ready to return inside.

She gave me a doubtful look but didn't pry further. A light flashed on in a second-floor window of the house next door, catching her attention. "Who's vacationing there? I'm not used to seeing that house so dark and quiet."

It usually wasn't this time of year. Music would be blaring, with light in all rooms blazing. "A woman from the States rented the place for the summer."

"Which state?"

I lifted a shoulder, surprised I hadn't thought to ask Carla. "No idea. She seems nice, though. You might meet her. She watches the kids play on the beach."

Natalya yawned, nodding, then gestured toward the slider. "It's late. I'm going to bed."

I reached for her hand when she started to walk by. She took mine without looking up at me and I pulled her into my arms. I almost sighed because the contact felt so good. Fist-bumps and neck hugs from the boys were great, but they didn't stave off the loneliness.

Natalya folded her arms around my waist and I buried my lips in her hair. The embrace was platonic until I let my lips linger, following the part down the middle. She stiffened and I let my arms fall away, afraid I'd crossed some unspoken line. The shower incident was almost fifteen months ago. You'd think it had never happened at all.

She retreated a step and looked up, her eyes searching my face. The skin between her brows bunched. "Let's grab some beers after work tomorrow. We can talk about what's bothering you." She grinned.

My mouth tilted up at the corner. "Beers sound great."

"But not the talking." She wagged a finger at me. "Now I know something's going on with you. Don't worry, I won't push it. Yet." She walked into the house and I followed. We said good night in the kitchen and I watched her walk down the hallway. She stopped and studied the pictures on the wall. I knew which one had her attention. A photo of her and Raquel at our wedding, bent over in laughter. Both of them beautiful in their dresses. Raquel in white and Natalya in lavender. She touched her fingers to her lips then the glass. Then she disappeared into the bathroom.

I tossed the bottles in recycling and went upstairs to write. Doctor's orders. But what started as a daily exercise in hopes of recovering my past had evolved during the last six months into a tool of survival. Should I lose myself to James, my memories would still be here.

CHAPTER 9

JAMES

Present Day
June 22
Los Gatos, California

"Aimee."

Her name fills the room before he realizes he spoke it out loud. The agony from not seeing her, hearing the smooth richness of her voice, folding her lean frame in his arms, the press of her feminine curves against his solid plane, floods the hollowness inside him. It nearly brings him to his knees.

The bottle slips from his fingers, lands with a thud on the wool carpet. Amber liquid bleeds into the cream fibers, soaking the sole of his bare foot. He barely feels it. Every sense is sharply tuned to the woman in the vehicle parked out front.

The headlights turn off; then after a few ticks of the ugly, ancient clock behind him, a family heirloom someone had the terrible sense to leave behind, they turn on again. It's as though Aimee's trying to decide what to do.

She's going to leave.

Like his beer-soaked foot, James hardly registers his long stride consuming the distance between them, or the front door slamming into the wall because he opened it with such force. He swore to himself he wouldn't contact her. She has a husband and a child. He doesn't want to disrupt her life, further complicating the mess Thomas created. He doesn't want her hurting any more than she already has. Hurting just as much, if not more, than he is.

But here she is, after years of separation for her and what seems like months for him, and nothing is going to stop him from getting inside that car. He wants to feel her nearness. He wants to hear her voice.

He knocks hard on the passenger window. She bucks in her seat, turning toward him as she white-knuckles the steering wheel with both hands. A complicated stew of emotions ravages her face, visible under the misty glow of the streetlight that floods the vehicle's interior. He sees the same longing he feels deep into the marrow of his bones, along with a haunting regret. But there is also disappointment in, and resentfulness toward, him. His heart crumbles a little more. He hurt her and betrayed their trust. He'd kept so much from her. He'd been so ashamed.

"Aimee." He rattles the latch. "Unlock the door." His pulse races. He can feel it throb in his throat. His skin is hot and uncomfortable. Sweat drenches his armpits. "Please." He rattles the latch again.

The lock clicks and he hauls open the door, sliding inside. He shuts the door behind him and plasters his damp back against the leather to stop himself from crashing into her. His lungs heave and nostrils flare as though he sprinted a 10K. A quickening tightens his chest as he breathes her in. Jasmine and orange blossom. Aimee's signature scent. Much more powerful than the memory.

Their gazes meld across the center console, and something electric rushes through him, a flash flood of emotion. He heatedly whispers her name, his own expression worshipful.

A river of brown, wavy hair—hair he used to twine around his hands when he kissed her deeply—falls gracefully over her shoulders.

The Caribbean-blue orbs he knows so well swim in pools of unshed tears. Her lashes glisten—the pale, delicate skin encircling her eyes, puffy. She's been crying for some time. There are teardrop stains dotting her jeans.

He watches his hand reach for her. He wants to caress the concave of her cheek, kiss away the tears, wind his arms around her, and never let go. But she's no longer his to care for, to soothe away the worry. The gold band on her finger, bright like starlight in the glow of the street lamp, is a grim reminder. She's no longer his.

His arm drops into his lap and her gaze follows. "You're shaking."

"Because I want to touch you so badly," he rasps.

She shifts her face away, revealing her profile. The soft slide of her nose, the quiver of her chin. With the base of her palm, she wipes away the moisture that makes her cheekbone shine.

"Aimee." His own eyes dampen. He blinks rapidly, fighting the burn. "Aimee, baby. Say something."

She briefly squeezes her eyes shut and James curses the endearment that slipped from his tongue. He doesn't want to scare her away.

Her breath hitches on a long inhale. "I've been driving in circles for the past two hours."

"Baby . . ." This time he ignores the slip. He doesn't like it when she's upset or sad. Make that devastated.

She wipes her face again. Her hand trembles and his restraint shatters. He grasps her fingers and his tears fall.

For an instant she tugs her hand, startled by the contact, only to grip his palm tightly. She turns fully toward him, tucking her nearest leg underneath her. "I've known for a while that you remember again."

"How long? Since December?" And she never reached out to him.

She nods. "Kristen called me after you called Nick. I always wondered if you'd recover. Carlos didn't think so. I mean, you didn't think so. But I still wondered. I also wondered what it'd be like when you came back. I've wondered that since the beginning," she quietly admits.

"Since Mexico?"

"Yes, since I found you." She glances out the front window with an unfocused gaze and James wonders if she's back with him in Puerto Escondido. All he knows about that visit is what Carlos wrote in the journal. Aimee had been honest with him and herself before she left. It had been achingly difficult to read, but he admired her strength. He didn't like it, but understood why she had to walk away from him.

"I wasn't sure how I'd feel living near you and not be with you. Would I realize I was still in love with you? Would I leave Ian to be with you?" Her voice diminishes until barely audible. She moistens her lips and stares at their joined hands, her fair Irish complexion a vivid contrast to his deep tan from years living under the Mexican sun.

"Nick called yesterday and told me you're here." She motions at the house. "With your sons. And suddenly . . ." She pauses, lips parted as though figuring how to word what she has to say. James gives her hand an encouraging squeeze and she looks up at him from under her lashes. "Suddenly I didn't have to wonder anymore. I knew. I can't invite you over for Saturday-night barbecues. And I won't go to Nick and Kristen's house for their pool parties. Not if you're there." Her mouth contorts into a watery grimace and James wilts inside. She's right, though. Still, it doesn't hurt less hearing it. It'll be awkward for both of them.

"I wish . . . I wish I'd listened to Lacy. I could have found you sooner." Her shoulders shake as she cries harder, forcing out the words. "But she was so odd. She scared me and I didn't know her, and the thought of you still alive . . ."

"Honey . . . darling, don't," James soothes. She's beating herself up and he feels every verbal punch. He knows of Imelda's friend, the one who approached Aimee at his funeral. Imelda told Carlos everything she knew about how Lacy, whom she'd known as Lucy, convinced Aimee to seek him out. Imelda had finally gathered the courage to draw Aimee out. She was weary of the deception and willing to risk Thomas's ire and Carlos's hatred for the sake of his well-being. He was entitled to the truth. James shakes his head. "Don't blame yourself. You can't blame yourself."

She bites her lower lip, absently nodding. James shifts his hand, twining his fingers between hers. "Aimee." He whispers her name again and again. He can't stop saying her name, even murmurs it against her skin when he brings their linked hands to his lips.

She whimpers. "Kristen said you were at the café this morning. That's why I wasn't there. I couldn't be there in case you . . . showed up. I was . . . I was afraid." She stops and a fresh current trails down her cheeks, thin streams that soak her lips and cling to her chin. A few tears spill onto her lap, further staining the tight jeans that adorn her legs. Legs he desperately craves to have cradling his hips.

Before he can make sense of what he's doing, James unlatches her seatbelt and drags Aimee onto his lap. He wraps one arm around her waist and burrows a hand through the curls he loves so much. Cupping the back of her head, he offers his shoulder for her to cry on. To his shock, she kisses him instead, crying into his mouth.

God help him, he kisses her back. The connection strikes him with tremendous force. He's missed her terribly. Her taste, her touch, her scent.

Her.

They pour everything they are, everything they have, and everything they've lost into the kiss. Tears mingle as they cling to each other, shaking in each other's arms.

He breaks the kiss and cups her face, pressing his forehead against hers. There's so much he has to say, so much he needs to explain. He knew it bothered her he never liked discussing his parents, or what it was like growing up in a home where a parent's love had to be earned. Nothing was freely given like the affection the Tierneys doted on Aimee. It had been especially difficult keeping from her the truth about Phil, that he is his brother, not a cousin, as his entire family led everyone to believe. Each of them had been disgusted in their own way that his mother had an incestuous relationship with her brother. James, though, he'd been ashamed. His family and the way they treated each other, the way his mother disregarded his art, and the way his father dealt out his punishments. It all embarrassed him.

Looking back, though, he understood why Phil's favorite pastime had been knocking around his brothers. His mother refused to recognize him as her own in public. He might have been Donato Enterprises' CEO's son at the time, but to the outside world, the mother who birthed him was a mystery. Uncle Grant never talked about her. He never admitted he'd slept with his own sister, not until Phil and James saw them more than wrapped in each other's arms.

James makes a rough noise of despair in the back of his throat. Words gush into his mouth. He wants to explain why he followed Phil to Mexico. How Donato Enterprises would go under if Phil continued to pour drug money into the company's accounts. The Feds would confiscate their assets. James would lose everything, including his own dreams. With his investments depleted, he wouldn't be able to open his gallery, and he wouldn't be able to support the life he believed his future wife deserved—not on an artist's salary. Phil didn't have to assault Aimee to get to him. The trade laundering would have been enough to destroy him. It almost ruined Thomas.

But those aren't the words that tumble from him. He kisses Aimee's forehead, her temple and cheekbone. "I'm so sorry I left you. I never should have left you," he says, and Aimee sobs harder. "I'm sorry for so many things. I should have told you about Phil. I should have been there for you, helped you heal—"

Aimee cries out, and before James can comprehend she's gone, she's back in her seat and buckling her seatbelt, leaving behind a cold and empty space where her body had been pressed against his. James feels just as frigid and hollow inside.

Tears cling to her chin. He wipes one off with his finger and she flinches. She grips the steering wheel with both hands and starts the ignition.

"Aimee?" He hesitates over her name. He feels her pulling away from him and she's taking his heart with her.

"I love you, James," she sobs without looking at him. "I will always love you." She lifts her Caribbean blues and locks onto his brown eyes. "But I love Ian. I love him so much. We have a beautiful daughter. We named her Sarah, after Ian's mom. We're a family, a very happy family."

His heart lands on the floorboard. She's killing him. He knows deep down inside they will never be together again, but hearing her say the words knocks the wind out of him.

He can't breathe. He has to get out of the car.

James snaps the latch and shoves open the door. He unfolds from the car before he does something stupid, like yank her back to his lap or switch seats and steal her away into the night. He quietly shuts the door and stares down the street, unsure what to say next, or what to do.

Where to go.

He doesn't want to return inside. The house doesn't feel like his. It will never feel like home, not like the house he once owned with Aimee.

The passenger window slides down. "James?"

He forces himself to look at her one last time, because this may truly be the last time. He's come to realize he can't live near her and not have her.

She leans toward the passenger seat to look up at him. "I forgive you."

His soul withers. He nods tightly.

She releases the brake, shifts into gear, and drives away. James dips his hands into his front pockets and watches her until the taillights flash and she's disappeared around the corner. Disappeared from his life. His fingers curl around the engagement ring he's kept with him since December. The ring she'll never wear again.

He wants to curse the world.

He wants to beat the crap out of Thomas.

His phone vibrates with an incoming text. Thomas has been buzzing all evening. *What the hell does he want?* He digs out his phone. Four text notifications light up the screen.

Phil's release date is confirmed for next Tuesday.

Talking on the phone with him now. He wants to move back into Mom's house.

Damn, James, I swear I didn't tell him, but he knows you're alive. How the hell does he know?

He wants to see you. He wants to talk about what happened on the boat in Mexico. What did happen?

CHAPTER 10

CARLOS

Five Years Ago
June 25
Puerto Escondido, Mexico

Señora Carla showed up at El estudio del pintor this afternoon. She'd seen Julian at the beach with his friends and he told her where to find my gallery. She said she wanted to see my work, but I think she was lonely.

"Your work is so different," Carla said with fascination. She wore white cropped pants and a pink blouse, tailored and expensive-looking. Several bracelets dropped from her sleeves, landing on her wrist bone when she lowered her arm. Diamonds glittered as she moved.

"Different from what?" I asked, rolling my sleeves as I approached her.

She lifted an angular shoulder. "From what I expected. They're bright and dynamic."

I glanced at the painting she admired, a surfer riding a colossal wave. I'd taken an impressionistic approach, using palette knives. The canvas was a study in blue, the surfer a weightless body as though he were flying down the wave's glassy surface. Which was the feeling surfers described when they caught the ultimate wave, and what I set out to achieve in my painting. That feeling of floating on air.

She moved to the next painting, another rider skimming the crest of a smaller wave ahead of the fold, his body a silhouette against the setting sun. "The unity of your scenes and hues . . . the approach you take . . . your perspective . . . the overall tone . . . they convey . . ." She tapped a curved finger against her chin and looked askance at me. "I'm trying to find the right words."

I rested my hands on my hips. "Try this. How do the paintings make you feel?"

"Make me *feel?*" Lips, tinted the color of the pink lemonade Julian loved to drink, parted. She swiveled her neck back to the painting. She was quiet for a moment. "It makes me wish I'd joined my sons when they surfed."

I glanced down at the glazed concrete floor, hiding my smile at the image of Carla on a surfboard. I cleared my throat behind a fist, my brows rising. "You want to surf?"

She looked appalled. "Goodness, no." Her shoulders rose and fell on a resigned breath. She plucked a promotional postcard from the holder beside the painting. "I had no interest watching them. It's not as though they'd do anything productive with it."

Like compete at master-level tournaments. I bit into my lower lip, trying not to pick apart Carla in the way she analyzed my paintings. Every interest and activity of Julian's fascinated me, and it would be the same with Marcus as he grew older.

She flipped the card over, read the painting's description, then tucked it back into its slot. "You have a bold and fresh style. Your brushwork is very skilled."

"You sound like an art critic." And critical of her sons, which might explain why she vacationed alone. She said she'd once had three sons. She hadn't said they'd died.

She smoothed a hand over cool silver hair and patted the flyaway pieces into place. Tied at the nape, her hair fell in a straight line parallel to her rigid spine. Carla's posture and refined features spoke volumes. As cliché as it sounded, she came from money.

"I'm not a critic. I try not to be."

My eyes narrowed slightly as a thought occurred to me. Assuming she did come from money, her youth would have been filled with dance recitals and music lessons. Art lessons. I looked at her fine-boned hands. "You're an artist."

She laughed as though my statement were ludicrous. She slowly shook her head. "Not for a long time. Not since before—" She stalled and walked away.

"I bet you used to paint."

"In another life." Her hand fluttered over a driftwood carving of a fishing boat. She lifted her face to look over at me. "I haven't painted since I was younger than you."

"Why did you stop?"

She shrugged a delicate shoulder.

An idea formed and I grinned broadly. I clapped my hands, the noise a loud echo in the gallery. She startled. I thrust a finger in her direction. "You have to paint again. Right now."

Her mouth fell open, her expression almost comical.

"It's never too late to learn to paint. Or, in your case, start again."

Her hand plucked the top button on her blouse. "But . . . but . . . I don't paint."

"You used to. Why not start again? You're on vacation."

The corners of her mouth angled down. She clasped her hands at her chest, fingers interlaced. She was nervous, maybe a little scared. What had made her give up her art?

The need to ease her discomfort had me closing the distance between us in two long strides. I grabbed her hands. Her fingers felt as if she'd been outside far north of here in cool, brittle air. I gave her hands a reaffirming squeeze. "I have a studio upstairs where I teach classes. Pia!" I called over my shoulder. Carla tensed and I gave her a quick smile.

Pia, my receptionist, peeked over the worn pages of her romance novel. *Dios!* I wish she'd hide the cover from our clients. "Watch the shop," I told her. "I'm teaching Señora Carla how to paint again."

"*Sí*, Carlos." She grinned at Carla before her face disappeared behind the book.

Carla pressed her lips into a thin line of disapproval.

I bent my arm and pulled her hand through, then gestured toward the door. The studio's entrance was up a flight of stairs outside. "This way."

Her step faltered when we reached the courtyard. She glanced up the spiral metal staircase. "I'm not so sure about this . . ."

I raised a finger. "One painting, then I won't bother you again."

Pia popped her head out the door. "Don't forget about your three o'clock appointment," she reminded me in Spanish.

I glanced at my watch. Two fifteen. "Let's see what we can manage in forty-five minutes."

She hesitated, then dipped her chin with a determined nod. "I'll give you forty-five minutes."

I grinned and led her upstairs before she changed her mind.

~

To my surprise, Señora Carla decided to stay when I excused myself for my appointment. I'd demonstrated some brushwork techniques, a crisscross stroke to create depth, layering light colors over dark for an uneven coverage effect, and stacking thin layers of translucent colors that mimic the look of glass. She picked up the techniques like a gifted athlete who'd taken several seasons off to recoup from an injury. And she wanted to paint flowers. I borrowed the bouquet Pia's boyfriend delivered to the gallery the day before for their one-year dating anniversary. With an exaggerated wink, I promised I'd return the vase before the flowers died.

"Things disappear around you, Carlos," Pia grumbled, waving her book with the soft-porn cover at me. "You're a squirrel. You take things and hide them in that beach house of yours. What're you doing? Storing for winter? Preparing for the apocalypse?"

Yeah. Mine.

"I only take home newspapers and books, and that's after you read them."

She hugged the romance novel. "You can't have this one."

My eyes went wide. "No worries there, Pia." I closed the door behind me and hurried upstairs, taking two at a time. Once I'd arranged a scene for Carla to paint, I returned downstairs to meet a buyer who'd commissioned an acrylic for his restaurant. When we finished I returned to Carla. Engrossed in her painting, she startled. I rested a hand on her shoulder and frowned. She was trembling. I peered down at her. "Is anything wrong?"

She gestured at the canvas with elegant fingers. "It's been too long. It's horrible."

Was she joking? An amateur admirer wouldn't know the difference. Her color-mixing ability was genius. "It's an excellent start," I said as though advising a student and not wanting to discourage her. In truth, I was beyond impressed. She had skill.

Her hand arced over the palette of mixed oils. We'd started with a medium she was familiar with as opposed to acrylics. She breathed deeply. "I forgot how much I love this smell."

I laughed. Only a serious artist appreciated the pungent, chemical odor of pigment. I patted her shoulder. "You've missed this." I glanced down, almost missing her nod. "Good, because there's something we must do." I went to the storage closet.

"What must we do?" A note of panic lifted her voice.

I spun around and held up a finger. *"Uno momento."* Then I flashed a big smile. Her eyes widened. I could only imagine what went through her mind. She probably thought I was crazy. Though in my defense, I did get a little zealous when a new student showed passion and promise.

I shook out a handled paper bag and loaded it with beginner brushes, three blank canvases, and a starter oil set and returned to her. She looked nervously at the bag. "We, Señora Carla, are going to make sure you keep on painting. Take these back to the house."

"No . . . no, no, no." She waved a finger. "This was a one-time trial. I can't . . ." She looked from me to the bag in my hand.

"You can, and I insist you continue. You're brilliant. Leave your painting here until it dries." I motioned at the wet canvas. "Come back next week and I'll give you another lesson. And you"—I jabbed a finger at the palette board, and the corner of my mouth twitched—"can give me a lesson in pigment mixing."

She dipped her chin and smiled. It quickly disappeared, replaced by a frown.

"The second-floor loft at your house has excellent natural light and the windows in that room are huge," I suggested.

"They are."

"Perfect spot to set up a studio for the summer."

She plucked the button on her shirt's collar and looked away.

"Carla," I whispered, then took a gamble, "there's no one here telling you not to paint."

The studio door flew open and in walked Natalya. Carla scooted away, putting some distance between herself and the supplies I insisted she take home.

Natalya smiled at me, the room suddenly feeling warmer and more alive with her arrival. My pulse quickened and my mouth went dry. I'd left that morning before she woke, first for a long run before the day got too hot and unbearable, and then here to the gallery. She looked stunning. Tawny waves danced wildly around her face. Skin flushed from the heat outside. She wore a muted sundress that hugged all the curves I longed to paint. I longed to do other things, too.

She closed the door behind her and gripped the strap of her messenger bag that crossed her chest. "Pia said you were up here."

"And you found us." I held out my arm. "Come here and meet my neighbor for the summer."

Natalya walked over to my side. I rested my hand on her lower back and looked down at her. A bit of black clung to her lashes and a touch of gloss glazed her lips. I cleared my throat and looked away. "Nat, this is Señora Carla."

Natalya extended her hand. "*Buenos días*. Nice to meet you."

Carla briefly clasped her fingertips. Her gaze shifted from Natalya to me and back.

"And this is Natalya Hayes," I introduced. "She's my—"

"Is she your girlfriend?" Her voice came out shrill.

Natalya and I exchanged a look. "No," we said simultaneously. What made her think that?

Probably me. I grimaced. My expression when Natalya walked in told her everything. *Grrreat.*

I raked fingers through my hair. "She's family. My sons' aunt," I clarified.

Carla's gaze jumped between us again. "Oh . . . oh." I could almost see her mind figuring the connection between the bunching of her brows then widening of eyes. She knew my wife had passed. She smiled, her expression apologetic as she reached for her purse. "I should go." She glanced anxiously at the door.

Looping my fingers through the handles, I offered her the bag of art supplies. "Don't forget this."

She glared at me.

"Is this yours?" Natalya moved around us, closer to the easel with Carla's canvas. "It's very good."

Carla kneaded her purse. "Thank you." She eyed the bag. I shook the contents. "Very well." She snatched the bag. "It was nice meeting you, Ms. Hayes. Thank you . . . Carlos." She hesitated over my name, then turned to leave.

I picked up a paintbrush and rolled it between my hands. "I'll pencil you in for the same day and time next week." She stopped at the door and I pointed the brush at the bag. "There's a store on Avenida Oaxaca that has premium art supplies. Just in case." She scowled. I held up my hands and shrugged. She opened the door and left.

I turned back to Natalya and smiled, close-lipped, brows high.

"She's interesting," Natalya said.

"That she is," I agreed. "She's incredible, though." I pointed at the painting with the brush. Natalya tugged it from my hand.

"You're going to poke out someone's eye."

"She hasn't painted for a long time and it took some coaxing to get her up here." I started cleaning up the supplies Carla used. "How'd it go with Mari?"

She gathered her hair and twisted the mass into a makeshift ponytail, letting it fall over one shoulder. She fanned her face with her hand. It always took Natalya several days to get used to our dry heat.

"The meeting went well. How late can the Silvas watch the boys?"

All night. The thought skidded into my head like a mountain bike careening downhill. My face heated. "Let me check with them. They owe me." I sent a message.

"And you owe me a beer."

I looked up from the screen. "Gale agreed with Mari's terms?"

"Nope." She looked sheepish.

I tucked the phone into my back pocket. "You haven't told him yet."

She shook her head. "But I did bring Pia a stack of new books."

I narrowed my eyes.

"Thriller novels. As in no skin on the covers."

"I owe you more than a beer."

⁓

"Mari's designs are radical," Natalya was telling me as we walked to Alfonso's, a bar up the street from the gallery. "She showed me five drawings. I texted them to Dad during the meeting and we picked three. Here, let me show you."

We stopped at a corner. Tourists crowded the street closed off to cars, heading home from the beach or out for the evening. I moved behind Natalya, looking over her shoulder at the screen. A rowdy group passed, bumping into us. I wrapped an arm around her waist to keep us balanced. She didn't tense or move away and I glanced at her curiously. Her attention focused on her phone.

"Here we go." She showed me the first sketch, a mosaic of sunburst designs in yellow and orange.

I cupped her hand and tilted the screen so there wasn't a glare. She leaned back against my chest, and without thinking twice, I ducked my head into the crook of her shoulder. She smelled like the beach and something exotic. I inhaled deeper. Tangerines. *Damn, that's sexy.*

She jerked slightly away and twisted her neck to look up at me. "Did you just smell me?"

Heat flamed my face. Thank God I had the permanent-tan thing going so she couldn't see how my cheeks burned.

"Omigod. Do I stink?" She sniffed her armpit and I laughed. She fanned her shirt. "I forget how hot and dry it is here."

"You smell fine, Nat." More than fine. I squeezed her hip. "Show me the others."

She flipped to the next image, a floral-and-ocean-wave montage done in black and white, and the third, an undersea scene of fish and octopi. "This is my favorite."

"Hmm, show me the first one again."

She scrolled back a couple of photos.

"That's mine."

She twisted in my arm to look at me again. Her expression softened. "You love the sun."

I nodded and a wisp of melancholy threaded through me, weaving around my heart. The world slowed around us, fading away until all that existed was me, Natalya, my conversation with Imelda, and the looming *what if* at the center of my life. When would the switch flip in my head? "Every sunset is one more day I had with my sons. Every sunrise is—"

"One more day where you remember the previous day," Natalya finished for me.

I let my arm fall from her waist.

She turned fully and rested a palm on the side of my face, her fingers curving into my hair and around my neck. I felt a slight pressure as though she tried to pull my face to hers. Her lips parted and I'd never wanted to kiss her as badly as I did in that moment. But her thumb skimmed my cheek and her expression turned to one of concern. "You've been thinking about the fugue."

"I'm never not thinking about it." I'm reminded every day when I sit down to write. It's the reason I write.

She frowned. "Then what is it? Did Thomas call you?"

"Not me. Imelda." I grasped her fingers and tugged her arm. "I'll tell you about it later. Let's go. I'm thirsty."

Packed and sweltering, I steered us to the bar. Music thundered from the speakers—a flamenco duo strumming their magic on guitars. Smoke from the grill outside clung to the ceiling, carrying the scent of Alfonso's famous beer-battered fish tacos. My friends Rafael Galindo and Miguel Díaz were parked at the bar. I knew them from the gym. We mountain-biked every few weekends, and when I could get away from the kids, I met them for beers.

I clapped Miguel on the shoulder.

"Hey, Carlos, my friend." He gave me a fist-bump then saw Natalya beside me. *"Mi bella novia americana."* He hugged her.

"There are two things you got right. I'm American and I'm beautiful."

"You break my heart." Miguel bumped his fist on his chest. "Since you won't be my girlfriend, how about showing me how you do the good stuff on the waves."

"In your dreams." She kissed his cheek. "Surfer girls never reveal their tricks."

I shook Rafael's hand. We exchanged a few words until I excused us and ordered two margaritas on the rocks. We took them to the patio, and Natalya commandeered a table as the occupants vacated. I cheered my glass.

"A toast to Mari and your company's new line of custom-designed longboards. Here's to your success."

Natalya sipped her drink. "Mmm, that's good." She dabbed the corners of her mouth. "I have no doubt they will be well received, and I'll figure a way for Dad to accept Mari's terms. But let's talk about you." She pushed her drink aside and leaned forward, hands clasped and forearms on the table. "What's going on with Thomas and Imelda? I thought he stopped calling you."

"He did." I glanced around the crowded patio. "Look, I can't talk about it now."

Her brows bunched. "Because it's too loud or because you're not ready?"

"Too public." I took a hefty drink. Ice tumbled against my teeth. I set the near-empty glass down a little too hard and motioned for the waitress, ordering us another round. I moved my chair closer and leaned toward her ear so she could hear me. "Do you remember last December when I asked you to adopt my sons?"

She snorted a laugh. "You were pretty drunk." I continued to peer at her and she stared back at me. "You weren't serious?"

"Have you given it any thought?" We hadn't broached the subject since. We avoided it like the shower incident.

"Of course not. Why would I adopt them when you're perfectly capable of raising them yourself?"

I tapped my head. "A man with no past, remember?"

"It's been over two years, Carlos, and you're still you."

"I have to take precautions."

"You'd take your sons away from yourself? God, that barely makes any sense." She combed fingers through her hair, holding the copper sheet off her face. "Do you still think you're as much of an asshole as your brothers?"

"Yes." How could I not be? I got myself into this situation, abandoned in another country. Then there was that story Aimee told me. I was appalled at my own behavior toward her. Who the hell does that?

Natalya let go of her hair and traced the rim of her glass. She didn't look at me. "I know you and Raquel didn't have much time together, but she couldn't have picked a better man for her sons."

"Is that all I am to you? Your nephews' father?" I pushed my back into the chair, my mood souring to complement my drink. "A brother-in-law?"

Natalya blinked, stunned by my tone and the way I'd twisted the conversation. I hadn't meant to ask that, not here, and especially not that way. But . . . there it was, out there, hovering between us like grill smoke. I waited for her to take in the now-obvious fact I had feelings for her or fan it aside as you would when smoke burns your eyes. My heart beat furiously.

Rouge tinted her freckled skin, starting at her cheeks and all the way down to the swell of her breasts. My mouth went dry and I lifted my gaze. She narrowed hers, her cheeks flexing from clamping her jaw.

Great. Now she's pissed. I shouldn't have said anything. She scooted back her chair and rose just as the waitress returned with our drinks.

My face tilted up. "Where are you going?"

Natalya slipped the bag over her head and shoulder. "I don't want to talk about this now."

"But you said—"

"Dammit, Carlos. You and James are the same guy." She stomped away.

I swore, tossing down bills and tossing back the margarita, and went after her. She'd thundered up two blocks by the time I caught up. I grabbed her upper arm and swung her around. "Why did you walk out on me?"

She wrenched her arm free and glared. "Don't you dare give up your sons. And don't you dare give up on yourself. Think how angry you'll be when you find out you gave them away."

"How do I know I'll even want kids?"

"Exactly. You don't. I'm appalled you're even considering it."

"What makes you think this is easy?" I asked, steel in my voice. "I'm thinking of their safety. I'll bet you, as James, I take them to California, right into the heart of that family that left me here." I point at my side where the bullet trail that looks like a pale tire mark across my hip hides under my shirt. "My oldest brother tried to kill me. Do you want your nephews raised around people like that?"

"Don't put it back on me. Don't make me feel guilty about my opinion."

I opened my mouth to object. It wasn't my intent to pile on the guilt. I wanted only for her to understand my point of view. But she stopped me with a cutting glare. I held up my hands and retreated a step.

She cupped her hands along her temples, exasperated. "This is so confusing." She sighed, defeated, and let her arms fall against her sides. She studied a crack in the concrete. "About your other question."

"What question?"

"You are a lot more than a brother-in-law to me."

Oh. That question. "Look, Nat, I didn't mean—"

She met my gaze and the longing I saw in her knocked me over like a surfer, wiped out while riding down the wave face.

"Nat . . ."

"I'm in love with you. I always have been. And I feel horrible that I took advantage of you."

What? I stared, just slightly taken aback. My mind worked in a million directions until I came up with the only thing that made sense. "That time in the shower? Why would you think that?" It had been one of the most amazing ten minutes I'd had in the last few years.

"Come on, Carlos. Are you really that dense?"

"Apparently so. Enlighten me."

She opened her mouth but snapped it shut. Her nostrils flared and she swung around, hair fanning over her shoulders. She walked away.

Now what? I tossed up my hands. "Where are you going?"

"Back to the house."

"But my Jeep's that way." I pointed toward the gallery.

"I'm taking a cab," she yelled over her shoulder.

I stood in the middle of the sidewalk, dumbstruck. What the hell had just happened?

∾

I picked up Julian and Marcus from the Silvas' and drove home to a dark and empty house. Natalya didn't answer when I tapped on her door. I cracked it open. A dull blue glow from the patio light outside revealed a room as empty as the house. Worried, I texted Natalya. She'd been angry, but not enough for her to stay out for the night. Maybe she decided to get a hotel room. That thought left me unsettled because I wanted to see her. We had to discuss Julian and Marcus. We had to talk about me. And we needed to address that huge revelation she dropped on the street like a couch falling off a moving pickup truck. She was not going to drive away from that.

When she didn't immediately reply, I called. From the corner of the room, I heard the phone vibrate. It was still inside her bag. She'd probably dropped her stuff and went for a walk.

It was late so I tucked the boys in bed and went to my room to change into shorts and a shirt; then I'd go looking for Natalya. She enjoyed evening walks and would most likely be strolling the beach. Or she could be running like a machine and kicking herself about what she told me.

I scooped hands through my hair. *Dios!* She was in love with me. Had been all this time.

And she'd never said anything.

Why not?

Curtains billowed outward from the windows, catching my attention. The slider to the balcony was open. I walked outside and found Natalya wrapped in a throw, lying on a lounge chair. The air had cooled. She stared off toward the ocean. Water lapped the shore, the sound out of sync with my erratically beating heart. Aside from Raquel, Natalya meant more to me than anyone I'd met in the past few years. She was my only friend, the one person I trusted. She was self-assured, compassionate, and as independent as she was beautiful, I adored everything about her.

I loved her.

But for reasons I couldn't figure out, she felt guilty about the one time she'd shared herself with me. She thought she'd taken advantage of me. She thought she'd seduced me.

Riiiight. I snorted.

I wiped damp palms on the back of my jeans and eased into the neighboring lounger, facing her. A lone tear leaked down her cheek. I brushed my thumb across the smooth plane of her face and she grasped my wrist, placing a kiss in the center of my palm. She let go and I made a fist.

Her chest rose with a deep inhale. "I have siblings in different countries, thanks to my globe-trotting, can't-keep-his-dick-in-his-pants father. I love my brother in South Africa and sister in Australia, but Raquel was my favorite. We were the closest."

"She felt the same about you."

Natalya tightened the blanket around her shoulders. "Julian's birth father was an asshole. Best thing he did was give up his rights so you could adopt him. I wanted to hate you when we met." She gave me an apologetic look. "Raquel fell so hard and so fast for you. I thought she'd gotten herself knocked up by another jerk. It was too quick and you were . . ."

"Damaged."

"No!" she exclaimed. "How could you think that?"

"I was pretty messed up."

Her mouth curved downward. "Yes, but it was obvious you loved her as much as she loved you. That's why I hated myself for being attracted to you. During those weeks after Raquel died, I fell in love with you, and then I practically forced myself on you. What kind of sister does that?" She shook her head in disgust and I wanted to fold her in my arms, kiss away the guilt.

"Nat," I said. She wiped her tears. "Nat, look at me." She did and her beautiful green eyes glittered in the moonlight. "You didn't force me to have sex with you."

"I went into your shower knowing you were hurting. I took advantage of that pain."

"We were both hurting. We both wanted to soothe that ache. I loved Raquel, and I'll treasure the short time we had together. But something happened between us in that shower. Something I don't think we can ignore any longer." I didn't think we *should* ignore it.

Her breath caught.

"I feel the same, Nat. I love you," I whispered, tugging the edge of the throw blanket. I wanted her in my lap where I could kiss her freckle-patterned skin and bury my face in the crook of her shoulder, breathe her in. I wanted to bury everything that could take me away from her and my sons, and just be me.

Without taking her eyes off me, she stood. The blanket slipped off her shoulders and pooled at her feet.

Holy shit.

"You're naked." Nerves, excitement, anticipation, every emotion that had my heart pounding and head buzzing, shot south.

A low, watery laugh escaped from her. She pushed my shoulders back into the chair and straddled me. I grasped her hips. The sensible side of me wanted to talk about this. Was she sure? How would this change our relationship? But the side of me that had been burning for two years was fed up with being ignored.

I skimmed my hands up her sides, curved my fingers around her nape, and kissed her. And damn, was she a good kisser. Her lips were exquisite and her scent intoxicating. God, I loved her scent.

My mouth moved over hers as she frantically unbuttoned my shirt. Then her hands were on my fly and that sensible side grasped her wrists. She dipped her chin and peered down at me. A flash of embarrassment brightened her eyes. A touch of vulnerability trembled her lip. I wanted to kiss it all away.

"I don't have protection," I managed to say, my voice sandpaper rough. It had been almost two years for me. There'd been no one since her and those ten glorious minutes in the shower.

She closed her eyes and shook her head. "We don't need it."

She was on the pill.

Air rushed from my lungs.

She skimmed her thumb along my bottom lip, and I nipped the soft flesh. Her eyes flared. Then her lips were on mine and I was lost.

Consumed by the desire she poured into me and my possessive need to take her. Right here. On the balcony.

Who cared who could see us?

We sure didn't.

She pulled down my zipper and I lifted my hips. Then I lifted hers, my thumbs grazing over a rigid line of skin inside each hipbone, and settled her over me. I wanted to ask about the scars I'd seen before when she wore a bathing suit and was just now touching for the first time. But the sensation of being inside Natalya stole my words away. We groaned, and started sliding against each other, our breaths coming faster. I thrust into her as though trying to reach that part of her she'd been keeping from me until tonight. When she'd laid bare her feelings and ran, as though expecting me to toss them back, gift wrapped and all, with a "No, thanks."

I'd done quite the opposite. I'd picked up her declaration and locked it inside where she'd left a piece of herself behind all those months ago. Because with Natalya, I felt whole. Undamaged.

∽

A short time later, Natalya lay on my chest, our heavy breathing easing into a steady rhythm. I grazed my fingers up her spine, in awe of what had just happened between us. I wanted more of this. The connection and of her.

She shivered. I reached for the blanket and draped it over us. Wrapping my arms around her waist, I kissed her forehead. She sighed and kissed my neck. "I've been thinking," she murmured.

So had I. About what I wanted for my sons, who I was, and what was next with Natalya. *Marry me* teetered on my lips.

"What about?" I asked.

She crossed her arms on my chest and rested her chin on her hands. Her lips were a kiss away, but when I met her eyes, I stopped. She chewed her bottom lip. The vulnerability was back.

"What is it?"

"You should go to California."

"What?" All the heat we'd built up dissipated as though a cold front moved in. Everything inside me chilled. My arms slid off her waist. "Why?"

"So you can find out—"

"Find out what?" I bit out the rude interruption. That my ID was fake and I'd get arrested boarding the plane? I shoved fingers into my hair and gripped the back of my neck.

She sat up, the blanket spilling behind her. "Who you are, that's what." Irritation and impatience hardened her tone.

At the risk of forgetting myself? I could see a face or landmark. I could hear a voice. Anything could snap me out of the fugue state.

"I don't travel."

"Listen, Carlos. I know you're afraid."

I tightened my jaw.

She cupped my face and I fought the urge to turn away. He may think it himself, but a man doesn't like to be told to his face he's scared.

"You've known about James for six months. Don't you think it's time you stop hiding from who you really are?"

"I'm not hiding. I—"

"Then you should go see Aimee."

"I—What?"

She stood, wrapping the blanket around her shoulders, her gaze skittering away. "She knows you better than anyone."

CHAPTER 11

JAMES

Present Day
June 25
Saratoga, California

James doesn't see any other option. He and the boys must go to Kauai. Natalya's home. Thomas wants James and Phil to meet at his office, but James doesn't see the point. He still doesn't remember what happened that day and as long as he doesn't, Phil will deny he fired the gun at James. What has James running from his brothers is Carlos's desperate plea to keep Julian and Marc safe. And he can't do that when the chance of coming home to Phil in the kitchen instead of his mother is anything greater than his remembering what had incited the fugue state in the first place.

He also needs a place to think, about where he and his sons go from here. Because he has come to accept he can't live in the same town as Aimee and not be with her. His decision to return to Los Gatos is just another in a long line of bad judgment calls.

But Nick thinks going to Kauai is a mistake. James's best friend told him as much in the Garners' backyard over the heat of the Bull grill searing their steaks. James had just happened to mention his relationship with Natalya.

"Is that wise?" Nick asks.

Staying at the house of a woman he'd been in love with? Probably not. They'd known each other for almost seven years. Been intimate for five, sharing a bed, their desires, and their fears. And other than the photos he'd seen on the wall, he can't recall her face, let alone a single moment spent in her company. No, staying at her house won't be awkward at all.

His stomach bottoms out as it always does when he thinks of her. Maybe he should get a hotel room.

"The boys trust her." He swirls the amber ale he's drinking.

Nick seems to consider this. He reduces the temperature on the grill and removes two steaks, leaving Kristen's and Julian's on a bit longer. He grilled hot dogs earlier for his daughters and Marc. Tongs in hand, Nick drags the back of his wrist across his sweaty brow. "Putting an extra thousand miles or so between you and Phil won't stop him from going after you."

He knows that. But avoiding Phil isn't the only reason he's leaving. He takes a massive drink from his beer. Deep in the pocket of his flat-front shorts, he flips Aimee's engagement ring on and off his fingertip.

"Julian and Marc will be safer there with her."

Nick almost drops Kristen's steak. "You're leaving them with her?"

"I haven't thought that far ahead."

"Now might be a good time to start." Nick looks pointedly at him. James flips him off.

But his friend is right. Here he is, running off again. He was reckless when he followed Phil to Mexico. And he was reckless when he approached Phil outside that dive beachfront bar.

James freezes, his mouth poised over the lip of the bottle, as a memory blinks in and out of his mind like a blip on a radar screen: Phil at a table with two other men. Locals given their attire, skin tone, and casual demeanor. The image is gone before he can make out the men's faces and the location. James squeezes his eyes shut. Forcing the images makes his head ache.

Kristen calls from the house that the salad and potatoes are ready. Nicole squeals at the patio table, followed by Marc's answering laugh. Nick adds the last steak to the plate and brushes down the grill, scraping off food bits. James picks up the plate to take inside.

"Like I said, the boys trust her. And from what I've read, I do, too."

⁊

Present Day,
June 27

Two days later, James and his sons are back at the airport and he's wondering about the woman he'll see in six hours. *She's family,* James thinks as he follows Julian and Marc through airport security. So far, she's the only member of his family who hasn't either screwed him over or tried to control some aspect of his life. Quite the opposite, actually. She's been more than a sister-in-law to him and aunt to his sons. The way he sees it, he owes her. Call him curious, but he wants to meet the woman who once loved him.

By the time they collect their belongings from the carry-on baggage conveyer and James puts on his shoes, Marc is dancing on the balls of his feet. "I have to pee." He cups a hand over his privates.

James motions to Julian. "Restroom, both of you, then breakfast."

After a visit to the bathroom and a brief battle with Marc to wash his hands, he orders hot chocolate and pastries for the boys and a coffee and oatmeal for himself. They take their food to the gate, which is packed with vacationers in a multitude of colors and tropical prints, and find a single seat by the window. Marc climbs up on his knees to watch the plane and promptly drops his doughnut behind the chair. He looks at James and his lower lip quivers.

"Idiot," Julian remarks at the same time he's splitting his doughnut. He offers the half to his brother.

"Thanks." Marc wipes a hand under his nose and bites into the doughnut.

James watches his oldest son sink to the floor, back propped against his pack, and is hit with that rapid free fall that comes with déjà vu as though he stepped off the edge of a diving board. He sees himself in Marc. How he curls his fingers as if holding a brush when he has the itch to paint. The tilt of his head when he's listening to something important. And the reverent way he looks up to his big brother as though Julian's words are gospel. But for the first time, he sees himself and Thomas in the way Marc and Julian interact. Julian is antagonistic and bossy toward his younger brother and James blames himself. The boys have been through several life-changing events in the last six months. But despite the upheaval, Julian still watches out for Marc while Marc continues to idolize his big brother. They're closer to each other than to him, which had been the same for him and Thomas with their parents.

He removes the coffee-cup lid and blows across the surface, recalling one event in particular when Thomas had saved his hide. James had swung by the art store after school one afternoon to buy new brushes and pigment tubes. But in his haste to get home and change clothes to meet Nick and their buddies for a pickup football game in the park, he'd left his backpack with the supplies on the couch in the great room. He arrived home a couple of hours later, sweaty, grass-stained, and muddy, to find Phil in the dining room skimming through his geometry notes. The textbook, cracked to the latest chapter James had studied, lay open at Phil's elbow. Phil had left the wide-open backpack on the chair beside him.

"What're you doing with my stuff?" James's gaze jumped from Phil to the backpack and back. He didn't want to make it obvious he was looking for the art supplies, but where were they? The shopping bag was gone. He heard his mother on the phone in the other room. Did she take the bag?

James glared at Phil, who glanced up casually from the notebook.

"Mom said you failed your last test. I thought I could help you study."

James narrowed his eyes. Math was his best subject. He might have missed two questions, and so what if Mom thought that was failing an exam. He didn't need Phil's help studying. And he sure didn't want Phil going through his stuff without asking.

James flipped the textbook closed, dropped it in his pack, and tugged the notebook from under Phil's forearm. It didn't budge. He tugged again and Phil slowly grinned, leaning back in the chair. He hooked an elbow on the chair back and nodded his chin at James. "Watchya been up to?"

"Football with the guys." He tucked the notebook away.

"That's all?"

James zipped up and shouldered the backpack. "That's all," he replied, leaving the dining room.

"I was only trying to help," Phil called after him.

James flipped him the bird over his shoulder. Then he swept through the great room looking for the shopping bag, first under the couch, then behind the table. His gaze skimmed the kitchen counters before he went to his room. He underhanded the pack onto the bed and stood there, rubbing his forearms. Had he left the bag at the store? No, he distinctly recalled stuffing it into his backpack before he hauled his ass home.

Too stressed to realize he was caked in filth, he sat at his desk and tried to study. He rolled the pencil between flat palms. He bounced the tip on the opened textbook. He shoved fingers into his crusty hair and squeezed. Complementary and obtuse angles blurred on the pages as his heart beat in his throat. His throat was dry and he wished he had a glass of water, but didn't want to get one in case he ran into his mother. The longer he sat there, staring at his homework, the more he believed his mother had searched his backpack and found them. It was only a matter of time before she'd realize he was home. She'd ground him for months.

A light tap rapped on the door. James twisted in his chair and stared wide-eyed at the door. It cracked open. The shopping bag appeared, swinging from a hooked finger. Seconds later, Thomas's wide shoulders filled the door frame. His brother shut the door behind him and tossed the bag at James. He caught it midflight.

"Where'd you find it?"

"On the floor in the dining room." Thomas launched himself on the bed, landing on his back, hands behind his head and legs crossed at the ankle. "I bet it fell out when Phil snooped through your books. What an ass."

"Thanks for covering mine." James shoved the shopping bag into the desk's bottom drawer, under a pile of old school notebooks. "He would've been a jerk about it."

"It's not his fault he is the way he is." His brother grabbed the baseball tucked inside James's glove abandoned on the floor by the bed. He shot the ball straight up, catching it before it landed on his nose.

"So it's my fault he went digging through my stuff?"

"He's just trying to get a rise out of you, but listen." Thomas tossed the ball again, then curled up, sitting on the bed edge and catching the ball in one move. Resting his forearms on his knees, he lightly juggled the ball side to side. "Mom dragged us along to the Valley Fair Mall a couple of days ago. We ran into Dad's secretary."

"Mrs. Lorenzi?" She was as cavalier as their mother and should have retired a decade ago.

"You know how Mom and Dad and Uncle Grant won't acknowledge Phil in public as Mom's son?"

"Yeah, so? What happened?"

Thomas shrugged. "You know Mom. She can't help talking about how great he is. 'My nephew this. My nephew that.'" Thomas mimicked the tone and cadence of their mother's voice. Then he scratched his head, ball in hand. "You'd think Phil would be cocky as shit with the compliments. He looked ill, and a little sad. I felt sorry for the guy."

James frowned. "What does that have to do with his being an ass?"

Thomas shrugged a shoulder. "I don't know. I got this feeling our parents and Uncle Grant are creating their own hell storm. One of these days Phil's going to get sick of us calling him cousin." His brother underhanded the ball and James caught it, putting it aside. Thomas stood and went to the door. "Does Aimee know about Phil?" His tone was curious.

James screwed his lips and shook his head. He was too embarrassed to tell her the truth. It disgusted him that his mother had sex with her brother. That would be like sleeping with Thomas if he were a girl. How gross was that? He still remembered the ridicule his family endured right before they left New York.

"Yeah, I think we've both done a good job sweeping that scandal under the rug. I haven't told anyone either." Thomas turned the handle and paused before opening the door. "Word of advice?"

James had turned back to his desk and homework. He cocked his head toward Thomas. "What?"

"Do the same about your art. You've slipped a couple of times lately."

James agreed. He'd gotten careless. He looked at the drawer where he hid the shopping bag. "If you didn't have to work for Mom and Dad's company after college, what would you want to do?"

Thomas was silent for a moment. "I don't know. I haven't really thought about it."

"If you did think about it?"

"Brian Holstrom's dad works for the FBI. He's told us some really cool stories." He shrugged, then held up his hand, fingers splayed. "Dinner in five." His brother shut the door, leaving James with exactly four minutes to clean up and one minute to get his rear to the table. He sprinted into the bathroom, thoughts of Phil rinsing away with the dirt and grime.

The loudspeaker crackles overhead, reminding James of where they are and why. Boarding would begin shortly for their flight. He nudges Julian's shin with the toe of his sneaker. "That was nice of you," he says, referring to the doughnut half Julian sacrificed. "You're a good brother."

Julian doesn't reply, just looks at him, then buries his face in his phone, cramming the rest of the doughnut in his mouth.

Standing beside his sons, James finishes his coffee and juggles his oatmeal, mixing in a packet of nuts and dried fruit. Flip-flops and loafers cross his line of vision while he eats. He scrapes the bottom of the bowl and takes his last bite when a pair of strappy, rhinestone slides fills his vision. They sparkle like crazy. Then he feels the owner's presence and his entire demeanor hardens. The pulse in his neck throbs. He doesn't have to see who's wearing the tailored sundress with the thin leather belt tightened at a slender waist as he draws his gaze upward. He doesn't have to look past the tiny pearl button at the neckline and into her pinched face to know who's standing beside him.

The oatmeal he just ate lands hard in his stomach. *What the hell?*

"Hello, James." His mother greets him with the closed-lipped curve of a smile.

For the second time this week, his jaw lands on the floor over her unexpected appearance. He has to stop himself from asking Marc to pick it up along with his dirty doughnut.

James gapes at the woman who lied to him and his sons for five years. The same woman who abhorred his artistic talent, so much so she'd ordered him to return the first oil-paint set Aimee had gifted him on his twelfth birthday. *A frivolous talent, James, and not worth wasting your time on.*

This came from the same woman who's an artist herself. A brilliant one, too. He'd seen the piece displayed in the upstairs hallway of their house in Puerto Escondido. Carlos had also described in his journals the other works she'd painted during her extended stays in Mexico.

His pulse pounds in his ears. "Why are you here?"

Claire's face twitches. Her barely there smile falters.

"Señora Carla!" Marc launches to his feet and hugs Claire, smearing sugar and sprinkles on her sundress. She doesn't blink an eye, but her smile is back, brighter and wider.

"Are you coming to Hawaii? Will you stay with us? Tía Natalya will be very happy to see you." Marc speaks rapid Spanish, unable to contain his excitement.

Julian looks up from where he's sitting and stares bug-eyed at Claire, just as surprised as James to find her there. He slowly rises to his feet, sliding off his headphones to drape around his neck. He glances to James, then back to Claire, and James knows it won't be long before his son figures out who Claire is, and what she's been hiding from him for years.

Claire kisses Marc's head, then does the same to Julian, who's slowly warming up. She hugs him, then meets James's hard gaze. "Do you mind if I join you?"

"Give us a minute," he tells his kids. He grips Claire's upper arm and hauls her a few seats away.

"James," she gasps.

He stops by the trash bin and tosses the oatmeal bowl, then launches into his mother. His teeth are gritted to keep his voice low and somewhat under control. "We might have had some messed-up friendship thing going on in Mexico, but fact is fact. You took advantage of my memory loss. Do . . . not . . . expect us to pick up where we left off."

"Watch your tone with me." Her eyes arrow left, then right, concerned they were making a spectacle of themselves.

James loosens his grip and lets his arm fall to his side. "Why are you here?"

Her polished nails flutter to the pearl button at her neck. "Thomas told me you were leaving. He thought I'd want to know." Her face softens. "You can use my help. The boys know me."

"As Señora Carla. I thought you weren't speaking with Thomas."

She grimaces. "We talk only when necessary. James, darling, please. You weren't home nearly long enough and Thomas didn't know when you'd be back." She glances around James. "I miss them. I haven't seen them since last December."

A chill rappels down his spine like a rock climber on a cliff face. "You were in Mexico last December?"

She looks surprised. "Of course I was. I went every year right after Thanksgiving. I'd stay through the Christmas holiday."

But he hadn't seen her. Which only meant one thing in James's mind. She'd known he surfaced and had left the country.

Over the speaker the attendant announces boarding for first-class passengers. Claire opens her purse and retrieves her ticket. "You aren't the only parent in this family worried about their children's welfare."

Since when had she cared about him? "A box of expensive paintbrushes doesn't make up for years of ignoring something I used to be extremely passionate about."

Claire snaps shut her purse. She frowns. "What do you mean 'used to be'?"

"You finally got what you wanted, Mother. I stopped painting."

She tucks her purse under her arm and averts her face. She watches the luggage being loaded onto the plane. "I'm still going. I have a ticket and a hotel reservation."

The gate attendant announces the next boarding group and passengers mill toward the gate. Julian looks impatiently at him and mouths

Let's go. James holds up a finger, a signal he'll be there in a second, then turns back to his mother. "I can't stop you. I can, and I will, determine when and how you interact with my sons."

"When do you plan to tell them about me?"

"I'm not sure I will."

"But I'm their grandmother. You have no right keeping me from them."

"Are you kidding me?" A short laugh rumbles from his chest. He gives his mother a look of disgust. "I have every right." He shakes his head, still laughing at her audacity, and returns to his sons.

Their row block is announced. "Grab your stuff, kids. Time to go."

"Where are you sitting, Señora Carla?" Marc asks once they're in line.

"I'm in the very front."

"Of course you are." James fumbles with the zippers on his pack, searching for their tickets.

Julian gives him a weird look. "What's your deal?"

"Life, Julian." He gives his son his ticket. "Don't lose it."

"Seriously?" he balks. "What do you think I'm going to do? Drop it between here and the gate?" A woman with a toddler rushes forward, bumping Julian's shoulder, knocking the ticket from his hand. It floats to the floor.

James snorts a laugh. He can't help it.

"Shut up," Julian mumbles. But his mouth twitches into a smile when he picks up the ticket.

James pats Julian's shoulder, leaving his hand there to rest as they inch toward the gate. To his amazement, his son doesn't shrug him off.

CHAPTER 12

CARLOS

Five Years Ago
July 8
Puerto Escondido, Mexico

I woke as the sun rose over the crest of the mountains to the east and ran my morning route, ten kilometers through the streets of Puerto Escondido with a finish on the hard-packed sand of Zicatela Beach. Broken clouds billowed overhead, revealing patches of golden blue, and electricity charged the air. Wind pushed inland.

Natalya was waiting for me as I walked up the beach, calves burning and body drenched. She sat on the half wall, drinking coffee. She was leaving in a few days. I'd drive her to the airport, kiss her good-bye, and make her promise me to call when she landed. She'd ask me again when I planned to fly to California.

I stopped in front of her and she smiled up at me. "Good morning."

Gripping the back of her head, I gave her a quick, hard kiss. "Good morning."

She wrinkled her nose. "You need a shower."

"Only if you join me." I sat beside her, groaning as I bent over to untie my Nikes.

"Hard run?"

"A good run."

She smiled and sipped her coffee. "I've been thinking."

I gave her a mock look of disbelief from my bent-over position. "That's impressive."

"Ha-ha." She playfully shoved my shoulder; then her expression turned pensive. "Work is going to be crazy for the next few months."

"Mari's longboards?"

She nodded. "Between production and marketing, I'll be pretty busy. I won't be back until the *torneo*."

"November?" That would be the longest time spent apart since we'd met. It would seem even longer now that our relationship had taken a new course. We moved her luggage into my room the morning after our first night together. She'd been in my bed every night since.

I slipped off my shoes and soaked socks, frowning at the unfamiliar ache in my chest. "You aren't having second thoughts about us?"

"No, not at all." She reached for my hand. Our fingers twined. "But about what I've been thinking . . . yes, I'm quite capable of that," she teased, and I grinned. "Assuming your trip to California works out"—she tapped her head in reference to my fugue and that I'd still be myself, as in Carlos—"would you consider visiting me? November seems so far away."

"I don't know, Nat." I slipped my hand from hers. "I haven't decided yet if I'm going."

"But you agreed to see Aimee. We talked about this."

"I don't know if I can go. I might not make it out of the country."

"You're still worried about your identification."

"I'd be an idiot not to be."

"Well . . . if Jason Bourne can do it, so can you."

"Who's Jason Bourne?"

She opened her mouth to explain.

"Never mind," I interrupted, pushing to my feet. I lunged a few paces away. Hands on hips, I turned to Natalya. "I called Thomas yesterday." Her mouth unhinged. "He said my identity is legit. When I asked how, he wouldn't tell me, not over the phone. He'll only explain in person."

"What did you say? Is he coming here?"

I shrugged both shoulders. "No clue. I hung up on him."

"Carlos . . ." She tossed up a hand. "Why?"

"Are you kidding me? This cloak-and-dagger shit is why I won't have anything to do with that family."

"You mean, your family." She gave an impatient roll of her eyes and stood, brushing off the back of her cotton skirt. "Like it or not, you're related to them, and there's only one way to find out *if* you're like them. Go to California. Go see how they live. Go meet your friends and find out what you're like. Go talk to Aimee."

"And when I find out I *am* just like them?"

She sighed, her gaze floating down the beach. "I don't know. Can we talk about this when you get back?"

I inhaled and briefly closed my eyes. "Yes." I could live with that. For now. Then an idea popped in my head and was out of my mouth in a flash. "We could just get married."

"Carlos . . ." Her face fell.

"I thought you loved me."

"You know I do," she vehemently whispered.

But not enough to marry me, or to move to Puerto Escondido.

I swung back around toward the ocean, not really seeing it. "Forget I asked," I said over my shoulder, because she was right. Best I get to know myself before getting attached to anyone else.

I heard Natalya sigh, then felt her arms around my waist. She kissed my spine and I covered her hands with mine. "We'll work this out,

Carlos. You'll see." She pressed her cheek against my back. "You're a better man than you give yourself credit for."

I looked up at the sky and disappearing sun. Thunder rumbled and I felt the vibration deep in my bones. Behind me, safe inside, the boys slept, the hour still early for a summer morning. Thomas said my identity and all accompanying paperwork was legitimate. How could I trust his word after all he'd put me through?

But if the paperwork wasn't forged, that meant I was legally Julian's father.

The realization came with some comfort. It also left me with a heavy heart. While I hadn't been inclined to trust Thomas, in this one instance I had no choice. Going to California was the only way I could put my mind at ease. It was also the best way I could learn about James. I just hoped I'd make it there and back with my identity intact, in my head and on paper.

CHAPTER 13

JAMES

Present Day
June 27
Lihue, Kauai, Hawaii

James can't sit still. His fingers tap the chair arm separating his seat from his sons', and his knees bounce. He borrows a colored pencil from Marc just so he can hold on to something. It isn't a paintbrush, but his fidgety fingers don't care. What he doesn't care for is why he's nervous.

Toward the end of the flight, Julian looks at him, annoyed, so James stands and paces the aisle. When the pilot puts on the seatbelt sign and announces their descent, his chest muscles spasm. He's finally meeting Natalya face-to-face. A woman who knows him intimately. Up until six months ago, their relationship was serious, like sexting and up-all-night-naked-under-the-sheets serious.

James groans and sinks into his chair, snapping the belt across his lap. He tells his sons to start packing their backpacks and helps Marc organize his colored pencils, picking up the ones that rolled onto the floor. Five of them, about the number of times he and Natalya have spoken on the phone since he surfaced. The first time had been the morning Julian climbed into the closet then dropped a metal lockbox on his lap. His son punched in the code and left the room. James found him downstairs bawling on the phone. While Natalya, back home in Hawaii, tried calming her nephew, James had been reading the documents and letters in the box. He then vomited in the toilet and called Thomas.

James felt like he would pass out. Panic and disbelief practically cut off his air supply. He wanted to book the first flight home. Instead, he reached a shaking hand toward the son he just met and demanded the phone.

"Who is this?" His voice came out strained, stretched rubber-band thin.

"I'm Natalya Hayes, your sister-in-law, an American like you. I live in Hawaii," she explained. He liked her voice. The last name sounded familiar. It evoked images of wetsuits and surfboards, of mornings riding waves in Santa Cruz. Julian ran upstairs, wailing. A door slammed. James took the phone outside. He needed air and light and a one-way ticket home. He needed Aimee. His breath shuttered out of him.

God, she was the one person he desperately needed to talk to, that he ached to hold to the point that the emptiness in his arms left him gasping. He had to stop himself from crying out in anguish.

"I know you're confused and I know Julian is upset," Natalya was saying in a voice that sounded barely under control. "He's angry, and he's going to be angry for a very long time. But he *is* your son. He knew this could happen. You prepared him for the possibility."

"What possibility?" he snapped, rubbing his forehead with the base of his palm.

"That you'd forget who he is. You've been living in a fugue state for over six years."

That's what Thomas had told him. It seemed preposterous. Unreal, like something out of a science fiction movie. He needed to research his condition and find a doctor as soon as he got himself out of Mexico.

"What about that other kid?" The one who woke him up jumping on the bed.

"Mar—cus?" Her voice cracked like hot glass when filled with ice. "He's your son, too."

"What the fuck am I supposed to do with them?" He winced. He hadn't meant to say that out loud.

"The same thing you've always done. Be their father."

"And their mother? My *wife*?" The word soured on his tongue. "She's dead?"

"Yes," she said simply. But James caught the notes of pain and loss over the roar of his own turmoil. Raquel had been Natalya's sister. He'd seen the marriage and death certificates. Despite his shock, he noticed she died on Marcus's birth date.

"I'm sorry." The apology was automatic even though he thanked God he wasn't hitched. It was a callous thought. But, holy shit, he could only take so much.

"Julian wants to come to Hawaii. I told him no, but I can be on the next flight there."

"No," he said too quickly. He paced the yard. "No, I need to think. I need time." She sounded nice on the phone, but she was a stranger to him. Could he trust her?

"You left yourself a journal. Take the time to read it. I think the answers to most of the questions you have will be there. And . . . James? I know you're scared, but so are your sons. They love you, and I hope you can find within yourself a way to love them again. They're good kids." She was crying by the time she finished; then she disconnected the call before he could thank her.

During their follow-up conversations, she was pleasant, even helpful. But this last one a few days ago? She was frozen-lake cold when he told her he was taking her up on her offer to bring the boys to Hawaii. Despite the icy reception, he reminded himself she had loved the man he used to be.

As Carlos, he had loved her and made love to her. But as James, he had read and reread every passage about their shared moments. He knows she eats an orange in the morning, peeling the fruit in a circular motion so the rind comes off in one long curl. He knows her scent is just as citrusy, and when mixed with the coconut sunscreen she applies throughout the day, that the aroma is intoxicating, even arousing.

The journal excerpts fascinated him, as did the woman. But they also screwed his stomach like a drill on an oil rig boring deep into the earth. The guilt he felt from being intimate with not one, but two women when he should have been with Aimee, often left him drowning in self-disgust. He almost stopped reading the journals for that reason alone. He already hated himself enough.

Once the plane lands, and as they file off, James wonders if he'll recognize Natalya by sight. Carlos had been sympathetic toward Aimee, but he hadn't been drawn to her. Will it be the same with him and Natalya? His heart bangs against his sternum like a gloved fist. He takes deep, meditative breaths, letting the air fill his cheeks as he exhales. Nerves and humidity dampen his armpits and the curve of his lower back.

He spots her immediately standing alone on the opposite side of the carousel in the Lihue Airport's open-air baggage claim. Trade winds lift the mass of burnished copper hair Carlos had described in detail. Burnt sienna. Cadmium orange. Terra rose. Yellow ochre. Her hair has all those paint colors and more. And he can't stop staring.

He doesn't alert the boys, who are occupied with the bags cruising at a snail's pace around the carousel, placing bets whose will appear first. He doesn't tell them he sees her because he wants the chance to watch her, unguarded before she notices him. He studies her like a model for one of his paintings. The sharp angle of her bent arm and the play of sunlight on her tanned skin. The long slope of her neck as it curves into her shoulder above the swell of her breasts. She tugs at the silver bangles adorning her wrists and she twines her hair into a makeshift ponytail, letting it fall over her shoulder. Again he has that sense of déjà vu, as though he's witnessed her quirks before. Though he knows that's impossible. She only seems familiar because he read about her.

Her gaze jumps from one person to the next around their carousel until landing on him. Their eyes lock and for a minute they simply watch each other. His heart drums but he doesn't move. Her chest rises sharply. She clutches the shoulder strap of her purse and walks toward him. His hands start to perspire.

Damn.

He breaks eye contact, wiping his hands against his jeans, then taps Marc on the shoulder and shows him who's approaching. He needs a moment to collect himself and Marc's a good distraction. Plus, he wants to observe how his kids react to her. Is she all that Carlos described? Does she love them the way he said she does?

"Tía Natalya!" Marc runs over and launches into her waiting arms. She covers his face in kisses and whispers in his ear. His son giggles and an odd sense of jealousy shifts through him. He wants Marc to react that way when he sees him.

Natalya clasps Marc's hand and walks toward James. Julian notices her and his face turns on its stadium lights. Marc spots his suitcase on the carousel and James grabs the handle. He turns around in time to see Natalya's reaction to his mother, who's joined them in baggage claim.

Natalya's face screws up. "Señora Carla?"

James drops the luggage. It lands with a thud on the tile. He holds his breath, waiting for his mother to sever the tenuous bond he's building with his sons faster than the snip of kitchen shears. Julian watches the three of them, his expression calculating. Thankfully, his mother doesn't correct Natalya. Rather, her entire demeanor changes. Claire smiles and pulls Natalya in for a hug. Natalya's brows bunch. She throws him a questioning look. He shoves a hand through his hair and glances away. He didn't plan having his mother in the picture when he met Natalya. How does he explain this to her?

"It's wonderful to see you again. How've you been?" Claire asks Natalya, holding her at arms' length.

"I'm . . . great. You?"

"Wonderful. Absolutely wonderful." She smiles at everyone. "We have much to catch up on. We'll talk once everyone is settled." Claire gives Natalya's hand a friendly squeeze.

"Okay." Natalya drags out the word. "I wasn't expecting an extra person, but I guess you can stay in my room with me."

Claire waves her hand. "Don't worry about me. I have a room at the St. Regis. Do you mind giving me a lift to Princeville? Or . . . should I get a cab?" She looks at James.

"I can drive you," Natalya says, then also looks at him as though wondering what to do about Claire.

James sighs and rubs his face with both hands. "Give us a moment," he says to his mother.

Claire smiles. "I see my suitcase. Julian, help me out."

Julian and Claire walk away in pursuit of the moving luggage. James turns to Natalya. "I didn't know she was coming."

"I don't understand. How do you know each other?"

"Her name is Claire. She's my mother."

Natalya backs up a step. "Your *mother*?" She watches Claire with an appalled expression and James imagines she's thinking about the amount of time Señora Carla spent with them. She'd fooled them all.

He scrunches his lips and nods.

Natalya just stares at him. "That's messed up."

The corner of his mouth lifts. "Which about sums up my family."

Marc pats James's hip. He points at the carousel. "Your bag."

"Thanks, buddy." He taps the bill of Marc's cap and turns back to Natalya. Her expression has changed, unreadable. James shifts uneasily. His mother's duplicity is probably sinking in, as well as the fact that Carlos hadn't trusted the Donatos, and here he is with their matriarch. It's probably also hitting her that she doesn't know *him*. He's not her

Carlos, just like Claire isn't Señora Carla. But the difference is that he never lied to her.

He casts Claire a look. "The boys don't know about her yet. With everything they've been through lately, I'm not sure how they'll take the news," he explains to Natalya, turning back to her. Their gazes meet again and he hears her sharp intake of breath. He feels it in an unexpected place deep inside him. He moves a step closer. She's welcomed him into her home and he wants her to feel comfortable having him there. He wants her to get to know *him*.

"By the way," he extends his hand, "I'm James."

She clasps his hand, quickly covering the tremble in her lower lip with a tentative smile. "Aloha . . . James. I'm Nat. Welcome to Hawaii."

CHAPTER 14

CARLOS

Five Years Ago
August 13
Puerto Escondido, Mexico and San Jose, California

It took two weeks after Natalya left for me to work up the courage to book my travel reservations to California, which I made for another two weeks out. Even though I gave myself time to prepare, nerves twisted my stomach days before my flight, and not solely because of my fear of traveling with my condition. Going to California meant that I trusted Thomas's word, that my identification wasn't forged and that I wouldn't be stopped by Customs and imprisoned or deported.

Despite my fears, I had to go. I had to learn whether I could trust James to care for Julian and Marcus. I also wanted to know more about why and how Jaime Carlos Dominguez came to be. Thomas wouldn't give me the answers over the phone. He had to tell me in person. If that was the case, then it would be on my own terms, which was why I didn't tell Thomas I was coming. I didn't want him censoring who and what I saw just to convince me to stay, or to provoke me from the fugue state.

The boys would stay with the Silvas while Pia would manage the gallery. Carla had been taking weekly classes from me, so the morning of my flight I went to her house to reschedule for when I returned.

She invited me upstairs. "I want to show you my studio."

I followed her up. "Wow!" Natural light spilled across the loft like liquid gold, but what astounded me was the number of paintings she'd produced in the last four weeks.

"I found the art store you mentioned."

"Yeah, you did." Three easels had been erected by the windows with canvases in various stages of completion. Paint tubes, brushes, palette boards, and mason jars filled with turpentine crowded the table in the middle of the room.

"I'm trying my hand at watercolors, too." She showed me a smaller table in the corner of the loft. She drew a brush from a jar and rolled it between her palms. The handle clicked against her rings. "I can't stop painting. It's like I'm making up for lost time."

The corner of my mouth lifted. I was well acquainted with the feeling. The glide of paint across canvas, the pungent scent of solvents, and the scratch of the palette knife through pigment. They lured me back to the studio like the scent of a woman in my bed. I thought of Natalya, back home in Hawaii. I missed her. November couldn't come soon enough.

I studied an oil canvas set aside to dry. The color layering was technical and advanced. "These are masterful." The brush clicked faster in her hands and I loosely gestured at it. "I do that, too, when I want to paint."

"Oh." Carla stared at the brush, then stabbed it into a mason jar and grasped both my hands. "Thank you for bringing art back into my life."

"You're welcome."

She grinned and released my hands. She capped an oil tube and a turpentine flask.

I picked up a clean brush and stroked the bristles. They snagged underneath a nail bed. "I'm curious. Why did you stop?"

Carla was quiet, her back to me. She sorted pigment tubes by color, then gracefully laid a hand over them. "My father didn't approve of a decision I'd made and the punishment was severe. He took away the one thing I was most passionate about."

"Painting. He made you stop?"

"He did more than that. He forbade it. He also threatened to disown me should he find a single paintbrush in the house." She raised a finger. Already thin-boned and delicate, Carla appeared smaller and more fragile with the admission. I sensed her withdrawal and my heart went out to her.

"I'm sorry," I said quietly, folding my arms. I cleared my throat with the intention of changing to the subject that had brought me there. My flight left in a few hours.

"I'm doing fine now. It was a long time ago. We lived in an old stone house in upstate New York with a large fireplace." She sorted clean brushes, aligning them in a wood case. She glanced over her shoulder at me and a sad smile curved her lips. "I used to love that fireplace, and I loved to read beside it. My father built fires during the winter that smoldered long into the night. That was until . . ." She paused and worried a paintbrush, fanning the bristles, then took a deep breath and put the brush away. "That was until my father gathered up my paintings. He built one of his roaring blazes. Flames shot up the chute. I could feel the heat on my cheeks from across the room. He ordered me to toss my canvases into the fire, and then he made me watch them burn." She snapped shut the brush case, but she didn't turn around.

My gaze roved over her paintings. Each one made it less obvious to the inexperienced eye she hadn't painted for decades. I had a difficult time believing the long hiatus. "You never tried painting again once you moved out?"

Carla shook her head. She angled her face toward me, revealing the right angles of her chin, the upward swoop at the end of her nose. "At the time, I was underage with a child my parents abhorred, and my father forced my brother, who was six years older than me, to raise him. I married a couple of years later, and soon had two more children. There wasn't time to paint, and eventually I simply lost interest. For a long time, everything about painting—the smell, the supplies, even watching someone else paint—reminded me of the horrible shame I'd brought upon my family. It still does."

She turned around and circled a hand in dismissal. "You didn't come here to listen to my pitiful life. What brings you here today, Señor Jaime . . . Carlos . . . Dominguez?" she asked with an air of formality and the touch of a smile.

Ever since I told her what the *JCD* stood for on my paintings, she'd been teasing me with my full name. She even threatened to call me Jaime when I pushed her skills with the brush. My mouth twitched. "Well," I began, "I have to reschedule your class tomorrow."

Her lower lip popped out. "That's a shame. I look forward to our time together. Is everything all right?"

My gaze dipped to the floor, where I toed a discarded paper clip. "Yes . . . yes, it's fine. I've had a last-minute opportunity to attend an art conference in Mexico City." I picked up the clip and flipped it through my fingers. Outside of Natalya, I didn't want anyone to know my destination. I used the same art-conference excuse I did with the Silvas and Pia.

"Sounds like a lovely adventure."

I grimaced. *If she only knew.*

Carla moved around the table and fiddled with a flower bouquet. She snapped off two wilting daisies. "Would you like me to watch your sons while you're gone?"

My brows arched. "Um, no . . . but thanks. The boys are staying with friends. I wanted you to know that we'll be gone for a few days. We can do two lessons next week."

She patted the flowers, shifted a few stems. I spotted a sticky note-pad on the table and jotted down the Silvas' phone number. "Just in case you need to get in touch. You already have my cell."

She read the note and put it aside. "I guess I'll see you in a few days, then."

I sure hoped so, because that meant my ass hadn't been hauled to prison, or I hadn't been refused entry back into Mexico. My chest clenched and palms dampened just thinking about everything that could go wrong over the next five days.

"Before you go . . ." Carla pointed at a room off to the left. "I'm having the devil of a time with my wireless connection. It keeps cutting out. Will you take a look for me?"

I glanced at my watch. "Sure," I said, and followed her into the guest room.

❧

Five Years Ago
August 14

The captain announced our descent into San Jose and soon we were taxiing to our gate. I'd called Natalya during the layover in Los Angeles as soon as I went through Customs. The officer had scanned my passport, asked the nature of my stay (visiting family), where I was staying (downtown San Jose), and the length of my visit (four days). After a brief moment of eye contact, he stamped my passport and welcomed me to the United States of America.

Natalya and I both heaved a long sigh. She even laughed off the nervousness. But I had to wonder. How the hell did Thomas create a new identity for me in such a short time frame? He had the paperwork in Imelda's hands within a week or so after my accident.

After a short diversion to the men's room, I called Natalya again on my way to baggage claim. She picked up after the second ring. "You made it!"

"I made it." I sighed dramatically and she laughed.

"How was the last leg of the flight?"

"Quick. My seatmate left me alone this time." On the flight to Mexico City, the woman sitting beside me could tell I was nervous. She was gorgeous if caked makeup and tamale-red nails was your thing. She kept offering me gin and tonics to calm those nerves.

Natalya laughed. "Good thing, else I'd have to come rescue you. So . . . the plan is . . ."

"The plan is: shower, eat, bed."

"It's only two in California."

"Yeah, I know." I scratched my stubbled cheek. I hadn't slept at all on the plane or during the layovers. "I'm going to pick up the rental car and drive around for a bit. I'll find Aimee once I get my bearings."

My luggage flipped onto the carousel and I snagged the handle, releasing it and dropping the bag wheel-side down in one motion. "I'll call you tonight," I said, walking through the automatic sliding glass doors to the arrival pickup zone and straight into Thomas. I stopped dead in my tracks.

Dressed in a slate-gray suit, arms crossed, Thomas lounged against an obsidian-black metallic Tesla. He gave me a short wave and a tight-lipped grin.

"What time do you think you'll call?" Natalya was asking. "I'll make sure I'm back from the beach."

Every nerve inside me hummed at full throttle. Blood roared in my ears. My heart slammed against my sternum. *How the hell did he know I was here?*

"Nat, I'll call you back."

"Wait. What?"

I disconnected the call.

Thomas uncrossed his ankles and pushed away from the car. His hands slid into his trouser pockets. "Hello, Carlos. Welcome to California."

CHAPTER 15

JAMES

Present Day
June 27
Hanalei, Kauai, Hawaii

Julian and Marc climb into the rear seat of Natalya's open-top Jeep Wrangler. It's not lost on James she drives the same type of vehicle Carlos had owned. Claire grimaces when James orders Marc to scoot to the center. He insists Claire sit with the boys. "You wanted the chance to catch up with them." He smirks.

Natalya glances at him when he settles in the passenger seat. He buckles up and smiles over at her. She blushes before her gaze slides away. She slaps on a sunscreen-stained, flat-billed cap with the Hayes Boards logo, which is a surfboard riding the company name where the letters *H-A-Y-E-S* are styled to look like a wave. She shifts the Jeep into gear, her movements rough, and the vehicle jerks forward.

Other than responding to his questions in clipped phrases, Natalya is quiet during the forty-minute drive to Princeville. Her reception as cool as her tone the other day on the phone. James reads her signals loud and clear. She isn't in the mood to talk . . . with him. He turns his interest to the passing scenery. From azure waters, airbrushed clouds, Jurassic Park–like mountains, and skyscraper palms, the Garden Isle is breathtaking. After six months in the dry Mexican heat, the last place he expected to find himself traveling to is another beachside community. But this island is different, almost effortlessly beautiful. He can feel the *mana*. The spiritual vibe is almost tangible. The air is heavy with humidity and the scent of plumerias. He sees now why Natalya wanted Carlos to visit. Kauai is magical. A living painting.

Natalya keeps her gaze focused on the Kuhio Highway as they curve around the island. She doesn't willingly talk to him so he steals glances at her profile. The freckled constellations across her cheekbones and nose intrigue him. The defined limbs that tell him she can probably keep up with him running trails as easily as she surfs the waves. And the hair that spins madly around her head like Indiana Jones's whip. It all fascinates him. As does the woman. Would she be the same as the image Carlos painted in his journals?

Her row of sterling bracelets jangle as she downshifts, turning off the highway. They cruise through Princeville to the hotel, leaving the Jeep idling at the lobby doors. A valet assists Claire from the vehicle.

"Are you all staying with us?" the valet asks James when he unfolds from the car.

"No, just her." He nods in his mother's direction and slips the valet a bill after he points out her bag.

"Do you want me to pick you up later for dinner, Carla?" Natalya asks.

She hooks her purse strap on her bent elbow. "No, thank you. I'll settle in here for the day. How about I join you in the morning for breakfast?" his mother asks Natalya, but her eyes are on James. He really doesn't want her joining them for anything, but what can he say without raising questions he isn't prepared to answer? Julian's watching him closely, that inquisitive mind of his ticking.

James shrugs and walks to Natalya's side. "What time should I pick her up?"

"Don't worry about me," his mother dismisses him. "I'll take a cab."

"Breakfast is at eight."

"Wonderful." Claire waves good-bye to his sons and gestures for the valet to follow.

Julian thrusts a chin in her direction and Marc waves back. *"Buenos días, Señora Carla."*

"Do you mind waiting a second?" James asks Natalya.

She points to an empty spot in the parking lot. "I'll be parked over there."

James claps the door's open window edge twice. "Thanks. I'll be right back."

Natalya drives away and James goes after his mother. He places his hand on her midback and shuffles her into the lobby. The valet hurries behind with the luggage.

"James," Claire says between clenched teeth when he directs her off to the side. The valet hovers nearby.

"Excuse us a moment," James tells the valet.

"Yes, sir. Ma'am, your bags will be at the concierge when you're ready."

James pivots back to his mother. "I don't know why you're here or what you're up to—"

"I'm up to nothing more than a visit with my grandsons."

His eyes narrow. She rolls her eyes. "Fine," she huffs. "I'm here to make sure you don't give up those boys."

He jerks back. "Why would I do that?"

"Carlos was afraid you'd do something like this. *He* told me things. We had a good friendship."

"Because he didn't know who the hell you were."

Claire averts her gaze. "Fair enough." After a moment, she breathes deeply and pushes back her shoulders. "I'm going to check in and have lunch. A manicure sounds nice, too." She inspects her nails, then walks away.

James rubs his face. He needs a shower and a shave. And food. What he doesn't need is his mother's dramatics. He groans into his cupped palms and leaves the hotel.

Back at the Jeep, he runs into more drama. His sons moan and groan. They rub their stomachs, complaining about unbearable hunger pains.

"We don't have any grocery stores or restaurants on the island," Natalya tells the boys as he slides into his seat. She catches his gaze and her eyes sparkle. "We have to pick our fruit from trees and slaughter our chickens."

His sons look at their aunt in disgust.

"Eww," Julian says.

"Haven't you seen the chickens running wild?"

The boys nod.

"Catch one and it's yours. We'll eat it for dinner."

"I was wondering about that," James remarks. Chickens and roosters dotted the roadsides and flocked in parking lots. He'd noticed the feral birds during their drive.

"Hurricane Iniki in '92. It wiped out the chicken farms," Natalya explains, shifting into reverse. James grips the dashboard as the car lurches. "Chickens aren't easy to catch and the island doesn't have any natural predators so their population exploded. Now they're just annoying pests begging in parking lots." She points at a flock.

"More like built-in alarm clocks," James quips, thinking of how many roosters he saw.

"You have no idea." Natalya shifts into gear and they leave the parking lot. "I know of the perfect spot to grab lunch." She yells at the boys over her shoulder.

"Do we get to kill chickens?" Marc excitedly yells back.

"No," James and Natalya answer in unison. They glance at each other. He skims his eyes over her face and she frowns. He sighs, running a hand through his wild, wind-blown hair as he settles back in his seat, and wonders what about Carlos had appealed to her because she certainly wasn't liking him.

They eat from a food truck parked on the main road that runs through Hanalei town. He watches how his sons interact with Natalya as she guides them through the menu of kalua pig, poi, and taro smoothies. She handles their disgruntled faces and objections over the unfamiliar food choices as he assumed she would navigate a rogue wave, with skill and finesse. Despite their complaints, Natalya insists they be adventurous. "Trust me," she says, and they do.

Carlos trusted her implicitly, and watching her with his sons is like the pages from his journal coming to life. For a brief moment, he looks away, the pang in his chest burns hot and deep. He wants his sons to trust him, to love him like they'd loved him when he was Carlos.

He pinches away the moisture from the corners of his eyes and takes a deep, calming breath. Then he places his own order, leaning over Natalya's shoulder. The cashier totals their bill and he hands her a few bills at the same time Natalya pulls out her credit card.

"I've got it," he tells her.

"I'm quite capable of paying."

"I'm sure you are. Money's not the issue. This is—" He stops. Natalya's face has gone blank. "What is it?"

"You'd mentioned that once, as Carlos. Apparently, money isn't an issue with *you*." She slaps the card on the counter ledge.

James frowns and tucks his money away. He bites back the urge to correct her. He's not swimming in an ocean of cash. More like a rain puddle. He joins his sons at a metal table and sits on a plastic patio chair. They eat quickly. The boys are anxious to see Tía Natalya's home and go to the beach. He follows them to Natalya's car and grabs her door as she goes to close it. He positions himself in the triangular space between her and the door. "Hey, back there, I wasn't trying to flash my cash."

She grips the steering wheel with both hands and sighs. "I know. It's just . . ."

"I wanted to take care of lunch. You're my host."

"And you're my guests."

James smooths a hand over his head and grips the roll bar. "Look, I know I'm not Carlos—"

"No, you're not."

"—but I think it's in the kids' best interest we at least try to get along."

She flattens her lips and nods. "You're right. It's just . . . this is hard. And honestly," she says, rolling her hands on the wheel, exposing her open palms, "I don't agree with what you're doing."

His chest goes cold. "Which is what?"

"I don't want to talk about this now. Get in the car. The kids want to swim."

Natalya's house could have been a short walk from where they ate lunch. After a couple of quick turns, they're on Weke, a road that parallels Hanalei Bay. Many of the homes are modest, villas reminiscent of vintage postcards, but the properties are large and the location premium. Natalya turns onto a long driveway. They pass a small bungalow and stop in front of a larger island-style home painted the color of the lush, tropical foliage surrounding the property, which is narrow and deep. Beyond the yard is the greenery of Waioli Beach Park and the Pine Trees surf break.

And she has issues with his wealth?

She explains the house has been in her family for several generations. Her grandfather purchased the property decades ago. Her father now owned the house, but he lived in the bungalow situated in the front corner of the property with mountain views.

So what if they both lived in the homes they grew up in? At least they have one thing in common. Not that he's looking for any, and living in his parents' old house isn't something he plans to continue doing.

The main living quarters are on the second level. Downstairs is the garage, a workshop for her boards, and Natalya's home office, where James would be sleeping on a sofa bed.

"Come on, kids. I'll show you to your rooms."

"Then the beach, right?" Julian takes the suitcase James hands him.

"You bet." Natalya playfully punches Julian's shoulder. He tries to punch her back and she dodges him. When he goes after her again, she wraps him in a headlock and smothers his face in kisses. He squirms and whines like a baby and once again, that green little snake of envy slithers through James. He slams shut his door.

Upstairs, an open-air lanai stretches the rear length of the house. Both the master suite and living area open to the lanai and face the bay. The kitchen and boys' rooms, decorated as though they live there permanently, which gives James pause, face the mountains. The furniture is Spartan with a Bohemian flair, but the stainless-steel appliances and media center are top-notch. A staircase leads down to the office and a full bath for his use. Another staircase off the deck drops to a patio with a barbecue and smoker. From his perspective, James thinks as he takes his suitcase downstairs, Natalya's house is equipped with the right essentials.

Forty minutes later, rooms assigned and inspected, bags unpacked and bathing suits on, they traverse the yard and park to the fine, tan sand of Hanalei Beach. The water's rough, so they walk toward the pier until Natalya finds a spot where she's comfortable for them to swim. The boys drop their towels and crash into the surf, thrilled to be back in the water.

"The ocean calls to them," Natalya says beside him.

He glances down at her capped head. She wears the same dirty baseball cap that looks as if it belongs on a trucker. The hem of her multicolored cover-up floats in the breeze, dancing around her thighs. Long, muscular, tanned thighs. He swallows and looks back toward his sons as they splash each other. He relishes the heat of the sun and warmth of the sand under his feet. Considering how desperately he wanted to get as far away from Zicatela Beach as he could, he wants to dive into these waters and forget what little he could recall of the last seven years and just *be*.

"La'i lua ke kai."

He swings his head toward Natalya as she peels off her cover-up. "What does that mean?" He forces his gaze away from her athletically lean form, but not before he catches the matching puckers of scar tissue just inside her hip bones. His hand involuntarily touches the scar on his face.

"'The sea is calm. All is peaceful,'" Natalya translates.

Marc splashes Julian. Julian dunks his younger brother. "That's not peaceful," James says with a laugh.

"But the energy is. They love the ocean. Everyone in my family does. Water is life. Life is family." She squints up at him from under the bill of the cap and flicks his shirt collar. "I don't think Carlos owned one shirt with a collar."

James takes in his white Under Armour polo and gray flat-front swim trunks that look more like stylish shorts than something he'd wear to the beach. His attire isn't anything different from what he usually wore to the beach, and it isn't what he would have worn in Mexico.

"I'm not Carlos," he murmurs. It comes out sounding like an apology, and in a way, he regrets he can't be the man she loves.

"I know. I have to keep reminding myself of that." There's a touch of melancholy in her voice and something shifts inside him. He reaches for her but she steps out of reach, her back already turned toward him. She whips off her cap and charges into the ocean, grabbing his sons around their waists, and all three of them go under.

James watches from the shore, feeling overdressed and out of sync with his family. Out of place in his own life.

CHAPTER 16

CARLOS

Five Years Ago
August 14
San Jose, California

Thomas swung open the passenger door with a flourish and gestured inside. "Let's go for a ride."

"I'll pass, thanks." I tightly gripped the phone. It buzzed incessantly. "How about I meet you at your office tomorrow?"

Thomas leaned on the door. "Come on, Carlos. You look like shit and I bet you're hungry. The least I can do is buy you lunch."

As if he hadn't done enough already. "How did you know I was coming?"

"Isn't that the million-dollar question?" He smirked. "I'm ready to talk if you're ready to listen. Last time you threw a temper tantrum." He scratched his cheek where I'd punched him last December.

I wasn't in the mind-set yet to meet with him. I had my own game plan. Plans Natalya and I repeatedly drilled through. Spontaneity wasn't in the rule book, and neither was a tour with Thomas as the guide. I spun around, looking for the rental-car kiosks. "I'll get my own car and follow you."

"You have no idea who anyone is or where you should go. Get in the fucking car, little bro, or I call my buddy over there and he'll put you back on the plane to Mexico."

Near the door to baggage claim stood a man. He wore a golf shirt, casual pants, and wraparound sunglasses. He looked like any other traveler at the airport except for his demeanor. It screamed government. He watched us cautiously.

Fear coursed through my veins, turning me cold. I looked around the airport, the flow of cars in front of me and the deafening noise of a jet overhead, and I saw no other choice. Either we created a scene or I went with Thomas.

I dumped my bag at his feet as if he were a parking valet and slid into the front seat.

"I wish you would have called me. I'd have had more time to prepare," he said, and slammed the door.

My phone vibrated again and Natalya's face lit the screen. I tapped the red icon, sending her call to voice mail; then I powered down my phone. Hopefully she'd forgive me later. I also hoped it wouldn't be the last time I recognized her face.

"Where are we going?" I demanded when Thomas sank into his seat.

He finished a text, tossed his phone aside, and pulled from the curb. "Lunch, and if you're up for it, a trip down memory lane."

"Not interested."

"That's a load of shit. Why else would you come home?"

"This isn't my home, and it's none of your business."

Thomas stopped hard at a red light. I slapped my hand on the dash to stop my forward momentum.

"Where you're concerned, it is my business. Your situation is my fuckup and I intend to fix it. Simple as that. Besides, we're family. Aren't you the least bit curious about your sons' uncle?"

"Leave them out of this." I yanked on the seatbelt I'd forgotten to buckle.

He glanced at me, then back at the road. "I bet you're here to see Aimee. She filed a restraining order against me."

My mouth twisted. Served him right.

"She and Ian recently married."

"Good for them."

Thomas stole a glance at me. "You don't care, do you?"

I shrugged a shoulder.

He swore colorfully. "There's no way in hell I want to be anywhere nearby when James finds out she married someone else. He'll be out for blood." He chuckled, humorless. "My blood."

"Let's hope for both our sakes that never happens."

"How about Nick? Are you planning to see him, too?"

"Who's Nick?"

He smacked his forehead. "Keep forgetting you aren't you. He's been your best friend since we moved here from New York."

"How old were we then?" I asked before I thought better not to.

"You *are* curious." He wagged a finger at me and changed lanes, slowing the car as we exited the freeway. "You were eleven. I was thirteen and Phil fifteen, maybe sixteen. Can't recall."

At the mention of Phil's name, I had the sudden urge to flee. I gripped the door handle.

"He's in prison for another five years or so. When he was indicted for laundering, he plea-bargained for a shorter sentence and struck a deal with the Feds to tell them everything he knew about the Hidalgo cartel. He'd be locked away for ten or so years otherwise. After the shit he put me through, I'd do anything to keep him there. That's why I'm hoping James remembers what happened in Mexico. Other than that wound on your hip, I don't have proof Phil took a shot at you. It's his word against mine." He nudged my upper arm. "Hey, man, you okay?"

"Pull over." I blew out a breath, feeling light-headed.

"Lunch, remember?"

"I've lost my appetite."

"Hang tight. We're almost there. Barrone's is your favorite. You always loved eating there."

Fury punched through me. "What part of 'I'm not interested' about any trips down memory lane did you not get?"

Thomas held up a hand in surrender. "We're just eating and talking. I'll drop you off at your hotel when we're done. I won't bother you again while you're here."

"Why do I find that hard to believe?"

Thomas chuckled. "Fair enough. You don't trust me, I get that. But understand this: since we were kids, I've always had your back. I'll never stop looking out for you."

I thought of Julian and Marcus. They were five years apart and Marcus was still too young to play ball and hang out with Julian and his friends. But his face did light up when Julian paid attention to him, and his head swung like a bobblehead toy looking for his brother when Julian wasn't around. Would they become closer as they aged? Would Julian stick up for his younger brother? I couldn't fathom what life had been like between Thomas and James. I didn't feel a familial connection.

Thomas turned into the restaurant's parking lot and eased into a spot. Despite the urge to eat and run, Barrone's was good. We stuck to neutral topics while we ate, with Thomas doing most of the talking. He told me about how he was rebuilding Donato Enterprises, acquiring new clients in Asia and South America. And he complained about how *our mother* had been on him to marry and procreate. Someone needed to take over the business when he keeled over. Then he asked about my art and sons.

I pressed my back into the chair and tossed the napkin on the table. "Is Julian my son?"

"Of course he is. Why wouldn't he be?"

"The adoption. Was it legal? Am I legal? You said my ID is real. How is that possible?"

Thomas glanced around the dining area, then leaned on his forearms and lowered his voice. "Your situation is unique. I couldn't talk about it in Mexico and we really shouldn't discuss it here, in public. But I don't know how much more time you'll give me, so here it goes.

"Phil eventually confessed his association with the Hidalgo cartel. He told me about the laundering, how long he'd been placing fictitious orders and shipping our merchandise over the border, and that you'd told him we knew about it. That Donato Enterprises and the DEA had struck up a deal and had a sting operation in place. The Feds wanted Phil's broker in hopes it led to the whereabouts of Fernando Ruiz. He runs the Hidalgo cartel.

"Phil didn't know I was in Mexico looking for you when he first called to tell me about your so-called fishing trip and that you were lost at sea. At the time, I'd just found you at the hospital. You'd been there a few days and were still delirious, so I didn't tell Phil I'd located you. His original story, before he confessed everything, was that you fell overboard and disappeared. That's the story I went with when we—we, as in the DEA—had to make it look like you'd died. I think he tried to kill you, or he was pressured to kill you."

"By whom?"

"Phil confessed one more thing." Thomas tapped a finger on the table. "He was meeting with a couple of the cartel's lieutenants when you walked in on them. After some brief conversation you were taken to a back room. Phil says they had you in there close to an hour and when they brought you out, you were barely conscious. Your nose was broken and the side of your face"—he points at my scar—"was torn up and bloody. He said it looked like someone had hit you with a two-by-four. That's when they hauled you out of the bar and put you on a boat to dump your body. Phil doesn't think you confessed to the cartel about our deal with the DEA and I don't think so either because you didn't know the particulars. But he does think the guy who tortured you is the same one the DEA has been after: Fernando Ruiz. Phil never saw him, but thinks you did. And should they learn you're still alive, they might try to kill you again. Everyone else is biding their time to find out who you saw and what you heard. You might have information that can lead us to the whereabouts of Fernando Ruiz. Assuming we're lucky, we'll capture him without your help; then you can leave the program without worrying whether you should look over your shoulder the rest of your life. You can leave the program at any time. It's your life. I was the one who insisted you be placed into it. I argued you could be a credible witness at Fernando's trial once he's captured but that your life's in danger in the meantime. I also wanted to keep you hidden from Phil. We needed him to focus on his job for the cartel, not searching for you."

I stared at him as if he'd told me the plot of a summer blockbuster and not the sequence of events that led me to who I was today. The scar on my face throbbed and the slash on my hip burned, the only physical connections I had to that day's events. Wounds the doctors and Imelda thought had happened when I swam ashore. From waves tossing me against the rocks. It was the way my mind interpreted it happening in my dreams.

"What is this program you're talking about, and who is Jaime Carlos Dominguez?"

"You are. You're in Mexico's witness protection program. Lucky for you, a measure authorizing benefits that include new identities was recently signed into law. Due to the situation, I called in some favors and submitted an urgent request. You had me listed as your power of attorney and you were in no condition to make decisions about your life at the time. The government issued your identification paperwork but I bought your gallery and house. I opened and funded your accounts. I created your backstory. I remade you to save you," Thomas explained, punctuating each statement with the tap of his finger on the tabletop.

"Why Mexico? Why not relocate me here?"

"There or here, you'd still need protection until Fernando Ruiz is captured, tried, and convicted. Hiding in plain sight, that's the foundation of any witness protection program. The fugue provided an extra layer. We hid you from you."

So James would leave Phil alone and they could carry out the sting operation.

The waitress brought Thomas the check and he thanked her. He glanced at the figures and reached for his wallet. "You can't *ever* tell anyone who you truly are. You must remain hidden until Ruiz is captured and you can provide a testimony."

"What if James doesn't remember anything?"

"Then I recommend we bring you and your sons home and set you up in witness protection here. Until Fernando is captured, the Hidalgo cartel needs to think you dead, or they'll send someone else after you."

I drank deeply from my water. What a mess. "Where does Imelda figure into all this? Does she know about everything?"

"She doesn't know you're in the program. I convinced my contact to let her play the role of your sister because she was well established in the community. She had credibility, so I made her part of your backstory. People knew her and would believe her. They would believe who you are, and in turn, you'd continue to believe yourself. I didn't foresee she'd get tired of pretending since we had a financial arrangement. I thought she'd come to me first."

"She was afraid of you."

He shrugged, indifferent. "Still, I should have predicted what she'd do." Thomas snapped for the waitress, who took the bill and Thomas's card. "Have you done any further research into your condition?"

I slammed the water glass a little too hard on the table. "No . . . why?"

"I've read some papers. Your condition isn't an easy one to treat."

"I don't want treatment."

"Yeah, I read about that, too. Guys like you don't want to recover their original identity. Why is that, do you think?"

"Other than the fact we'd be exchanging one set of memories for another? How about our previous selves were assholes?"

The waitress returned with the final tab. Thomas signed the check and tucked away his credit card. "James was a better man than me."

"Still doesn't change the fact I prefer the man I am now over him."

"Is your life really that much better?"

"You tell me. I have nothing to compare it to."

Thomas inhaled, nostrils expanding. "I thought it was at one time. I helped set you up so you had the life James aspired to have, but now . . ." He moved his hand up and down, measuring me. "You're scared."

"Cautious."

"Weak."

My hands curled into fists. "Untrusting. Are we through here?"

Thomas leaned back in his chair and crossed his arms. "I came across some interesting cases during my research. You know there aren't any meds available to help you."

"I don't need help. I'm fine the way I am."

"Have you tried hypnosis?"

"We're done here." I stood.

Thomas expelled a long sigh. He looked across the room, his gaze not focused on anything in particular. He knocked on the tabletop and stood. "I'll take you to your hotel."

On the way out, Thomas's phone buzzed. He glanced at the screen, then at me. "Excuse me, I have to take this." He answered the call as we walked to the car. "You're ready?" He paused, listening. "I'll be right over."

He frowned at the phone as he disconnected. "I have to swing by our warehouse. It's a new location, but it's on the way. Do you mind? It'll only take a moment."

"Sure." As long as it got me closer to a hot shower, clean bed, and a moment of privacy to call Natalya.

We drove to the warehouse and Thomas parked in back. "I'll only be a few. Interested in coming inside?"

"I'll pass. Thanks."

Thomas studied me for a moment. "Suit yourself." He opened the door and left.

I watched him punch in a code in the box by the door and heard the click as the lock released. Thomas went inside and I waited in the car. Five minutes later, I was still waiting. Ten minutes later, I got out of the car and paced. Twenty-five minutes later, angrier than a hornet's nest, I decided to go inside and haul his ass out.

Then I remembered the door had an automatic lock.

I knocked and no one answered. I banged on the door. Still, no one answered. I yanked the handle and the door flew open. "Whoa." I stopped the door's momentum with my foot and peered inside. It was pitch-black.

"Hello?" I listened. Somewhere off to my left, plastic crinkled.

I moved into the warehouse. The door slammed behind me. I skimmed a hand along the wall, found the light switch, and flipped it on. A high-wattage bulb buzzed on a few feet from my face, blinding me.

Shit. I held my forearm above my eyes.

"Carlos." A disembodied voice said from beyond the light. "Look at me until I say something."

I lowered my arm slightly and squinted. "Who's there?"

"Don't talk. Just listen. Listen . . . listen . . . listen." The voice soothed in an even cadence. "In a moment, I'm going to say one, two, three, and when I do, I want you to nod."

I listened and waited.

"One . . . two . . . three," came the monotone voice.

I nodded.

"Now continue to nod, and as you nod I want your eyes to close. I want them to feel heavy like you've stayed up too late. You're tired, Carlos."

I weaved.

"Your eyes feel heavy . . . they're very heavy . . ."

My eyelids closed.

"Go to sleep . . . you should . . . sleep."

I crumpled to the floor.

☙

The buzz of heated whispers reached me as the darkness in my head ebbed. I forced open my eyes, which felt like ripping duct tape off a flesh wound. Light emanated from overhead. It wasn't blinding like the one I swore flashed in my face a moment ago, but it did burn. My eyes watered and my forehead throbbed. My limbs felt heavy as though pinned to whatever I was lying upon. I tried moving my head toward the voices. Pain shot across my temple.

Damn, that hurt. I groaned.

Whispers faded and a face appeared above me, blocking the light fixture. He looked familiar.

"What's your name?"

I frowned and moaned again.

"What's your name?" he asked in firmer tone.

My name? My name is . . . my name . . . my . . . name . . . is . . . "Carlos." The word scraped over dry vocal cords.

"Shit." The face disappeared and the heated whispers buzzed again.

I willed my arms to move. Stiff plastic crinkled underneath. I cradled my head. When had it ever hurt this bad?

Once, I thought. In the early days after my accident.

I blew out a breath as memories shimmered into view. The accident, therapy, my wife, her death, my sons. Thomas, that asshole. Natalya.

Oh man. I needed to call her. Focusing on the light overhead, I tried to get some control over the pain.

Voices rose, transitioning from a buzz to a hiss, moving faster. Two, or maybe three, people were here with me, and they were arguing. The ligaments around my ears tensed as I tried deciphering their words through the pain.

"Memory inhibition . . . brain imbalance . . . need a neural image from prior to the episode."

"Not possible. Can we try again?"

"Not here . . . shouldn't have come . . . lose my license . . . bring him to me."

I tried sitting up. Pain shot from my head and down the ridges of my spine. A long, low groan emanated from my chest.

"What's wrong with him?"

"The suggestion hasn't worn off yet."

"You gave him a headache?"

Someone cursed, then sighed, long and impatient.

"What else can we do?"

"Nothing really, other than pinpoint the stressors. Go from there."

There was a long pause before, "I think there might be another way. I've got to get him to the hotel before his tail thinks something other than a tour is happening."

Whatever they were talking about, I wasn't going to find out. I curled on my side and dropped. My nose, chest, and knees connected with the cement floor.

"Gah!" I slid my knees inward and cupped my nose.

Feet thundered to my side. Hands grasped my armpits, hauling me back onto the plastic-covered couch I'd been lying on. I propped elbows on knees and dropped my face in my hands. My nose throbbed. I cautiously touched the bridge.

The couch dipped beside me. "I doubt you broke it."

My brain finally caught up and connected the voice beside me to Thomas. "Muck you," I said, the words muffled in my hands.

"I didn't mean to take so long. I was just leaving when you came inside."

"What happened?" My head screamed and I squeezed shut my eyes. I still saw that blazing light every time I closed them. Its shape and intensity seared into my retina.

"You flipped the switch on the torchlight, tripped over the cord, and hit the floor. You went down harder than a steel beam dropped by a crane. Scared the shit out of me." He chuckled uneasily.

I lifted my head and looked around. "Where is everyone?"

Thomas gave me an odd look. "Who?"

"The other people who were here."

He slowly shook his head. "There isn't anyone here but us."

"I heard voices . . ."

Thomas's mouth slid into a curve and I slammed mine shut. I knew exactly how that statement made me sound. *Crazy.*

"How are you feeling?"

Nausea coiled in my stomach like the snake of a brother sitting beside me. I didn't believe a word of his, but I wasn't in the condition to argue.

He clapped my shoulder. "Let's get you to the hotel."

I slowly stood and promptly lost my balance. Thomas grabbed my upper arm and I shook him off. "Don't touch me." I started to walk toward the door. "Just . . . leave me . . . the fuck . . . alone."

He held up both hands. "Sure thing, bro."

∾

Thomas dropped me off at the hotel without any further suggestions about visiting the house we grew up in or checking out the offices of the legacy our parents had left us. But he did want to talk and offered to buy me a cocktail at the bar.

I wanted to pop three aspirin, take a shower, and call Nat.

I didn't ask Thomas again about the people I swore had been at the warehouse with us. And the farther we drove away, the more I wondered exactly what had happened. Shrouded under the thick haze of a migraine, the incident grew fainter with each passing moment.

Thomas stopped in front of the lobby entrance and I got out of the car. He popped the trunk and the valet removed my bags.

"Carlos." Thomas leaned across the front seat and offered his business card. "Call if you need me or have questions," he said as if he'd just sold me a life insurance policy.

Maybe he had. *Something* had happened at the warehouse and I had survived intact. I was still Carlos.

His face turned serious. "I've missed you."

"Yeah, sure," I muttered, and shut the door. Thomas drove off and I tossed his card in the trash.

Once checked in to the room with my luggage and carry-on dumped inside the pencil case–size closet, I popped three aspirin, swallowed them dry, and took a shower. Scalding water drenched my hair and poured over my shoulders. I watched it course down my abs, creating rivulets across my groin and thigh. It swirled down the drain, carrying a day's worth of travel grime into the sewers. The vein in my head throbbed and I gritted my teeth. *What the hell happened today?*

Anytime I thought about that warehouse and tried to recall the voices that had whispered around me, no matter how blurry the images and indecipherable the words, the skull buster in my head cranked up its jackhammer. I pressed fingers into the corners of my eyes, sorely tempted to dig them from their sockets to relieve the pressure.

I flipped off the water and toweled off my bone-weary body. Neither the shower nor aspirin helped. I felt like shit.

Wrapping a towel around my waist, I went to sit on the edge of the bed and called Nat. It went straight to voice mail. I disconnected and called again a few seconds later. This time I left a message. "Crazy day. I'm fine. I'll tell you about it later, but right now I need to crash. I love you."

I ended the call, sent a quick text with my room number since I'd promised to do so earlier, and tossed the phone onto the bedside table. It skidded over the edge and onto the floor, but I didn't care. I was too tired.

Groaning, I fell back onto the pillows. My eyelids dropped and I slept, through the night and well into the next day.

CHAPTER 17

JAMES

Present Day
June 27
Hanalei, Kauai, Hawaii

That evening, they barbecue chicken—chicken Natalya purchased at the local fresh market. The sun sets in a vibrant array of lavender and gold. A spectacular sight, one he'd paint should he have the inclination to do so, which he doesn't.

Natalya watches the sun drop below the horizon and he feels a similar drop of disappointment in himself. She'd longed for him to paint her sunset.

James steals glances at her from where they eat on the lanai, twirling his fork like he does with paintbrushes. Conversation between them has been stilted, and at times he's convinced she keeps the chatter going with his sons so she doesn't have to engage with him.

"Today was awesome, Tía Nat." Julian yawns the announcement and Marc follows suit. He rubs his eyes. "Can we catch some waves tomorrow?" Julian asks.

"I want to build more sand castles." Marc yawns again.

James covers his own yawn. They are used to a later time zone. Puerto Escondido is four hours ahead of their current time. He rises and collects the plates. Natalya reaches for them.

"I got it," he says. "Why don't you help them get ready for bed?" He remembers reading that she likes to participate in the nightly ritual during her visits to Mexico. He takes the dishes inside.

There isn't much to clean. Aside from the salad, which the boys had a hand in assembling, the cooking had been done on the grill. He finishes quickly. Natalya is still with his sons, so he returns to the lanai to have a few moments to himself, and he keeps walking, down the stairs, across the yard, and through the park. He sits down where the long blades of grass meet the cool sand and listens to the ocean. He matches his breathing to the rhythm of the waves and thinks about the years he's lost, his instant fatherhood, and how he won't feel settled until he's settled things with his brothers, which could land Phil back in prison. He has the scar, a stark line across his hip, but he doesn't have the memory. Yet. He wants more proof than Thomas's conviction Phil tried to murder him.

His mother won't take kindly to another family scandal, not after what she's been through. Apparently she had a breakdown after his death. Sending her oldest son back to prison might send her back to the "retreat" Thomas took her to the summer after James had been "lost at sea." But at this point he doesn't care. His sons' safety is his top priority, and he wouldn't put it past Phil to threaten them to get back at him. Because Phil has lost as much as James. His place in the family, his birthright to Donato Enterprises, and five years of freedom.

The ocean plays its song, reeling his mind back to Puerto Escondido and her violent shore that lures experienced boarders. They ride her waves, a race to the beach before she devours them whole.

James feels himself go under, spinning, his world going dark until he's standing at a table in a dive bar. The sunlight is murky and the air thick with cigar smoke.

"You walked into the hornet's nest, Jim."

He glanced down at Phil, dressed in a black shirt and teal shorts. Phil took after their mother's side of the family more than he and Thomas did, which made sense considering both his parents were from that side of the family. Phil turned those hawkish features up at him, his mouth twisted in a cynical grin. He slowly shook his head. Dark Ray-Bans hid his eyes, but James knew they'd be narrowed in warning. Phil had told him not to follow him into the bar. His brother slowly shook his head, dipping his chin, seeming more fascinated with the bottle cap he spun on the tabletop. James's stomach bottomed out. He knew whatever happened next was his own damn fault. He swore at his impatience. Raged at his own anger and drive for vengeance.

"Is this the guy you were telling us about?"

James's gaze swept over the other two men. The one who'd spoken and sat beside Phil had an arm across his bloated stomach, his hand tucked under his other arm, hidden from view. James crossed his arms, hiding his clammy hands. He didn't want to think about what the man kept out of sight from him and the other patrons in the bar.

"No, Sal," Phil said, his tone adamant. "That's my other brother. Jim was just leaving."

The second man, decked in a silk shirt and linen trousers, forearms inked, kicked out the empty chair. It hit James in the shins. "Why don't you have a seat?"

"Mind if I have a seat?"

James blinks and looks up, disoriented. A beer bottle hovers in his line of vision. Condensation beads on the side, and sweat dots his hairline. He takes the beer and adjusts his position so his forearms rest on his knees, and Natalya eases down beside him. "How are the kids?" he asks.

"Marcus fell asleep in the middle of the story and Julian was already out before I went to his room."

He sips the beer and flavor explodes in his mouth. His eyes widen at the citrus and mango taste. He checks out the label.

"Beer, Hawaiian-style." Natalya drinks hers.

"It's . . . different." He prefers darker brews, but on an evening such as this, where the humid trade winds are more pleasant than the blistering heat of Puerto Escondido, he welcomes the change.

"What were you thinking?"

He frowns. "When?"

"A moment ago, I called your name and you didn't hear. Maybe you were just ignoring me." She laughs softly, nervous.

"No, I wouldn't do that." He plucks at the corner of the label. "I was thinking about my brother. Nothing in particular." He tries to grab the memory again, but it's like grasping smoke. Details recede like the tide with every passing second.

His skin pricks. He senses Natalya watching him, so he angles his body toward her. The night sky casts her skin in blue. His expression is questioning, inviting her to ask him anything. She must have plenty on her mind.

Her eyes buzz over him; then her chest rises with a deep inhale. "I'm going to come right out and say this. It's very hard for me to look at you and not see Carlos."

"My conservative clothes and shorter hair aren't enough to differentiate us?" he quips, trying for humor in hopes of unbuckling the tension he'd felt strapped around her since their arrival.

"I wish it were that simple, but no. For a long time, Carlos saw his situation differently than I did. He separated himself from you. He talked of you as though you were a brother or cousin."

"How do you see me?"

"You're the same person. Almost," she adds as an afterthought. "The same blood pumps through your veins. You have the same heart and same soul. So, tell me, James Charles Donato. Who are you?"

He doesn't know. There isn't much of his old life left. He gulps back his beer.

"Come on," she prods. "You have to give me something. What makes you different from Carlos?"

"I don't collect newspapers?" he points out.

She nods, considering. "That is something. But you know he did that for you?"

James palms the sand and lets it rain between his fingers. There'd been more stacks of newspapers than he cared to count, boxed away in the garage in Mexico. Left behind by Carlos for James, so he wouldn't miss out on one day's worth of news. He'd tossed them without opening the boxes. The clutter had been overwhelming. It only added to the staggering number of issues he had to contend with.

"There are quite a few similarities between you. You both run, God knows why."

James chuckles despite his heavy mood. He finishes his beer.

"You both paint."

"Not anymore."

"Why?"

He lifts a shoulder. "Not feeling it."

She studies him for a moment. His skin itches from the way she watches him. He's not her Carlos, and he's tired of being compared to a man who no longer exists. He's already compared himself enough with Carlos. He pushes the bottle into the sand beside him and considers returning to the house. Maybe they should talk tomorrow. His mood has darkened with the night sky.

Natalya digs her feet into the sand and wiggles her toes. "I was four when my mom passed. My dad didn't surf for a long time. There he was, at the pinnacle of his professional career, and he couldn't compete. Surfing is like any sport. It's about where your mind's at." She taps her forehead. "Dad's mind hadn't been on the water, so he decided to take some time off and mourn. Then he took another year off to start his company. But the ocean called to him, and in time he was back on the water and winning titles because when he went back, he was ready to go back. Now he has a booming business, travels the world sponsoring tournaments, and has a gal in every port."

"You and Raquel were sisters, right?"

"Half sisters. Dad's a free spirit. He's always been open about his relationships. I love all my siblings."

"How many do you have?" James recalls reading something about her family, but not the details. These would be his sons' aunts and uncles. Their family.

"My sister, Tess, is in Sydney, Australia, and my brother, Calvin, is in South Africa. He's the baby. I'm the eldest."

"How old are you?"

"Thirty-three."

"You probably already know I'm thirty-six. I feel like I'm thirty."

"Hmm, I wonder why."

He taps his temple. "In my head, I'm drinking a beer with an older woman."

Natalya looks at him with a blank expression; then a laugh bursts from her chest. He grins. "Couldn't resist."

"Anyhow, there's a point to my story."

"Which is what?"

"You're not ready to paint."

"Well . . . ," he says, rising and brushing off his shorts. "Send me a memo when you figure out when that'll be." He means it jokingly but the crass undertones are unavoidable.

"Oh, I already know." Her tone matches his. She stands and takes his empty bottle. "You'll start painting again when you stop hating on yourself and your life."

He tenses. Carlos didn't write anything about Natalya's bluntness. Other than telling her last December he didn't need her help, he can't figure out what he's done to deserve the icy attitude she keeps tossing his way.

"You've got me all figured out." He crosses his arms. "What's your story? Who the hell are you, Natalya?"

"Didn't Carlos write all about my deep, intimate secrets?"

James clicks his tongue. "Ah . . . so you know what he wrote about in the journals."

Her face turns crimson in the pale light. "I've read some parts." She takes a deep drink of beer and he doesn't have to guess about the parts she's referring to. Like his paintings, Carlos's writing was very detailed.

"Awkward." The word echoes in her bottle. She looks sad and he can't help feeling like an ass.

"I don't remember anything about, um . . . us." He motions between them.

She presses her lips tight and nods. Her eyes glisten. "Maybe it's for the best. It'll make tomorrow easier."

"What happens tomorrow?"

"I call the attorney so he can start drafting the adoption papers."

CHAPTER 18

CARLOS

Five Years Ago
August 15
San Jose, California

A muffled noise echoed through the room. It sounded like a hammer pounding nails into walls, but felt as if it were happening inside my head. White-hot pain shot across my scalp.

Thump, thump, thump. I peeled open sleep-crusted eyes to a dark room. I blinked and blinked again, trying to adjust to the pitch-blackness.

Thump, thump, thump. "Carlos!" My name came through the walls.

Memories from last night, or lack of them, scattered inside my brain like tumbleweeds on an empty road. No direction and completely at the wind's mercy. At some point in the morning hours, I'd closed the privacy shade to block the sunlight. I couldn't see shit.

I ground the heels of my palms into my eye sockets.

Thump, thump, thump. "Open the damn door, Carlos, before I call the front desk and demand they do it for me."

"Coming," I croaked. I rolled out of bed, stumbling to a knee. The migraine that burned like a forest fire had waned during the night, but my body ached, muscles stiff from sleeping hard the last few hours.

I pushed to my feet and felt my way to the door, hands in front of me seeking walls. I jammed my big toe on the desk chair and swore. The impact radiated up my shin. I shoved the chair I didn't remember leaving out back under the desk.

Thump, thump—

I fumbled with the lock and opened the door.

Nat's eyes rounded like a cat caught off guard. She gasped, then the tension melted. "You're here. Thank God." Her gaze lowered and her eyes went buggy again. "You're naked." She slapped palms against my chest and pushed me back into the room. The door slammed shut behind her.

At the skin-on-skin contact, my brain woke up. So did my body.

"Nat," I groaned, my arms going octopus around her. I pushed her against the wall and pressed my entire length against her. "You're here." *You feel goddamn amazing.* I kissed her hard. My hands roamed up her shirt and cupped her breasts. My hips rocked. I groaned again.

She gasped. "Carlos."

"Right here." I bit her neck.

"Ow. Carlos." She smacked her hands on my shoulders.

Impatient devil, I thought with a growl. I fumbled with the fly of her jeans. She wedged a knee between us, right into my lower abs. "Oomph."

She squirmed from my arms and moved out of reach. "What the hell, Carlos?" she fumed and flipped on the light.

"Gah!" I squeezed my eyes shut.

"What the hell do you think you're doing?"

I squinted at her. She looked stinking mad, her face tomato red under the freckles, with her fists on her hips. She was so damn gorgeous and hot, and it was freaking wonderful to have the one person in the world I trusted to be here with me. It only made me more aroused.

"I'm on fire for you, Nat." I motioned at my groin.

She scowled and looked at the messy bed. "Have you been asleep this whole time?"

"Uh . . ." I squeezed the back of my neck. My gaze darted to the bed, rumpled sheets heaped on the floor. "Yeah."

Her nostrils flared. "You probably have to pee."

At the mention of that bodily function, my bladder roared and arousal died.

"What happened to you?"

"I have to piss." I flipped on the bathroom light and kicked shut the door.

"Brush your teeth, too," she hollered. "You reek."

I relieved myself, washed my hands, and splashed cold water on my face, hoping the chill dissipated the Tule fog condensing inside my head. I couldn't think or focus. Then I brushed my teeth, twice, and slipped on boxers and a shirt before returning to Nat.

She had opened the curtain and turned on the air to circulate the room's staleness. She'd also straightened the bed. The sheets were back on the mattress. She was now flipping through a small paper pad and looked up as I approached. She flipped the paper back in place.

"I've been beyond worried about you. I've been calling and texting since you hung up on me."

My gaze jumped to the nightstand. "Where's my phone?"

"Here." She handed it to me. "I found it on the floor along with my gazillion unanswered texts and calls."

I launched the screen, saw the queue of notifications, and tossed the phone on the desk. I sagged onto the chair. "I forgot to unsilence it before I crashed."

"I doubt you would have heard them. You were sleeping like the dead. Do you know how long I banged on the door? Ten minutes," she answered at my clueless expression.

I scrubbed my face, rough with stubble. "Sheesh, Nat." I hated that I made her worry, and that she had to fly out here and check on me. "I'll pay you back for your flight."

Her eyes protruded and mouth pursed. I guess that remark annoyed her because she stomped to the window. She folded her arms and watched a plane come in for a landing. "God, Carlos, I love you but don't scare me like that," she said after the plane touched down on the runway. She swiped a finger under each eye.

I wanted to weep with her but figured I'd already disgraced myself enough in her presence. *Horny bastard.*

"Come here," I said, opening my arms.

She curled on my lap and rested her head on my shoulder, tucking her face against my neck. Our arms went around each other and for a few moments, we just sat there. It was bliss.

"I'll try not to scare you like that again." It wasn't a definitive promise considering I was terrified myself. I kissed her gently, hoping to reassure us both.

She shifted on my lap, settling deeper. "Don't worry about my flight. I'd planned to fly into LA on Monday anyhow."

I nibbled her ear. "What's in LA?"

"The year's Miss Malibu Pro. She lives in Santa Monica. Dad and I are meeting with her about licensing our new longboards."

Miss Malibu Pro hosts a longboarding invitational. "The ones with Mari's designs."

"The very ones. But I don't want to talk about that." She leaned back in my arms and cradled my neck. Her thumbs caressed my jawbone. I heard, more than felt, the scratch of her skin on stubble. The line between her brows deepened. "What happened to you yesterday?"

"I don't know. I can't remember." My heart marathon raced with the admission.

"Amnesia can't remember? Or, I-drank-too-much-and-blacked-out can't remember?"

"The latter, but without the benefit of alcohol." I gently squeezed her jean-clad thigh. "Thomas was waiting for me at the airport."

Natalya's mouth parted. "What? How?"

"Maybe my ID triggered a flag when I went through Customs." She inhaled sharply and I kissed her nose. "Don't worry. No one was there to arrest me. But Thomas was somehow notified I'd be there. I also think I'm being watched while I'm here."

"Carlos." She sounded alarmed.

"Thomas offered to show me around and meet up with old friends. He figured I came because I was curious about myself."

"Which you are," Natalya supplied.

"Yes, but I told him I wasn't. He took me to lunch and . . ." I frowned, my thoughts turning inward as I tried to capture yesterday's events. Some eluded me.

"And what?" Natalya's fingers tapped the back of my neck to get my attention.

"Thomas didn't tell Imelda and Aimee the whole story about James." I then told Natalya, and when I finished, a mix of incredulity and distress marred her delicate features.

"My God, Carlos. You need to get back on the plane and get to your sons right now. Your life could be in danger." Panic raised her voice with each word.

I gave my head a hard shake. "No, I don't think it is. Phil is in prison and doesn't know about me. As long as he and the Hidalgo cartel believe James is dead and Carlos can't remember what happened, I'm of no value to anyone."

"You are to me. And Julian and Marcus."

"Yes, I know. But listen. There's more. After lunch Thomas got a call. He had to swing by some warehouse before taking me to the hotel. I remember waiting in the car for him and then . . . and then . . ." My brows furrowed. "Then he was dropping me off at the hotel."

"You can't recall anything between waiting in the car and arriving at the hotel?"

I lifted Natalya off me and paced the room. "No. And my head hurts like a mother anytime I try to think of what happened."

"Something did happen because you wrote about it."

I stopped midstep. "I did?"

Her face took on a green hue as she flipped through the pad.

"What is it?"

She pressed the notepad to her chest as though she didn't want me to read it. "I think Thomas did something to you."

"Let me see that."

She reluctantly handed over the notepad, then twisted her hand in the mass that haloed her head.

I rapidly flipped the paper, skimming the words I'd written down at some point during the night. I'd used the entire pad. Nausea rose swiftly, followed by a wave of light-headedness. I sank onto the bed edge and swore. "This is why Thomas had to tell me about my ID in person." I waved the pad in the air. Paper rustled, fanning with the movement. "He wanted me to come to him and he was ready for me. The bastard had me hypnotized."

I tossed aside my notes and shot to my feet.

Thomas was my brother. He was also my sons' uncle. A man they'd be exposed to should my screwed-up head figure out how to fix itself. Because James would want to return to California.

I paced to the window. The sun was already three-quarters across the sky. My gaze shot to the clock by the bed. 3:45 p.m. I'd slept away the day.

"Now do you see why I want you to be their guardian?"

"Carlos—" she started.

"Do *you* want Julian and Marcus exposed to people like that?" I gestured wildly at the notepad.

"Of course not."

"They will be. That's the family they'll celebrate their holidays with. That's who they'll spend their summer breaks with. That's who will want *my* sons working for their business."

"You don't know that."

"That's James's fucking family, Nat. *My* family." I smacked my chest.

I shoveled both hands into my hair and gripped tight. My gaze zigzagged from Natalya to the clock, and then to the notepad before coming to a skidding halt at the closet. I stomped across the room and hauled out my suitcase. In the bathroom, I gathered up my belongings and dumped them inside.

"What're you doing?"

"Packing. I'm going home." Then I remembered that I reeked.

"Carlos?"

I picked out clean clothes, grabbed my toiletries again, and went to the bathroom.

"Carlos!"

"What?" I snapped from the doorway.

Her cheeks took on a rosy hue. "There's more going on here, Carlos," she said firmly. "About your feelings and the way you feel about James and the Donato family."

"What is that supposed to mean?"

"Your reaction toward them is fierce."

"It's warranted, Nat. My brother had me hypnotized against my will."

"Yes, I understand why you despise him. But when it comes to your sons, you have this primal need to keep them safe."

"That's part of being human, and my being a father."

"Not every father feels the same. Otherwise there'd be a lot fewer cases of child abuse and neglect in the world today."

I shifted my clothes under my arm. "What are you getting at?"

"Has it occurred to you James felt the same way about his family as you do? His oldest brother nearly raped his fiancée. You've told me about the dreams you used to have of Aimee before you knew who she was, and the terror you felt about not being able to protect her. Don't leave until you learn about James. Because if you used to be anything like the man you are today, and I have to believe you are, James will give up his own life keeping Julian and Marcus safe."

CHAPTER 19

JAMES

Present Day
June 27
Hanalei, Kauai, Hawaii

"Whoa, whoa, whoa!" James lunges to his feet. The back of his legs itch from grass and sand, but he ignores it. "What in the world are you talking about?"

Natalya tilts her head. The glow from the house lights outline her silhouette, leaving her face dark. He can't read her expression.

"The paperwork. What's it for?" he asks more specifically.

"Guardianship of Julian and Marcus. That's why you're here, isn't it?"

He raises bent arms. "No!"

"But you said on the phone . . ." She stalls.

"I said what?" He moves a step closer.

She frowns and takes a deep, shaky breath. "Jeez, this is confusing. I was talking about Carlos, not you. It's that every time I look at you, I see . . . him."

While today is the first time he's seen her in person, she's been around him for years. The reconstructive surgery to his face helped

Aimee separate him from Carlos in her mind, but to Natalya, he looks identical to the man she loved.

Her shoulders bow and chin lowers. "This is so weird."

He slides his hands into his pockets and ducks his head to look up at her. "If it helps any, I'm floating in that same boat." Seeing her is like seeing a character from a novel come to life. He's read so much about her. Knows numerous intimate details, such as why she wears scars on her lower belly and that she hurt as much as the women her father left behind when he traversed the globe.

His eyes have slowly adjusted to the night sky and he sees a flash of white appear when she quickly smiles. A light breeze ruffles her skirt and he's quite taken with how beautiful she is. His body has made love to her. His hands have touched every secret fold. And his mouth has worshipped every feminine curve.

His mind, though, can't recall a damn second of it, and strangely, James regrets that.

Natalya gathers her hair, gives it a twist, and drops it over her shoulder. "Let me rephrase so this isn't confusing to either of us. Carlos didn't want his sons raised around the Donato family. He didn't trust them, and that includes you. He was also convinced you wouldn't want to be burdened with two kids you didn't ask for. He asked me to assume legal guardianship. He told me he was going to give you an 'out clause'"—she air-quoted—"by writing in his journal that I would take your kids should you not want to raise them. When you called and said you want me to watch your sons—"

"Not indefinitely." He slices a hand outward in the space between them. "Maybe just a week or two, if that. But let's get back to Carlos. There's one thing we can agree upon, and that's my family. I don't trust my brothers anywhere near *my* sons."

Natalya releases a long, steady breath. She smiles gloriously. "I'm so relieved to hear that." He now realizes why she gave him the cold reception at the airport. She thought he was unloading his sons on her.

"My mother, though, is another story."

"Yeah." Natalya rolls up on her toes and back. "That was a shocker. I can't believe Carla is your mother. Should I be worried?"

He itches the back of his neck, then his elbow. "I can handle her. The boys don't know about her, and I'm not sure how they'll handle the news." He takes the empty bottles from Natalya and motions for her to follow him back to the house. Mosquitoes are biting. "They're already mad at me because I'm not their *real* dad. How do you think they'll feel when they learn the old lady next door that bought them ice cream and churros isn't who they thought she was either?"

"I can't say, but Señora Carla loved your sons, which means your mother loves her grandsons. We take risks and do things we can't necessarily explain for those we love."

Natalya's statement couldn't be truer. James has been guilty of that on more than one occasion. He feels like a hypocrite when he says, "But she lied to them."

"That bothers you."

"Immensely." Because he lied to Aimee for years about his family, and look where that got him. He yanks a hibiscus flower off the bush they pass and twirls the stem. "You?"

"Yes, but . . . I understand why she did what she did. Carlos wouldn't have let her near them had she told him the truth. I also don't think she visited just to see them."

"No?" He spins the flower stem.

"She spent most of her time with you, James. She was there to see you. You're her son, a son she thought had died. I assume Thomas eventually got around to telling her about you. Can you imagine how she felt?"

"They aren't talking. Not regularly, not like they used to."

"No surprise there."

A breeze moves between them, ripe with rain and heavy with salt. Natalya stops near the bottom step of the stairs that lead up to the lanai.

She turns to him. "I assume you love your sons since you aren't giving them to me."

"Unconditionally."

"I told Carlos you would." She briefly smiles, then absently scratches at the wood banister rail with a fingernail. "I remember Carlos telling me how nervous Carla was around you during her first visit to Mexico. Imagine how you'd feel learning Julian or Marcus was still alive after you buried your child's body. That's emotionally intense."

She has a point. "I still don't trust her."

Natalya takes the flower he's mutilating and tucks it over her ear. "Give it time. She's your *ohana*, your family, and 'family means no one gets left behind, or forgotten.'"

His mouth twitches. He tugs another flower off the bush beside his thigh. "You're quoting *Lilo & Stitch* to me?"

"Very good. I'm impressed."

"I have a six-year-old."

"Yes, you do." She cups his hand in hers, silently asking for the flower. He gives it to her and she tucks it over his ear. The tickle of petals across his cheekbone, the barely there touch of her fingers against sensitive skin, and her warm breath on his chin have him sharply sucking air. Sensations shoot through his body, waking him up as though he'd been hibernating for years. She looks at the flower, then at him, and smiles brilliantly. He blushes like a teenager and guilt drips through him like paint spooling off the tip of a brush.

Aside from Aimee and their frenzied, gut-wrenching parting several days ago, he hasn't been touched or kissed by a woman in longer than he can remember. That hug with Kristen doesn't count. It was completely platonic and quite awkward. Then there are the stiff-armed hugs he gets from Marcus, who seems to break the contact faster than he makes it. Aside from those, James hasn't really been hugged by another human being, let alone held by a woman, in what seems to him like years.

Oxygen shuttles from his lungs. He touches the flower. "Thanks." His voice is strained, heavy with emotion he barely understands.

This time Natalya blushes. "So . . . why *are* you here?"

He cocks a brow. "Vacation?"

"Why don't I believe that?"

A gust of wind sends a chill across his skin. He suddenly feels tired, bone-weary, as though he hasn't slept in months, which he hasn't. He was either worrying about keeping his sons safe, or how their upheaval would affect them in the long term, or how to nurture their father-and-sons bond. He isn't a bad guy and is tired of them treating him as such. But right now, he just wants to sleep for days. Surprisingly, here, in Hawaii, with his brothers thousands of miles away and Natalya by his side, he finally feels as though he can do so. He feels like he's in a safe place.

It dawns on him as to the root reason he brought his sons here, and it's much less complicated than the impulse to flee Phil until he can get his bearings or to avoid Thomas from hounding him about a three-hour time block he may never recapture. Quite simply, James came to Kauai because he had nowhere else to go. He didn't have anyone to turn to who completely understood what was not just going on around him, but what was wrong with him. He has no one except Natalya. Maybe he can find comfort in that thought. Or, maybe he's only seeking her friendship. He has yet to find whatever he's looking for, but perhaps he can find it here, in paradise, with the help of a woman who is neither a stranger nor a lover, but for the moment, simply his *ohana*.

It starts drizzling and Natalya turns her face to the sky. "It's going to pour. Let's go inside."

In the kitchen, James drops the bottles into the recycling bin. He yawns deeply. "I'm going to turn in. Thanks for the beer, and the talk."

"Sure, that was nice." She glances toward the stairs that lead down to the first level. "I hope you don't mind I put you in my office. My dad is expected back soon and we usually meet there to catch up when he returns from his business trips. I can have the boys bunk together and move you up to one of their rooms if we become too intrusive."

"I should be fine." She had him on a pullout sofa in her office. She'd made the bed and left out towels and soap for the adjoining bathroom.

"Do you have everything you need?"

"I think so." He starts moving toward the stairs, then stops. "Thanks for letting us stay."

Natalya is staring at him, watching as he leaves. Her shoulders rise and fall on a long breath; then her eyes lift and meet his. "Of course, you're family."

"Ohana."

She smiles. "Yes, *ohana.*" She twists her hands.

The gesture makes him uneasy. "Everything all right?"

She nods and circles a hand as though erasing her thoughts. "You move like him. I mean, you move like yourself. I guess I expected there to be more of a difference than just your names."

"We *are* different. I bet by tomorrow evening you'll kick me out because I'm too much of a snob for you." He points at his collared shirt.

She laughs. "I doubt that. But, speaking of tomorrow, I have work to do. I hope you don't mind that I have to encroach on your space."

"Not at all. I'll take the boys exploring."

"Well . . . um . . . good night, then." She moves toward the hallway that leads to her room.

"Good night, Natalya." James watches her go. Carlos would have kissed her good night. Or taken her to her room. Made love to her until they crashed, gasping and sweaty, on rumpled sheets. He read those passages multiple times, often wondered how different Carlos was in bed. *Would Natalya sense the difference should she close her eyes?*

He inwardly groans. Why is he even thinking of sleeping with her? They just met.

With a tinge of embarrassment, he scratches at the back of his head and turns away.

"James?"

He swings back around.

"Julian told me you're leaving him and Marcus here."

When will Julian understand he won't abandon them? "What else did he tell you?"

Natalya comes back into the main room. "He doesn't believe you want him. And Marcus believes anything his brother tells him."

James swears. He rubs his forearm, scratches the bite on his elbow. "I'll be honest; it was rough those first few weeks when I surfaced. Getting our lives in order hasn't been easy. Okay, it's been extremely difficult, and that's putting it mildly." He slightly smiles with the admission. "But they're my sons. I love them, and I'll never leave them behind. I just wish they'd believe that."

When James initially came to, he and his sons had been confused and scared. While Carlos had prepared Julian for the possibility it would happen, it didn't make the situation any less frightening. Or had Carlos's instructions to Julian. He'd told his son he might forget him and need help being a father again. He'd also warned him that James might not want them and they could go live with Aunt Natalya. James could kick his other self in the ass for that. The kid was ten years old at the time. What had he been thinking?

"I don't know what Carlos told his sons, but he thought you might be like your brothers." She looks him up and down. "You aren't like them, are you?"

"Hell, no."

"Knew it." She reaches for his hand. "I want to help you."

"How?" He watches her trace the lines on his palm. That slightest touch buzzes through him. He feels it all the way up his arm. His throat thickens with unshed emotion.

"My nephews trust me. Let them watch how we interact and see that I like you. Let them see that I trust you." She lifts her gaze and meets his. "Maybe they'll do the same."

"Maybe," he murmurs, staring at her. He can see why Carlos loved this woman. And she just admitted she likes him, James. "Thank you."

"May I ask you something?"

He nods.

"May I hug you?"

"Ah . . . sure." He opens his arms and she walks into his embrace, settling her ear above his heart. He stands there, arms out, pulse thrumming, unsure what to do. Does he hug her back? Should he hold her? Then he feels her body heat seep into him. He finds it comforts him and he releases the breath he wasn't aware he held. He folds his arms around her.

Natalya hums, a contented sound. Then after a few beats, a few meditative breaths, she whispers on a sigh, "Same heart."

CHAPTER 20

CARLOS

Five Years Ago
August 15
Los Gatos, California

Several weeks after Aimee showed up in Mexico and Imelda told me what she knew of my situation and the role she played, I received a package in the mail from Thomas. An iPhone. Aimee had downloaded James's contacts, music, and photos from his iCloud account when Thomas got word to her the phone was for me. Just in case I found use for it.

I hadn't, until now.

I'd brought the phone with me and charged it while I showered. Natalya brewed coffee and when the phone could be powered on, she scrolled through James's contacts. Then she looked through his photos.

"There are a lot of pictures of you and Aimee," she said, her tone flat, giving me the phone after I'd dressed. She twisted her hair, her attention drifting to my phone on the desk where there were plenty of snapshots of us.

"Hey," I murmured. My hand cupped her face. I skimmed my thumb over her freckled cheek, the skin as smooth as expensive bedsheets. "I love *you*." I kissed her gently, then rested my forehead against hers. "You."

She nodded. "I know. It's just . . ."

"You don't have to come with me."

"Yes, I do. Someone has to protect you so you aren't knocked over the head again."

We both laughed uneasily.

"Have you looked through the pictures?"

I shook my head. Seeing James's life through his pictures was a gamble with my mind I didn't want to take.

She moved away from me and grabbed her purse. "I found the address where you lived. We should go."

We now sat in the car Natalya had rented, parked one house down from the one I owned, or *had* owned. Two boys played catch on the lawn, and the woman sitting on the porch was not Aimee.

"She must have moved," Natalya surmised.

I'd told her on the way over that Aimee and Ian had recently married. That part of my conversation with Thomas I did remember.

A dull ache burned across my forehead. I scooped out the two aspirin I'd brought with me from my front pocket and dry-swallowed them.

Natalya passed over a bottled water. "How many have you had since I woke you up?"

I chugged half the bottle. "Six, I think." I screwed on the cap and returned the bottle to the center console's cup holder. "They aren't helping."

"Maybe we should go to the hospital."

"No. No doctors. I don't want anyone else messing with my head. I don't want to forget my sons." I grasped her hand and kissed the inside of her wrist. "Or you."

"God, you're stubborn. No doctors, unless your headache gets worse. Promise?"

I leaned across the front seat and kissed her. "Promise."

She turned on the ignition "Where to next? The café?"

The dash clock read 5:56 p.m. "We don't have time. The café closes at six."

"So, what's the plan?"

I rubbed my forehead and closed my eyes against a wave of light-headedness. "I was thinking Aimee's parents' house. They can tell us where she's living. But I need to eat something."

She shifted into gear and pulled from the curb. "Let's call it a day, then."

"What a waste of time," I complained, grinding the heel of my palm against my head.

Natalya shot me a concerned look. "We'll visit the Tierneys tomorrow. Tonight, I'm buying dinner. Then I'm giving you a back rub."

"Just the back?"

She snorted and playfully knocked my shoulder. "Let's get some food in that belly of yours, then we'll see what happens."

⟨∘⟩

It was midmorning when I rang the Tierneys' doorbell. Natalya stood beside me, our shoulders brushing. I tightly grasped her hand. She rubbed my forearm. I loosened my grip.

"I'm as nervous as you." She pressed closer.

Light footsteps approached the door and after a moment's hesitation, the lock flipped and the door opened. A smaller, older version of Aimee greeted us. Blue eyes, bright and wide under a head of chicly spiked salt-and-pepper hair, darted from me to Natalya, then back to me. She stared, blinked several times, then fell back a step and gasped. Her hands cupped her mouth and nose, and her eyes sheened.

"Mrs. Tierney?" I asked.

She lifted her hands away from her face. "James?"

Natalya's nails dug into my hand. I glanced at her. She'd gone pale.

"Carlos." I offered my hand.

"Yes, of course . . . Carlos." She gripped my hand with both of hers. "Carlos," she repeated, chewing on the name. "You look different than . . . I never thought." She pressed her lips, her chin quivering, and released my hand. She touched her hair, pushed down the silver cuff she wore on her wrist, and glanced over her shoulder into the depths of the house. She discreetly swiped her tears.

"Oh my," she murmured. "I'm a bit overwhelmed."

I imagined finding me on her doorstep was like seeing a ghost. They'd attended James's funeral and the burial afterward.

Natalya tugged my arm.

"This is Natalya Hayes, my—"

"I'm his sister-in-law," she said, looking at me. I frowned and she shook her head, then extended her arm. "It's nice to meet you."

"Catherine." Mrs. Tierney looked a bit dazed.

"May we come in?" I asked.

"My goodness, where are my manners? Come in, come in." She opened the door wider.

Natalya went first, and I hesitated. Panic sliced through me. What if I recognize the rooms? What if there are pictures of Aimee and me? What if I suddenly forget who I am and remember everything I was?

Natalya glanced at me over her shoulder and squeezed my hand so I'd know to read her lips. *It's okay,* she silently told me. I moved into the entryway and turned a full circle. Aside from an oil painting of an old railroad track I recognized as James's—it was his artistic style and signature in the corner—I didn't see anything familiar. I exhaled and smiled reassuringly at Natalya.

Catherine closed the front door, watching us. The way Natalya stood beside me, our hands clasped. The secret glances at each other, which apparently weren't so secret.

"She's more than a sister-in-law."

"I love her."

Catherine's mouth curved downward. She nodded. "I can't imagine what life must be like for you with most of it missing. Everything your family did to you . . ." Her chin quivered. "You're still welcome here. You'll always be family to us." She turned to Natalya. "I'm glad he has you."

Natalya adjusted the purse strap on her shoulder with a trembling hand. "Thank you," she whispered.

"I'm happy you aren't alone," Catherine said to me. Tears flooded her eyes, fell in ribbons over weathered cheeks. Her shoulders shook; then she broke into a full-on cry.

"Oh!" Natalya exclaimed. She hugged Catherine as the older woman sobbed on her shoulder.

"Cathy?" A voice boomed through the house.

"In here, Hugh." Her voice broke through her tears.

Heavy footsteps echoed through the house. A large man appeared around the corner. "Why are you crying?" Hugh asked his wife. I watched with distorted amusement as his expression changed from confusion to shock when he saw me. "Jesus Christ."

"Not quite, but I guess you could say we've both risen from the dead."

Natalya smacked my chest. "Carlos."

Catherine grasped my wrist. "Will you stay for Sunday lunch?"

"Cathy, I don't think—"

"Lunch?" I asked, then noticed the dining room table set for four right before the front door burst open.

"Hello! We're—here." Aimee's voice dropped midsentence, the last word coming out as a thin whisper. She stopped abruptly in the doorway, her blue eyes as deep as the sea, and brunette curls that flowed over her shoulders like a waterfall. She made an odd noise in the back of her throat. "Carlos."

Ian appeared behind her. "Move aside, honey, or I'm going to drop—" His gaze caught mine. Where Aimee's face had paled, Ian's went hard and red. A flash of fear darkened his eyes.

"Don't worry," I said. "I'm still Carlos."

CHAPTER 21

JAMES

Present Day
June 28
Hanalei, Kauai, Hawaii

Wired for an earlier time zone, James wakes before the sun. Rain drums outside, as it did on and off through the night. He changes into the running shorts and shirt he set out the night before and laces up his Nikes. It's been too many weeks since he left the boys alone. Last winter he just didn't care. He'd take off for a ninety-minute run and think nothing of leaving a five-year-old with an eleven-year-old who threatened daily he'd hitch a ride to the airport. His mind was damaged and the world he knew had moved on without him. He had to get outside and run, hard and fast until his lungs burned and calves cramped. So he did.

This morning, though, he runs for pure enjoyment, that rush of adrenaline that comes as the miles build. Because this time, his boys are safe, sleeping soundly under their aunt's roof.

He slips on his iWatch, swipes over a text message from Thomas without bothering to read it, and preps the settings for his run. It will be a good one, and he plans to make it a long one.

He runs toward Kuhio Highway, maintaining a steady pace past homes shrouded under grayness. He knows the trees overhead and lawns yawning outward from the road are as green and bright as an acrylic painting. He saw them yesterday while driving to Natalya's house. Where Carlos had loved the heat and rustic appeal of Puerto Escondido, its air pregnant with salt and dust, dry like the surrounding hills, James prefers the vintage feel of this beachside community. Hanalei is a 1950s postcard and running past the storefronts, elementary school, and little green Wai'oli Hui'ia Church, is like going back in time. As he eats up the miles, his shoes pounding the rain-drenched asphalt, he lets his mind wander. Back to the hours he pushed himself in football conditioning, running sprints, leading the pack. Then his mind meanders further. Back to the time they lived in New York and everything changed.

James was nine that Thanksgiving weekend when he, Phil, and Phil's friend Tyler had walked in on his mother with Uncle Grant, Phil's dad, in the woodshed, their limbs roped around each other and clothes askew. After a stunned moment, Tyler grabbed Phil's collar and dragged him away. Grant ran after them, pleading for his son to wait.

James's mother straightened her skirt and gripped his shoulders. "You have to forget what you saw," she pleaded. "Your father can't ever know, and you can't tell Thomas. Promise me."

How was he supposed to forget this?

His mother shook him when he didn't answer. "Promise me."

He did, but it wasn't through him his father eventually heard about James's mother and her brother in the woodshed.

Phil had been told at a young age his mother abandoned him, leaving his father to raise him as a single parent. But after the shed incident, Phil went looking for his birth certificate. He'd always thought his mother and aunt had the same name, but after seeing his father and aunt together, the truth of his parentage was there in his aunt's crisp penmanship, handwriting he recognized now that he was older. *Claire*

Anne Marie Donato. Unfortunately for Phil and the rest of James's family, Tyler was with Phil when he found the birth certificate. Shortly after Phil learned the truth, so did their friends at school, and eventually their small community, and their church. Soon the corridors and cubicles of Donato Enterprises, which had been headquartered in New York at the time, were buzzing about the Thanksgiving debacle. Because news about Grant Donato and his sister was gossip too shocking not to spread.

Disgraced, his father, Edgar, packed up the family and moved them across country, but not before he negotiated a windfall of a deal that landed him as the second largest shareholder next to Grant. He opened Donato's western division, which eventually became the company's headquarters upon Uncle Grant's death. Strangely enough, Edgar still loved his wife, but he loved the company more.

Although Phil hadn't been aware of it at the time, it was because of that deal and what he'd witnessed in the woodshed that had lost him any chance of inheriting Donato Enterprises.

Gasping as much from the memories as from pushing his body, James reaches Haena Beach Park quicker than he initially calculated. He ran the six miles from Natalya's house at race pace. He bends over, hands on knees, lungs heaving. Sweat drips off the ends of his hair, his nose and chin, and lands in the grass. Phil changed with the knowledge of his parentage. Hell, they all did. In the end, though, Phil accomplished what he set out to do. The Feds seized a majority of Donato Enterprises' assets and James lost Aimee. It would be easy to blame everything on Phil, but all three of them—Phil, Thomas, and James—lit the fuse that blew their family apart.

With James hidden in Mexico, Phil locked up in prison, and Thomas rebuilding Donato, he wonders if the past few years have only been the eye of the storm. What does Phil want with him? Has he burned off his need for revenge or is he still out for blood? Or could it be something else entirely? Damn, he wishes he could remember what happened inside that dive bar and on the boat.

As much as he would love to stay in Kauai, he knows he must return to California and meet with Phil. Find out the truth about what happened the day his mind crashed. If Phil indeed tried to kill him, James is in full agreement with Thomas. They have to do everything possible to lock Phil back up again.

⁓

On the run back into Hanalei, the sun's morning rays peek through low-lying clouds and shimmers through the tree canopy, casting golden hues. His fingers twitch as though holding a phantom brush. For a moment, maybe two, he considers Googling where art supplies are sold on the island until he remembers Carlos's acrylics, paintings as vibrant as the floral color palette in Natalya's backyard. Canvases painted with a skill he can never hope to replicate.

Natalya loved Carlos's work. Three of his pieces hung in her house. Scenes from Puerto Escondido, and none of them had a sunset.

In Hanalei, he stops for coffee, ordering one for himself and Natalya, then returns to the house. He leaves his shoes on the lanai and opens the glass slider. Raucous laughter and banging pots fill the rooms. He follows the noise and the sweet, syrupy scent of pancakes to the kitchen. He finds Natalya at the stove spooning batter into an iron skillet. Julian pours bright-pink juice into plastic cups and Marc waves a butter knife in an imaginary sword fight as he sets the table. His mother slices fruit with the skill of an executive chef.

He blinks, and if he weren't holding steaming cups of coffee, he'd rub his eyes because he clearly questions his vision. First the egg sandwiches in Los Gatos and now this. Since when has his mother enjoyed working in the kitchen? He doesn't recall ever seeing her cook anything. Their housekeeper left their after-school snacks waiting for him and

Thomas on the kitchen counter. She was the one who cooked their meals. And, dear God, what is that floral tent his mother is wearing? It's so bright that it shimmers.

Claire slides the blade through a ripe papaya and catches his gaze. She gives him a smile as dazzling as her attire. "Good morning, James."

His mouth parts. "Uh . . ." He can't take his eyes off her. The outfit, which he figures is a swimsuit cover-up, makes her look young, and artsy, and fun. She wants to be the fun grandma.

She puckers her lips, the fine lines deepening.

Ah, there's his mother.

"Really, James. Close your mouth. The geckos I've seen running around here may think it's a new home."

Yes, it's definitely her.

Marc giggles. He snorts in merriment.

"You think that's funny?" James asks wryly.

Marc nods. "Uh-huh."

"Hilarious," Julian drawls in a flat tone.

"Julian," Natalya warns.

James looks at her from across the kitchen. His hands sweat from the coffee's heat. Natalya smiles. *Good morning.* Her lips shape the words. A rubber band loosely holds her hair in a messy bun at her nape and purple semicircles prop her green eyes. She's the only one among the lively bunch who looks tired. It can't be any later than eight, but everyone aside from her is functioning on Pacific time.

She flips a few pancakes onto a pile of others and turns off the stove. Then she beckons him to follow her into the main room.

"You don't have to cook for us," he says when she starts straightening magazines on the coffee table.

"I don't mind." She relocates them to the shelf under the TV console. "The boys love to help in the kitchen."

That's news to him. Though he doesn't necessarily cook any meals. They mostly eat out. He sets down the coffee cups and makes a mental note to go to the grocery store today. He misses barbecuing and enjoyed helping with dinner last night.

"Your mom got here about an hour ago. She knew the boys would be up early." She sorts the drawings Marc left scattered on the couch. He joins her there and picks up his son's colored pencils. "And no," Natalya says, giving him a crooked smile, "they don't know who she really is. I'll leave the big reveal up to you."

"Thanks." James grimaces, aligning pencils on the coffee table. One drops to the floor and rolls toward Natalya's bare feet. She hands it to him, which he adds to the pencil queue, then sits down on the couch. "I didn't think you'd tell them."

"Claire's not keen about that. Gosh, it's weird calling her that." She kneels on the floor and looks under the couch for wayward pencils, finding two. "Did Marc bring any paints?"

James shakes his head. "I didn't want him to make a mess."

"I have a vinyl tablecloth. He can use the kitchen table or the patio table on the lanai. The toy store in Princeville sells art supplies." She scratches the base of her scalp with a pencil. "My dad called this morning." Her crooked smile appears again. He likes the way it looks on her. "He woke me up, not your kids, in case you're wondering."

"I wasn't, but is everything all right?"

"Yes, he's fine. He's flying in earlier than I expected. Like this afternoon."

"Ah. Are you telling me or warning me?"

She chuckles nervously and sits beside him. Her attention falls to the pencils, which she nudges back and forth. "I was kind of hoping he wouldn't arrive for another few days so it could be just us for a while. By the way, how long do you plan to stay?"

Indefinitely.

The word appears on his tongue faster than he can come up with a more realistic answer. He presses his mouth closed to keep from saying it, though he wishes it were true. Life in California isn't what it used to be, and the one person he wanted most who is there is no longer his.

But he knows he must return soon.

"I'm thinking a couple of weeks, if you don't mind."

"I don't mind at all. You're welcome to stay longer. In fact, I'd love for you and the kids to stay longer. I haven't seen them for a while. They don't start school until August, right?" He nods and she rests a hand on his forearm. "Will you stay?"

"I think the boys will like that."

"What about you?" Her gaze searches him. "Do you want to stay?"

James thinks of the engagement ring in his suitcase, which he'll probably transfer to his pocket after he showers and changes. He thinks of his sons eating in the kitchen and how this woman beside him offered to help bring them all together.

"Yes, I want to stay."

"Excellent," she says, smiling. "Though you might change your mind when Dad arrives."

"Have we met yet?"

"Once. At your wedding."

His stomach drops and his mind jumps to Aimee and the wedding they never had. Instead, she spent that special day they'd reserved on their calendar for almost a year at his funeral and burial. Then he remembers Carlos married Raquel.

"What happened at the wedding?" There wasn't much information in the journals. At that time, Carlos hadn't been writing as though the journals were a life preserver.

"Well . . ." Natalya rubs her hands and stands. She picks up Marc's backpack and pulls out his books. She stacks them on the coffee table. "Dad's a womanizer and he was harassing Imelda, the woman you were told was your sister," she adds when he frowns. "He wasn't being too obnoxious. But she was annoyed, so you clocked him."

James's brows shoot to his hairline.

Natalya unzips each pocket. She shoves her hand inside and adds whatever she finds to the growing pile on the coffee table. "When you were Carlos, it didn't take much to get you fired up. You were a very physical man."

She ducks her head and the loose bun comes undone. Her hair falls forward, obscuring her face, but not fast enough. James caught the blush tingeing her cheeks. She's embarrassed; nervous, too, judging by the way she's searched each pocket more than once.

James stands and takes the pack. He wants to tell her she doesn't have to be nervous around him, but she looks so darn uncomfortable that he's concerned he may spook her and she'll retreat behind her cold front again.

He sets the backpack aside. "I take it your dad doesn't like me very much."

"Not really."

For some reason, the admission makes him laugh.

"What's so funny?"

He laughs harder. He wipes the corners of his eyes. "Oh God. I can't tell you how good it is to hear I'm not the only one with a screwed-up family. Here I thought you were perfect." His tone is light and teasing.

"Well . . . he *is* your father-in-law."

His eyes bug. "Good point. Don't worry about him, though. I'll do what I can to make amends. God knows what that'll be."

"Just be yourself. He'll like you."

He fights a smile as he looks down at her. He catches the scent of her lotion Carlos wrote about more than once. Warmth coils inside him as he breathes her in and his pulse quickens.

"And James?"

"Hmm?" he asks, his gaze transfixed on the line of her collarbone that disappears under her shirt's neckline. He has the urge to kiss the dip between that bone and her shoulder.

"You stink."

"Oh jeez. I ran twelve miles today." His face heats. He chuckles and moves back, circling to the opposite side of the table.

"Is that for me?" She gestures at the coffee.

"Yes. I picked them up at the roasters a couple of blocks from here." He gives her a cup.

She lifts the lid, blows across the top, and takes a cautious sip. Her eyes open wider. "How did you know the way I like my coffee?"

"It's your favorite, right?" A touch of coconut milk with a shot of macadamia-nut syrup.

"Yes, but . . ." She traces a finger around the lip, looking uncomfortable. He can tell she's thinking about Carlos's journals. Maybe he shouldn't make it obvious about *how much* he knows about her. The situation between them is already weird enough as it is.

"It doesn't seem fair you know so much about me and I have to get to know you all over again," she says, her thoughts aligning with his. But there's an invitation in her observation.

"Do you want to, though?"

She taps the cup rim and nods.

He smiles, pleased she does. He picks up his cup, toasts hers, and sips through the lid opening. "Don't worry about your dad. I'm looking forward to meeting him." He grins broadly. "Again."

❦

While Julian surfs with his aunt, James borrows Natalya's car and takes Marc and his mother grocery shopping. They barely make it through the produce aisle before Marc starts complaining. He's bored. He wants to build sand castles at the beach with Tía Natalya. And he wants to color.

"Help me select the zucchini," James suggests, bagging the squash he plans to grill.

Marc slumps, arms hanging loose. "This is booooring."

James pushes the cart to the tropical fruit bin. Marc reluctantly follows, his flip-flops sliding along the linoleum floor. James selects two pineapples and compares their weight. "I can't tell which one is ripe." He had no problem selecting a cut of meat to go with potatoes and salad. Aimee always did the shopping for the other stuff. She'd been the cook in their relationship.

"Smell them." Claire drops a bag of spiny maroon fruit in the cart. James sniffs each pineapple. "Scent or no scent?" his mother asks.

"This one smells sweet." He bounces the pineapple balancing in his dominant left hand. "And this has no scent."

His mother points at the unscented pineapple and he returns the sweet, overly ripe pineapple.

Marc peeks inside the cart and points at the spiny fruit. "What are those?"

"Dragon fruit," Claire says.

"Whoa." He pokes the fruit. "Do dragons eat them?"

"Maybe," Claire says, playing along. "We'll try one when we return to your aunt's house." She inspects the apple-bananas, a smaller, more flavorful banana varietal, as noted on the label James reads beside the price. He adds the pineapple to their groceries.

Marc swings from the cart. "Are we done yet?"

"Almost. We'll go to the toy store next."

"How about I take him there now?"

"What?" James tightens his grip on the cart handle.

"*Sí, sí, sí!*" Marc tugs Claire's hand. "I mean, yes! Let's go." He tries dragging Claire away.

"I won't wander off with him. I have no car."

He scowls, and not because he suspects his mother will leave with her grandson like she thinks he believes. *He* wants to spend time with Marc.

"You don't want to help me shop?" he asks his son.

Marc vigorously shakes his head. He tugs Claire's hand. "Let's go, Señora Carla."

His mother grimaces at the name and James can't help humming a laugh at her expense. Then he leans his forearms on the cart handle, narrowing his eyes, watching her.

She gives him a perturbed look. "I won't say anything. Both you and Natalya have been quite clear about that. But James," she adds, letting Marc tug her away, "grocery shopping isn't how Marc wants to spend time with his father."

James ducks his head and sighs. He hates to admit it, but his mother is right. "Give me twenty minutes. I'll meet you over there."

She finger-waves good-bye. "See you soon."

James watches them leave, their clasped hands swinging between them, and wonders when his son will voluntarily do the same with him. Once they're out of sight, James checks the time on his phone. Voice-mail notifications litter the screen, one from his buddy Nick and several from Thomas. He slides the phone back into his pocket, making a mental note to call Nick later. Thomas can wait. Though he is curious if Thomas knows their mother tagged along to Kauai. Probably not. Thomas might be keeping their mother updated about his whereabouts, but he doubted she returned the favor.

James shrugs. Not his problem, he thinks, pushing the cart toward the meat department. He's dying for a steak.

⁕

Thirty minutes later, James stands in the doorway of the Spotted Frog Toy & Art Supply, a quaint nook of a store. Rows of display shelves overflow with an assortment of puzzles, games, books, and paints. His gaze darts around the shop and a brush of panic sweeps through him. There's no sign of his mother and son. He's ten minutes late and they've already come and gone. But where to?

James glances around the shopping plaza. Marc's attention span is shorter than the colored pencils he loves to draw with. His mother promised to stick nearby so she must be wandering through the shops to keep his son occupied. His gaze strays toward the parking lot and his hand slides into his pocket to fist the keys. Could he trust her not to leave?

He wants to, but this is a woman who lied to him and his sons for five years. He reluctantly pulls himself away from the paints, brushes, and canvases and goes in search of them. After scoping out the women's clothing boutiques, the stores where he expected to find his mother and an extremely bored son, he finds them in an empty retail space, and only because he heard Marc's laughter.

He utters a sigh of relief, forcing the panic to subside, and watches his son from the doorway. Marc shuffles from wall to wall, answering Claire's questions. *How many paintings? What will the paintings be of? Will he keep the same ceiling lights or install new ones? How many employees? Where will he paint? What will he name his gallery?*

El estudio del pintor, Marc replies. *Just like his papa.*

Then he sees his papa standing there. Marc's excitement disappears like the eraser bits he brushes off his drawings. James feels his heart drop to the floor with those tiny particles. He wants Marc's smile back. He wants his son to look at him with the same excited expression he had when talking about Carlos. He wants his son to call him *Papá.*

He moves into the space and Claire turns around. "Good, you're back."

"What're you doing?" he asks her.

Marc shuffles to the far corner of the room and picks up a bag. James notices the toy store's logo.

"Marcus was telling me about the art gallery he wants to open when he grows up. Weren't you, Marcus?"

"Sí, Señora Carla." He nervously glances at James and clears his throat. "I mean, yes, Ms. Carla."

Claire makes a sound in the back of her throat. "Well, gentlemen, it's dreadfully hot in here. I'll meet you at the car." She glides to the door and slows as she moves past him. "This space would make a lovely gallery. The lighting is perfect."

After listening to his mother for half a lifetime tell him painting was frivolous, James forces himself not to gape. Who *is* this woman? Why did she change her tune after all these years?

Perhaps they're all changing.

"Mom."

Claire swings around and arches a trimmed brow.

"Thanks for watching Marc." *And for encouraging him to paint,* he wants to add. But the emotion in his throat is too thick. It's too much of a reminder as to what she didn't do for him.

She dips her chin and then she's gone, walking around the building and toward the car.

A plastic bag crinkles behind him. James glances down at Marc's wide-eyed, open-mouthed expression. "Ready for the beach?"

"*Sí*, I mean, yes."

"Me, too. And Marc?" He holds out his hand. "As long as you understand and speak English, which I know you can, and do so very well, you can speak whatever language you want around me."

Marc beams. *"Gracias, papá."* His son clasps his hand and James looks away when they leave Marc's imaginary art gallery. His eyes burn as though he's been looking directly into the sun.

CHAPTER 22

CARLOS

Five Years Ago
August 16
Los Gatos, California

Lunch with the Tierneys was . . . awkward. Catherine kept up a steady chatter during the meal of grilled salmon and summer greens. She sat at the end on my left, opposite her husband, Hugh. Natalya, who picked at her fish like a bird, sat on my right, her hand clutching my thigh. I didn't think anyone at the table was comfortable and I knew Natalya was having second thoughts about my spending time with Aimee. I was, and I sure hadn't expected to have an audience when I met with her.

Aimee sat across from Natalya. She didn't look at either of us, and she didn't participate in the conversation. Ian was opposite me. He didn't take his eyes from me as Catherine peppered me with questions. *How many children do you have? What are their ages? What sports do they like? Do you enjoy Mexico? Are you still painting? What do you paint?*

Safe questions, that is until Ian leaned forward on his elbows and clasped his hands. "Why *are* you here, Carlos?"

Aimee set down her fork with a loud clatter. "Ian, don't."

Hugh cleared his throat and dipped his head. His hands were loose fists alongside his plate.

Ian looked at his wife. "It's a fair question, and one we all want to know." He looked around the table.

Natalya flipped her hand over on my thigh and grasped mine. I gave hers a squeeze. This was it, the reason we came. It was time to lay it on the table, literally.

"I'm sure you're aware of my condition." I spoke to everyone, but kept my gaze level with Ian's. "I can remain like this, as Carlos, for the rest of my life. Or, I can revert to my original identity as quick as a finger snap."

Natalya made a low noise in the back of her throat when I snapped my fingers for effect. I stroked my thumb across her knuckles.

"Aimee told me a little about what happened to you." Catherine's gaze shifted briefly to Aimee. "What can trigger you to be . . . oh, I don't want to use the word *normal* . . . ugh, which I just said. But what can make your identity revert to James?"

"It's different for each person, and usually when that person is ready to deal with the trauma that caused the fugue. Really, though, anything can trigger me to surface. Familiar surroundings, visiting with family and friends."

"You're taking a risk coming here," Hugh stated.

"Yes," Natalya immediately said.

"Which makes me wonder why you *are* here." Ian folded his arms on the table edge. "You were darn adamant last December. You didn't want anything to do with your former self."

"I don't trust anyone in the Donato family. Including James," I added, sneaking a glance at Aimee. She exhaled a choppy breath and stared at the barely touched food on her plate.

"You shouldn't trust them," Ian agreed.

"If I revert to James, I lose every memory of my sons. James won't know them, he wouldn't have asked for them, and he may not want them, yet he'll still be their father. I can't ask anyone in the Donato family about James and the type of man he is. Will he be a good father? Is he a decent human being? Or, is he like his brothers? Can I trust him to raise my sons?"

Ian leaned back in his chair. "Thinking about what you're dealing with messes with my head. No offense." He held up a palm.

"None taken."

Catherine reached over and laid a hand on my forearm. "James was nothing like his brothers. We adored him."

"I'm relieved to hear that. But I have questions."

"I can't do this." Aimee rose quickly. She tossed her napkin on the table and shoved back her chair. Ian grabbed it before the chair back hit the buffet cabinet.

"Excuse me." Aimee left the room.

Ian watched her go. When the front door opened, he stood and, excusing himself, quickly followed after her. The door slammed behind him, rattling the dining room window.

Through that window, we watched Aimee and Ian argue on the front lawn. Their arms flailed in exaggerated gestures, mouths moved, chests heaved, and faces turned red and stern.

"Do something, Hugh," Catherine said.

"Like what?" He stuck a forkful of salmon in his mouth, manipulated a bone through his lips, which he set on the edge of his plate. "Ian's got a handle on this."

Outside Ian fisted his hair, elbows raised. He walked in a tight circle.

Catherine sighed, a mixture of concern for Aimee and exasperation with Hugh. Aimee started to cry. Ian tried to comfort her and she pushed him away.

"Hugh," she snapped, "you're her father."

"And he's her husband. There isn't any way I'm getting in between that." He jabbed a fork at the window.

I folded my napkin. "We shouldn't have come."

"Nonsense," Catherine said. "You're family. It's that we never expected . . . your being here . . ." She sighed. "We're just surprised, that's all."

Aimee thrust out her hand. Ian shoved his hand into his pocket and held a set of keys above her hand. They stared each other down until Ian dropped the keys in Aimee's hand, where they disappeared in her fist.

Ian returned and stopped in the dining room doorway, arms crossed. He stared at his feet until Aimee came inside and stood beside him. Then he lifted his face, directing his attention at me. "I don't agree with what she's doing, and I'm not comfortable with her taking you anywhere. Seeing you has been quite the shock. For all of us."

"For God's sake, Ian," Aimee bit out, her eyes red rimmed and face puffy. "I want to show you something, Carlos. Will you come with me?"

Natalya swiftly rose to her feet. She glanced down at me, panicked. We both knew what happened the last time I went off alone.

I stood and wrapped an arm around her waist. Her breast pressed into my side. "I'll be fine," I whispered in her ear. "I doubt she'll try to hypnotize me."

Natalya pressed a flat hand to my chest. "That's not funny."

"We won't be long, Natalya," Aimee said with an unmistakable edge to her tone. She might be married to and in love with Ian, but she didn't like Natalya with me, not with the way she visibly seethed underneath her barely controlled exterior while she watched us.

Ian glanced at his watch. "You've got an hour; then I'm coming to get you."

Aimee lifted her face to the ceiling, exasperated. "With what? I have the car. Dad, make sure Ian stays put."

Hugh's brows lifted over the rim of the wineglass from which he was drinking. He waved a fork at Ian's empty chair. "Have a seat, son. You and Cathy can now interrogate Natalya."

"Hugh," Catherine huffed, annoyed. Ian kissed Aimee's cheek. He whispered to her, then returned to his chair. Catherine got up from hers. "Would you like another glass of wine, Natalya?"

"No, thank you."

"Well, I need one. So do you, Ian." She patted his shoulder as she passed behind him, heading for the kitchen. "Actually, I think we need another bottle."

I cupped Natalya's cheek. "I'll be fine."

Her eyes searched mine. "What if where she's taking you triggers James?" she asked in a low voice meant only for me. "And then you're with her and you forget about me . . ."

I kissed her mouth hard, stopping her words. "I love you, Nat." Then I left with Aimee before either of us could change our minds. Besides, I was tired of having an audience. I came to California to meet with Aimee. She was the one I wanted to see more than anyone.

Aimee drove their minivan, taking sides streets to a freeway. She was not Thomas, and she'd been a pawn in his game to keep me hidden, but my palms were still sweating. I couldn't stop my heart from hammering. She hadn't told me where we were going despite my asking. "You'll see," she'd answered, fighting her tears from falling. I figured it was too difficult for her to explain. Yet, I still went with her.

She exited the freeway a short distance later to an expressway. She talked sparingly, pointing out landmarks here and there. I didn't notice anything that might have meaning to me, and from her tone, they weren't of consequence to her. Her comments were solely meant to fill the void between us.

After a few miles she turned uphill, weaving along residential roads. I had a moment of panic, thinking she was taking us to the meadow she once told me had been her favorite place to be with James, a place that meant much more to both of them. And the one and only place I imagined could yank me from my fugue state. James had proposed to, and Phil had accosted, Aimee in that meadow. It was an emotionally intense spot for everyone.

But my worries slipped away to be replaced with another form of panic. She turned onto the driveway of a cemetery.

I clutched the door handle, knowing exactly where she was taking us.

We followed the road through the grounds and she eventually pulled into a parking space and killed the engine. "It's over there." She pointed across the lawn, then opened the door and got out of the car. She tromped across the lawn without looking back.

I unfolded from the car and followed. She stopped about twenty-five meters in and moved aside when I joined her. She pointed at a granite headstone.

JAMES CHARLES DONATO
BELOVED SON

Birth and death dates followed.

I slid my hands into my back pockets. I should have felt angry looking at the stone, and I should have felt some sort of connection to, or sense of loss toward, the woman standing beside me. The man I used to be had lost everything. Instead, I felt a bone-deep fear that Natalya could be right. Would I recognize her when I got back to the Tierneys' house?

I glanced from the headstone to the car and back and swallowed the rising panic. "Is anything buried here?"

Aimee hummed a laugh. It sounded cruel and was filled with loathing. "A coffin full of sandbags." Part of Thomas's stratagem to fake my death, she told me, and I had to remind myself she didn't know the full story. Based on what Thomas explained to me yesterday, Aimee and anyone else close to James had been told the bare minimum of what they needed to hear.

"Leaving you behind in Mexico was the hardest thing I've ever done. But it was the right thing."

Afternoon sunlight peeked through the tree canopy. Shadows of leaves danced on her clothes. Warm light played off the outline of her profile. It reflected in the shimmer of tears that moistened the soft tissue under her eyes.

"I love James. I will always love him. And for the most part, he treated me very well. In the end, though . . ." Her voice slid away. She swiped a finger under an eye and hummed uneasily. "You know what happened."

"I wish I could apologize on his behalf." I wished I could beat the crap out of James for what he'd asked of her. How he'd expected the love of his life to bury what happened with Phil until Thomas and the DEA could carry out the sting operation. For not allowing her to heal the way she needed to.

She sucked in her lower lip. "There are three reasons why I've been able to forgive James." With her arm down by her side, she splayed three fingers. "One, I had to put the past behind me. Two, James was fiercely loyal to me. He was protecting me the best way he knew how, and that was by doing what he thought he could to keep Phil away from me. But Carlos," she lifted her head, her eyes a piercing blue in the shadows, "I have to believe James is dead. He is dead to me."

My chest rose and fell with a deep, settling breath. "That's the third reason, isn't it?"

She pressed her lips between her teeth as though holding the emotion inside and nodded. "I don't know what I'd do, or how I'd feel, were you James, and you moved back here. That scares me. I've never told Ian, but I know it's something he thinks about."

I took two steps back and one forward, rocking on the lawn. What would James do? I had to assume he'd return home as soon as he could. Would he bring the boys with him or leave them behind?

"You've mentioned James wasn't like his brothers. Other than how he handled the situation with Phil, was he a good man?"

"I wouldn't have spent as many years of my life with him as I did if he wasn't. There were things about his past, things that happened before he moved to California when we were kids, that he kept from me. I have to believe he did that because he was ashamed. But I'd trust him with my life, even after what happened in the meadow."

"My sons . . . should something happen to me . . ."

"James will be angry and hurt. He will feel like everyone bailed on him, but he would never give them up."

Aimee had built a new life with Ian, a man I sensed she loved deeply. What would happen to them when James returned? Would he try to win Aimee back? He'd already left Aimee behind, but then that hadn't been intentional. It probably never crossed his mind he wouldn't be back for his wedding.

What about Natalya? Would she give him up, or fight for him? James wouldn't know her.

"Would you leave Ian for James?"

"I honestly don't know. But I can tell you this. For Ian and me to be truly happy together, I can't live near James. There's too much history. Ian trusts me, but I know he'll wonder, and that's not fair to him." She rested a hand over the lower region of her belly. "It wouldn't be fair to our child."

"You're pregnant."

"Yes," she said quietly. Her mouth turned downward and she looked at the headstone. She'd probably imagined for as many years as she and James dated telling him that news. For one day they would be married and she'd birth his children. But here he stood before her, but not really him, and she was pregnant with another man's child.

Her eyes sheened and I agonized about what to do. *This must be so damn difficult for her. I shouldn't have come.* Instead, I opened my arms. "Come here."

After a slight hesitation, she leaned against me and I folded my arms around her as she cried on my shoulder.

A breeze swept through the trees, rustling branches, giving flight to Aimee's hair. Sunshine brightened the tint of red threaded in her curls and suddenly, with Aimee in my arms, I longed to be with Natalya with an intensity I hadn't felt before. To hold her tight while making promises I'd never let her go. That I'd never leave her, or forget her.

But on the heels of that need came an unbearable reality. While I could make those promises to Natalya, I wouldn't be the one breaking them.

Aimee soon eased from my embrace and pushed the curls from her face. "Must be the hormones." She wiped her damp cheeks.

I slightly nodded. "Congratulations."

She reached a shaking hand for me only to let it fall to her side. She gestured at the headstone. "Anyway," she said with a wistful sigh, "I wanted you to understand how I feel, and showing you this is the only way I knew how. Knowing this headstone is here helps me keep the past in the past. And James is my past. I had to let him go."

∽

The following morning, Natalya flew to Los Angeles and I left for Oaxaca. We didn't talk much about our afternoon with Aimee, Ian, Catherine, and Hugh, but that night we'd made love fiercely and exhaustively, until the early-morning hours. I buried myself deep inside her, convinced that loving her this intensely, I could imprint her on my soul and it would be impossible to forget her when I surfaced from the fugue. Because how could James not sense how deeply I loved her?

In flight, I thanked the attendant for the tequila on ice I ordered and finished the drink in three gulps. The fermented agave sliced a heated path along the back of my throat and settled my churning stomach. It did nothing for the dull ache in my head I'd had since meeting with Thomas.

As we flew across the United States–Mexico border, my mind coasted over the past couple of days. Thomas surprising me at the airport and shocking me further over the machinations he helped the governments of two countries put together in a matter of a few short weeks—days, even—to keep me hidden in plain sight. I thought how Thomas had me hypnotized and the hours missing from my trip. There was something he believed I might have seen and he wanted that information. There was the awkward meal with the Tierneys and Ian's fierce protectiveness toward his wife. I'd feel the same had I been in his place.

Then my mind cruised to Aimee's parting words. On the way back to the car, she stopped me with a gentle touch of her hand. "James wanted children," she told me. "He would have made a wonderful father. He was loyal to those he loves, and he'll protect those he loves. He will do what needs to be done to keep them safe. He did so for me. But Carlos—" She tightened her grip on my forearm. Fear tinged her ivory cheeks, sharpened the blue in her wide, opened eyes. "James and Phil have unfinished business. One of these days, Phil will be out of prison, and I wouldn't be surprised if he goes after James. He'll be angry, and may still feel cheated, not just out of the family business, but from the years he lost in confinement. That's how Phil will see it. He'll use anything and anyone to hurt James. Whatever you do, keep your sons away from him."

Outside the plane's window, patches of clouds floating over the dry, brown hills of Mexico passed underneath the belly of the plane. I'd left home afraid I couldn't trust James with my sons. But while I was returning with the reassurance James would make a good father, would even come to love Julian and Marcus as I did now, I still wasn't sure I could fully trust him. I wasn't sure he could keep the boys safe.

Hell, with the knowledge I now possessed, I wasn't sure *I* could keep them safe.

CHAPTER 23

JAMES

Present Day
June 28
Hanalei, Kauai, Hawaii

After a quick excursion with Marc back to the art and toy store, where they purchase paints, brushes, acrylics, canvases, and portable easels because there's no better time than the present to start Marc's art gallery, they return to Natalya's. James pulls into the driveway behind a truck that's seen its share of saltwater. Three surfboards angle up from the rear bed. Julian's shooting hoops with an older man whose long, athletic strides and sinewy frame forecast the body Julian's growing into. Gale Hayes, retired world-class surfer and the owner of Hayes Boards. This man is his son's grandfather. His father-in-law.

He's also the one Carlos punched in his face at his wedding.

For once, he's thankful he can't remember.

Gale catches Julian's rebound and pitches him the basketball as James cuts the engine. He squints at the car, hand raised to block the high sun. James exits the car, and Gale, lowering his arm, approaches him with a purpose.

Oh boy. This should go well, James thinks grimly. He shuts the door, pushes back his shoulders, and thrusts out his hand. Might as well reintroduce himself, and then apologize on behalf of his other self. "Mr. Hayes, I'm—"

"James, yeah, I know." Gale clasps James's hand and claps his upper arm. Weathered skin folds under a dusting of strawberry-gray whiskers, revealing teeth tinged yellow with age. Julian dribbles the ball up behind him, listening to their conversation. Gale grips his hips and widens his stance, ducking his head against the sun's glare to peer at James. "Nat tells me you don't remember anything about the last seven years."

James lifts his Maui Jims to rest on his head. His eyes immediately tear from the intense daylight reflecting off the light-colored asphalt. "Aside from the past six months, not a thing."

Gale grins. "Then we're going to get along just fine. Although"—he loosely grasps James's upper arm—"it's a shame you don't remember Raquel."

Julian's dribble slows. He's angled his body away, acting as though he doesn't care, but James knows he's listening intently. "She's the mother of my sons, and for that reason alone, I'll always be grateful."

Gale nods and pats James's arm. "She was a good woman."

A car door shuts behind James, and Gale cranes his neck to get a better look around him. Green eyes the same color as Natalya's widen. "Who is this lovely beach bunny?"

James turns around in time to see his mother blush.

Marc swings from the Jeep's roll bar. "She's *papá's mamá.*"

The dribbling stops. Julian gawks at his brother. "Don't be stupid, Marc. She was our neighbor."

"It's true. I heard *papá* call Señora Carla 'Mom.'"

Julian swivels his head and glares at James.

234

James's heart drops to the ground. He swears under his breath. Marc had heard him. And he was old enough to connect the dots. He watches the color drain from Julian's face, how his hands flex, fingers splayed and bent gripping the ball. Emotions come in a quick succession of waves, rippling across his face—disbelief, fear, anger, and then the worst. Betrayal. James knows that feeling well.

Julian's body tenses. He chucks the ball at James, hitting him in the ribs.

He grunts, choosing to absorb the impact of Julian's anger rather than deflecting the ball. He catches and holds the ball against his chest.

"You're an asshole," Julian shouts. He takes off toward the beach at a full sprint.

"Aren't you going to go after him?" Claire asks, her voice pitching high with her dismay.

"In a moment. He's been angry with me for a long time. He needs to run off some steam."

James gives the ball to Gale, letting it roll off his fingertips. His mother glowers at him. "It's probably for the best," she says sanctimoniously. "They would have found out sooner or later. I should have told them—"

James holds up a finger, stopping her. "What you did in Mexico is a whole other matter. Right now, I need to go talk with my son."

James finds Julian about a football-field length down the beach crouched under the shade of a palm, elbows parked on knees and head buried in his arms. James eases down with a long sigh to sit beside his son; then he unlaces his shoes and dumps the sand. Taking off his socks, he stuffs them in his shoes and digs his heels into the sand in search of the cool granules underneath.

Julian lifts his head. He wipes his damp face with the base of his palm and glances away. His lungs rattle and shoulders vibrate.

James quells the instinctual urge to hug his son. He'll be twelve soon, on his way to becoming a young man. Instead, he picks up and inspects a dead leaf.

"Why—" Julian snorts. He swipes the back of his hand under his nose. "Why didn't you tell us she's our grandmother?"

James twirls the leaf. "Because I didn't know. I couldn't remember who she is and she never told me. I don't think she told any of us because I didn't read anything in the journals that would make me think Señora Carla was my mother." He phrases his words carefully. He wants Julian to perceive him and Carlos as the same man. He wants Julian to see *him* as his father, which means he must do the same. As Natalya told him years ago, and again last night, "same body, same heart, and same soul." Just a damaged mind he was doing his best to fix.

"I didn't know Señora Carla and my mother were the same person until she showed up at our house last week."

Julian swipes his nose again. He picks up a twig and jabs it into the sand. "I bet you were mad at her."

"I'm still mad," James says, staring off to the ocean. The sun has passed the day's highest point. Their patch of shade shifts away. Sweat beads along his hairline. He feels a drop trickle down his spine. "I'm angry with my whole family. Not you and Marc," he clarifies at Julian's quick intake of breath. "Just my mother and brothers. But you know who I'm angriest with the most?"

Julian shakes his bent head. He jabs the twig harder. It snaps.

"Myself." He's made more than his share of poor decisions, each one leading him further away from the future he and Aimee had plotted like a road trip. But each mistake had brought him closer to Julian and Marc. "I wish more than anything that I remember the years I forgot." Julian's chest rattles and James presses on. "I wish I remembered your mother, and everything you and I did together."

Tears roll freely down Julian's face. They drop into the sand, creating divots. James gently knocks his bent knee against Julian's. "You know what?"

"What?" Julian sniffs.

"I was smart. I wrote everything down, and I remember reading all about us and our time together in Puerto Escondido. And as I read, pictures formed in my head like real memories."

Julian nods, considering. "Why did you have to change?"

"I don't know, Julian. My mind is sick and I'm trying to heal."

Julian frowns. "How did it get sick?"

He shrugs. "I can't remember. I don't know what made me forget being James, and I don't know what made me forget being Carlos."

Julian blinks. His lower lip trembles. "Are you scared?"

"Very much so."

"Me, too."

James rubs his son's back. "It'll get easier for us, I promise. But whether I go by the name of Carlos or James, I'm still your father. *Yo siempre voy a ser tu papá.*" I will always be your dad.

Julian sucks in a ragged breath. Fresh tears flow like a clear stream over rivers rocks. "I still wish you remembered everything for real."

"Me, too." And he honestly did.

"Do you wish you remembered Tía Natalya?"

James dangles his hands between his knees. "Yes."

"She's very sad you don't. I heard her crying last night."

Something James can't explain twists inside his chest. He's been so focused on putting some distance between them and his brothers until he has the chance to think straight that he didn't consider how difficult his being there, sleeping under her roof, must be for her.

"She loves you."

"I know," James says quietly. The way she looks at him, reaches out to touch him only to pull back, how she feels she must ask to hug him and not just do it. She's opened her home, given them sanctuary without asking for anything in return.

Julian traces his finger where he'd been jabbing the twig. "I miss our home."

James doesn't know how he should respond to that. They'll never move back to Mexico. He doesn't belong there. And he isn't in a rush to return to California. He doesn't feel like he belongs there either.

"Can we live here?"

James arches a brow. "In Hawaii?"

"Tía Natalya wants us to stay."

"Do you like it here?"

Julian extends his arms to encompass Hanalei Bay's crescent beach. He gives James a look like he's nuts not to consider otherwise. Julian grew up living beside the ocean. It makes sense he's drawn to this one.

James fists the sand, then lets it spill between his fingers. "It is pretty nice here."

Julian buries his toes. "I didn't like California."

"Hey, I didn't say no. But we should get Marc's opinion, too, before we decide."

A watery smile pulls Julian's mouth wide. Then he frowns and the smile disappears. He watches a trail of ants hike the hills and valleys beside him. "What's Señora Carla's real name?"

"Claire Donato."

"What should I call her?"

"Why don't you ask her?"

"Why did she lie to us?"

"She was afraid I would have sent her away."

"Would you have?"

James opens his mouth to say yes but stops himself. He debates telling Julian the truth else he continues to see him as the bad guy. The one who's tearing their family apart when all he's really trying to do is put the pieces together. Then he remembers what got him into this mess. Withholding the truth. And he was starting to despise his shame more than the flaws that make him human. One of those being he has a terrible relationship with his mother.

"Yes," he finally says. "I would have sent her away."

Julian opens his mouth and closes it. James watches his son's mind tick.

"Will you send Marcus and me away?" he hesitantly asks in a voice tinged with fear.

There it is, James thinks on a long sigh. What Julian has feared most these past six months. In quite a few entries, Carlos commented on his fear that James would abandon his sons. Carlos had expressed that fear with Julian. Talk about a heavy load of responsibility on shoulders so young.

James faces his son. "Look at me," he says, and waits for Julian to lift his head and wipe his eyes. "I will never send you and Marc away. I'll never leave you either."

Julian inhales a sob and nods.

"I've never stopped loving you. Even last December when I first couldn't remember you. I loved you back then. You're my son, Julian. You will always be my son."

Julian sucks in another sob. His body vibrates as he cries. James drags his son against him. Then he just holds him.

◦~◦

Marc's eating at the kitchen table and Natalya's storing condiments in the fridge when James and Julian return to the house. She lifts her head above the fridge door when she hears their arrival. "I made lunch." She nods at the plates on the counter.

James lifts a brow at Marc, amazed he's devouring the Spam-and-pineapple sandwich.

"Muy bueno," Marc exclaims around a mouthful of food.

"If you say so, kiddo." James eyes the sandwiches. He has his doubts.

"Gracias, Tía Natalya." Julian selects a plate and takes it to the table.

"Thank you," James says to her from the doorway. "I'll take care of dinner."

She nods. "I put away the groceries for you." Natalya twirls the bread bag closed and puts the loaf in the pantry. "And your mom"—she lowers her voice, her gaze darting to the boys—"went back to her hotel."

James isn't surprised. She's next on his list of family discussions and she knows it, too.

"She left with my dad."

He stuffs his hands into his pockets. "Really?"

"He's a womanizer, remember? Don't worry." She waves a hand. "It's platonic, I'm sure. She wanted to freshen up, and Dad offered to drive. By now, they're probably having lunch, cocktails, and a dip in the pool."

"That doesn't sound platonic to me." James doesn't know what to think about this development. His father passed shortly before his own disappearance. Granted, his parents had never been close, even slept on opposite ends of the house in later years. But he never thought of his mother being with someone other than his father or uncle—*Ugh! Don't go there.* He moves into the kitchen and peeks inside his sandwich. He hasn't had Spam since college, and only because his dorm roommate dared him.

"I put your art supplies in Marc's room. I'll show you." She drops dirty utensils in the sink.

James follows her down the hall. She's showered recently. Damp hair is clumped into a messy bun. A smattering of freckles speckle her shoulders like paint drops. She wears a loose lavender tank top and white cutoff shorts. Sleek, toned, and tanned legs stretch to the floor. He can't look away from those legs. His fingers twitch, the way they do when he needs to paint. He wants to paint her legs. He wants to . . .

"James."

He jerks his head up.

She frowns and he inwardly squirms. Heat warms his chest. "What?"

"You bought a lot of stuff." She moves into Marc's room and opens a cabinet. The supplies crowd two wide shelves, enough to keep Marc busy for weeks.

"Yeah, I did." He gives her an embarrassed look.

"One would think that you're planning to stay awhile." She closes the cabinet and swivels around. She leans her shoulder blades against the cabinet and crosses her arms. "Or that you plan to start painting again."

James hears the hope in her voice. He rubs his nape and sinks onto the edge of Marc's twin bed. "I want to spend time with Marc doing what he enjoys doing. We'll see where the painting takes me from there."

She looks out the window, tugging a tendril behind her ear. Her gaze focuses beyond the glass and she slowly blinks once, twice. Then she pushes away from the cabinet, moving toward the window. "My room has the best natural light. You're welcome to paint there," she offers without looking at him.

James admires her profile. The high forehead and feminine slope of her nose. Freckles adorn the bridge, spilling down her cheeks like autumn leaves. His fingers twitch again. This time he wants to do more than paint her. He wants to touch her. In his mind, it's been over a year—and in actuality, seven years, given James's identity was buried that long—since he's touched a woman. For a man who's more physical than reserved, tends to feel more than think, and responds more empathically to the emotions of others, seven years is a very long and lonely time. It's one hell of a dry spell.

"You wouldn't want the smell in there while you slept."

"That's right. I forgot about that."

"I was thinking we could paint on the lanai. It's not serious artwork, just a way for Marc and me to hang out together."

"Your mom, too? You bought three easels."

He did, but only as an afterthought. James clasps his hands between his thighs. "That's a good question. I've never painted with her."

"But in Puerto Escondido—"

"Before that. Did you know she despised my painting?"

Natalya frowns. "How could she? She's an incredible artist."

"I didn't know that until I read the journals." He brings forth those entries about Señora Carla and the time she spent painting with Carlos. Anger and sadness mix like paint as he recalls several of the paintings he packed and shipped to California had been hers. As Carlos, he'd hung them on his walls in his house. His mother never displayed a single painting of his.

"She had her reasons, which I understand more so now since she told Carlos. But she did everything she could to keep me on track for a career at Donato Enterprises."

"How did you paint, then? I've seen your work. It's obvious you've been painting for years."

"Aimee's parents set up a studio for me in their house. I'm self-taught."

At the mention of the Tierneys, Natalya shifts uneasily. "I met them."

His gaze catches hers. "I know."

They watch each other for a moment until Natalya's attention dips to a spot on the teakwood floor. She undoes the bun, and damp hair spills over her shoulder. James sucks in a quiet breath at her natural beauty.

"Do you miss her?" There's a hitch in her voice.

"Yes."

"Do you still love her?"

He nods.

Natalya rolls her lips inward and stares at her glossy coral toenails. "How was your talk with Julian?"

He blinks at the subject change. He wants to tell her Aimee had let him go, that she moved on, and that every day, every single waking moment, he's trying to do the same. To build a new life from the rubble of his previous life. But now is probably not the best time. He's still working through his emotions.

"We had a good talk. He got a lot off his chest. We both did."

Natalya twists her hair. Her hands shake and her lips pull into a contorted smile. "Okay, then . . . um . . . I guess you've got everything under control with the boys, after all." She angles her head at the door. "Unless you need to use your room right now, I have some work to do." She turns to leave.

James frowns, not at all liking her mood change.

"Oh." She snaps her fingers, stopping in the doorway. "I saw the steaks you picked up. I can help with dinner, unless you've got that under control, too."

"I'd like your help," he says, standing. He takes two steps toward her. "Natalya, what's wrong?"

Her lower lip quivers and she raises a hand, stopping him. "I have to get to work," she whispers harshly before leaving.

He hears the thump of her feet bounding down the hall, then the slide of the glass door opening to the lanai. She hadn't gone to the office where he'd slept last night. Instead, she raced outside and away from him.

CHAPTER 24

CARLOS

Three Years Ago
July 11
Puerto Escondido, Mexico

The sky was a patchy blue. Outside, shadows came and went, while inside, the interior light held an even brightness throughout the studio. Perfect for mixing colors. I added cerulean blue and emerald green to my palette and mixed the two colors with a touch of titanium white to soften the tone. I inhaled deeply. Pigment fumes, a pungent blend of octane, damp earth, and magnolia flowers, filled my sinuses. The odor sent a rush through my head.

Painter's high, I thought, smirking.

The color wasn't exactly right, so I added a fingernail size of cerulean blue. A satisfied warmth moved over me as I watched the color blend into the hue I'd set out to achieve.

Slender hands curved around my waist, glided up my ribs to my chest. Long, delicate fingers undid a button, and then another. They dived under the edge of my shirt and caressed my skin. My heart pounded under those wandering fingers. Blood pulsed to my center and my breath left in an abbreviated rush. I groaned.

Lips pressed between my shoulder blades. The heat of her breath warm through my shirt. I turned in her arms and looked down into a set of eyes that matched the color on my palette.

"Aimee."

"Kiss me," she asked, and I did.

She finished unbuttoning my shirt and I unzipped her dress. Clothes fell to the floor and we followed. I rolled onto my back, pulling her on top. She kissed her way down my chest, tracing the hairline past my navel. My head fell back and eyes closed. *God, her mouth feels so damn good.*

That was all I could think, all I could feel. And I wanted to watch.

Lifting my head, I opened my eyes. Aimee was gone and I was no longer in the studio at our house.

Instead, I looked up into the barrel of a gun held by my eldest brother. I watched his mouth move and I barely made out the words.

Get up!

Get up or Aimee's next.

My face felt like a pile of bricks had landed on it. Nausea roiled in my gut like a skiff bobbing on rough waves. Beneath me, the surface rose and fell. I gripped a thick rope hanging nearby and tried to pull myself up. Pain shot through my shoulder and down my arm. I yelled, dropping to my knees. White sneakers faded in and out in my line of vision. Hands hauled me up. Lips pressed to my ear. "Swim." And then I was flying, and next, sinking. A coldness like I'd never known before seeped into my bones, forcing my legs to kick. One arm flailed. I had to get to Aimee. I had to get home.

I want to go home.

I woke with a start, gasping.

A dream. It's just a dream.

I swung my legs over the side of the bed and sat there, head buried in my hands. My fingers clawed my scalp as I waited for my pounding heart to slow. I massaged my temples to coax the headache that rarely left, only eased, to go away. It burned, as did the long, thin scar on my hip.

My hand skimmed over that scar, and the last image I'd seen in my dream seared in my head like the thick tissue on my hip. Bullets whizzing past, their long, bubbly wake widening and dissipating in the ocean's rise and fall. Searing pain in my side as one of those bullets hit their mark.

Fingers slid down my sweat-damp back. Chills raised the hair on my arms and legs.

"Same dream?" Natalya asked in a groggy voice.

"Yeah." I pushed to my feet, knees cracking, to go to the bathroom as much as to get away from her touch. My heart still raced and my body was damp out of fear for another woman's life. A woman I had once loved as desperately as the air I breathed.

I popped two aspirin and drank them down directly from the faucet. I caught Natalya's reflection in the mirror as I swiped the water from my mouth. She leaned against the door frame, arms crossed.

"That bottle was half-full when I got here two weeks ago." She nodded at the container.

I glanced inside before spinning on the lid. Fifteen pills left. I needed to go shopping today. Then I remembered Julian and I were mountain-biking in the hills. I'd have to swing by the store on the way back.

"Have you seen a doctor yet?"

I turned around and shook my head.

"Carlos." She dragged out my name, coming into the bathroom, and glared up at me. "They're getting worse. And at the rate you're going"—she shook the bottle, and the few aspirin remaining rattled inside—"you'll have an ulcer to match that ache in your head."

I trapped her in my arms and buried my face in the curve of her neck. "It's not my forehead that aches right now." I kissed her bed-warm skin, hoping to distract her. Hoping to distract me and all my aches, because my brain really was on fire. That damn dream got more vivid each time and my headaches were always intense in the hours following.

I scooped up Natalya and carried her to bed. We fell onto the sheets. I could tell from the way she kissed me she was in the mood to talk. I wasn't. It was three-fucking-a.m. and my head hurt like a mother.

She gently nudged my shoulders and kissed my nose. I sighed and flopped to my back, arms spread wide as I stared at the ceiling fan overhead. Bad idea. The room spun like a merry-go-round and my innards hitched a ride, spinning along with it. I draped my forearm over my brow and breathed through the sourness in my mouth.

"Why won't you see a doctor?"

"We've been over this before, Nat." I didn't want anyone prodding my head and administering tests. One surprised hypnosis experiment had left a jackhammer without an "Off" switch drilling my brain. I had no intention to be a willing—or unwilling—participant in any further psychotherapy sessions.

Natalya flopped on her back. "I could kill Thomas."

"You and me both." I lifted my arm to look at her. She tugged a sheet over her breasts and buried her fingers in her hair.

"I can help you find a doctor who makes house calls. You can be examined here and I'll stay by your side. Just in case, you know?"

"No. I don't want to be examined." I got out of bed and paced to the slider door. It was pitch-black outside and the only thing I saw was my reflection, my face ragged and worn with deep tension lines, a train track across my forehead.

"Don't tell the doctor what's really wrong. Make up an excuse, like you have chronic migraines or something."

"I *do* have chronic migraines."

"Which means you need prescription medication so you stop popping aspirin like jelly beans."

I shook my head. "No."

"Maybe it's stress that's causing the headaches. Have you considered antidepressants or anxiety meds?"

"No drugs," I said, slicing the air between us. "They're too addictive."

She gave me a look. While aspirin itself isn't addictive, we both knew my reliance on those pills to manage the pain was pretty close to an addiction.

Natalya lifted her gaze toward the ceiling. She was frustrated with me and I didn't blame her. *I* was frustrated with me. She let her hands fall into her lap. "I understand why you don't travel, and I get why you don't want to see a doctor. What I can't figure out is why you insist on living with the pain when you can do something about it. Think of your sons."

"I am." I stomped to my bureau where my laptop was charging. "I think of them and their future with a father who can't remember them every goddamn second of the day. Someone who may always have to be on the run with them."

"You don't know that, Carlos. It's been several years and no one has come after you. I don't think anyone from that cartel knows who you are, let alone that James is still alive."

"Not yet." Phil was still in prison and still believed me dead. *What will happen when he discovers the truth?* Because instinct told me one day he would.

Natalya sighed, exasperated. "Tell me how I can help. I want to help you."

Marry me. Adopt my sons. Run far away with them so James or anyone in the Donato family can't find them.

"Look, I'm tired. I don't want to talk about this right now." I yanked out the charge cord and grabbed the laptop.

"Where are you going?"

I turned in the doorway at the note of panic in her voice. She'd risen to her knees, white-knuckling the sheet with both hands. For a splinter of a moment I wanted to drop the laptop and dive back into bed with her. Reassure both of us that everything would be fine. But those were promises I couldn't keep.

"I'm going downstairs. To write."

She sat back onto her heels, but she still gripped the sheet. "I don't like arguing. Please don't leave. Come back to bed." She patted the pillow beside her.

"Go to sleep. I'm just going to the kitchen." I pulled the door closed behind me, leaving it open a crack. I walked past Marcus's room, then Julian's.

"Dad?"

I backtracked to his room and poked in my head. His Captain America night-light cast a soft blue glow, chasing shadows into the corner.

"Is it morning yet?" Julian sat up in the middle of his bed and rubbed his eyes.

"Almost. We have a few more hours before sunrise."

He flopped back onto the pillows. "I'm going to ride down the mountain faster than you."

"I'm sure you will. Get some sleep."

He yawned. "Good night, *papá*."

I bounded down the stairs to the kitchen and fired up my laptop. While I waited, I sorted through yesterday's mail, adding the latest magazines to the pile along the far wall. The newspaper didn't have any articles I thought would be of interest to me later, so I dropped it in the recycling container.

Once the laptop was ready, I opened my Cloud account and uploaded the twenty or so pictures I took yesterday—photos of the boys and Natalya at Julian's *fútbol* game—then I added them to the folder where I was storing this month's images. I had files for everything—photos, journal entries, financial statements, legal documents, and other important instructions. I even wrote notes about what I did on a daily basis, whom I loved (Natalya and my sons), whom I trusted (Natalya) and whom I did not (Thomas and Imelda). Everything was in meticulous order. Because that hypnosis session Thomas forcibly subjected me to? It hadn't just brought on the headaches. It woke the Jekyll to my Hyde. My other self was fighting his way to the surface, and I knew, without a doubt, I didn't have much time left.

∾

"Slow down."

Julian hunched low over the handlebars and leaned into the turn. I coasted behind, picking up speed. The loop through the foothills was mostly paved and we'd ridden it many times. For an eight-year-old, Julian was fearless on his bike.

I moved up alongside him. "Ease up. Stay in control."

He tackled another turn, putting slight pressure on the brake.

"Looking good."

Air howled through our helmets. Sunlight glared overhead and heat steamed our backs. Sweat dripped off my chin. We'd started early, and though it was still morning, the day was already hot, dry, and dusty. Good thing we only had another couple of kilometers, all downhill. We'd ridden hard. This father-son time with Julian was great, and I wouldn't change it, but damn. For the life of me, I couldn't pedal out of last night's nightmare. It was as though I'd been there. The throbbing, mind-numbing pain in my skull left me reeling with nausea, and that gun in my face scared the shit out of me.

I motioned for a water break and we slowed to a stop on the side of the road.

Julian gulped down his water and let out a long, well-earned sigh. "Can we take the trail?" he asked, referring to the dirt path that paralleled the road in some spots. It was narrow and littered with divots and overgrown vegetation.

"Think you can handle it?" We'd already ridden more than five kilometers, some of that uphill on dirt and cobblestone roads.

He pointed at himself with both hands. "Hello . . . I'm the fastest halfback on my team."

"That you are." His athleticism and competitive drive always amazed me. I washed back a couple of aspirin and a sudden wave of dizziness overcame me. I stumbled to the side, almost dropping the bike.

"Ten out of ten." Julian rated my lack of finesse.

"Ha-ha." I shook my head to clear the fog and checked my watch. We'd make it back to the car in less than twenty minutes.

He bounced his bike's front tire. "Ready?"

"Yep. Take it slow, though." The fog wouldn't lift in my head and the last thing I wanted to do was crash and burn in the bushes. Julian wouldn't let me hear the end of it should that happen.

After glancing both ways, Julian crossed the road and about twenty or so meters downhill, he disappeared over the embankment onto the trailhead.

I returned the water bottle to the holder, got on my bike, and crossed the road. Then I was sitting on a boulder with my head between my knees.

What. The. Fuck?

Pain sliced through me when I lifted my head. I moaned. My skull felt like a watermelon split open on hot pavement.

I looked around. The bike lay in the road beside me and Julian was nowhere in sight.

"Julian?" I hollered, standing. *"Julian!"*

Where was he?

I turned a 360 in the middle of the road while drowning in mounting panic. "Julian!" I yelled again. Then I remembered the car. Julian and I had an agreement that we'd meet at the car should we get separated.

I jumped on the bike and raced down the hill, eating up the kilometers. The Jeep was parked in a dirt lot at the base of the road and Julian was crouched against the rear passenger tire. *Thank God.* I hopped off the bike before stopping and ran toward him. The bike crashed into the car's bumper and I skidded the last few yards.

"Julian!" I knelt before him. "Are you hurt?"

He lifted his head. Tears streaked his dirty face like tire tracks in mud. "You know my name?"

"What's that supposed to mean? Of course I know your name."

"But you didn't back there. You took off right after you yelled at me."

Every nerve ending inside me went ice-cold. I stopped breathing and stared hard at him for what seemed like an eternity. Then I sucked in a big gulp of air and gripped his shoulders as terror gripped me. "What did I say?" He hiccuped a sob. "What did I say?" I yelled.

"You asked who I was and when I said I'm Julian and that I was your son, you said . . . you said . . ." He was full-on bawling, unable to get out the words.

My fingers dug into his triceps. "I said *what*?"

"You said you didn't have a son."

CHAPTER 25

JAMES

Present Day
June 28
Hanalei, Kauai, Hawaii

James stands outside Natalya's office debating whether he should interrupt her. She obviously returned. He can hear her on the phone. He can't stand the thought he's the reason she was upset earlier. He doesn't know how he'll make her feel better, but he wants to see that quirky half smile on her face again. But her voice rises with determination. She's in the middle of negotiating the price on something so now is not the time to disturb her.

He returns to Marc's room and selects an assortment of paints, brushes, blank canvases, and the portable easels. He heads for the lanai, passing Julian in the main room, who's sprawled on the couch. Headphones clamped over his ears and feet propped on the couch arm, his fingers fly across his phone's screen. A multicolored beach ball sits waiting on his stomach.

Julian slips off the headphones when he sees him and holds out his phone. "This guy keeps texting me. Says he's Uncle Thomas. He wants you to call him."

Kerry Lonsdale

James unloads the art supplies on the coffee table and takes the phone. He immediately recognizes Thomas's number. It shouldn't surprise him his brother would stoop low enough to reach him through his son's phone number. It was exactly the contrived tactic Carlos did not want his sons put in the middle of.

But James is partially to blame. He's been ignoring him. He reminds himself to call Thomas later, else he'll show up at Natalya's door.

"Have you called or texted him back?" he asks his son.

"I've only texted Antonio since we've been here."

James checks the phone log. He skims through their exchange, then taps the information icon beside Thomas's phone number and selects the "Block This Caller" link. He gives Julian back his phone.

"He won't bother you anymore," James says with the wry thought he should do the same on his phone.

Julian tucks the phone into his pocket and bounces the beach ball against his raised knees. "What's up with you and your brother, anyway? He seems nice. I mean, he was nice to me and Marcus."

"When was that?"

Julian dramatically rolls his eyes. "Last December, when Uncle Thomas visited. All you guys did was yell at each other. I thought Señor Martinez swore a lot."

Señor Martinez was the father of one of Julian's soccer teammates. His mouth flew as freely as the ball was passed around the field.

But those first weeks last December had been the worst weeks of his life. He hadn't felt such rage toward his family since Phil assaulted Aimee. Had Phil hit James's head any harder so that he didn't wake, he would have . . . *Ugh!* He doesn't want to imagine what would have happened.

He sighs, releasing the anger the memories bring back, and sinks onto the couch beside Julian. He presses his back into the cushions and stares at the ceiling. Julian sits upright and hugs the ball. James rolls his head to look at him. "It wasn't easy between us last winter."

Julian shakes his head.

"You know a little about my memory loss. Someday, when you're older, I'll tell you why I think I lost my memory."

"Why not now? I'm almost twelve."

James leans forward, elbows on his thighs. "You've watched the news. There are some scary people out there, and some scary things happened to me."

Fear darkens Julian's expression, a passing cloud of emotion. "Like what things?"

James debates how much to tell him. "My brother knew I lost my memories but he didn't tell me who I really was."

Julian's brows knit. He bounces the ball once, then again. "Maybe he was trying to keep you safe from the scary people. Maybe he wanted to keep an eye on you, like you're always telling me to watch Marcus so he doesn't do anything stupid or get himself hurt. Uncle Thomas *is* your big brother. Big brothers are supposed to look after little brothers."

James absorbs the impact of his son's words. "You know, you're a pretty smart kid."

Julian bounces the ball on the coffee table. James snags it on the upswing.

"Hey!"

He holds the ball from Julian's reach. "Not in the house." He sets the ball on the floor.

Julian groans and flops back onto the couch.

Marc walks into the room. Bread crumbs and spilled juice mar his shirt like splattered paint. Mayonnaise streaks his chin. He spots the arts supplies and his face brightens. "Are you going to paint, *papá*?"

"I am. Do you want to paint with me?"

"*Sí!*"

"Go wash your hands and face. I'll meet you on the back deck."

Marc runs to the bathroom.

"Want to paint with us?" James asks.

Julian scrunches his face. "No way, dude." He slips on his head-phones and slides out his phone, back to texting his friends.

⁓

Aside from art classes taken during college, James has never painted with anyone. And aside from the Tierney family and the few friends who frequently hung out at Aimee's house while growing up, no one knew about James's art. Painting has always been a solitary venture. He never discussed his work, and aside from the canvases the Tierneys hung on their walls, and later on the walls of the home he rented with Aimee, he never displayed his work.

But he had dreamed.

He visualized owning a studio, teaching others what he'd learned and fine-tuned himself. He imagined his paintings on display at galler-ies. And he dreamed about painting with his own children, where he'd encourage their talent, not repress it.

As Carlos, he achieved those dreams. Would he be able to do it again? He thinks of the retail space in Princeville. Puerto Escondido wasn't his home and California isn't his sons' home. He isn't sure it's his home anymore either. Maybe they could start a new life here.

James glances at the house. His gaze roams over the yard and trails to the beach. They already had a foundation in Kauai. Natalya is family. She's his sons' aunt and his sister-in-law. She was his lover.

Thoughts lunge to Aimee, his one true love, and he feels that famil-iar dull pang in his chest, like bumping an old contusion into a sharp corner of furniture. He wonders if he's capable of falling in love with someone else when he still loves Aimee.

Carlos wanted him to fall for Natalya. He'd spun every phrase and polished each word in that damn journal so that James found himself caring for a woman he had yet to meet face-to-face. *But to love her?* He doesn't see how that's a possibility when Aimee still owns his heart.

He will admit, though, he'd been envious of Carlos for the time spent with Natalya. He'd also been envious of Carlos's artistic talent, which has kept James from his own art. *That's going to stop today,* he thinks. He's going to paint with the freedom he never allowed himself previously, and he plans to teach his son to do the same. No more hiding.

James sets up the easels in a corner of the lanai and positions two patio chairs in front. He's arranging paint tubes and brushes when Marc joins him.

"What are you going to paint, *papá*?"

"We"—James corrects his son, handing him a set of brushes—"are going to paint that palm tree, the tall one in the middle." He points across the yard.

Marc's mouth forms a small circle as he takes in a cluster of palms of varying sizes. "I've never painted a palm tree before."

The corner of James's mouth twitches. Marc painted animals, boats, and trucks. "There's no better time to start than the present. What do you think?"

"Can I put birds in my trees?"

"Sure, why not. Now, look at the greens in the tree. Which colors should we use?" He gestures at the array of paint tubes.

Marc scratches the tip of his nose. The skin bunches between his brows and for an instant, James sees Natalya in his son. It's the first physical connection he's been able to make between his son and the woman he married six years ago. She was beautiful like her sister and James regrets his son will never have the chance to know his mother.

Marc selects the cadmium and sap green tubes and shows them to James.

"Excellent choices." He claps his son on the shoulder and pulls out a chair.

Marc sits and swings his legs. "Are you going to teach me what you taught the other kids at your studio?"

He glances up from where he's adding dabs of paint on the palette boards. "I taught kids?"

"Lots of them."

He doesn't recall reading anything about kids in Carlos's workshops, but the news makes him happy. While in the fugue state, James had been a man he could admire: a devoted father, a loyal spouse, and respected individual within the community. Perhaps he can be that way again.

"Yes. I'm going to teach you what I taught them."

Marc grins broadly and the bond James has started to sense between them strengthens.

❧

A few hours later, palm-tree paintings complete and tropical-bird paintings started, Claire and Gale return. His mother's laugh floats from inside the house, making his skin tighten. Then he realizes his mother is giggling and he twists around, looking for her. Never in his life has he heard his mother giggle. The laugh rises in volume as she opens the glass slider and joins them on the lanai.

Behind her, he sees Julian follow Gale. He asks his grandfather if they can go surfing. Claire approaches him, blocking his son from view. Her cheeks are rosy and the smile she wears softens her usually harassed face. She stands behind Marc and admires his painting. "Very nice," she remarks before turning to James.

He holds his breath as though waiting for a compliment, and he fumes, especially when her gaze narrows and lips twist.

He looks away, silently tolerating her scrutiny, which further irritates him. He drums the brush handle on his thigh and stares at the horizon. Glassy blue and bleached yellow tint the sky. Water glitters like decorative white quartz. The sun has sunk lower and soon the cool colors will warm to purple and orange. He thinks of Natalya. She's wanted him to paint her sunset.

Claire clicks her tongue and his back stiffens. "You've done better."

James tosses the brush on the easel ledge. "I'm a bit rusty." He stands and straightens his shorts. Moving aside the chair, he dunks the tips of the used brushes in a jar of turpentine.

"I'm not done yet," Marc says, painting faster.

"You have time to finish. I have to start dinner."

James removes his painting and replaces it with a clean canvas. Below them, Julian and Gale cross the yard, surfboards tucked under their arms. James calls out and they turn. "Back in an hour," Gale hollers up to him.

James waves, then repositions his chair in front of the easel. He invites his mother to sit.

Her eyes cast down to the chair, then slowly lift to meet his. "You want me to paint?"

He turns back to the table for the unopened art box and holds it out for his mother. Her face pales and he can guess exactly what she's thinking. The box is almost an exact replica of the one Aimee had gifted him on his twelfth birthday. The one Claire demanded that he return.

Her fingers flutter to the top button of her shirt and her lips slightly part. He can sense she wants to paint but is unsure of her next move, especially since it's him encouraging her to do so. They'd probably never talk about their issues and they'd probably never be as open with each other as she'd been with Carlos. He also doubts he can forgive her. They don't have that kind of relationship. But he can live with a truce between them. The art box is his white flag, as the premium art brushes she'd gifted him last week was hers.

"Marc wants to paint with you," James says.

"*Sí, Señora—*" Marc stalls, paintbrush poised before the canvas, a glob of paint clinging to the tip. Marc looks from Claire to James and back.

Sensing his distress, James asks his mother, "What should the boys call you? Grammie?"

Her eyes widen in horror. "Goodness, no. *No!*" She waves a hand in dismissal and forces a smile. "Nonna is fine. Call me Nonna," she says to Marc, snatching the art box from James.

James tucks his hands into his pockets and ducks his head to hide the smile that creeps onto his face.

"Nonna," Marc says, tasting the word on his heavily accented tongue.

"It's Italian," Claire explains, flipping open the art box.

Marc smears this brush across his canvas, leaving a trail of blue. "Am I Italian?"

"Yes. You're also Mexican."

Marc sits straighter. "I am? Radical, dude," he says in a voice that mimics his grandfather.

Claire grimaces and James chuckles, leaving the two to paint.

In the kitchen, James removes the steaks from the fridge and selects spices from the pantry. He arranges the steaks on the counter so they'll warm to room temperature; then he goes looking for the potatoes. He finds them in a basket on the pantry floor. He's scrubbing them in the sink when Natalya joins him in the kitchen.

"How about some salad and veggies to go with those meat and potatoes?"

"Sounds great." James grins at her over his shoulder.

They work in tandem, forearms brushing as Natalya rinses tomatoes beside him, and he's hyperaware of every move she makes. The way she pauses while slicing when he reaches across her for his own knife, and the way her breath hitches when he rests a hand on her lower back, coaxing her to move aside so he can hunt for a bowl. He catches her scent, the faint essence of tangerine that's unique to her and makes him ache with a familiarity he doesn't quite understand. His mind doesn't remember her, but perhaps his body does, which might explain why he feels so at ease around her in such a short time.

She makes a sudden turn into him, knocking his elbow. The cap to the grilling spices he was attempting to screw on fumbles from his fingers.

"Sorry," she murmurs as they both lower to the floor. Natalya captures the cap where it's rolled behind her feet. She drops it into James's hand with shaking fingers. Their eyes meet and hers dart away.

The fading sunlight casts a warm glow to her freckled cheek. Her hair is a palette of reds and golds, which together make the copper he's determined to paint. He can't resist any longer. He touches her hair.

She sucks in a breath and jerks away.

He drops his hand.

Pushing against her thighs, she stands. James rises more slowly, sensing a new tension inside her. "You all right?"

She grips the knife and slices through another tomato. The blade connects hard with the board. She slices again. "We lost a contract today," she says after a moment. "Usually I can predict when that'll happen." Finished slicing, she drops the knife in the sink. She rinses her hands, then roughly dries them with the dish towel.

James sets down his knife and swivels around to face her. He shifts his weight against the counter edge, leaning back on his hands. "Anything I can do to help?" He wants to know more about what she does during the day, more than what he's read about in a journal.

"No, it's a done deal." She folds the towel and glances at the oven clock. "How much longer until dinner?"

James glances at the marinating steaks. "About forty-five minutes."

She lifts a shaking hand and scratches her scalp. "I'm going to take a shower." She leaves the kitchen, brushing past him so fast he feels a breeze.

His gaze falls on the sliced tomatoes, their juice bleeding onto the cutting board, the lettuce head, still whole, and the zucchini wrapped in the produce bag. Salad and vegetables forgotten, something had chased Natalya from the kitchen, and he's positive her swift mood change has nothing to do with the lost contract.

CHAPTER 26

CARLOS

Three Years Ago
July 21
Puerto Escondido, Mexico

I swirled a brush through the cadmium yellow and tried to focus on the final touches of a painting a local restaurant had commissioned. Another sunset to match the other three in a private dining room: *El otoño*, *El invierno*, and *La primavera*. Autumn, winter, and spring. I'd deliver *El verano* in a few weeks, once the canvas dried.

Sweat dotted my brow and pooled in my lower back, just above the waist of my jeans. The air conditioner was working overtime but it was still hot as a mother inside the studio. I fanned my shirt. The headache didn't help either, although it no longer felt like the sledgehammer it had been. I finally went to the clinic for a prescription after last week's blackout. The doctor reasoned dizziness and dehydration caused the blackout and my headaches were from stress. But I hadn't told him my full story, and, ten days later, I was still shaken by the ordeal.

So was Julian. Every day since, he'd asked if I knew that he was my son, which only reinforced what I'd always feared. James wouldn't want Julian and Marcus because he wouldn't think of them as his.

Because I was a stubborn ass—Natalya's words, not mine—and refused to do the research, she got in touch with Dr. Edith Feinstein, a neuropsychologist in the States. Natalya described to the doctor what she knew of my condition and mentioned the blackout as well as my nightmares, which had been on my mind throughout the entire ride with Julian. Without examining me, Dr. Feinstein could only postulate that my nightmares were dissociative memories and I'd experienced a flashback. The traumatic emotions the nightmare evoked may have triggered the flashback, and for those terrifying ten minutes I'd experienced a different identity state. I might have been James or someone else entirely. I just wasn't me.

Their conversation went on for more than an hour. Dr. Feinstein explained some things we already knew. My condition was the result of a psychological trauma, not a physical injury. That was why I could speak, write, and read in Spanish. I could run marathons without remembering how I trained. It was also why I could paint like a professional artist. Because James could do those things. The only thing missing was my past, which was locked up tight in my head. It was why people with my condition could easily pick up and start new lives. Or in my case, step into a life that had been fabricated for me.

Dr. Feinstein asked Natalya if I was interested in treatment. Hypnotherapy might unlock the memories and I could go back to my life as James. When Natalya declined on my behalf, the doctor noted that whether or not I elected to proceed, I might not have a choice. My mind would decide when it was ready to heal. It would know when I was ready to confront the stresses and trauma that had pushed me into this state. The switch could be today, tomorrow, or years from now. And the transition to my previous identity would be quick.

Before they ended the call, Dr. Feinstein had one last word of advice. I'd taken it as a warning, one that had driven me in the early hours of the morning to document every single detail about my life. On some level, I would sense when I'd be ready to confront my demons. The increased frequency and improved clarity of the nightmares, and now the blackout, were possible indications my mind was preparing. She advised Natalya, being my significant other, as Natalya had introduced herself, that she needed to mentally and emotionally prepare herself. When my transition happened, our lives would be seriously disrupted. I'd likely experience severe depression, grief, and shame. There might be mood disorders, suicidal tendencies, and an inclination toward aggression.

Great. I'm going to be an asshole. Just one more thing for me to worry about, I thought, tossing aside the paintbrush.

Behind me, sandals scuffed across the hardwood floor. The essence of coconut sunscreen reached me before Nat's arms folded around me. She rested her chin on my shoulder. I lifted her forearm to my lips, tasting salt and the bitterness of lotion.

"I don't want to leave you." There was a concerned edge in her whisper.

"Then stay." I unfolded her arms and tugged her around in front of me, settling her between my legs. The stool I was sitting on put me at eye level with her.

She clasped her hands behind my neck. Her thumbs stroked my scalp. "You know I can't."

Meetings, travel, big deals to negotiate. A tournament in South Africa. A visit with her younger brother. She'd be back in Puerto Escondido for a brief visit in September, and again in November for the *torneo de surf.* Between those visits, we'd text and FaceTime, talk on the phone. Despite that, September seemed a long time away, especially when all I wanted to do was hold and kiss her. Move deeply inside her warmth. Marry her, and convince her to adopt my sons.

I kissed her, achingly soft and agonizingly slow. I felt the tingle from the metallic taste of her medicated lip balm, but I didn't care. I poured everything I felt for her into that kiss. My love, compassion, and fears. Her fingers dug into my neck and her pelvis ground into mine, urging me to deepen the kiss, to take her one last time before she boarded the plane.

"Marry me," I whispered against her lips. She whimpered and I asked again. "Please marry me."

Her lips released mine. She pressed her forehead to mine and murmured my name. This hadn't been the first time I'd asked.

"Do you love me?" I hated the emptiness in my tone.

She stepped from my embrace and my hands fell to my lap. Cool air swirled into the space she left. My gaze washed over her as she took interest in the paint drops on the floor. She twisted her hair. Emotions played on her face, confusion and uncertainty. I lifted her chin and we watched each other for a moment. "Nat, do you love me?"

"Yes. With all my heart."

"Then why won't you marry me?" I asked. Then, unexpectedly, I thought of her scars, battle wounds I never asked about, figuring she'd one day be brave enough to tell me. I'd waited long enough. She'd told me she was on birth control. Maybe there was something more going on. "Can you have children?"

She stiffened. "I hope so."

"But your scars?"

She frowned. "My scars?"

I skimmed my thumbs along the inside of her hip bones. "Did you have surgery?" Her mother passed from ovarian cancer. "Were you sick?" I didn't like that she would have kept such a thing from me were that true. I still needed to know.

"Sick?" She looked down at my hands where they clasped her hips. "I got those while surfing." It was my turn to frown. "A wave pushed me into some sharp rocks when I was seventeen. They punctured my skin and it hurt like a bitch, but that has nothing to do with why I won't marry you."

"Then what is it?" I practically growled the question, frustrated for an answer.

Her whole body wilted. "I want to marry you, I really do. It's just . . . I'm afraid you're only marrying me for the kids' sake."

"*Dios*, Nat." She didn't think I wanted her. "I love you. It's you I want every goddamn second of the day. There's no one else I want to be with."

"You say that now."

My hands fell from her. I slid off the stool and backed a step away. *God, I'm an idiot.* "You're afraid I'll want to be with Aimee."

"It's a logical fear, Carlos. You're convinced the fugue will end. You're also convinced James won't want your sons or that he'll be unable to keep them safe from your family. Us getting married puts me in the exact same predicament as Julian and Marcus. I'm scared you'll just leave me behind, too."

"Nat . . ." My world crashed. She turned away, looking as lost and forlorn as I felt. I wanted to punch something. Life was so goddamn unfair because Nat was right. I shoved a hand into my hair and gripped hard.

Her phone buzzed with an appointment alarm. She looked at the time. "I have to go." She put the phone away then gave me a long look. Reaching out, she skimmed her fingers along my unshaven jaw. I captured her hand and pressed my lips to her palm, holding her there.

"Let James decide what he wants," she said, locking her gaze with mine when I released her hand.

I shook my head hard. "I can't do that. I don't care what Aimee told me. I can't see that guy she described." Yet I wanted to tie her to me. I ground my teeth and looked away.

"Hey." She coaxed me back with the gentle touch of her fingers on my face. "If he doesn't want the boys, or if he doesn't think he can keep them safe from his family, then, yes, I'll adopt them. I'll give them a good home. You can put that in your journal so James knows."

I put both hands on her face and kissed her hard, somewhat desperately. "Thank you," I whispered. "Thank you." I would take whatever she was willing to give me.

"I love you, Carlos."

I hugged her tightly. "I'll always love you."

She murmured in my ear then said good-bye, stepping from my embrace. I grasped her hand, her fingers falling from mine as she backed away. The door closed behind her, leaving me alone with my paints and the words she whispered after my declaration that I would always love her.

I hope you do.

CHAPTER 27

JAMES

Present Day
June 28
Hanalei, Kauai, Hawaii

They dine on the lanai under a darkening sky with the heady scent of barbecue in the air. During the meal, talk is lively between his sons and their grandmother and grandfather. Gale and Julian compare their rides on the waves; then Marc takes his turn sharing his first experience using "grown-up" paints. In between steaks cooked to perfection and ice cream for dessert, Claire enlightens the table about her travels to Italy. She became an expert at haggling over furniture prices. Other than a smile or small exclamation to acknowledge a feat Julian or Marc shares with the group, Natalya has been quiet. James also notices she intentionally sat between his sons. He'd deliberately set her plate beside his, hoping for a chance to talk with her, but she moved it to another place setting when he went back to the grill for Gale's steak.

After dinner, Natalya kisses the kids good night and escapes to the kitchen. James takes them to their rooms and tucks them into bed, which amounts to a fist-bump and a "See ya in the morning, Pops" from Julian. Marc still wants a story. As expected, he falls asleep against James's shoulder halfway through the book. Next time he'll start reading from the middle so they finish the story for once.

Gale has taken Claire back to her hotel, so he goes looking for Natalya. She's still in the kitchen, rinsing dishes. He joins her at the sink, grabs a towel, and wipes down a pot drying in the rack.

Natalya glances at him, her rubber-gloved hands elbow deep in soapy water. "Thanks, but you don't have to do that."

He gives her a funny look. "I made the mess."

"You cooked. I'll clean. It's how we—" She presses her lips tight and scrubs harder.

"It's how we always do it," James finishes for her, his tone gentle. "I'd still like to help." He puts the pot aside and picks up another.

Natalya puts her hand on the pot, stopping him. "I'll do it." She glances over her shoulder. "Why don't you grab a beer and go relax on the lanai."

Outside, and out of the kitchen. James may be a little slow catching up on the six-plus years missing from his life, but he knows when he's not wanted. Abandoned for years in a foreign country taught him that lesson well.

He refolds the towel and moves aside to lean against the counter. He folds his arms, crosses his ankles, and watches Natalya. She scrubs with rough, jerky movements. Moisture shines on her cheek where she scratched herself with a gloved hand. She's rushing through the dishes and refuses to look at him. She's obviously uncomfortable around him.

"Do you want us to leave?" he asks before he thinks better of it. He and the boys can get a hotel room for a few days. Then what? Where would they go? None of them wants to return to California, but that's where they'll probably end up. He should start looking at real estate listings since there's no way he'll stay in his parents' old house. It holds too many memories he prefers to forget. He never liked that house.

"No . . . no, I don't want you to leave." Natalya adds a dish to the dishwasher. "It's just—" She scratches her forehead with the back of her hand.

"It's just what?"

"I can't do this." She closes her eyes and James gets a sickening feeling in the pit of his stomach. "I thought I could but it's too hard." She snaps off the gloves, tosses them into the sink, and leaves him standing there, bewildered at her abrupt departure.

The front door slams. "Nat?" Gale calls.

Feet bound down the hallway.

"Nat? What's wrong, hon?"

James pictures Gale calling down the hallway for her. He rubs his forearms; then, realizing what he's doing because he always rubs his arms when he must make a tough decision, he rubs his face instead. Stubble scratches his palms and he groans into his hands. He was tired of feeling unsettled, and now they have to leave once again.

He should pack tonight so they can go first thing in the morning. The longer they stay, the harder it will be for Julian and Marc to leave their aunt and grandfather. Leaving Kauai is the best option, and it makes him angry. His sons will hate him all over again.

Gale saunters into the kitchen, spinning a set of keys around his index finger. He takes a long look at James. "Want a drink?"

James sighs. "Yeah."

Gale tosses the keys on the counter, where they slide into the backsplash. He opens a cabinet. "Scotch?" he asks, showing James a bottle of Macallan.

"Sure."

"When it comes to women, I'm not the most committed guy," Gale says. James arches a single brow and Gale chuckles. "Ah, so Nat's told you some stories."

"A few," he says, although he knew more about her father from what he read in the journals.

Gale selects two lowballs from another cabinet. "Ice?" James nods and Gale goes to the fridge. "I'm also, by no means, an expert on women."

"What guy is?" James scoffs. He dated Aimee for a decade and there were plenty of occasions when he had no clue why she was upset with him.

Gale pushes a glass against the ice lever. The ice maker rumbles to life and cubes tumble into the glass. "Kylie, though, that's Nat's mom," he clarifies. "She was my first and only. Only real love and only wife."

He peeks over at James as he unscrews the liquor cap. "I know what you're thinking," he guesses. "I did love Raquel's mom, but it wasn't the same. It wasn't the same with the mothers of my other kids."

James hadn't been thinking of Raquel, but as he watches the amber liquid splash into their glasses, he does find himself wondering. "Do you think a man can love more than one woman in his lifetime?"

"Sure he can."

"I'm talking about that deep, all-consuming love, like what you felt for Kylie." And what he feels for Aimee.

Gale spins the cap back on the bottle. "Depends on the man and the woman he wants. I wasn't so fortunate; then again, I didn't want to find that love again. You've got to want it. In here." He thumps his chest then gives James a glass. They toast and James tosses back half of it. The liquor sears, warming his gut.

Gale swirls the ice in his glass. "What I'm trying to say, and doing a piss-poor job at, is—"

"Natalya's like her mom," he murmurs to himself.

"What did you say?"

"Your daughter is like her mother. She wants commitment." She doesn't want to be left behind, not like her father had done with the mothers of her siblings. It's why Natalya always did the leaving, and why she never moved to Mexico and married Carlos. She knew when he came out of the fugue he would return to the States. He would leave her. Exactly as his father had done with the women in his life.

Gale watches him for a long moment. He sips from the glass without taking his eyes from James. "Nat may be unfamiliar to you, and it may seem strange being with her. But your *not* being with her, not talking to each other, not touching or kissing, and all that other stuff couples in love do, well, that's weird for the rest of us, especially for Nat.

"You and I might not have seen each other since Raquel's wedding, but Nat talked about you over the years. A lot. And she's hurting."

James watches the ice bob in his glass. "I know." He could punch himself that he hadn't figured that out earlier.

"She knew this day would come, you not remembering her. Thinking about it, though, and experiencing it? Well, like the waves outside those doors, they may look and sound the same, but when you're up there on your board, each one is a different ride indeed."

James recalls the passage when Carlos first met Aimee and learned of the fugue. He'd been outraged and conflicted. He didn't have any interest in learning more about his original identity or his relationship with Aimee, which, from what he's read about his condition, is typical of people with dissociative fugue. The fear of losing one's current self is palpable and Carlos had been terrified. He couldn't remember Aimee and he didn't want to remember Aimee. It had driven her away.

The same would happen with Natalya.

His sons will be devastated if she doesn't want to see them because having him around is too difficult for her to bear. His situation with Natalya is different from Carlos and Aimee. Carlos prepared him for this. He left behind passages filled with his wants and desires. He drew such a detailed picture, inside and out, of the woman he loved, and gifted it to James in hopes he could find it again. But can a man love a woman when he still loved someone else?

"Do you care for Natalya?" Gale asks.

"Yes," James answers.

"I don't get much about what's going on with you up here"—Gale waggles a finger by his temple—"but I think you still love her here." He puts a hand over his heart. "That brain of yours just needs to heal and catch up."

"That's what I'm trying to do, sir." It's why he is here.

"Well, then." Gale sets his empty glass in the sink. "I'm done with the mush talk. I've said my piece. Time to hit the sack. That son of yours is one crazy beast on the waves. Wore me out today."

"Good night, Gale." James follows him to the front door so he can lock it behind him.

"One more thing." Gale stops in the doorway. "If you feel anything for Natalya, go to her." His gaze slides toward the hallway. "You can figure the rest out later."

After Gale leaves for his cottage at the front end of the property, James finds himself outside Natalya's bedroom. Head bent, ear to the door, he lightly knocks with the knuckle of his pointer finger. He hasn't figured out what he'll say. He figures they'll talk, discuss how to make their relationship work—whatever relationship that is—so he doesn't have to uproot the kids again.

He knocks again, a little louder this time. She doesn't respond, so he cracks open the door, wondering if she's even in the room. The last time she seemed agitated, she'd taken a walk.

"Natalya?" he calls quietly.

He steps into the room, his vision slowly adjusting. It's dark except for the yellow glow of light that outlines the bathroom door. Great, she's getting ready for bed and he's invading her privacy. Talk about overstaying his welcome. He feels like a cad and goes to leave when his gaze lands on her. She's tucked in a chair in the far corner of the room, legs curled underneath. Moisture glistens on her high cheekbones like a coat of fresh paint.

Now he really feels like an ass. He made her cry. "Natalya?" He moves farther into the room.

She glowers at him and he stops. Wiping away the moisture with the heel of her palm, she unfolds from the chair and goes into the bathroom. Light briefly drenches the bedroom as the door swings open then slams shut. James sighs, defeated. He's not welcome. He starts to leave but a noise has him turning back around. Natalya stands outside the bathroom door, watching him. She dabs the corners of her eyes with a tissue.

"I apologize," he says. "My being here bothers you."

"Here at my house or here in my room?"

The corner of his mouth lifts. "Both?"

She sighs, long and wistful, and her arms fall to her sides. "I can't tell you the number of times I imagined you standing right there. And here you are"—she lifts an arm slightly—"looking at me as if you just met me."

James's heart cracks a little. The urge to soothe her powers him forward. "Natalya."

She holds up a hand, stopping him. "There were so many nights while you were in Mexico and I was here that I fantasized about our making love in *my* bed for once." She closes her eyes. "I desperately want to be with you and you won't even hold my hand."

Her breath hitches and she bites her lower lip. Her eyes well and a tear spills over, followed by another. "I told myself I could do this, that if you came out of the fugue, I could be your friend. I could help you sort things out with the kids and be there for you should you need me. You know what?" She stares vacantly out the window in the direction of the beach. "I used to crush it surfing fifteen-foot waves. That's not an easy feat, but it's a cake walk compared to what happened yesterday."

"What happened yesterday?" he asks uneasily.

She lifts her face and her brilliant green eyes meet his. She drinks him in as though he's completely lost to her. "The hardest thing I've ever done in my life was shake your hand at the airport and act as if we just met when all I wanted to do was run into your arms.

"I haven't seen you since November and it's killing me." She thumps her chest. "Killing me that you haven't kissed or hugged me. You used to hug me as though you were afraid to let me go. God . . ." She sucks in a ragged breath. "I want you to touch me. I just want you to hold me." Her voice breaks on the last word.

James desperately wants to hold her, too. She's destroying him. But he isn't the person she truly wants. He isn't her Carlos. He cares about her, but he doesn't love her, not the way Carlos did, or the way she expects him to. He isn't sure he can love like that again.

"I'm sorry, Natalya. I'm so, so sorry I'm not the man you want me to be."

As the words leave him he feels as if he's apologizing for so much more. For demanding Aimee bury Phil's assault. For not listening to Thomas when he told James to back off on Phil's case. For chasing Phil to Mexico without asking for anyone's help. For uprooting his sons from their birth country. And for not remembering how much he once loved Natalya.

Overwhelmed by his own emotions—anger, despair, grief, and shame—he lets his gaze slide to the room's door out to the lanai. God, he's an asshole for coming to her room, but at this moment, he needs to get out. Run, bellow, rage, or even punch something. "I should leave." He shouldn't have tried to fix what was wrong with them because he royally sucks at repairing relationships.

"I love you, James," she says when he grips the doorknob. "I loved you as Carlos and I love the man you are now."

His arm shakes, rattling the knob. He lets go and turns to look at her. She stands alone in the middle of the room, her face tear-streaked, hands twisting a ratty tissue. "You're a brilliant human being and a wonderful father. I knew you would be."

Go to her!

A voice shouts in his head, and for a split second of insanity he wonders if it's Carlos.

She gives him a sad smile, and it's as though everything settles into place. Carlos gave him the gift of his memories in the form of the written word. *I am you,* he'd written.

That's when it hits him. James *is* her Carlos.

He crosses the room in three long strides and grabs her up in his arms. She cries out, tensing at the quick, unexpected contact. Then her hands latch around him and he feels her melt. He tucks his head into the crook of her neck, curving his body around hers as though he's her shelter, and groans against her skin, a cry of anguish. It's been far too long since he's held anyone, or that anyone has wanted to hold him.

His hands glide up her back and he realizes that she's shaking. They both are. Large, hoarse sobs rack her body as her fingers dig in his hair and he just holds her. He drags his mouth over her shoulder, her neck, and then the shell of her ear. That feeling of having a woman who loves him touch him, hold and caress him, rocks him to his core. His own eyes well.

Natalya presses her lips to his shoulder. He feels the heat of her breath through his shirt, then the nip of her teeth against the skin exposed above the neckline. The sensation ripples across his corded muscles, and he groans. He roughly breathes her in—her distinct, warm scent and the salty, musky aroma of her arousal—and he suddenly wants nothing more than to have her. He *needs* her.

Her lips move over him. She murmurs his name—*James*—and God help him, his heart beats faster and his blood runs south. She tugs his shirt, and heat bursts through his body. Every part of him ignites, like a dry forest after years of drought.

"I want you. I want you so badly." She tugs his shirt again.

"I know, baby." But he keeps his shirt on.

"Kiss me," she breathes against his mouth. And he does. He allows himself that one thing. It's almost his undoing.

Every passage in the journal describing what it feels like kissing Natalya pales in comparison to actually kissing her. He wants her with the desperation of a man who's been lonely for years and the longing of a man who's lost so much.

But he had started his relationship with Aimee based on lies and half-truths. He kept secrets guarded for years, and in the end, he had destroyed them. As ashamed as he is of his family, as well as his own behavior, he won't make the same mistakes. Whatever this is with Natalya, whatever it has the chance to become, must start right. She needs to know who he is, not what she learned of him through Carlos. And she needs to know what he's done.

He cups her face and slows their kiss. Natalya whimpers, and when he lifts his head, she blinks up at him, confused. Her lips are wet and swollen, and it takes all his willpower not to dive back in.

"What's wrong?" Her eyes search his. Apparently she finds an answer, and her face falls. "You don't want me."

"No, that's not it at all. I do want you. Can't you feel how much I want to be with you?" The corner of his mouth lifts as he pulls her hips tighter against him.

Her eyes shift left and right, looking into each one of his. "Then why won't you . . ." She stops as it dawns on her. Her shoulders drop, and she seems to shrink an inch or two. She lifts a shaking hand to his chest and rubs a pinch of his shirt between her fingertips. "It's too soon for you." She smooths her hand along his shirt.

He clutches her hand to his chest. "I can't believe I'm saying this, and my body is raging at me for stopping, but, yes, I need more time."

"O . . . kay," she murmurs. Her gaze casts downward. Rejection mars the passion that had put a blush on her cheeks mere seconds ago.

He pulls her against him and cradles her head. His fingers dive into her glorious hair. "I'm not saying no, Natalya. I just need to figure things out. Just give me a little bit more time to catch up on us."

∽

Present Day
June 29

James slowly wakes with the previous night on his mind. He's slept with three women in his lifetime and can only recall one. Aimee. As for Raquel, he doesn't know too much about her, which pains him because she's the mother of his sons. The journal entries at that time hadn't been as detailed as those that came after Carlos learned about his original identity. What James does know is that he once loved her immensely, their mutual affection immediate and intense.

His thoughts move to that woman's half sister. Natalya. They spent the better part of the night on the lanai, drinking beers and talking. She told him about her fears. As much as she wanted to marry Carlos and be a mother to Julian and Marcus, she'd been afraid to commit, terrified he'd see her as another burden, or an obstacle that kept him from returning home when he surfaced from the fugue. He'd divorce her for Aimee. Because that's the woman James loves.

When Natalya asked, he told her he had seen Aimee. Just last week and not fighting for her had been one of the most difficult decisions he's made. But it was the right one. She had moved on and was in love with and married to another man. He then shared the parts of his past he'd kept from Aimee. His family's shame when their community and church on the mainland's East Coast shunned them because his mother loved her biological brother and had a child. It was why his family relocated to California. They wanted to start fresh where the family's scandal and his father's humiliation remained hidden. He explained how it had been beaten into him and Thomas to never acknowledge Phil as a brother in public.

It was after three a.m. when Natalya fell asleep on the lounge chair. James carried her to bed, and when he turned to leave, she grasped his hand. "Please stay."

He did, stretching out on the bed as she curled into his side. With his arm around her and her hand resting over his heart, they fell asleep. It's where they lie now. It can't be later than six in the morning, which leaves him wondering why he's awake. He slowly opens his eyes in search of a clock when what feels like a foot jabs him in his side.

He grunts and his eyes shoot wide open. The room is a dusky yellow gray. His internal clock tells him it's not even close to six, more like five thirty. Under the sheets, his hand searches for the culprit that jolted him awake and latches onto a small foot. He yanks up the sheet and peers underneath. Marc is sprawled on his back between him and Natalya, mouth wide open and face relaxed. He's sound asleep.

The sheet flutters down and he flops his head back on the pillow. His gaze finds Natalya's across the bed. She's curled on her side, folded hands tucked under her face, watching him. She shyly smiles and whispers, "Good morning."

He rolls to his side, careful not to disturb Marc. "Morning." Worried he said too much last night or that what he said—how he treated Phil when they were kids and how he handled Aimee's assault but still carries around her engagement ring—might have Natalya looking at him differently this morning now that she's had time to digest their conversation, he offers her a cautious half smile. "I didn't mean to keep you up so late."

"That's all right. Thank you for talking."

"Thank you for listening." He smiles and she smiles back. He can't recall the last time he's woken up with his conscience feeling clear. He realizes being up front with Natalya has a lot to do with that and he wonders if that's how their relationship has always been, open and honest. No secrets. "Is it always like this with us?"

The tan skin between her brows folds and she blinks a few times. "No," she whispers with a slight hesitation as though she's chewing on her response. "Usually, when we were together, we're frantic, as if we couldn't get enough of each other in the time we had together. I visited a lot for weeks at a time, so it's not like we didn't see each other. It was more like you knew your time as Carlos would end. Despite that, it was still good between us. Like crazy good." She plucks the edge of the pillowcase. "I love being with you in that way."

He holds her gaze for a long moment, then grins broadly. "Thank you. But that wasn't what I was asking."

Her face turns crimson. "No?"

James sweeps a hand over them lying there in bed. "Is it always like this? Is there always a kid crawling into bed? I don't remember reading about that," he teases, lifting the sheet to show a sleeping Marc underneath. He couldn't resist. Her reaction was adorable and her cheeks turned the prettiest shade of rose.

Natalya buries her face in the pillow and groans. "I'm so embarrassed."

He chuckles and nudges her shoulder. "In all honesty, I suspected it used to be pretty awesome between us. Don't forget, I kept a very detailed journal."

"I know." Natalya groans the word, her face still smashed in the pillow.

"I guess that's why my wanting to talk last night took you off guard."

"Yes."

He can't help goading her further. "We spent more time screwing than sleeping, didn't we?" He also guessed she was used to spending their nights together naked under the sheets, not fully clothed, and having deep conversations that lasted for hours.

The back of her head bobs up and down. She mumbles something he can't make out, but it sounds as if she said he wasn't a good sleeper. That made sense, because Carlos often had nightmares and, at one point, excruciating headaches.

"Look at me."

"Uh-uh."

"Nat." The nickname rolls unhindered off his tongue. He prods her shoulder.

She rolls to her side and he props up on his elbow to look down at her. He cups the back of her head and his thumb traces the hairline along her temple. "Seriously, though, is it peaceful like this in the morning? We've slept for less than three hours, but I feel more rested than I have in months. *Years*," he adds with a smirk.

"Like I said, you didn't sleep well, so, no, it wasn't like this. But I do like this." She motions between them. "Do you?"

"Yes, very much." His thumb drops to her lips and so does his gaze. He thinks about kissing her when they both get a strong reminder they aren't the only people in bed. Marc shifts under the sheet and his elbow connects with Natalya's breast.

Her eyes grow saucer round. "Ow." She rubs the tender spot.

"Roll this way, kiddo." James drags Marc closer to him. "What time did he crawl in here?"

"Four thirty, I think." She yawns. "I'm going to need a nap today."

"I'll take one with you," James says, yawning. Then it occurs to him there's more than one way to interpret what he said. He gives her an embarrassed smile. "I meant that I need a nap, too."

She laughs softly. "I got that. You're welcome to sleep here with me."

They watch each other as the room lightens and the birds announce the day. Their hands meet over Marc's sleeping form. "Thank you," he says.

"For what?"

"For not giving up on me, and for convincing me not to give them up."

"Your sons?"

He nods. "In Mexico."

"I knew you'd love them."

"Unconditionally."

James leans down to kiss her. A shrill noise shatters the moment. He tenses. Marc groans under the sheets.

"Sorry," Natalya says, rolling away. "I'm expecting a call from the mainland."

She frowns at the screen and answers the call with a question. Her gaze cuts to James before she hands over the phone. "It's for you. It's Thomas."

CHAPTER 28

CARLOS

Seven Months Ago
November 27
Puerto Escondido, Mexico

Señora Carla seemed unusually bothered by the dry, damp heat. She was especially weary of the crowds. Last summer, Julian had convinced her to visit during *Fiestas de Noviembre*, so Carla moved up her usual holiday stay in Puerto Escondido by several weeks.

The *torneo de surf* was this weekend. Tourists packed the beaches, streets, and restaurants. Hoping to give her some reprieve from the tournament's noise, traffic, and the day's weather, I invited her to the gallery. Upstairs, after cleaning up from a workshop, we decided to spend the remainder of the afternoon painting. Unfortunately, my air conditioner was dying and the ceiling fans only moved stagnant, warm air.

Carla stared beyond the blank canvas, her eyes glazed and skin flushed. She fanned her blouse, a bright flamingo-colored linen, and patted her damp hairline and neck with a folded hand towel. She sighed, exasperated, and set aside her still-clean paintbrush before going to the bank of windows. For a few moments, she watched people mill below; then she opened a window. Air heady with the smell of sunbaked fish, rotting fruit, and sweat gusted into the studio, sucked in by the overworked air conditioner. Loud shouts, high-pitched laughter, acoustical music, and the rev of a motorcycle disrupted the studio's solitude.

Carla's face contorted into a look of disgust. She slammed closed the window. "Do you like living here, Carlos?"

"*Sí.*" I swirled a brush tip in the ultramarine blue and stroked the color across the canvas. The small fishing boat surfing on a sea of blue was slowly coming to life.

She studied me from across the room as though considering me to model for her next painting. I arched a brow. She fanned her face with the towel. "Why do you live here? This place is dreadful."

"Dreadful?" I said on a laugh.

"Have you always lived here?"

I opened my mouth to tell her no and hesitated. The brush, heavy with paint, hovered a mere inch above the canvas. My hand started shaking so I set the brush down.

Carla waited for me to say something. Other than Natalya, Imelda, and Thomas, no one else in Puerto Escondido knew about my past and the condition I suffered. Not even my sons. Thomas had warned me to not reveal my identity to anyone. For reasons I couldn't explain—maybe it was because Carla had once been open with me about her relationship with her art—I wanted to share my story with her.

"Can I trust you?"

"What kind of question is that? Yes, you can. I'm your—" She stopped and motioned at herself. "I'm your friend."

I looked at her for a long moment, considering, then nodded. "You are my friend, and I'm grateful for your companionship," I said, then admitted, "I have lived elsewhere before. California, to be exact."

A small gasp reached me. Carla's fingers fluttered to the neckline of her blouse, fussing with the pearl-size button.

"I had an accident and can't remember anything about living there or the people I knew. I can't recall anything about myself. My real name is James." I gave her the highlights of my condition.

The flush discoloring her neck and chest faded into a chalky white. She weaved slightly on her feet. I grabbed a stool and reached her in three paces. She settled on the seat and clutched my forearms. "Why wouldn't you return to California? You don't belong here."

"James doesn't, but I do. So do my sons." I gently removed her hands, feeling overheated myself. Sweat dripped down my spine, plastering my shirt to damp skin. I strode to the far wall and adjusted the thermostat. "This is our home," I said, arms out to encompass the room and the greater town around us as I walked back over to her.

"What about your family in California? Don't you miss them? Surely you must miss your mother." She whispered the last word.

"It's hard to miss someone I don't remember."

Her mouth slightly parted before she averted her face. She stared out the window.

"As for my brothers," I continued, pulling up a stool beside her, "I don't trust them. I'm not sure I trust James."

She turned back to me. "How can you trust anyone at all if you can't trust yourself?"

"Because I don't know the man I'm supposed to be."

"I'm sure your mother misses you desperately and would want you to come home."

"I'm not sure she knows I'm still alive. If she does, where is she?"

"You don't want to go find out?"

"No," I said too sharply. Every new thing I learned about my past moved me one step closer to reverting to my original identity. That was something I would never be ready to do.

I returned to my canvas and dropped dirty brushes into turpentine and tightened caps on paint tubes. White-hot pain shot across my forehead. I groaned. Squeezing my eyes shut, I dug my thumb and forefinger into the corners of my eyes.

I heard the scrape of a chair and the rustle of clothing.

"Your headaches are because of your fugue," Carla said beside me.

I dropped my hand and looked at her. "I think so," I said, even though I didn't have a doctor's confirmation. Perhaps the headaches were residual from Thomas's hypnosis session.

She frowned. "They're getting worse."

"They were manageable for a while, but lately, yes. They've been worse, more frequent, and . . ." My voice trailed off. I grabbed a brush and drummed the handle on the table.

"And what?" she encouraged.

"I have to tell Julian about me."

"Why would you ever do that?"

"He needs to know what to do when I forget he's my son, and what will happen if I don't want to be his father."

Carla turned two shades paler. Her mouth worked, trying to form words.

"Natalya will adopt Julian and Marcus," I said, anticipating her question. "They'll go live with her."

"In Hawaii?"

I nodded.

A veneer slid over her face, making it impossible to read her reaction. Her gaze jumped around the studio and landed on her purse. She went to pick it up. "If you'll excuse me, I'm going to the house to rest."

I watched her walk toward the exit. "Carla?"

Her long, bony fingers gripped the doorknob and she angled her chin in my direction.

"Is something wrong? Have I somehow upset you?"

She looked down her nose at me. Gone was the woman my family befriended and my sons looked up to like a grandmother. In her place was the woman we'd first met on the beach five years ago.

"I'm perfectly fine. It's just entirely too hot and uncomfortable in this studio." She left, the door softly closing behind her.

CHAPTER 29

JAMES

Present Day
June 29
Hanalei, Kauai, Hawaii and San Jose, California

Short on time, James packs frantically. Natalya comes into the room with two steaming mugs of coffee as he comes out of the bathroom. He tosses his toiletries case into the packed suitcase on the bed.

"What time's your flight?"

"Eight forty-five." He has two hours.

"Oh! We've got to hurry." She sets down the mugs. "It'll take at least forty-five minutes to get to the airport."

"I've called a cab."

"Are you sure?"

The hesitation in her tone has James glancing up from where he's zipping closed the roller. Natalya rubs her hands. Her gaze flutters from him to the suitcase. She chews her lower lip and he slowly straightens.

"I'm coming back," he says quietly.

"I know, it's just . . ." She looks away and traces one of the mug's rims where the coffee sits on the desk.

"It's just what?"

"Is it shameful for me to admit I'm scared?"

He could write the book on shame. "No." Because he was scared himself. "Trust me, I am coming back. My sons mean too much to me. You . . . I want to see you again. A lot."

"I want to see you, too, but that's not what has me worried. How much did Carlos put in the journal about my conversation with Dr. Feinstein?"

"Enough, I assume. The passage was fairly extensive. I've also talked and met with a few medical experts myself."

"Then you know your fugue can recur."

Their eyes meet across the room. "Yes."

Although rare, there have been documented cases where a person can have not just one repeat episode, but multiple. Once again, he'll be left with a blank slate in his head while those around him are left with nothing but heartache and memories of the man he used to be. It's why one of the psychologists who evaluated James recommended therapy. There's likely more at war in his head than solely the fear Carlos felt in his nightmares when Phil threatened to go after Aimee. That imagery could be symbolic of a greater issue from his past, possibly from his childhood, his mind had buried.

And here he is, running straight to the man both he and Thomas believe was the trigger that tossed James into the fugue state. They also believe Phil tried to murder James. Phil has yet to admit that, and fortunately for him, James can't remember most of it.

In less than twenty-four hours of his release, Phil showed up at Donato Enterprises this morning. He was there when Thomas arrived at the office. Thomas first thought Phil was looking for employment. Instead, he was looking for James, and seemed very determined to find him. He wouldn't tell Thomas why, and when Thomas proposed the three of them meet for dinner this evening, Phil wasn't keen on the idea.

His business is with James and James alone. Which is why James needs to get to California before Phil comes to them.

Natalya blinks rapidly. She averts her face. He feels her despair as though it's his own, right smack-dab in the middle of his chest. An imaginary fist that squeezes his pulsing heart. He crosses the room and embraces her.

"I will come back," he whispers into her hair.

"I'm not afraid you won't come back. I'm afraid you won't remember to come back."

That fist drops his heart into his stomach. "Should something happen to me when I see my brothers—"

Natalya shakes her head. "Don't say that. I have to believe nothing's going to happen to you."

He leans back to look down at her. She blinks away her tears. "Nat, honey, the last time I thought that about Phil, I lost six and a half years. The last time I thought that about Thomas, he hypnotized me without my consent." He needs to be realistic about his situation. He needs to prepare, mentally and emotionally. So does Natalya. "My sons, Nat . . . I need you to keep them safe for me. And if I don't come back . . ."

"You will. You'll find your way. I have to believe that. Remember Stitch. You're my *ohana.*"

Family.

Where no one is left behind or forgotten.

His mouth twitches. "You're quoting Disney movies again."

Despite the tears, Natalya cracks a smile. "I'll keep your sons safe."

"You're leaving us?"

James and Natalya jerk apart. Julian stands rigid in the doorway. How much did he hear? Enough, judging by the stew of emotions contorting his face: disbelief, anger, and rejection.

Betrayal.

His hands are fists at his side. His gaze cuts from Natalya to the suitcase on the bed and up to James. "I knew you'd leave us. I hate you.

I want my old dad back." He takes off. James hears the door slam to the rear yard.

A horn blares in the driveway. The cab is here. James shoves both hands through his shower-damp hair. He eyes the suitcase then starts to go after Julian.

"James." Natalya blocks his way. "You'll miss your flight. I'll go talk with him and explain why you're leaving. I'll tell him you're coming back."

"He won't believe you." He yanks the suitcase off the bed and sets it upright on the floor. "He won't believe I'm coming back until I do come back."

"Then make sure you do." She hands him a sealed envelope.

"What's this?"

"A letter for you. From you."

His skin tightens behind his neck. "*From* me?"

"You made me promise to give it to you should you find your way back to me."

"You haven't read it?"

"No, but you told me about it once. Since we both know there's the slightest possibility you can forget again, maybe the letter will help you find your way back to us. Now go. Your cab is waiting."

James touches her cheek, traces her jawline, then lets his arm fall. He leaves the room, leaving Natalya and his sons, and possibly his memories, behind.

❧

James calls Julian upon landing in San Jose. The call goes to voice mail so he hangs up and sends a text: Call me.

He also sends one to Natalya. She immediately replies. James watches the three dots blink below his text as he exits the plane. He could kiss his phone when it comes through.

We're at the St. Regis, swimming and having lunch with Dad and Claire.

How are the kids? he responds.

Marcus is great. Having fun chasing Dad in the pool. Julian isn't talking to anyone, but he is here.

She attaches a photo of Julian on a lounge chair, headphones on, face in his phone's screen. Which means Julian has seen his text. James checks. Sure enough, the message shows it's been read.

Another text comes through.

I forgot to tell you I love you. I love you.

James stares at the message. Aimee regularly texted those words and he always replied in kind because he loved her beyond anything or anyone else in his life. She'd been his one and only. He cares for Natalya, but he still carries around Aimee's engagement ring, for God's sake.

With that thought, he feels the ring burn in his pocket, as though the platinum is molten hot, reminding him it's still there. Aside from showering, running, and swimming, it hasn't left his person in more than six months. He even had it on him when he spent last night with Natalya. What kind of man does that?

One who isn't ready to forget his past, that's for sure.

His thumbs hover over the keyboard and he finally texts back a message before sliding the phone into his pocket.

I'll call you tonight.

James hires a cab. He doesn't want to return to his parents' house, but he has a couple of hours to kill before meeting Thomas and Phil at the restaurant. He lets himself into the stale house through the front door. He drops his suitcase and carry-on in the entryway and heads toward the kitchen for a glass of water.

He walks through the main room and movement in the corner of his eye snags his attention. "Jesus Christ." James's heart rockets into his throat.

Thomas lounges on the leather sofa swirling a lowball of whiskey on ice. James doesn't have to smell it to know it's Johnny Walker.

"I found an unopened bottle in the library. I think it's leftover from Dad."

Then it had been there for some time because their father died more than seven years ago.

"What the hell are you doing here?" *And how did you get in?* James had changed the damned locks.

Thomas takes a leisurely sip. "Have you remembered anything about that day in Mexico?"

Seriously? That's what this is about? "Some."

"Does it help me?"

"I doubt it."

Thomas blows through his lips. "That's unfortunate."

James moves into the room, growing more uneasy by the second. "Fernando Ruiz is behind bars. My life is no longer in danger from his cartel, if it ever was. There isn't anything further I can add to the DEA's case because that case has been resolved. What difference does it make whether I remember or not?"

His chest expands on a deep inhale; then he speaks slowly, punctuating each word, his voice rising with each sentence. "I want to know what happened on that damn boat and the role Phil played. Because I want Phil's ass back in prison. I want Mom to cut him off. I want him fucking out of our lives."

A chill moves up James's spine. "Where's Phil?"

Thomas peers into his glass. He tilts it back and forth.

"Thomas. Where is Phil?"

James's phone rings. He looks at the screen. Julian's face flashes. His gaze snags in Thomas's the same moment he answers the phone. The same moment Thomas says, "Kauai." And at the same moment Phil greets him on the other end of the line.

"Jimbo, long time no chat."

~

Present Day
June 30

God, we crossed paths midair.

James paces the back deck. He wants to hurl, he's so disgusted with himself. The fear, it's eating him alive. He hasn't changed, as though six-plus years in a fugue state hadn't taught him enough of a lesson. Once again, he got on a plane and chased Phil halfway across the globe, leaving his loved ones thousands of miles behind, unprotected.

After several phone calls that went straight to voice mail and even more unanswered texts, he finally gets in touch with Natalya. She's home with the boys, thank God, not at the St. Regis where his Find My Phone app displays the location of Julian's mobile.

"How did Phil get his phone?"

Through the phone, James hears her call for Julian. She gets back on some seconds later. "He says he left it in Claire's room on accident. Your mother took him and Marcus up there to shower and change. We ate a late lunch at the hotel's restaurant."

But they're home now. Thank God.

"Do you want me to go back and get it?"

"No," he exclaimed, his heart racing. "Definitely not. Don't go there tomorrow either. Come to think of it, lock your doors and windows. Promise you'll stay there until you hear from me. Don't let my mother come over either. Tell her you and the boys are busy all day. I don't want her bringing Phil with her."

"Why is he here, anyway? What does he want with you?"

"I don't know." James grips the back of his neck. "He's been pretty determined to have a face-to-face since he learned I was still alive."

"This doesn't make sense. Why doesn't he just call you? And how *did* he find out about you? You told me Thomas never told him. He didn't want anyone to know so he could keep you safe in Mexico."

"That's what Thomas told me."

"Do you believe him?"

It takes only one second for James to consider his answer. "Absolutely not."

"Could your mother have told him?"

"She's basically disowned him. They aren't on speaking terms, as far as I know."

"Well, they are now," Natalya says, stating the obvious.

James sighs. "The only thing I can think of that he possibly wants is vengeance. Like me, he's angry. We've both lost years because I was the idiot who walked into that bar after he warned me away."

"You never would have been at that bar if Phil hadn't abused his position at Donato. You never would have flown to Mexico if he hadn't attacked Aimee. Yes, you were angry, but Phil's the one at fault, not you."

"I won't have Phil hurting anyone that's important to me. Not again. Just promise me you'll stay home until you hear from me."

"James, a man who just got out of prison and never expected to be there to begin with isn't going to do anything that lands him back inside. And any man hung up on wanting any sort of revenge with his brothers isn't going to run back to his momma, who happens to love those brothers you think he hates so much."

Thomas joins him on the deck.

"I've got to go. Please promise you'll stay home."

"I promise. Be careful, James. I love you."

He knows she wants to hear the words, but he can't give them to her, not yet. "I'll see you tomorrow."

"I've booked us on a nonstop to Kauai first thing in the morning," Thomas says as James ends his call. "We land at ten and should be at the St. Regis by eleven, eleven thirty at the latest."

James taps the corner of the phone on the wood railing. He runs through his conversation with Natalya. Her questions have echoed his own. Thomas had him convinced Phil despised his brothers so much he would come after James once he learned James was still alive. Thomas was adamant Phil had tried to kill James. But Phil had failed, and should James remember, it gave Thomas the evidence he needed to send Phil back to prison. It also put James at risk.

But if Phil wanted to "silence" him, why go through the trouble of arranging a meet-and-greet? Why not show up at his door?

"What's going on, Thomas? What does he want?"

"The answer to that question is tucked inside that brain of yours. But if you ask me, Phil's going to do whatever he can to keep from going back to prison, even if it means threatening you and your family to keep you quiet. Come on, let's get some sleep. We'll deal with him tomorrow. Nothing we can do about it now."

James watches Thomas go into the house. He isn't sure he agrees with him, about the threats or attempted murder. Call it instinct, but there was something Natalya said. *What type of man runs back to his mother?*

Definitely not one bent on revenge.

$\sim$

James swayed back and forth. The world around him rocked and the air smelled of saltwater, rotten fish, and dried blood. His nose throbbed and his eyes hurt too much to open them.

A voice harshly whispered in his ear. "James. Wake up."

Someone shook his shoulder. He groaned. A motor revved louder. It vibrated his bones. Water sloshed back and forth. His hair was wet and clothes damp.

"We're almost there," came the disembodied voice again. "Wake up. You need to be ready. They're going to make me kill you. You've got to jump when I tell you and you better swim like your goddamn life depends on it. Come on, James. Wake . . . the fuck . . . up." Another nudge to his shoulder. "Think of Aimee. Think of me on top of her."

James groaned. Deep inside his mind he bellowed. Fury pumped through his bloodstream.

"That's it. Now wake up, get up, and get mad. It's the only way you'll survive."

"Tell him to get up," came a different voice, raspier.

"I'm working on it, Sal."

Phil.

"Get up." A booted foot nudged his side. That was Sal, one of the cartel's lieutenants who had been at the bar.

James grunted. He pulled his eyes open and tried to haul himself up with a coil of rope. Pain shot through his arm and he collapsed to his knees. Hands latched onto him and yanked him upright. He stumbled and grabbed the side of the boat. The boat bobbed up and down. His stomach did the hammock-sway, side to side. He took several deep breaths to keep from vomiting then looked up, straight into the barrel of a gun held by his oldest brother.

"Fuck you," James spat.

"Nah, little bro. That's what I'm going to do to your fiancée."

Sal glanced at his watch. "We're late. Shoot him and let's go."

James's heart lurched into his throat. The gun shook. His gaze tracked up the arm holding the weapon and locked onto the brother who should never have been a brother. Something flickered in Phil's eyes. A fleeting emotion twisted his face. The instant James recognized it as regret, Phil's mouth moved, making out one word. *Swim.*

"For Christ's sake." Sal made a grab for the gun. It fired.

James didn't think twice. He fell backward, over the side and into the deep blue water. Bullets flew past, leaving long, angry trails in the water. One sliced into his hip and he jerked. It stung worse than the smack of his father's leather belt.

He felt it again and again, then the tight grip of a hand in his hair that wrenched his neck backward. Instead of Phil's face contorted with remorse, he now stared at the blotchy, sweaty face of his father, Edgar Donato. A man who loved his wife despite the humiliation and shame she brought upon the family. He never left her either because he loved his position at Donato Enterprises and the legacy it would provide his sons more.

"What did you tell her?" he shouted into James's face.

He was talking about Aimee, the girl he'd met that afternoon. His mouth was still swollen and sore from the one punch he let that kid Robbie get away with. But now, bent over his father's desk with his pants around his ankles, his lower back made his mouth feel like a scratch.

"I didn't tell her anything, I swear."

"I don't believe you." *Smack.* "I don't raise liars and I can tell you're lying to me." *Smack.*

The belt's impact shot up his spine, vibrated his teeth.

He couldn't take anymore. His back was on fire and he'd lost count of the strikes. He wondered if there'd be more than welts this time. He swore he could smell blood.

The belt connected with his raw flesh and he sobbed. "*Ow!* Stop. All—all . . . right." He choked out the scream. He'd tell his father anything if it meant getting him to stop. "She asked how many brothers I had. I showed her two fingers. I didn't mean to. It was an accident. I only told her I had one. Honest, sir. I just told her one."

His father pulled back his arm, the leather belt swinging from his hand. James squeezed his eyes shut and braced himself. He wondered if someone could pass out from the pain. God knew he couldn't take much more. He heard the whir of the leather before he felt it. The impact sent him to his knees.

"Stop! Stop hurting him."

James looked up from his curled, half-naked position on the floor. Phil stood over him as he faced Edgar.

"We *are* brothers, whether you like it or not. We will *always* be brothers. But I'm the one you hate. Beat me."

James's father tossed aside the belt. "You disgust me. Get out of my sight. Both of you."

Phil leaned over to help him up and James pushed away his hand. He should be thanking him, but all he felt was humiliation. He stood on his own and pulled up his pants. God, he wished he'd never walked in on his mom and Uncle Grant. He hated them and he hated Phil. Phil was the reason his father punished him and Thomas. Why did he have to go and dig up his birth certificate to find the proof? Phil was the reason they were in California. Phil was the reason his father beat him. Everything was Phil's fault.

"You're *not* my brother," he said to Phil. "Stay away from me."

Just stay away.

"Wake up, sir."

Stay away.

"Wake up!"

James jolts awake. He blinks and looks up into the face of a woman he's never seen before. He doesn't recognize her or anything around him.

"Who are you?" he asks, panting.

She frowns.

"Where am I?"

CHAPTER 30

CARLOS

Seven Months Ago
November 29
Puerto Escondido, Mexico

How can you trust anyone if you can't trust yourself?

Carla's question had been haunting me for two days.

When I first learned the truth about my condition, there was no doubt in my mind I'd always be Carlos. I'd already been in a fugue state for nineteen months when Aimee appeared. Truth was, I'd been in denial. The enormity of my situation hadn't sunk in.

Days and months passed, and so did that belief, disappearing like mist over the ocean with the rising sun. With the headaches, the blackout, and Natalya's discussion with Dr. Feinstein, it became apparent that my mind was in the process of healing. The question was no longer *if* I surfaced from the fugue state, but when, and how, and where.

This unknown scared me.

I trusted Natalya to care for my sons. She'd keep them safe and raise them far away from the Donato family should, God forbid, James—rather, *I*—not want the responsibility.

I trusted Julian to watch over his brother. And I trusted him in that rebellious, preteen way of his, to not only help guide me back to fatherhood but make me want to be a father. It was an enormous responsibility, but Julian had a strong spirit. He'd also have his aunt's help.

Since the day I woke in the medical clinic more than six years ago, I'd had little faith in anything, except my art, or anyone, except my sons and Natalya.

You're the same man, Natalya had told me time and time again. *Same body, same heart . . . same soul.*

My headaches didn't respond to the medication like they used to. As Carla observed, they'd grown in frequency and intensity. So had my nightmares. They kept my stomach in knots and my heart palpitating long into the night.

It was time for me to take a gamble. It was time to put a little faith in myself. It was also time to trust that the man I was supposed to be would do the right thing.

I opened the metal lockbox I'd purchased online. Inside, I put my wedding certificate, Raquel's death certificate, and the boys' birth certificates. I added CDs of medical films and reports, keys, passwords to my laptop, computers at the gallery, and Cloud accounts, and a few thumb drives containing other important documents, as well as my journal entries up to that point. I included anything I could think of that would help me understand who I was, how I arrived in Mexico, how I lived, and who I loved. The latter of those items being summed up with one of my favorite photos, Natalya arm in arm with the boys, Playa Zicatela as the backdrop.

Finally, I wrote a letter and addressed it to James. I placed the unsealed envelope on top with Aimee's engagement ring. Then, with a heavy heart and a prayer to the all-knowing, I closed the lid, set the code—Julian's birth date—and went in search of my eldest son.

I had to tell him a story. I had to advise him of what to do when I forgot that I'm his father. And I had to teach him how to teach me to be a father again.

∽

Natalya was waiting for me out back. Facing the ocean, she sat on the half wall, her chin upturned toward the night sky. Stars glittered in the inky canvas, extra bright with the new moon. The breeze coming off the water lifted her hair, a wild mane I wanted to get lost in. I drank in the sight of her, absorbed every curve so that I'd remember the details later when I wrote about the day. She still wore her bikini after an afternoon under the Mexican sun. The turquoise strings peeked from under the white linen cover-up, twisting around her neck like a lover's embrace.

I thought about our future, wondering how many more times I'd gaze upon her with *my* eyes. Would I see her again? She was flying home tomorrow to wrap up year-end projects before the holidays.

A rush of emotion coaxed me to go to her. Sensing my presence, she turned to me and smiled. Her fingers twined through mine. "How'd it go?"

Wind chased up my back and ruffled her hair. I caught tendrils clinging to her moist lips and tucked them behind her ear, letting my fingers linger along the fine line of her neck. My gaze trailed them as they dipped into the crevice of her collarbone then skimmed over the swell of her breasts.

"He's overwhelmed," I answered. Julian had cried, I'd cried. I'd stayed with him until he fell into a fitful sleep.

"He'll have questions when it all sinks in." She parted her knees and I moved into the space she created.

"I'll answer anything he asks." I lightly kissed her forehead and her fingers pressed into my hips, holding me to her. "I love you, Nat."

"I love you, too, Carlos. I'll always love you, every side of you."

The backs of my eyes burned. My face tightened as I reined in emotions still raw from the long talk with Julian. Holding her hand to my chest, I whispered against her lips—"Same heart"—and kissed her thoroughly. In between those kisses, with our breathing growing heavy, I told her about the items I put in the lockbox.

"I wrote myself two letters. I put one in the box and the other I mailed to you."

"Me?"

"Don't open it. Save it for James."

Her breath snagged and she tensed under my roaming hands. "What does it say?"

I kissed her neck, tasted the salt of her skin, and prayed everything would work out for the two of us and my sons in the end.

"It says," I started, untying her bikini straps, "'Dear James . . .'"

Then I told her what I'd written in the letter as I made love to her for what I hoped wouldn't be the last time.

CHAPTER 31

JAMES

Present Day
June 30
Hanalei, Kauai, Hawaii

Thomas peers around the flight attendant leaning over James. "Nightmare? You were wigging out the other passengers."

The flight attendant rests a hand on his shoulder. "Would you like a cup of coffee?"

James straightens his rumpled shirt and sits up in his seat. "Yeah, that would be great." He barely slept last night and as soon as the plane took off, he crashed.

Thomas shows James his empty Bloody Mary glass. "I'm getting a refill." He walks to the front of the first-class cabin, leaving James to shake off his exhaustion and disorientation.

His hands are shaking, his pulse still pounding. That nightmare was a doozy. He hasn't thought about his father and their meetings with the belt in years. Memories best forgotten, he thinks, searching for his phone in his carry-on. His fingers find the envelope Natalya gave him and he pulls that out instead.

His name is written on the front. Odd that Carlos's handwriting is different from his, but he guesses he should expect that. They have different painting styles. The envelope's edges are worn, as though it had been stored in a drawer with other items bumping into it. Or perhaps Natalya often held it, wondering whether she'd have the opportunity to give it to him.

He tears it open and unfolds the stationery. The emblem printed on top is from El estudio del pintor, the gallery he sold in Puerto Escondido. Neatly penned on the paper is exactly what Natalya told him it would be. A letter *to* him, *from* him. As he reads, his hands continue to shake and his heart goes out to the man who somehow knew that his time was almost up.

Dear James,

When you woke up from the fugue state and realized you lost more than years of memories, I'm sure you were angry at the world and despised your brothers. You longed for Aimee and probably hated me. I'm the guy who refused medical treatment. I didn't want to remember who I used to be, because that meant I'd forget who I am. But I've slowly come to accept that the likelihood I'll come out of the fugue and become you again is definitive. I have also come to understand that there is more than the self-loathing and shame you feel with your failure to protect Aimee from Phil at play here. There is something deeper in your past, for I see it often in my nightmares.

It must be the explanation as to why the fugue has lasted as long as it has.

I urge you to come to terms with past mistakes, to forgive those who have wronged you, and find peace within yourself. You might discover that despite the losses, you've gained so much more: two incredible and talented sons, a woman who has remained at your side for years and loves you beyond anything, and the freedom of expression through your art. Perhaps you have already. And perhaps, you have also already found your way home. After all, you're reading this letter.

C.

James slides the key his mother left him at the front desk into the slot. The lock unlatches and he opens the door to Claire's suite.

Phil lounges on the couch, arms extended across the back. He wears a peach Hawaiian print shirt and white shorts with flip-flops. Always the tall, lean one of the three of them, prison has noticeably changed him. Deep lines etch a face that hasn't regularly seen the sun. He carries more weight around the middle and less hair on his head. What he does have is streaked with a lifeless gray. He sips a yellow, frothy cocktail with a blue paper umbrella and grins when he sees them.

James doesn't know what he expected to feel when he saw Phil. The rage that coursed through him when he'd seen his older brother covering Aimee would have been logical. As would the terror that chilled his veins when Phil put a gun in his face and ordered him to swim as if his life depended on it. Thank God he'd been running marathons since college and had been training for a triathlon. He never would have survived. James would also have understood animosity. It was because of who and what Phil is that he suffered through countless conditioning sessions with his father. Edgar Donato had successfully beaten the bitterness toward Phil into him and Thomas.

But he certainly hadn't anticipated remorse. Phil never asked for his parentage, and he never wanted anything more than to be considered a respected member of the family. He tried on several occasions to slip into the big-brother role and James had scoffed. The less he interacted with Phil, the less chance he'd make the mistake of thinking of him as a brother. It kept his lower back welt-free.

The man Phil is today is the man his family molded him into. All the extra bits—his anger, violence, and maliciousness—is the armor he wore not only to survive in this family but to let them know loud and clear exactly what he thought of them.

"Hola, amigos." Phil toasts his drink at them, then waves a finger at James. "You know exactly what I said. I hear you spent six years in Mexico. I knew you liked it there, but seriously? That's over the top."

"What do you want, Phil?" Thomas demands before James has the chance to.

"What do *I* want?" Phil looks at them both. He takes a slow drink and settles deeper in the couch. "Nothing. With you." His gaze narrows on James.

"Then why did you have us come here?"

"He didn't. I did." Claire walks into the room like the regal matriarch she is.

"Welcome to family therapy, Donato-style," Phil jeers. "It's a grand fucking family reunion."

"Do shut up, Phillip." Claire sits on the couch across from him in a flurry of multicolored silk. She smooths the tunic over her legs. "Dr. Brackman will be here in thirty minutes. He's a family therapist, and comes highly recommended. I flew him in this morning."

"You've got to be fucking kidding me." Thomas yanks off his blazer and tosses it over the back of a chair. His words and tone echo James's sentiments exactly. Thomas rolls up his sleeves as the jacket slides to the floor. He crosses the room to the wet bar.

"Thomas, really, your language." Claire straightens the toss pillows beside her. "Your father passed over seven years ago, God rest his soul, and we haven't sat together as a family since. I was not fond of his position on many things, or his methods. We need to discuss this. It's been forever since we talked."

"Forever is too soon." Thomas pours himself a scotch, downs it, and refills his glass. He raises the bottle and a brow at James.

"No, thanks." James picks up Thomas's blazer. A billfold falls from the pocket. He folds the blazer over the chair and takes the billfold to the window.

"I have some things to say, Thomas, and you're going to listen." Claire's tone is a mother's order. "I never agreed with how your father treated Phil. He's your brother. But I loved your father just as much as I loved your father, Phil. I adored my brother—idolized him, if you must know. He wasn't around much while I was growing up because he went to boarding school, then away to college. When he came home, though, there was a connection. We both felt—"

"God, Mom. Stop!" Thomas slices his hand through the air. "I don't think any of us want to hear that. I sure don't. What I do want to know is where the hell you were when Dad was beating us?"

Behind James, Thomas continues to lob questions and his mother complains. Why can't her sons get along? Why do they keep hurting each other?

Because there's too much history. They were never encouraged to treat each other with respect. In fact, quite the opposite.

James opens the billfold that holds Thomas's DEA identification. Why is he not surprised? His role in exports with Central and South America put him in the perfect position as the government's eyes and ears. Hiding in plain sight, as Thomas once told Carlos.

Outside the window is the crescent of Hanalei Bay. People dot the resort's beach like paint speckles on a white canvas. While he can't see it, he knows toward the far end of the bay is Natalya's house, tucked behind the palms. She's there with his sons, waiting for him.

He wants to be with them more than anything, especially as the tension between his brothers and mother escalates. Their voices rise, each trying to talk over the other. He knows they must accept and move past how they've treated each other. But right now, his sons are his priority. He wants to build a life for them, here in Kauai. He also wants a chance to get to know the woman who remained at his side, even with the knowledge he'd one day forget her. They are his *ohana*.

But his heart is heavy, and he still isn't sure he can return the love Natalya freely gives him. He wonders if he's entitled to another chance with his sons after everything he's put them through. He's made too many mistakes over the years.

He grips the taut muscles in his shoulder and slides his other hand into his pocket. His fingertip snags on Aimee's engagement ring. He holds the diamond solitaire to the light. The platinum band reflects a distorted view of the room behind him. As he watches Thomas argue with Phil and their mother, everything clears.

Had Aimee told him last week she wanted to file charges against Phil, he would have done everything in his power to make sure Phil received the justice he deserved. He'd still do it. Instead, Aimee forgave James for how he'd handled the situation. She's moved on.

How can he do the same? He's made too many decisions he regrets. Despising Phil during their youth when he should have loved him as a brother. Lying to Aimee for too many years. Not trusting Thomas to handle the situation with Phil. And following Phil to Mexico. That's his biggest mistake. One that cost him everything, and one that he can never turn back from.

He isn't sure he can accept these mistakes, which make him think of the letter from Carlos. The words run through his mind and in between the lines he finds the answer. While he does need to forgive those who have wronged him to move on, he needs to forgive himself above anything else.

"He practically bankrupted Donato and tried to murder James," Thomas bellows at their mother. "You expect me to carry on as though nothing happened?"

"What's done is done. We've lost too much of ourselves already," Claire pleads.

"I saved James," Phil defends.

"That's bullshit!"

"He's right."

Three sets of eyes turn to James. Phil grins. Thomas's jaw comes unhinged. "You remember."

"I've been remembering bits and pieces for a while now. But, yes. I remember." James fists the ring. "I'm alive today because Phil warned me to swim and when to jump. There was another guy on the boat. He's the one that shot me."

Disappointment twists Thomas's face. He stares at the white shag carpet, hands on hips. "Are you absolutely sure it wasn't Phil?" he asks after a long moment. "What about the back room at the bar? Did you hear or see anything?"

"I didn't see a thing, and I didn't hear anything about Fernando Ruiz or the Hidalgo cartel that would have helped your case, if that's what you're asking. They put a sack over my head and made me into their punching bag as they asked questions about the DEA's investigation, of which I didn't know much. I wasn't of importance to them. That's why they dumped me."

Thomas's shoulders sag and his face contorts into a masterpiece of regret. He'd never had to keep James hidden.

"Actually, I did witness something of importance."

Thomas lifts his face, his expression expectant, eager almost.

James looks at Phil. "At the risk of his own life, my big brother saved mine. Why, Phil? Why didn't you shoot me?"

Phil swipes a tongue across his lips. His eyes shift to their mother and back to James. "I couldn't do it. You're my brother." He looks at both Thomas and James, then holds his mother's gaze. "Ever since I learned you're my mother, I just wanted to be your son." Claire softly gasps and Phil turns to Thomas. "As for what I did to Donato Enterprises, I never meant for anyone to get killed. I only wanted you to feel the same loss I did when I didn't inherit my father's company. And James, I swear," he says, looking back at him, "I'll make it up to you someday. I'll even apologize to Aimee." He sets down his drink with a shaking hand, the first sign of vulnerability James has seen him exhibit since he discovered his parents in the woodshed.

Phil fists his hand and a mask falls back over his face. He extends his arms with a flourish and takes a dramatic bow. "That, ladies and gentlemen, is what I call relationship progress. Mom, your therapist will be proud." He meets James's gaze, his own sincere. "Thanks for remembering."

James crosses the room and gives Thomas the billfold. Their gazes meet and a general understanding passes between them. Thomas's secret is safe with him. Where James grew up wanting to be an artist, Thomas had wanted to be an agent. At least Thomas figured a way to do both, work for the DEA and oversee Donato Enterprises' operations. He then sets Aimee's engagement ring on the coffee table. Claire peers at it.

"Is that the ring you gave Aimee? She was never good enough for you."

"No, Mother," he says, heading toward the door. "I was never good enough for her. But I'm trying to make myself better."

She twists around. "Where are you going?"

"Home, to my family. Oh, one more thing." He snaps his fingers when he reaches the door, then points at Phil. "I apologize for how I treated you when we were kids. But if you so much as contact Aimee, go to her café, shop in the same fucking grocery store, or even breathe her name, I will serve your balls on a platter to local law enforcement." He may still do that after he discusses it with Aimee.

James quietly shuts the door behind him, leaving the hotel and all the crazy that makes up the Donato family.

∽

On the way back to Natalya's, James stops at the shopping center in Princeville. He snaps a picture of the lease sign in the empty retail space's window, then swings into the art store and purchases way too many supplies, including an extralarge canvas. He'll order more online later. He'll also research the school district and pick up registration packets.

It's late afternoon when he arrives at Natalya's house. He called ahead and they're waiting for him in the driveway. Marc barrels into his arms before he's fully out of the cab. James can't hug Marc hard enough.

The cab driver pops the trunk, revealing James's purchases.

"Whoa." Marc slides down James.

"What's all this?" Natalya asks as he unloads the canvas.

"I have a sunset to paint."

317

Her gaze jumps to his. She tugs the end of her hair and her eyes well. "Really?"

"Really." He pulls her against him and kisses her soundly, amazed at how much he missed her in such a short time, considering they've only known each other in person for such a short time.

He lifts his head. He wants to look at the woman who's been so incredible to him. Her face tightens with emotion and she lightly punches him in the shoulder. "Damn you, you made me cry."

"Maybe I shouldn't paint, then?"

"Oh no! You're painting my sunset. I've been waiting for years, and I'm not going to let you leave until you finish."

"What if I don't plan on leaving?"

Her surprised expression is almost comical until she bursts into tears. The emotion plows into James and his own breath hitches. "Come here, Nat." He holds her close as her arms squeeze him tight.

Over her shoulder he sees Julian cautiously watching them. "Give me a second," he whispers in Natalya's ear.

Julian slowly dribbles a basketball but makes no move to come closer. James watches Julian and his internal battle. Did his father honestly mean it when he said he'd never leave him behind?

James figures he'll make it easy on the kid. He asks Marc, who wobbles under its awkward size, to take the canvas, making Natalya giggle. James moves closer to Julian and opens his arms. "Come here, son."

Julian takes a step, bounces the ball, then takes another step. His mouth, which is pressed into a tight seam, quivers when he finally tosses the ball aside and walks into James's arms. "I love you, Dad."

EPILOGUE

CLAIRE

Six Months Ago
December 17
Puerto Escondido, Mexico

Claire Donato was tired of the oppressive heat of Puerto Escondido and the endless trail of ants marching up her walls. She was tired of the sunburns and the sand that always found its way into the wrong places. And she was tired of her grandsons calling her Señora Carla. What a dreadful name. Why she picked that one, she has no idea. It was a spur-of-the-moment decision. She never intended to interact with her son and grandchildren. She just wanted to observe, to see with her own eyes what Thomas finally confessed. Her youngest son was alive, but for his safety he had to remain hidden in plain sight. *Don't interact, do not engage,* Thomas had told her as if *he* were some sort of government agent.

Well, she'd visited Puerto Escondido more times than she imagined, and she'd let Thomas's charade go on long enough. She was sick and tired and disgusted from lying. Her son James—even though he didn't know yet he was her son because he still went by that ridiculous name of Carlos—had brought painting back into her life. The least any good mother could do was return the favor. It was time to bring James home.

She'd consulted a specialist, who advised that James needed to confront the stressor that had induced the fugue state. If Thomas was right, Phil was James's stressor. James needed to face his brother because hypnosis hadn't worked. She told Thomas it wouldn't, and he hadn't believed her. And because of his idiotic ploy, there was the chance she'd never see her grandsons again. Carlos didn't trust Claire's family. He wanted Natalya to adopt them. She couldn't let that happen. Ever.

Claire turned on her laptop, launched Skype, and accepted the call from the California Men's Colony for her weekly scheduled conference with Phil. She despised these calls, prearranged and with a time limit. But a mother must do what a mother must do. All her sons mattered. She just wished they'd all get along.

Once the call connected, she said hello to her son, then excused herself momentarily from the room. She needed a glass of water. It was dreadfully hot and her throat was parched.

But she didn't go to the kitchen. Instead, she waited unseen in the hallway for Carlos to arrive. She'd called him a few minutes ago complaining about her faulty wireless connection. She needed his assistance, she'd said.

Yes, it was a lie, but it was for the greater good of her family.

James would thank her later.

EPILOGUE

CARLOS

Six Months Ago
December 17
Puerto Escondido, Mexico

Carlos let himself in through the glass slider as he always did when he visited his neighbor.

"Señora Carla?" he called.

Classical music played softly. Vases of freshly cut flowers from the local market colored the room and perfumed the home's artificially chilled air, as did the faint chemical scent of pigment. Carla had been painting earlier.

"Carla?" he called again. He heard a faint noise in the other room, like a pen tapping on a desktop.

He followed the sound through the great room and into the den. Carla wasn't there but her laptop was powered up and on her desk. He'd quickly check into its wireless-connection issue then leave her a note. He was already late for a meeting with a new client at the gallery. The mayor had commissioned a painting for city hall.

Carlos jiggled the mouse before realizing the Skype app was already open with a connected call. A man dressed in an orange jumpsuit sat on the other side, leg propped on the table as he leaned back in his chair. He stared at the ceiling, his fingers drumming on the chair arm.

Where was Carla? She couldn't have gone far considering she had a call still connected. Obviously, she'd gotten her wireless to work without him. Perhaps the man on the other side knew where she'd gone off to.

"*¿Hola?*" he asked.

The caller dipped his chin and narrowed his eyes at the screen. His brows bunched in confusion; then his mouth fell open. "James?"

Carlos jerked back. His stomach bottomed out like a sinkhole.

Orange-suit man dropped his booted feet to the floor with a loud thud. He leaned forward, his face and shoulders filling the screen. He whooped. "It *is* you."

Carlos's gaze dove to the name stamped on the man's right breast. Donato, P.

Phil.

The name crash-landed in Carlos's head. Dread, sour and toxic, filled the empty space in his gut.

Phil hooted, slapping a palm on the tabletop. His image bounced on the screen—his steepled palms over his nose and mouth, his eyes going baseball-size on either side of his fingers. "You're alive. You're fucking alive."

Carlos worked his jaw. His hands balled into fists as the dread twisted and morphed into a level of rage he couldn't comprehend. Pain splintered through his head, leaving him unbalanced and seeing stars.

"Thomas, you sonofabitch," Phil said more to himself. He jabbed a finger at the screen. "He told me you were dead. Jesus, it's a miracle you survived at all considering how offshore we were. Ah, man, I thought you were a goner when I told you to jump, with your face being so messed up. They did a number on you. Sal, that tool that was with us in the boat, he took my gun. He shot at you, man. He shot at you!"

Phil continued to ramble, jumping out of his chair to lean in closer to the screen. Carlos's eyes bugged, the pain behind them unbearable. He weaved on his feet.

Phil thumped his chest. "I never planned to use it. I wasn't going to kill you. No way, man. You might have treated me like shit all our lives but I never would have killed you. Brothers don't do that to each other. I told you to swim. I warned you when to jump. I saved your ass, I saved you. Sal would have killed you. But not me. I couldn't pull the trigger. I just couldn't." Spittle rained on the screen, giving his lips an unnatural sheen. He flopped back into his chair and heaved a breath. "Besides, Mom would have kicked my ass if I harmed you, especially after what I tried with Aimee. Dude. My bad. But, shit, the whole family had teed me off. I was tired of being treated like crap by you guys. You can understand that, right?"

Nausea sloshed inside Carlos. He bent at the waist, hands on hips, and blew out large breaths. He started panting.

"It's great to see you, man," Phil was saying, "really, really great."

Carlos cocked his head from his bent-over position and glared at the laptop. Phil peered into the tiny camera narrowing his eyes. "You look different. They fixed your face, like a Racer-X-from-Speed-Racer-reconstructive-surgery fix. Damn, your face had been a mess when I last saw you. Your eye was practically sealed shut. How did you swim like that? Come to think of it, how *did* you get to shore?"

Carlos's chest rose and fell. His fingers dug into his kneecaps.

Phil scratched his cheek. "Fucking spectacular, man. I still can't believe I'm seeing you. All this time I thought you were dead, and there you are, in the flesh, hanging out with Mom.

"By the way, why *are* you there?" He gasped. "Have you been in Mexico this whole time?"

Carlos gritted his teeth. Sweat bloomed over every inch of skin. Muscles cramped. His entire body was shaking. He straightened to his full height and stared down at the laptop.

Phil whistled. "Boy, you look madder than a penned-up bull. You must be really upset with me. But, hey"—he raised both hands in surrender—"I'm a reformed man. I take full responsibility for everything, including that little finger number I did on your fiancée." He wiggled his fingers, then cleared his throat. "Oops, ex-fiancée. I was a bit messed in the head back then." He pointed at his temple then clapped his hands together. "Tell you what. When I get out of here, I'll make it up to you. I owe you big-time. You helped me see the light, so to speak. I'll find you and we can—"

Carlos roared. He grabbed the laptop and threw it at the window. Glass shattered.

He looked madly around the room, panting, fists balled. Home. He had to get home.

And this place wasn't home.

EPILOGUE

JAMES

Present Day
July 31
Hanalei, Kauai, Hawaii

James fills another bucket alongside Marc and flips its end over. He lifts the bucket slowly so the damp sand retains the shape.

"Put another one here, *papá*." Marc points to the far corner of the castle they built together.

"You got it, kiddo." James shovels sand back into his bucket.

After they set up the second tower, James cranes his neck, gazing off in the distance where Natalya and Julian are surfing. The waves are heavy today, thanks to an offshore storm. Perfect for riding, Julian told them.

Today is probably the last afternoon for some time for Julian to surf. They've been living with Natalya for more than a month. Thanks to the Silicon Valley real estate market, his house sold quickly in Los Gatos and well over the asking price. He should start looking for a condo, but it's been nice staying with Natalya. He transferred his belongings to her room several weeks ago and she wants them to move in permanently. They still need to talk about taking the next step in their relationship, and he wants to do that soon. Because thinking about a future with her warms his heart and makes him ache—a good ache—in all the important places.

Construction on the gallery begins in a few weeks. Tomorrow the boys start school. Soon, their afternoons of beach play and surfing will be filled with homework and soccer practices. Even Marc, who is going into the first grade, has shown interest in playing.

James takes a deep breath of ocean air. In a short span of time, he's changed names, acquaintances, homes, and countries, but their lifestyle remains the same. They're back to the daily grind, which is perfectly fine with him after what they've been through.

Julian and Natalya paddle their arms, aiming for the stickiest part of an approaching wave. The water peaks beneath them, and as if in sync, they pop to their feet and direct their boards down the face of the swelling ocean. James stands to watch, holding his breath as he shields his eyes from the sun's glare. Natalya once described surfing to him as one of the best feelings in the world. Besides sex, of course. It's like being on top of the world and part of the ocean all at once.

"Is that your wife?"

James glances down, surprised to find a petite woman standing beside him. Her white cotton sundress swirls in the wind, dancing around her ankles. She braces a hand on her head so the wide-brimmed hat doesn't fly away. Large, round white-rimmed sunglasses shield her eyes from the late-afternoon sun. Platinum hair flutters around her cheeks. She smiles at him and James feels himself grinning in response.

"Not yet." He turns back to Natalya. "Someday, maybe." And the thought leaves him feeling anxious, and warm, and at peace, all at once.

He thinks of the letter Carlos had written him. The words often return at unexpected moments, a subtle reminder of how blessed his life is now. Carlos's last wish had been that he could find his way back into Natalya's arms. And he has. He's also enjoying falling for her all over again.

"Sounds to me like you can see the future," the woman teases.

"Much better than I can my past," he quips, not expecting this stranger to understand.

"I have ways of helping people rediscover their past."

A chill runs through James, leaving him slightly shaken. "What are you? A psychologist?" He knows he needs therapy, but is it that obvious?

A secret smile touches her lips. "I'm a friend."

"Grandma! I found a crab. Come look."

The woman beside him grins. "That's my granddaughter." She nods with her chin toward a young girl digging where the tide kisses the sandy beach. She waves at her grandmother again.

"Coming," she calls, and slides a hand into a side pocket. "I believe you know someone who might need this, James. He's been looking for me." She hands him the card, facedown.

James stiffens at the sound of his name and watches the woman join her granddaughter. Frowning, he flips over the card.

LACY SAUNDERS
PSYCHIC COUNSELOR, CONSULTANT & PROFILER
MURDERS, MISSING PERSONS & UNSOLVED MYSTERIES
HELPING YOU FIND THE ANSWERS YOU SEEK.

"Dad! Dad! Did you see that?"

James lifts his head and smiles at Julian. He tucks the card into his pocket, where it disappears but isn't forgotten. Julian and Natalya trudge through the sand toward him and Marc, boards tucked under their arms. Exhausted and dripping wet, they drop their boards and sit down.

"I'm beat," Natalya laughs, falling backward on the sand, arms stretched wide.

James sneaks up on Marc and grabs his son around the waist, tossing him over his shoulder. Marc squeals and kicks his legs. James laughs, and with a squirming Marc on his shoulders and happiness in his heart, he joins the rest of his family.

COMING JULY 2018

EVERYTHING WE GIVE

AUTHOR'S NOTE

In January 2016, CNN reported that Mexico released figures on the country's drug war, which it had been aggressively fighting since 2006. It was estimated that at least eighty thousand people had been killed between 2006 and 2015.

Drug cartels continue to fight over territories, and many drug-related deaths go unreported. Many more people are missing or have simply disappeared. While Mexico has had a witness protection program in place, it wasn't until 2012 that president Felipe Calderón signed into law a measure that expanded the program's benefits. For their protection, crime victims and witnesses are now eligible to receive new identities.

ACKNOWLEDGMENTS

This book is for each and every reader of *Everything We Keep*, for traveling with Aimee on her journey to find James—and herself along the way. Thank you for reading and sharing my passion for this series. I hope you enjoyed James's story and can breathe a sigh of relief. He and his sons finally got their happily ever after.

The writing community is a tremendous network. There is always an accessible expert to tap somewhere. Many thanks to these authors and attorneys, for either their knowledge or pointing me to the right resource: Kasey Corbit, Matt Knight, and Catherine McKenzie. Thanks for answering my crazy questions, from trade-based laundering and property seizure to child custody, immigration, and foreign adoption laws. Any mistakes are mine and for the purpose of making the information work within the story.

For my dear friend and critique partner Orly Konig-Lopez, thank you for the calls and e-mails as I brainstormed story ideas back in this book's infancy. For Michele Montgomery, thank you for introducing me to Matt Knight and his *Sidebar Saturdays* posts.

For the Ladies of the Lake and the Tiki Lounge, your enthusiasm and support never cease to amaze me. I am grateful for every text, e-mail, and Skype call of encouragement. You keep me writing.

For Kelli Martin, thank you for your editorial guidance, the "happy news" phone calls, and emoji-filled e-mails that make me laugh and appreciate how much I enjoy working with you. For Gabriella Dumpit, thank you for sending flowers when I ventured into synopsis hell. For Danielle Marshall, Dennelle Catlett, and the entire Lake Union team, thank you for all the publicity and support you put behind my projects.

Many thanks to my agent, Gordon Warnock, and Fuse Literary Agency for everything you do on my behalf, especially the screenshots you tweet with the red *Wow!* when my books' rankings increase. Those are awesome! This journey has been incredible, for which I'm truly grateful.

For my parents, to whom this book is dedicated: Thank you for believing, and thanks, Mom, for reminding me every so often how I once told you I'd write a book one day. That day has come and then some. Love you both!

Last, and certainly not least, many thanks to my husband, Henry, for keeping me grounded and (somewhat) sane. Much love to you and our kids, Evan and Brenna.

BOOK CLUB DISCUSSION QUESTIONS

1. *Everything We Keep* ended with James surfacing from the fugue state. What did you think happened next? Did you expect him to return to California with his sons?

2. How do you think James handled his relationship with Aimee? Should he have pursued her, or was he right to let her go?

3. Claire showed up in Mexico only to observe her son, but ends up not only interacting with him, she returns every summer and Christmas holiday. She obviously didn't want Carlos to know who she was for fear he'd send her away. Why do you think she kept coming back after the way she treated James? Were you surprised she was an artist, too?

4. As Carlos, James put a huge burden on his son Julian. Not only did James prepare Julian for his possible change, but he asked Julian to help him become a father again. Considering Julian's age at the time (eleven), did James do the right thing? If you were in a similar situation, how would you have prepared your children?

5. Julian remarked that older brothers are supposed to protect their younger brothers. What do you think of Thomas and how he treated James? Were his revelations surprising? Do you think he had James's best interests in mind?

6. In the end, the reveal shows Phil had protected James. He warned him when to jump overboard. Did Phil's actions surprise you?

7. At the beginning of the story, James has lost so much: his childhood sweetheart, his career, and six years of memories. By the time the story ends, it's apparent he's gained so much more: a new love, two sons, and his art. How did this change him? What did he learn along the way?

8. Many themes are presented in this novel: loss, love, resilience, family, forgiveness, and acceptance. Which theme resonated the most with you?

9. The story ends with a mysterious appearance from Lacy, the psychic who propelled Aimee on her own journey. She gives James her business card. Whom do you think the card is for? What do you think James will do?

ABOUT THE AUTHOR

Photo © 2013 Deene Souza Photography

Kerry Lonsdale is the *Wall Street Journal* and #1 Amazon Kindle best-selling author of *Everything We Keep* and *All the Breaking Waves*. She resides in Northern California with her husband and two children. Learn more about Kerry at www.kerrylonsdale.com.

Two months before his wedding, financial executive James
Donato chased his trade-laundering brother Phil to Mexico
only to be lost at sea and presumed dead. Six and a half years
later, he emerges from a dissociative fugue state to find he's
been living in Oaxaca as artist Carlos Dominguez, widower
and father of two sons, with his sister-in-law Natalya Hayes,
a retired professional surfer, helping to keep his life afloat.
But his fiancée, Aimee Tierney, the love of his life, has
moved on. She's married and has a child of her own.

Devastated, James and his sons return to California. But Phil
is scheduled for release from prison, and he's determined to
find James, who witnessed something in Mexico that could
land Phil back in confinement. Under mounting family
pressure, James flees with his sons to Kauai, seeking refuge
with Natalya. As James begins to unravel the mystery of his
fractured identity, danger is never far behind, and Natalya
may be the only person he can trust.

LAKE UNION
PUBLISHING

9 781477 823972